1987 MIAMI X GENERATION

Book 1
New Edition
MGX BOOK SERIES

Copyright © 2020 KM Mitten

ISBN: 978-1-7345712-5-7

Book cover graphics by Scott Mitten

Miami Generation X 1987 Book One

New Edition

This is a work of fiction. Names, characters, events, and incidents are the products of the author's imagination. Any resemblance to actual persons, living or dead, or actual events is purely coincidental.

For more information, go to mgxbook.com

Author KM Mitten / MGX BOOKS LLC

Welcome to the MGX Series

Where it all begins in the summer of

1987

Table of Contents

Prologue

My name is Samantha, and I live in the city of freedom, Miami. Many people who live here have come from somewhere else. Miami must be one of the biggest melting pots in the United States. A majority of the people who live here have come from Cuba to escape Fidel Castro and his government. The island of paradise has been turned into a communist country. I also have many friends and neighbors whose families originated from other Caribbean islands and Latin America. All who live here have come with one main goal — opportunity. Many of the people who moved here only spoke Spanish, but Miami quickly adapted to the change, and a new type of language was formed, Spanglish. Whatever word, you do not know in English, you say in Spanish. Whatever word, you don't know in Spanish, you say in English. Everyone in Miami quickly found a way to communicate, and Spanglish is a language I still speak today. This place is my home.

I am a teenager living in paradise. My parents are from up north, where they get tons of snow every winter. For me, every winter in Miami is enjoying the pool or beach and wearing shorts all year round. My parents are recently divorced, so I live with my mom. Tonya is my best friend. I met her when I was five years old. My mom and her grandmother, we call her Abuela, would take us to the pool on the weekends to play together. Eventually, we ended up spending every day with one another playing with dolls at her place or Atari at mine. That is also when Tonya gave me the nickname Muñeca, which means doll in Spanish. I often taught her words in English, and she would teach me words in Spanish. A few times, they were bad words, and of course, I would always remember them. I guess that is when we began speaking Spanglish.

Chapter 1 Summer Break

Tonya and I are 14 years old now, and we're practically sisters. Currently, we are enjoying the last couple of weeks of our summer break before returning to school. This year we will be in the ninth grade, so it's our last year in junior high. I can't believe we're going to be freshmen. We finally have a title, and before you know it, we will be in high school. I can still remember our first day in seventh grade. Tonya and I had to ride the school bus instead of our parents taking us to school. We had seven classes to get to on our own. We had no idea where we were going. Every class I had, all the students I spoke to were just as lost as I was. We were all from different schools. Everybody was a stranger in every classroom I entered. I don't often speak with strangers; it's usually difficult for me because I'm an introvert. However, the fear of being late for my next class, looming over my head, made it very easy for me to open up and talk to everyone. I just wanted to know where to go next. The whole first week was crazy and confusing, but by week two, I knew where all my classes were, and I got to know many of my classmates. I became close friends with several people, and we're still close today. Tonya and I go to the same school, and we live in the same neighborhood, so basically we have the same friends. Tonight, we're going to spend the night at our girlfriend Daphne's house. She's having a slumber party, and my mom has agreed to drop us off.

My mom is very close friends with Daphne's mom; her name is Carmen. She's totally eccentric, and we love to be around her all the time. Our friend Daphne is just like her mother, only younger.

On the ride to Daphne's house, my mom told us it was good for us girls to have one another to lean on while we're going through our teenage years. I don't know exactly what she meant by that.

It was a compliment, I think. So, I said, "Thanks, Mom," as I looked back at Tonya, with my eyebrows raised. She just shook her head with her shoulders raised and palms up, which meant she wasn't sure either.

When we arrived at Daphne's house, her brother Arturo was outside with a friend working on a car. He stopped what he was doing to run over to my mom and say hi. As I stepped out of my mom's car, Arturo offered to help me with my duffel bag. After handing him my bag, I headed for the trunk to help Tonya grab our sleeping bags and pillows. Then we waved bye to my mom and followed Arturo into the house. Daphne, Maria, Monica, and Denise were waiting for us in the living room. All the girls screamed with excitement the minute we walked through the door.

That's also when I overheard Arturo's friend ask, "How many girls are coming over here tonight?"

"This is it, Michael. Six girls. Why do you sound so annoyed?" Michael said something else, but I couldn't make-out what he told Arturo. Then I saw his friend Michael walk out the door. Arturo yelled out, "Mom, I will be back later."

In the living room, there was a large burgundy sectional sofa where we all sat down. "Daphne, now that everyone's here, tell us what you have planned for us to do tonight?"

"Well, Denise, I thought we could rent a movie from the video store, or go to the movies."

The minute we arrived at the video store, we all headed for the comedy section except for Daphne.

She remained at the entrance leaning up against a

wall staring at a cashier. I walked back over to her and asked, "Are you okay?"

Daphne just nodded her head yes, while continuing to stare at this guy behind the counter. "Daphne, are you sure that you're okay?"

Sounding annoyed, she quickly responded, "I'm fine, Sammy."

"Alright, then help us pick out a movie." Daphne followed me back over to the comedy section, and the six of us were quickly able to agree on a movie. However, by the time we reached the counter to check out the video, Daphne had become motionless and tongue-tied. It took all five of us to drag Daphne out of the store.

When we arrived back at Daphne's house, the six of us found a spot on the couch and got comfy. We watched the movie, and Carmen ordered pizza. Later on, when the film was over, Daphne helped us set up our sleeping bags on the floor in her living room. Then the six of us sat down on top of our bags to play Gin Rummy when Maria asked if we could play truth or dare instead.

"None of us want to play that again, Maria. The last time we played that, you girls made some crazy concoction that Sammy had to drink, and it made her sick."

"I know a game we could play, Denise,"

Denise had a skeptical look on her face before asking Tonya, "What game?"

"It's more like a discussion than a game, but it's totally entertaining."

"Fine, what is the discussion about?"

"Denise, it's about sharing your most embarrassing moment."

"Tonya, no, I don't want to participate in this either."

"Come on. It will be a lot of fun, Denise."

"No, I'm not interested, Tonya."

"Well, it sounds like fun to me."

"It is Daphne, you'll see."

"Great, I believe you, Tonya, and that's why I think you should go first."

That's when Tonya began to complain about going first to Daphne, and Denise was cracking up the whole time.

"If it's so much fun, you shouldn't have a problem with going first, Tonya."

"All I'm saying is that this is your house, Daphne, so it's only right that you go first."

Then Monica stood up and said, "It's not a big deal. I can go first." We learned a lot about each other from that discussion, and eventually, the conversation ended with talking about boys. I found out Denise, Monica, and Maria have already had a boyfriend. I still haven't, and neither has Tonya or Daphne. That night for the first time in my life, I fell asleep thinking about boys and what it would be like to have a boyfriend.

We only have two weeks of summer left before we have to go back to school, and I'm trying to keep up with my routine. Every day I hang out at the pool with Tonya, which is in the center of our complex. I have very fair skin, so even with sunscreen, I've had a sunburn on and off all summer long. I also currently have strawberry blonde hair instead of my natural auburn red color. Thanks to spraying peroxide in my hair every two weeks, and I noticed that I'm looking more fit too.

I'm sure it has everything to do with the number of laps I swim at the pool each day. The boys in my neighborhood have been spending their entire summer at the pool along with us, and they taught Tonya and me how to do the butterfly, backstroke, breaststroke, and freestyle. As soon as we learned all four strokes, we began to participate in the relay races and enjoyed it so much that it became part of our daily routine. I take these races seriously and usually put on a one-piece bathing suit to compete. Okay, that wasn't completely honest. Lately, I have been feeling shy about my appearance, so I prefer the one-piece over a bikini. It just makes me feel way more comfortable with my body concealed as much as possible.

At least that was the case until today when I was walking to the pool wearing my two-piece bathing suit. Julio, who is my neighbor and also Monica's brother, saw me and stopped to stare at me. I didn't know what was going on at first, so I stopped walking and stared right back at him.

Then he pointed at me before asking, "What is that?"

"What is what, Julio?"

He kept staring at me with a strange look on his face before asking me again, "What is that?"

Then I noticed he was pointing at my chest. That's when I instantly felt insecure and tried my best to keep my composure while I calmly unwrapped the towel from around my waist, as Julio stood there, gawking at me.

It took me a couple of seconds with my hands shaking to be able to re-wrap the towel around me by placing the towel under my arms and pulling it across my chest.

When I was finished, Julio's mouth dropped open, and I raised my chin up before I walked off, shaking my head at him.

Julio kept calling my name, and I heard him say, "Sammy, please come back here to let me explain what happened."

No, I thought to myself. I'm not going to stand there and listen to what Julio has to say. Why should I? He has made me feel awkward over my appearance, and I'm totally upset by it. All I need to do now is continue walking until I reach Tonya's front door.

I knocked on her door, but there was no answer. I was about to walk away when I heard, "I'm coming, Muñeca." Tonya answered the door, and of course, like usual, she was on the phone. I walked inside as Tonya jogged back down the stairs to her bedroom.

She has the longest phone cord that I have ever seen with two extensions added on to it. Tonya also had her own phone line in her bedroom. Which meant all of her calls ring into her room only. The rest of her grandparents' house has a different number. I feel as though she is one of the luckiest girls I know.

Probably because I have a beeper and although I can take it with me everywhere. Sometimes it's hard to find a payphone and even harder to wait for one that's working or available. Tonya was given a choice between having a beeper or her own phone line. She made the right choice for her since Tonya is always on the phone.

"What's this, Tonya?"

"Oh, I just got that, Muñeca. It's an answering machine. My mom's boyfriend gave it to me on my birthday, and I have a great idea."

"Of course, you do, let's hear it."

"We should make a voice recorded message together?"

"Alright, what do we have to do?"

"Give me a second to get the cassette tapes out of this box."

Tonya took out two cassette tapes and placed them in the machine. Then she pressed the record button. It took us about five different recordings until we had a recorded message that we both liked. Tonya then asked me to run upstairs to call her room from the kitchen phone. She wanted me to hear how the recording sounds over the phone. The phone rang four times before the answering machine picked up. The recorded message was: "You have reached Tonya and Sammy. Tonya's not home right now. Obviously, she's hanging out with Sammy, somewhere. Please wait for the beep to leave a message."

When I heard the beep, I decided to leave a message telling her what happened between Julio and me. By the time I hung up, the phone Tonya was standing behind me with her arms out. With my head now resting on Tonya's shoulder and tears streaming down my face, I admitted how Julio made me feel.

"Muñeca, why are you crying over this?"

"Tonya, I don't know, I guess it's because he made me feel embarrassed. Plus, I really don't think they have changed that much since yesterday, do you?"

"No, but Muñeca-"

"Yesterday, we were all playing in the pool, and Julio didn't notice anything different, and today it was like he was in complete shock or something."

"Oh, Muñeca, my cousins did the same thing to me over Christmas last year. I had a dress on, and it was tight, so it revealed my chest and my booty. My cousins kept asking me, when did this happen to you?"

I laughed as they pointed at me asking questions, but inside I felt humiliated and angry."

"How were you able to forgive them?"

"Honestly, it seems like it happened overnight to me too, Muñeca. My family was just surprised, and it's no longer a huge deal anymore."

"You never let on that you felt insecure about it, Tonya, not even to me."

"Well, I was after that conversation for a few months to the point I was wearing oversized sweaters to conceal everything."

"Wow, Tonya, how big were those sweaters?"

"What?"

"I just can't believe you found sweaters big enough to conceal all that booty," I replied with a smile.

"Oh, really, Muñeca, well, I can't believe you finally have boobs."

"Hey, I'm surprised by that myself. Thanks, Tonya. You made me feel a lot better."

I reached out to give her a hug, and as I pulled away, Tonya asked, "Are you headed home now?"

"Yeah, I think so, but I will call you later."

"That sounds good, Muñeca. Before you leave, can you do me a favor?"

"Well, that depends on the favor."

"Muñeca, I'm totally serious."

"Okay, shoot, Tonya."

"Stop being ashamed of your body. You're beautiful, Muñeca. Learn to embrace your appearance and work on your confidence."

"Look, it's not going to happen overnight for me, Tonya, I've always been shy, to begin with, but I will try."

"Good, that's all I'm asking, Muñeca."

"Okay," I replied while walking out the door.

As I was walking back to my building, I heard, "Sammy, come on now. I'm sorry."

It was Julio. He walked up to me and was now standing right in front of me. I stood still, looking down at the ground.

"Please don't ignore me, Sammy."

I released a very loud sigh before I finally looked up into his eyes and asked, "What do you want, Soccer Player?"

"I, I, I," he was stammering now to get the words out. While he was trying to explain himself, I noticed the worried expression on his face. Oh, and I could tell he was nervous because he kept wiping the palms of his hands on the pockets of his shorts. Then there was this whole thing where he kept staring into my eyes. I stared back, of course, and felt lost until he said, "I'm sorry, Sammy." That grabbed my attention, and Julio turned his eyes away from me for a second.

He swallowed once then blurted out, "Sammy, I was checking you out from over there." He pointed to the clubhouse behind us. "Honestly, I thought, Oh man, she's cute. Who is that? I swear all I saw was your form. The sun was shining on you, which made it difficult to see your face."

"Great, so you're telling me that you need glasses, Julio."

"Maybe, I do, but I like what I saw. That's why I walked over to you, but I didn't realize it was you exactly, and when I did, it took me by surprise. Which is why I ended up asking you a really stupid question."

"Yes, you did, Julio, and like I said before, you must need glasses."

"No, I don't. You're very pretty, Sammy."

"Okay, Julio, I've heard enough."

Julio was making me feel uncomfortable with everything he was saying. No boy has ever told me this kind of stuff before, so I don't know how to act or what to say. Then I looked down and realized I left my towel at Tonya's house. All I had on was my two-piece bathing suit and chancletas. Now that was totally shocking, and I was beginning to panic, but I didn't want to reveal how I was feeling to Julio.

In order to keep my composure, I quickly lifted my head and said, "Thank you, Julio, for the explanation and apology. Bye now."

The following day was Sunday. My Mom was called into work, so I offered to make us dinner tonight. I was about to head out the door with Daisy when the phone rang. It was my mom calling to let me know that she was still at work. I told her that's not a problem; I can delay making dinner for another hour. Then she mentioned I should take Daisy out for her walk now. I just agreed, and after I hung up the phone, we headed out the door.

Daisy was a gift from my brother Tommy. He gave her to me when she was just a puppy, and she has grown up to become a very big girl. She is all black, with white going down her chest and etched around each of her paws. Daisy has been the best gift I have ever received with her big heart filled with unconditional love. When I headed outside with Daisy, we followed the sidewalk out to the entrance of the golf course. Beside the golf course is a dog walking path. Daisy and I were walking on this path when I saw a bunch of boys playing soccer and decided to sit down to watch them play. I was under a tree with Daisy beside me when I saw Julio run past us, kicking a soccer ball. That's when my mind drifted off, and I remembered my mom telling me things about the Sanchez family. Starting with how Lewis failed the ninth grade, so he has to repeat it again this year. He was supposed to move to California, but he will remain here to repeat the ninth grade instead. Lewis, along with his brother Eddie, has moved into their aunt Pilar's apartment, which happens to be next door. Pilar is Julio's mom and my mom's best friend. At least they did not have to move too far. Before their father moved to California, they used to live in my building.

Come to think of it. I have not ever seen Julio and Lewis away from one another until yesterday. I started to giggle, thinking lucky me – I ran into Julio not once but twice without Lewis.

While I sat there watching Julio chase a soccer ball, I began to notice how much he has changed too. He's definitely taller, at least 5'9", and his legs are so muscular, especially his calves. They look like little rocks in his socks. Julio was fast on the field. It appeared as though nobody could keep up with him. I felt mesmerized watching him run back and forth on the field until Daisy barked. I turned my head to look over at her, and she was sitting up with her tongue hanging out on the right side of her mouth. "Oh, Daisy, what am I doing here?" She barked again before placing her head down on my lap. Which was her way of indicating she wants me to pet her.

As I began to pet Daisy, I told her how I felt because I can tell Daisy anything, and she doesn't judge me. "I don't know what's happening to me, girl. It all started yesterday when Julio mistook me for someone else. Prior to that, he was just another annoying boy in the neighborhood until he apologized to me, and that's when it happened. I noticed Julio's piercing brown eyes. They held me captive like nothing I had ever experienced before, and I was lost the entire time he spoke to me. It has to be his tan, right? I mean, we have known each other for over six years, and his eyes never caught my attention before. It's hard trying to understand all of this, so thanks for allowing me to vent my frustration."

Daisy licked my hands, and I went back to petting her for a moment before saying, "We need to get back home, Daisy. "I'm sorry, girl. I know how much you like sitting out here. The problem is I can't handle staring at him anymore."

I placed my hand on the grass to push myself up. Then I saw a shadow on the grass close to me. I looked up, and I was suddenly looking into Julio's brown eyes, which made me feel uneasy with my nerves setting in. Julio was smiling down at me, and my stomach began to tighten.

"Hey, let me help you up, Sammy." Julio extended his hand out to me, and he pulled me up onto my feet. I just kept repeatedly thinking to myself in a sheer panic he caught me, he caught me for sure checking him out. While I stood there, staring up into his eyes, feeling lost all over again. It must have taken me about a minute before I remembered to even thank him for offering me his hand. My mind was all over the place, and I just felt silly, so I waved bye to him before walking away.

Less than a minute later, while back on the dog path, I heard, "Well, what do you think, Sammy?"

Ut-oh, I thought to myself before turning around to see Julio standing a few feet away from me. "What do I think about what?"

"Do you think I play well enough to have earned your nickname?"

"To be completely honest, I am confused, Julio. I don't know what you're talking about."

"Your nickname for me is Soccer Player, right?"

"Oh, I get what you're asking me now. Yes, you play very well, Julio, or should I continue calling you Soccer Player?"

His whole face lit up, and I instantly felt relieved that he didn't bust me checking him out. Then we just stood there in silence, staring at one another until Alex ran up to Julio. He whispered something and took off back out onto the field.

"I'm assuming you have to return to the field now, Julio, and I have to get home, so enjoy the rest of your game."

Chapter 2 Back to School

I woke up the minute I heard my mom knock on my bedroom door. "Sam, are you awake yet?"

"I'm awake now, Mom."

She walked inside my room, saying, "Good, get up before you're late for school. As it is your very lucky, I'm off today, kiddo."

"Really, why is that mom?"

"Since I'm off today, I can take Daisy out for her walk while you get ready for school. By the way, Sam, you only have about thirty minutes left before you miss the bus."

"Oh no, I must have slept through my alarm clock." I quickly jumped out of bed to head for the bathroom. On my way back to my bedroom, I felt relieved that I listened to my mom last night. She suggested that I pick out what I plan on wearing to school today, and I did just that before going to bed. I don't have much time to style my hair, so I pulled up the sides and tied them in place with a scrunchy. Next, I applied my blue eyeliner, mascara, and bubble smelling lip-gloss. When I saw the time on my alarm clock, I ran into my closet to get dressed. First, I put on my stretchy black pencil skirt with a white tank top. Then I reached back into my closet to grab my long sleeve black lace blouse that I put on over my tank top. Dressed and ready to go, I grabbed my Ziplock bag filled with my jewelry off my dresser and my backpack prior to heading out the door.

While walking to the bus stop, I pulled open the Ziplock bag to put on my earrings. In my left ear, I have three piercings, and in my right ear, I have two. I filled all of the holes with CZ studs except for the bottom hole on my left ear.

There I only wear my dangling silver cross earring. By the time I reached my

destination, which was, of course, the bus stop, I had put everything on. Now I was wearing three silver bangles on my right arm along with eight black rubber bracelets and two Swatch watches on my left arm. There were usually around fifteen of my neighbors waiting with me for the bus. I looked around for Tonya and did not see her anywhere. Then my beeper went off, and I had to dig through my backpack to find it. While attempting to locate my beeper, I could hear Tonya's voice behind me. I turned around to say good morning when she spoke first and said, "Muñeca, I don't know why you have a beeper? You don't ever call anyone back, so maybe you should get your own phone line."

"How am I supposed to call someone back from the bus stop? Do you see a payphone anywhere around? And why would I want my own phone line, Tonya? The whole point is that I don't want to be bothered? Which means I won't ever answer the phone."

"Are you saying I'm bothering you, Muñeca, whenever I call you?"

"No, that's not what I'm saying at all, Tonya. Although you are starting to bother me right now."

"How can you say that to me?"

"Tonya, how can you be so talkative this early in the morning? You're beginning to give me a headache." I spun around to face Tonya, and I could tell by the look on her face that I had hurt her feelings.

"Wow, Tonya, I'm sorry I didn't mean to say all that."

"Muñeca, I accept your apology because I know that you're not a morning person."

"No, I'm not. Nevertheless, I will be awake and able to function in about an hour." That is when our school bus arrived, and I boarded the bus with Tonya right behind me. We shared a seat, and Tonya went right back to talking non-stop.

"Isn't it wonderful that Patrick is still our bus driver?" I just nodded my head, yes. Oh, did you remember to bring your registration slip for school Muñeca?

That's when I dug through my bookbag and pulled out my Trapper Keeper. "Why did you pull that out?"

"Because I put the slip in here, Tonya, or at least I'm hoping I did."

"Well, you better find it, Muñeca, or you won't know what room you need to report to first."

When I pulled open my Trapper Keeper, the Velcro made this magnificent tearing sound. Julio turned around immediately and looked down on my lap before saying, "Hey, nice folder."

I looked directly into Julio's eyes and told him, "You mean Trapper Keeper, right? It's not just a folder."

Once I said that Lewis, who happens to be Julio's cousin, turned around in his seat to face me. I took in a deep breath and blurted out, "What do you want, Lewis?"

"Wow, excuse me, Ms. Trapper Keeper. I didn't mean to bother you." Lewis and Julio both turned around in their seat in front of us laughing. I just stared at the back of their heads, wishing I had a pair of scissors in my hand to cut off that rat tail Lewis has growing on the back of his head. All of the rappers in school have this rat tail, and some of them braid theirs or spray it a different color every day.

"Lewis, why do you have that rat tail?"

"Because it's cool."

"Sammy, that's not true. Lewis is lying to you."

"Oh yeah, then why does he have it, Julio?"

"My cousin thinks it brings him good luck."

"Yeah, because the chicks love it," Lewis replied, laughing before he continued to say, "And that to me is good luck."

"I never knew that before Lewis, how many girlfriends do you have?"

Lewis stopped laughing and became serious. "Just so you know, I happen to speak to lots of chicks, Julio."

Tonya smiled at me before saying, "Yeah, but I'm sure they don't speak to you, Lewis." I high-fived Tonya, and Julio was cracking up laughing.

Now Lewis was clearly upset when he told Julio, "I can't believe it. You're laughing at me, bro. I'm you're cousin."

"Primo, I know I'm sorry, but it was funny, and she was only teasing you. I'm just as guilty of it as she is, so don't take it to heart, Lewis." Julio turned around in his seat, facing us, rolling his eyes and shaking his head. When Lewis suddenly turned around to see what was going on.

"Julio, what are you saying?"

"Me, nothing," Julio answered as he closed his mouth and blew out his cheeks.

"Bro, what are you doing now you look like a frog?"

"Actually, he looks more like a blowfish.

"Tonya's right, you do look like a blowfish, Julio. I never realized that before. I can't wait to get home to tell Alex and Eddie." That's when the three of us began to laugh, and Julio became serious. If there's one thing, we all know for sure, it's that you don't say anything to Alex or Eddie. They will call Julio a blowfish for the rest of his time on earth.

It was finally time to exit the bus when Tonya asked me again, "Where is your homeroom?"

Before I could answer, Lewis turned to Tonya and asked, "Can I walk you to your first class? Tonya turned to me instead of answering Lewis.

"Look, if you're worried about Sammy, I can have Julio escort her to her classroom. Come on. It's the first day of school. I can show you around Tonya, so you don't get lost."

"Lewis, I have been going to this school for two years now. Why would I need you to take me to my homeroom?"

"Like I said, so you don't get lost, Tonya." She shook her head as she started to laugh, and when she looked over at me again, I nodded my head yes.

"You know what, Lewis? You make me laugh, so yes."

"What? Really?" Lewis was incredibly shocked.

"Yes, if you really want to Lewis."

"I do. I want to walk you to your classroom," Lewis replied, completely serious now.

"Okay, then let's go." Lewis put out his hand to Tonya, and she took it before they walked inside.

Julio turned to me and asked, "Sammy, do you want me to walk you to your classroom?"

"No, Julio. I'm fine."

"Oh, alright, because you know I don't want you to get lost, walking from the school bus to your homeroom."

We both laughed, and Julio said, "I can't believe that line Lewis used worked on Tonya."

"How can you not? Julio, your cousin, has the rat tail of good luck, which brings him chicks, remember?"

"Oh yeah, that's right. I forgot all about that tail, Sammy."

He suddenly stopped laughing and began to stare into my eyes. As I stared back at him, I began to feel hypnotized by those dark brown eyes of his. The bell rang and instantly got my attention, so I took off, running towards my homeroom. I was running down the hall, feeling lost. I haven't ever locked eyes with a boy like that before. Now I was unable to remember the room number to my classroom. I could only recall that it was in the same wing as the band room. If I didn't hurry up, I was going to be late. When I saw the band room on my left, I noticed the first classroom on this wing was to my right, so I stopped. I read the number above the door and knew it was my classroom. Feeling relieved, I reached down for the handle and heard someone say, "Let me get that for you." The door was pulled open for me, and I walked inside. When I turned around to say thank you, nobody was there, and the door was closed. I turned my head around to face the classroom and heard, "Sammy, over here." I looked over to my right and saw Daphne waving me over. I quickly sat down at a desk beside her.

"Oh, wow, I can't believe it. Sammy, how did you get Greg to leave the band room?"

"Who's Greg?"

"The guy who just held the door open for you."

"Oh, I didn't see him or get to thank him. In fact, I don't even know him."

Daphne was facing the door looking like she was daydreaming.

"You don't know who Greg is, Sammy?"

"Oh, hi Maria, I didn't see you there. No, I have no idea who Greg is. Maybe if you describe him to me."

That is when Maria went into a description of a tall guy with black hair and green eyes.

"With the most handsome smile I've ever seen," Daphne added.

Maria just laughed at Daphne before continuing with her description, "Greg always wears the best smelling cologne. He's a rocker. He has every heavy metal t-shirt that exists."

"Yeah, he sure does, and that's why we would be perfect together," Daphne said with a smile.

Maria looked over at Daphne and asked, "Can you explain to me why you'd be perfect together."

"Certainly, because we both like rock music and concerts."

Maria shook her head before asking, "Daphne, since when have you liked rock music?"

"Since now, Maria."

"Just one more question, Daphne."

"Fine, what is it, Maria?"

"When have you been to a concert?"

"Well, I've never actually been to a rock concert, but I would go with Greg if he asked me."

"Oh, and since when do you listen to rock music, Daphne?"

"I watched Headbangers Ball all summer long on MTV. I'm a fan now, and I like all of the bands. Bon Jovi, Def Leppard, and Cinderella."

"Wow, I guess you're a true rocker now, Daphne."

"Yes, I am Maria, and I'm glad you realize that."

The bell rang for class to begin, and our teacher took attendance and passed out our school schedule. Once I had my schedule, Maria asked me if she could see it. I handed it over to her, and it turns out we all have lunch together, so we agreed to meet up again in the cafeteria. Maria also noticed our lockers are in the same stack beside one another right outside this classroom. As soon as the bell rang, all three of us ran over to our lockers. I slapped my padlock on the door before I took off down the hall towards my next class. My second class is Physical Education. I do not like the idea of having P.E. for my second period, yet I don't have a choice.

The day has been moving rather quickly for me, which I'm thrilled about. I just completed my fifth class and was on my way to lunch. The minute I walked inside the cafeteria, my beeper went off. Which meant I had to dig through my backpack to find it. After viewing the number, I realized it was Tonya. She left a two-digit code after the phone number to indicate it's urgent. At first, I thought it was rather weird, then I began to panic, realizing something must have happened to her. Perhaps at PE or maybe she's sick. Why else would she be beeping me during school? I left the cafeteria headed for the nearest set of payphones. While thinking if they don't work, I will head to the office and try asking someone if I can use a phone in there; after all, it's urgent. By the time I reached the payphones, I had put my quarter in the slot before I had even picked up the receiver. Then I heard Tonya laughing behind me.

"So finally, you were going to call me back, Muñeca." I turned around, still feeling jittery and nervous.

"Tonya, what happened to you? Are you okay?"

"Yes, of course, I'm fine."

"Then why did you beep me, Tonya? What's so urgent?"

"The phones are still working even now. They didn't turn them off yet, and did you know the payphones at school only cost ten cents?"

"Tonya, I didn't know that, and I don't care."

"Well, I found out today that you can use the payphones during school hours but only today. Tomorrow the payphones go back to being turned off during school hours."

"Wow, that's totally not interesting, Tonya. I'm going back to the cafeteria to eat now. Are you coming with me?"

"No, I already ate." Then Tonya held up a yellow piece of paper signed by her teacher. It's a hall pass to use the bathroom. I was subtly disappointed and realized we wouldn't have lunch together this year, either.

"Tonya, you obviously have the first lunch session. That means you already had lunch while I'm standing here hungry. I'm leaving to get something to eat."

"That's fine. I need to get back to class anyways. Enjoy your lunch, Muñeca, and I'll see you on the bus."

"Great, I'm totally looking forward to our next encounter," and I rolled my eyes.

"Come on, Muñeca, you're not that annoyed with me, are you?" I nodded my head yes as she reached over and hugged me. I managed to peel her off of me before I took off back down the hall. When I walked back inside the cafeteria, Daphne ran over to me.

"Hey, where have you been, Sammy? Is everything okay?"

"Everything's fine, Daphne. I just had to take care of something really quick."

"That's okay. I just came over to check on you and to let you know where we're sitting." Daphne pointed to the table where Maria was seated.

"Thanks, I'll be over there in a minute." Daphne headed back to the table, and I joined them with my lunch tray a couple of minutes later.

The minute I sat down, I had this feeling like somebody was watching me. I looked around the lunchroom and noticed this guy staring at me from across the room. He was tall and skinny with a golden tan, green eyes, and long hair. Even when I looked back at him to give him a strange look, he would not stop looking at me, and I became uncomfortable to the point of feeling insecure about my appearance. I was starting to wonder what the heck was wrong with me that he wouldn't stop looking at me. Maria and Daphne were in the middle of talking about their classes when Daphne asked me, "Hey, where's your next class, Sammy?" I was so busy staring back at this guy that I did not bother to answer Daphne's question right away.

Daphne stood up and waved her hand in front of my face until she got my attention.

"I'm sorry, Daphne," I was —"

"Staring at the guy over there, Sammy?"

"No, it's not like that."

"Oh, no, then what is it like, Sammy?"

"That guy keeps staring at me, and he's making me feel uncomfortable."

"Well then, maybe you should stop staring at him, Sammy."

"Maria, I just want him to know how it feels."

"Yeah, I don't think that's working, Sammy. If anything, he probably thinks that you are interested in him. I mean, that's what I would think if I saw you staring at me like that, and I was some guy."

"Whatever, Daphne, maybe your right."

"Sammy, eat you haven't touched a thing on your plate."

I knew Maria was right, so I looked down at my plate, and that is when my stomach began to rumble. I shook my head as I stood up. "Sammy, where are you going?"

"To throw my tray away." When I left the table, I asked myself, why did a complete stranger make me feel so insecure, and why do I care about what he thinks of me? I had no answers, just questions for myself.

When I arrived back at the table, I didn't bother to look at the guy again. Instead, I asked the girls, "Have you ever been so hungry that once you finally get to sit down and eat, you have lost your appetite?"

"Yes, that's happened to me before, Sammy. I completely understand where you are coming from."

"No, you don't, Maria, that was anorexia." Maria's eyes became glossy as she turned her head away from Daphne and started to cry. "I'm sorry, Maria, but you're my best friend, and you really scared me. You actually scared all of us, including your family. You could have died. I just don't want that to happen again. Maybe I should not have been so quick to voice my opinion. If I hurt you, I'm sorry."

Maria turned around to face Daphne. "What you said is true, and I'm grateful you stood by me through all of it, Daphne. It's just hard for me to face the truth sometimes that I have an eating disorder, and it's even harder to talk about it."

The bell rang, which meant it was time to get to our next class, and we only have eight minutes to get there. I said bye to the girls before I took off down the hall and thought to myself, where am I going. I forgot to look at the schedule before I left the lunchroom, so I had no idea where my class could be. I stopped long enough to reach into my bookbag to locate the paper with my list of classes. Finally, I found it, and I hadn't realized my next class was on the second floor. I just passed the staircase, so I had to walk back over to the stairs. I spotted Tonya and Lewis ahead of me, holding hands. I stopped right where I was on the staircase. It was such an awkward moment because I wasn't sure what was going on with them. I just figured Tonya would tell me later, but for now, I don't want to know.

When I finally arrived in front of my classroom door. I had a rather bizarre encounter. It started with me reaching for the doorknob and placing my hand on top of someone else's. Shocked and surprised, I let out a squeal as I pulled my hand back. Before I could look up, I heard, "Here you go, my lady," in a guy's voice. As the door opened, I looked up at the guy this time holding the door. Now it turned out I recognized this guy, but I did not know from where. He was standing perfectly straight, waving his hand for me to walk inside. It seemed as though he got the wrong idea and thought that I was checking him out. I know this to be the case since the guy whispered, "Do you approve?" I intuitively knew what he meant, but I tried to play it off, and I looked back at him like he was crazy.

Once I was inside the classroom, I told him, "Thank you for holding the door for me." Then I decided to sit as far away as I could get from this guy. That was until Daphne showed up.

"Sammy, why do we have to sit back here in the last row?"

"What do you mean, Daphne? Is there something wrong with this row?"

"No, it's just that I had a chair saved for you over there."

Daphne pointed to the chair that was right beside Greg. "I tried to wave you over, and I even called out your name."

"I'm sorry, Daphne. I was distracted by this guy at the door when I walked into the classroom —"

Daphne interrupted and said, "You mean Michael?"

"Oh, that's who he is. Thanks, Daphne"

"Michael's in character today."

"What do you mean he's in character?"

"He's a drama student, so he's still in character from his drama class."

"Daphne, today is the first day of school. Do you really think they had the drama students acting out a play today?"

"Nope!

"Then how is he in character?"

"Sammy, he has been in that character since last year. Michael was in a play that took place during the Renaissance era, and I think he uses it to get girls."

"Wow, Daphne, that's not charming or suave. That's just ridiculous." We both laughed, and I asked, "How does your brother put up with him?"

"Easy Michael is my brother's best friend, and Arturo accepts Michael for who he is."

"And who is he?"

"Michael's a great guy. You just have to get to know him to understand him, Sammy."

The bell rang, and our teacher asked everyone to have a seat and be quiet while he took roll call. Daphne opened her notebook and began to write. She tore the paper out of her notebook and folded the paper up into a triangle. Then she flicked the triangle to me. I opened the note and read, "Did I ever tell you about my family vacation to Fort Myers when my dad was in town?"

"No," I simply wrote. Then I folded up the paper and flicked it back to Daphne. She unfolded the piece of paper and began to write and write and write some more. After about ten minutes of writing, Daphne ripped out another piece of paper from her spiral notebook before folding it up and flicking it back. It read, Michael went with us on our two-week family vacation. The whole time we were in Fort Myers, my brother Arturo and Michael kept walking up to girls and using pickup lines from Michael's plays. My brother and Michael quickly realized the girls eat this up like crazy. They had tons of girls after them all summer long. Michael's beeper kept going off, so Arturo and Michael spent most of their time on the payphones speaking to girls. Sometimes the payphones wouldn't stop ringing. Guess who would be on the other line? If you guessed girls, you would be right. The girls they called previously from the payphones would call them back all day long. It was as if they were at home using a house phone or something. It was definitely crazy, and since we were on vacation, girls were coming and going all day long, either on the payphone or in person. They only gave out Michael's beeper number to the girls, so when our vacation was over, he needed a new beeper. Michael's dad bought him another one, but only his parents have the number.

I wrote back, "That's cool, but is Michael back to being a Casanova and giving out his beeper number to every girl he meets or did he learn his lesson?"

Daphne read the note and laughed. Then she wrote back, "Michael says he has two beepers. The players' beeper and the parents' beeper." After I read the last note, a piece of paper made into a rectangle with a pull tab landed on my desk. I picked it up and looked around the room. Michael was waving his hands and motioning for me to give the note to Daphne. I handed the cute little note over to her, and she quickly read it and rolled her eyes.

I opened my trapper keeper, to a blank piece of paper where I wrote, "What's wrong?" I tapped on the paper with my pen to get Daphne's attention. She looked over and read what I wrote before shaking her head and tossing the note from Michael into her purse. Daphne opened her spiral notebook to a blank sheet of paper and wrote back to me.

It merely read, "Michael spoke to my brother, and he's picking us up after school today."

The bell rang, and I told Daphne, "That sounds great, no waiting on the school bus to drop you home after a bunch of stops. You wouldn't hear me complain; that's for sure." I slid the straps of my backpack on over my shoulders as I left the classroom. My first day back to school was over, and I was ready to go home.

Patrick greeted me when I was boarding the bus and asked: "How was your first day back to school, Sammy?"

"Good, I'm just a little tired, and I'm glad you're our bus driver again this year, Patrick."

"Me too, Sammy. Now you can sit back and relax after everyone is on board, we will be on our way. I walked to the back and sat down on the opposite side of the bus to ride home. I opened the window to let out some of the hot air before I sat back down to stare out the window. That's when I spotted a dark blue Camaro playing music really loud. When I saw the driver, I was shocked. It was the same guy who was staring at me during lunch today.

My stomach started to flip out. Then I said, "Oh crap," out loud when I assumed he spotted me because he was waving and looking in my direction. I decided to duck my head down, but I ended up turning my head to the side instead, and I spotted a boy waving back to him. Suddenly I felt relieved and silly all at the same time because I recognized the boy. He was

the same boy sitting at the table directly behind me in the cafeteria today. That means this guy was not staring at me during lunch. I just assumed that he was, and I was wrong, which means Tonya was right. I need to work on my insecurities and stop worrying about what everybody thinks of me. The world does not revolve around me, and everything is not about me. I laid my head back and closed my eyes until I heard, "Muñeca, how was your first day back to school?" Tonya sat down beside me, waiting for an answer to her question.

When Patrick asked, "Is everybody ready to go?"

Everyone answered yes, so Patrick closed the doors and took his seat behind the wheel. That is when I had this sudden impulse to ask Tonya what's going on between her and Lewis, but then I thought maybe it's not my business, and Tonya can tell me when she's ready.

On our ride home, Tonya talked about how her day went, and I was anxiously waiting for her to bring up Lewis. However, she did not mention Lewis once during the whole conversation. Which is why I probably blurted out, "What's going on with you and Lewis?"

Tonya's face became serious for a moment, yet she never answered the question. Instead, she continued to speak to me as if I had not asked her anything about it. I walked off the bus, wondering why is she keeping this a secret from me.

Fall is over, and winter is here. It's already December, and today was my last day of school until I return on the fourth of January. I love this time of year. It's already in the 60s, well, sometimes. On those days, I've been enjoying wearing sweaters and turtlenecks. I like wearing darker colors, black, brown, red, burgundy, and of course, purple. I love being able to wear a dress with black tights and boots. It just looks really classy and chic to me.

Daphne, Maria, Denise, Tonya, and Monica are supposed to come to my place tonight. We're trying to plan a night out together at our favorite winter place in town. It's a forest filled with lights and amusement park rides. The girls and I have been going there together for the last two years. One of my favorite things to eat at this place is the freshly baked cinnamon mini donuts. The stand is in the mid-center of the park. There's always a line to get a bag of these delicious donuts. Once you have your bag, you can just munch on them as you continue walking down the path through the trees filled with lights.

The girls all showed up an hour after my mom came home from work, and she ordered pizza for us. As soon as our dinner arrived, my mom mentioned how beautiful the weather was outside. Of course, Tonya took that as a suggestion that we should eat our pizza outside by the pool. Everyone thought that was a great idea, and we all headed out the door with our two boxes of pizza, paper plates, napkins, and our drinks.

After everyone sat down at the picnic table, Tonya brought up the outing. "Girls, I think this year should be a little bit different."

"What do you mean by different, Tonya?"

"This year, I would like to invite some of our other friends to join us, Denise."

"Can you be more specific, Tonya, by telling us who it is that you want to invite?"

"Just a couple of guys, Maria."

"A couple of guys, Tonya. What guys? You know what, nevermind. I'm sure I know who you want to invite already."

"Muñeca, I knew you were going to get like this."

"Get like what, Tonya? "

"Aggravated Muñeca."

"Only because you want to invite your crush to go out with us, Tonya?"

"Who's her crush, Sammy?"

"Daphne, I think Tonya should be the one to reveal that to you, not me. "

"Tonya, who are you crushing on?"

"Nobody, Muñeca, is exaggerating Daphne."

"Could it be that one of the guys you want to invite Tonya is someone that you are secretly dating?"

"Sammy, what are you talking about? Tonya isn't dating anyone."

"Maybe she is Daphne, but she's keeping it a secret from us."

"Muñeca, all I will admit to is having dreamt of holding hands with a guy while surrounded by the beautiful lights as we walk through the forest."

"Is that what you want me to believe, Tonya? You only hold hands with him, that's all?"

"Yes, that's all, Muñeca."

"Tonya, why haven't you told me about this before?"

"You didn't ask, Muñeca."

"What are you two talking about?"

"I don't even know anymore, Maria."

"Okay, if you say so, Sammy."

"While Tonya and Sammy have their own conversation that no one understands. I just want to admit that I've had dreams of not only holding hands with a certain guy, but I also wear his jacket in my dreams to stay warm as we walk through the forest, holding hands." All of us just stared back at Daphne with a blank look on our face. Then Daphne said, "It's just a dream, girls. Besides, Greg doesn't even know that I exist. How can I wear his jacket?"

We were all cracking up except for Maria. She sat up in her chair and reached across the table for Daphne's hand. Then she told Daphne, "The minute you find the courage to speak to Greg, things will be different, and he will know that you exist."

"I don't know about that, Maria, but that would be great."
"Wait, you haven't spoken to your crush yet, Daphne?"

"No, Denise, because every time I get around Greg, I feel nervous. I want to talk to him, but I cannot think clearly whenever he's around me. That's why I haven't spoken to him yet."

"Tonya, if you want to invite boys, that's fine with me. I do not care who comes. I'm there to see the lights, and I don't know about the rides."

"Does that mean you're not going to ride anything, Denise?"

"Honestly, I don't care about the rides either. I just want those cinnamon donuts."

"I agree with Denise," Monica said. "I just want to see the lights and eat donuts. You have to admit they are the best thing in the park."

Maria finally chimed in, saying, "It doesn't matter to me. I'm there to hang out with you girls, and that's it."

"Well, I heard they raised the entrance price."

"My mom and I heard the same thing, Denise, so my mom offered to take me by the forest tomorrow to find out the cost of admission."

"That's great, Sammy let me know."

"For sure, Denise, or you can come with me tomorrow."

"Maybe I will, I'll let you know."

"Okay, so what have we decided?"

"What do you mean, Daphne?"

"Monica, I'm asking if we're inviting boys to go with us."

Tonya stood up and announced, "If you want boys to go, raise your hand. If you don't mind, raise your hand. If you don't want them to come, then leave your hand down."

As we all looked around the table at one another, I noticed everyone had their hand up except for me. "Okay, so we're inviting boys," Tonya said with a smile.

"Can I ask a question."

"Yes, of course. Go ahead, Denise."

"When are we going, Tonya?"

"We still haven't set a date yet. Do you have a date in mind?"

"No, but that's something I need to know ahead of time. Even though we're out of school, my parents work Monday through Friday, so I still have the same curfew. Home by ten o'clock on weekdays and eleven o'clock on the weekends. Plus, I watch my siblings while my parents are at work."

"What if we go tomorrow? It's the weekend, and you can spend the night at my house, Denise?"

"I don't know, Sammy; I need to speak to my parents about that tonight."

"Now, I have a question for you, Tonya."

"Sure, Monica, what is it?"

"Who are the boys you want to invite?"

Tonya looked down at the floor, before answering, "Your cousin and your brother." Everyone was stunned by Tonya's answer, except for me.

About a minute later, Monica asked, "Which brother and which cousin?"

That is when I blurted out, "Lewis and Julio." Tonya smiled while nodding her head, yes.

Monica replied, "Great, I just hope for your sake Tonya that it's Lewis you have a crush on, or you might be disappointed."

Now Tonya was grinning when she said, "Well, I guess that I should also mention that I want to invite Greg."

"How are you going to do that, Tonya? When you're not even friends with Greg."

"You're right, Muñeca. I am not. However, Julio and Lewis are friends with Greg, and they can invite him."

"Tonya's right, Sammy. Greg is best friends with my little brother Julio, and he has become like family to all of us."

"That's great, Monica, and now that brings me to my next question."

"And what would that be, Tonya?"

"I just wanted to know if there is someone you would like to invite?"

"Thank you, Tonya. Yes, I would like to invite my brother Alex and my cousin Eddie. Think of them as chaperones for Lewis and Julio."

Tonya was shocked, I could tell by her expression, but she regained her composure and simply replied, "Monica, that's great. Be sure to invite them."

"Hey, can I invite my brother, Tonya?"

"Of course, Daphne, please do."

"Denise, is there anyone you would like to invite?"

"Nope."

"Maria, how about you?"

"Yes, my brother, Alvaro."

Monica's face suddenly lit up, and she smiled. Tonya replied, "That's awesome, Maria. I would love to hang out with Alvaro." Monica instantly spun her head around to face Tonya with an angry look on her face. At the same time, Daphne stood up and announced her brother was here.

That's when we all stood up beside her to say goodbye. Daphne, Maria, and Denise gave us each a hug before they took off running toward Arturo's car.

"Girls, I'm leaving too. I have to take Daisy outside for her walk." I hugged Monica, then Tonya, and I left.

The minute I walked in the door, Daisy jumped up on her hind legs, giving me kisses. "Are you excited to see me, girl, or do you need to go outside? I'm pretty sure you want to go outside for a walk, so give me a second to grab your leash."

Daisy practically pulled me down the stairs and out onto the grass. The Lawnmowers were here earlier today, and Daisy enjoys the smell of the green after it has been cut. She was in the middle of inspecting the field when all of a sudden, Daisy jumped and took off running. She pulled me out onto the sidewalk, and I had a death grip on Daisy's leash as she dragged me behind her. I yelled out, "Daisy, slow down. It's okay, girl," but she was like a runaway train, and I was the caboose still attached. Julio was ahead of us, and before I could warn him, he turned around and caught Daisy mid-run. He picked her up and dragged me along with Daisy straight smack into his chest. Before I said anything, I just stood there for a moment, out of breath with my heart racing. Finally, I stepped back from Julio, ready to explain what happened until I noticed his eyes shining down on me. Feeling captivated and yet mystified, I simply stood there staring up at him. It was crazy. We hadn't said a word to one another, but our eyes were locked on each other. Then Daisy barked and broke the spell we were under.

"Sammy, I'm sorry I forgot that I was holding her. Do you want your dog back?"

"Yes, of course, thank you for getting her under control for me. Daisy was spooked by something on the grass, and her behavior was totally unexpected."

Julio attempted to hand Daisy to me, and I backed up, asking, "Could you just set her back down on the grass for me? Daisy weighs close to a hundred pounds."
"Oh, of course."

Julio set Daisy down on the grass, then asked, "May I walk with you girls?"

"Sure, I don't think Daisy would mind."
She looked up at us with her tongue hanging out on the right side of her mouth.

"Daisy looks like she's smiling.

"Your right, I think she likes you, Julio."

"Well, I like Daisy, too."

Daisy stopped to do her business, and I caught Julio staring at me again. I quickly turned my head away, but I wanted to talk to him, so I said, "I'm going to the forest with the girls this weekend, most likely on Sunday. You and Lewis are going to be invited."

"Really, are you going to invite me, Sammy?" I looked up, at Julio and our eyes locked for a second before Daisy took off down the sidewalk again.

"No, Tonya will invite you and your cousin."

"Do you want me to go, Sammy?"

"You can go. I guess. I mean, I'm okay with boys coming with us."

Julio stopped in front of me and squinted up his face before asking, "Do you usually have a problem with boys going out with you places?"

"I don't know; I haven't gone anywhere with boys before except for my brother or Daphne's brother."

"Oh, I see. So you haven't gone out with a boy you like?"

"No."

"Have you ever had a boyfriend?"

I looked down at the sidewalk and, feeling utterly nervous, I answered, "No." Now, this is going to sound strange. Although I was nervous, I was also starting to feel a bit excited at the same time by his intrusive questions.

"Have you ever kissed a boy?"

"Ummm, No, I haven't."

"Do you like anybody right now?"

This question made me lift my head up and look him straight in the eyes before answering, "I'm not sure yet, maybe."

Julio smiled at me as he bit down on his bottom lip. We remained there on the sidewalk, just staring at one another again until Daisy pulled me away. Now Daisy and I were practically standing up on this hill looking down on Julio. Oh man, I was grateful Daisy brought us up here. The energy I was feeling between Julio and I had become intense, and I needed a moment. Especially after answering that last question. Julio must have known how I was feeling, and therefore he didn't ask me any more questions. However, he had a big smile on his face the rest of our walk together.

When I walked in the backdoor with Daisy, my mom was in the kitchen and asked, "Sam, are you feeling alright?"

"Yes, Mom, I feel fine. Why?"

"You have a strange look on your face."

Then I thought to myself a strange look, what does she mean? I took off toward the bathroom when I heard my mom ask, "Can I take the leash off, Daisy?"

"Yes, please, thanks, mom." I bent over the sink to look at my reflection and thought, Wow, what in the world is going on with me? How could I forget to take the leash off Daisy? Then I spotted a pimple on my chin and thought of Julio. I immediately ran into my mom's room.

"Honey, is everything alright? You look upset."

"I am upset. I have a pimple on my chin, mom, and I can't let anyone see this."

She started laughing while I was standing in front of her. Mom, why are you laughing? I'm being completely serious. I don't want this on my face. Can you please take me to the pharmacy?"

My mom laughed even harder before saying, "I'm sorry, honey. I am only laughing because it's like Deja vu all over again. Your brother had the same reaction to his first blemish. Your life is going to be filled with lots of these little surprises. It's a part of growing up, Sam, and I do understand. See, when I was a teenager about your age, I already had terrible acne all over my face. You and your brother are extremely fortunate not to have the same problem I had to deal with."

"Mom, I'm sorry you had to go through that, but I still don't want anyone to see this pimple on my chin tomorrow."

"Why? What is going on tomorrow, Sam?"

"Nothing is definite yet, but we might be going to the forest, and we're inviting boys to go with us."

"I didn't realize boys would be going. You never mentioned this before, Sam."

"Mom, I didn't know about that until today."

"Well, who are these boys?"

"Monica's brothers and both of her cousins."

"You mean Pilar's kids?"

"Yes, mom."

"Well, I approve of them, so who else has been invited?"

"Daphne's brother Arturo and I think his best friend."

"Arturo is Carmen's kid, and his best friend Michael is a wonderful person. Now is there anyone else?"

"Yes, this guy named Greg, and Maria is inviting her twin brother Alvaro."

"And which one of these boys have you worried about that pimple on your chin Sam?"

"Oh no, Mom, it's not like that at all. It's more like I don't want anyone to see this pimple on my chin because... "Nevermind, can we just go to the pharmacy, please?"

My mom sat back on her sofa, grinning at me before saying, "Of course, we can go, Sam. Be ready to leave in ten minutes."

"Thanks, mom." I ran into my bedroom to grab my purse and stopped at my window to take a look outside. I was looking over at Julio's building.

When I suddenly heard, "Sam, what are you looking at?" Startled, I jumped away from the window and tripped over Daisy. Now I was on the floor looking up at my mom. She had her arms crossed over her chest with a curious look on her face.

"Hi, mom. I was just looking outside at nothing, really."

"Are you okay, Sam?"

"Yes, I'm fine."

"How about Daisy?" I leaned over to check on Daisy, and she rolled onto her back for a belly rub with her tongue hanging out.

"Mom, I think she's fine too."

"Good, are you ready to go?" I nodded my head, yes, and my mom put out her hand to help me up. We went grocery shopping, and I found everything I need at the market. When we arrived back home, Julio and Lewis were outside. They saw us walking in the parking lot, both arms filled with groceries, and ran over to help us. Julio grabbed all the groceries from my arms, and Lewis took the groceries from my mom. I ran upstairs to unlock the door, and the boys walked in behind me.

"Thank you, boys, for helping us with our groceries."

"Anytime, Ms. Harris, I'm glad we could help," Lewis replied. Julio didn't say a word; he just stood there in my kitchen, staring at me.

"By the way, boys, we're going to find out the price of admission into the forest tomorrow."

In an instant, Julio had a smile on his face, and said, "That sounds great, Ms. Harris, thank you." Julio looked over at Lewis and saw a puzzled look on his cousin's face. Then he immediately turned to me and said, "We have to go now, Samantha, but I'll see you tomorrow." Julio quickly rushed Lewis out the door, and I realized Tonya still had not spoken to her crush with regards to joining us at the forest, which made me giggle.

"Sam, what's so funny? Why are you laughing?"

"Mom, they haven't been invited yet."

"Oh, I'm sorry, Honey."

"I'm sure it's fine, mom. Besides, they will be invited tomorrow, and everything will make sense to them afterward."

"Well, that explains it."

"Explains what, mom?"

"The strange look Lewis had after I said that."

"Yes, it does, mom," and we were both laughing as we put the groceries away."

I woke up the next morning relatively early for me. I had been tossing and turning for about an hour, attempting to fall back to sleep with no luck. I gave up when visions of Julio popped into my head, and I decided it was time to get up now. Daisy followed me back to my room after I took a shower. "Do you want to go for a walk? Is that why you're in here, Daisy? She sat down in front of me and handed me her paw. "Wow, you have never done that before, so I'm taking that as a yes." The minute we stepped foot outside, Daisy towed me down the stairs and over to her favorite spot on the grass. A couple of minutes later, she was continuing to sniff every inch of this area. Daisy was doing a thorough investigation of the green since her spot was trimmed yesterday. Tonya and Lewis even showed up approximately ten minutes later, and we were still standing in the very same place.

"Hey, Muñeca, what are you doing up so early?"

"I couldn't sleep anymore, Tonya, so I got up to take Daisy outside for a walk, but she won't leave this area."

"That's only because the grass was cut recently, and Daisy wants to take in the fresh scent. There's no need to worry she's not sick or anything like that. "

"Oh no, I realize that Tonya, especially after what happened yesterday."

"Why what happened yesterday?"

Lewis had a knowing smile suddenly appear on his face, and I replied, "Nothing, Tonya forget I even mentioned it."

"Okay, I will, Muñeca, but you should get up this early every morning to come jogging with Lewis and me."

"Exactly, when did you start jogging, Tonya?"

"A couple of months ago after Lewis invited me to go with him."

"And Tonya clearly loves it; she goes with me every morning. We head out at five o'clock if you ever want to join us, Sammy."

"Thanks for the invite, Lewis. I will be sure to let you know.

"It was great to see you and Daisy, but we have to start jogging now. I can give you a call a little later when I'm ready to go down to the pool."

"Sounds good, Tonya. I'll wait for your call." The two of them jogged off, and a few minutes later, I saw Julio. He walked out of his building, headed in our direction, so I turned around facing Daisy. I did not want Julio to catch me looking at him. Then Daisy spotted Julio, and she went crazy. First, she started barking, but then she began to pull me across the parking lot to get to Julio. Fortunately, he noticed right away what was happening and ran over to us. He kneeled beside Daisy and scratched her behind the ears, and she promptly settled down.

Julio was grinning when he looked up at me and said, "Good morning, Samantha, are you girls out on your morning walk?"

"Yes, we are. Thank you for getting Daisy to calm down. I don't know what's going on with her lately. For the last two days, you have had to come to our rescue, and that's totally embarrassing."

"Why? I don't mind playing the hero for you and Daisy."

Right after Julio said that I felt overwhelmed with joy, and it surprised me. I wanted to conceal how he made me feel, except I could not stop smiling. Knowing I had to say something, I asked, "So what are you up to?"

It was such a stupid question, yet that is all I could come up with. Julio stopped petting Daisy and replied, "Well, I was-"Before Julio could complete his sentence, Daisy sat down in front of him and placed both of her paws up on his shoulders.

"Daisy, what are you doing?"

Julio laughed and told me, "It's okay. I'm enjoying the attention." Daisy was rubbing her head against his chest, demanding him to continue scratching her. She even went as far as to give him kisses.

"Wow, I don't know what to say, Julio. Daisy must have a crush on you or something. She seldom gives kisses to anyone."

He laughed and hugged Daisy before standing up with a great big smile on his face. "Now, the answer to your question Samantha is that I'm speaking to you. Oh, and I should mention that I already have a crush on somebody else." He looked down at Daisy and said, "I'm sorry, girl, but it's true," then he winked at me. I do not know why, but that wink of his made me blush, so I bent my head down. Julio reached over and moved a lock of hair away from my face.

"Now that's better. I can see your eyes again."

I looked up at Julio and smiled, although my cheeks were beginning to burn from blushing. "I don't know if it's appropriate for me to say this to you...

"Say what, Samantha?"

"Several times yesterday, you made me feel a bit invaded, and it made me nervous. It's all those questions you asked. They were so personal."

He took his eyes off me and began to stare at the ground. "I'm sorry if I hurt your feelings, Julio. I'm not trying to make things awkward between us. I just wanted you to know how I felt, that's all. "

"You haven't made anything awkward, Samantha. I'm amazed that you opened up to me and told me how I made you feel."

"Are you really?"

Julio nodded his head yes as he cupped my chin and looked into my eyes. "Samantha, I want you to know that you make me feel things too." My curiosity was peeking, and I wanted to know what he meant by that, only I couldn't bring myself to inquire about it. Instead, I stood there, staring back at him.

When Julio removed his hand from my chin, everything instantly became clear to me. It was like magic. I went from feeling discouraged to courageous and asked, "Do you mind answering a couple of questions for me?"

Sounding surprised, he replied, "Not at all, Samantha. Ask me whatever you want."

"Great, what type of things do I make you feel?"

"I don't even know how to began to put it into words. I guess once I've figured that out, you will be the first one to know."

"Do you have a girlfriend, Julio?"

"No, but I want one."

"Have you ever kissed a girl?"

"Yes, but she wasn't someone that I wanted to kiss."

"What do you mean? Can you explain that to me?"

"Sure, I was playing spin the bottle at this party-"

"Nevermind, I understand, Julio."

He stopped walking and looked directly into my eyes and said, "Now, there is a girl that I want to kiss if she'll let me."

Once again, I felt insanely nervous, and I dropped Daisy's leash onto the ground. Julio bent down and picked it up. I held my hand out for the leash, but he didn't hand it back to me. Instead, he took my hand and asked Daisy if she would like to go for a walk by the lake. She barked and wagged her tail with excitement.

"Julio, should we be out on the golf course?"

"Don't worry, Samantha. The golf course won't be open for another hour. We have plenty of time to sit by the lake and watch the sunrise."

"There's a lake out here?"

"Yes, a big one, and I have a towel for you to sit on." Then I noticed the towel slung across his shoulders.

"Did we prevent you from going to the pool?"

"No."

"Well, that's what it looks like. I mean, you're dressed for the pool Julio."

"Okay, you caught me. I was headed to the pool to swim some laps, then something better came up."

"Alright, I guess we can go by the lake for a little bit. Afterward, I can join you at the pool if you want. I mean, I'm already going to the pool with Tonya."

Julio stopped walking and faced me. "I would love it if you would spend some time with me at the pool before everybody else shows up."

"Really? Why?"

"Samantha, I really like spending time with you. I'm enjoying getting to know you better, and I have some more questions to ask."

"That doesn't sound fun at all, Julio. Yesterday, I was beginning to feel like I was under interrogation."

"I'm just curious, and there are no wrong answers, Samantha."

Then let's make a deal, Julio. We can continue to ask each other questions. However, we need to remain honest with our answers."

"No, problem I've been honest with you this whole time." I turned around to shake his hand, and that's when I realized we were still holding hands.

"Julio, I can't believe you're holding my hand."

"I'm surprised you allow me to." We both stood there, smiling at one another when the intense nervous feeling came back flowing through me more potent than ever before.

"There were several times that I wanted to hold your hand like yesterday, for instance. I just didn't have the courage to do it."

"Today, you did. How did that change?"

"Samantha, I didn't even think about it. I just saw your hand and reached for it.."

"Have you ever held hands with a boy before?"

"No, Julio, I haven't."

"Do you know what was my biggest fear?"

"Not really, what was it?"

"I was afraid that you would pull your hand away from me."

"Julio, I didn't pull my hand away because I wanted you to hold it."

"Do you like me, Samantha?"

"Yes, of course, I like you, Julio. You're my friend."

He stopped walking, shook his head, and started to laugh.

"Why are you laughing?"

"Because you knew what I meant by that question, Samantha."

"Fine, do you like me, Julio?"

"Yes, very much, I have a crush on you."

"How do you know for sure that you have a crush on me?"

"Now that is an easy question, Samantha. It's the way you make me feel whenever you're around me."

"How do I make you feel?"

"Samantha, you make me feel nervous and excited. My best part of the day is when I've spent it with you. I can even tell you right now, getting to hold your hand has been awesome. It's also been the best feeling that I have felt so far. It is like a nervous feeling that has turned into energy."

"Do you realize you just answered my first question, Julio?"

He grinned and said, "I guess you're right, I did."

We made it to the lake, and Julio laid out his towel. He sat down on the towel first, then tugged on my hand. I took two steps closer to Julio, and he put up his hands. Julio eased me down gently until I was sitting down beside him on the towel. We looked up at the sky, ready to watch the sunrise when we heard a splash. Daisy had her two front paws in the lake prepared to jump in by the time we reached her. I tried to coax Daisy out of the lake when Julio leaned over me and picked her up. That's when I attached her leash, and we headed back home.

"Thank you for going on the walk with us, Julio. You did not have to walk me to my doorstep. I know you have to get home."

"Samantha, will you still meet me at the pool?"

"Yes, a little later, though. I can't go right now."

"Okay, beep me when you're ready to go. Do you have my number, Samantha?"

"No, I don't have your beeper number."

"If you get a pen, I'll write it down for you." I ran inside and grabbed a black marker. When I came back outside, I grabbed Julio's hand and wrote my number down instead. He was just standing there, grinning at me.

"You can beep me when you're ready to go to the pool, Julio. That way, I will have your number."

Now he looked shocked when he asked, "You want my phone number?"

"Yes, I want your number, Julio, so don't forget to beep me."

"I won't forget anything," and he looked down at his hand again, grinning before waving bye.

When I walked back inside, my mom was upset.

"Sam, why are Daisy's paws full of mud?"

"What do you mean?"

"Daisy jumped up on my bed, and my white comforter is now covered in brown mud."

"I'm sorry about that, mom I will give her a bath right now, and I'll wash your comforter too."

"While your washing, Daisy, I can make us breakfast. I hope you want pancakes, Sam."

Chapter 4 Who's at the Pool

At ten, I received a phone call from Daphne asking if she could come over. "That's fine with me, Daphne, but bring your bathing suit because I'm spending the day at the pool. As a matter of fact, I have to let you go now, or I'm going to be late."

"Late for what?"

"I'm meeting someone at the pool in a few minutes, so I've got to go."

"Are you meeting up with Tonya at the pool?"

"Yes, she will be there a little later."

"Oh, I see, then who is meeting up with you at the pool right now?"

"Julio."

"Is Julio at the pool waiting for you?"

"No, he told me he would meet me there in like five minutes when I spoke to him over the phone."

"Where's Greg? Is Greg coming over to his house today?"

"I don't know, Daphne. I guess you can ask Julio yourself when you get here."

"Fine, I'm leaving now, and I'm picking up Maria and Denise on the way."

"That sounds good. Bye, Daphne." After I hung up with Daphne, I called Julio's house. Monica answered the phone, so I told her the girls are coming over. Then I asked her to join us at the pool in twenty minutes.

"Sammy, I can meet you at the pool, but my brother left for the pool five minutes ago to meet up with you."

"In that case, I have to go. Thanks, Monica."

After I hung up the phone, I slid on my chancletas before running out the door. As I was heading down the stairs, someone grabbed my hand, and I screamed. Until I heard Julio from behind me say, "Samantha, stop screaming. It's just me." I turned around on the steps and looked up. Julio was standing one step above me, holding my hand. He kissed the top of it before saying, "I'm sorry, Samantha. I didn't mean to startle you like that."

"It's okay. I was just going down to the pool to look for you."

"Well, that's why I'm here. I thought we could walk down to the pool together."

"There's something I need to tell you, Julio, and that's why I was in a rush and haven't put on my bathing suit yet."

Julio's face went from a massive smile to a huge frown. "What happened? You don't want to go to the pool with me anymore?"

"No, that's not it. I want to go to the pool with you, but I thought you should know that I will not be there alone. My girlfriends will be there with me in less than twenty minutes."

"That's perfect, Samantha,"

"Really, why? What changed?"

"My brother and both of my cousins have decided to join us at the pool."

"Well, that sounds perfect. It will be like our summer spent at the pool all over again. Now I do not even know how to ask you this, Julio?"

"Ask me what, Samantha?"

"Is your friend Greg coming over to your house today?"

Julio released my hand before asking, "Why? Do you have something for my friend Greg?"

"Yes." His mouth dropped open, and suddenly Julio appeared to be very upset.

"Samantha, is that why you have been paying attention to me lately because you have a thing for my friend Greg?"

"No, I did those things because... I don't think I'm ready to tell you that, Julio."

"But, you're able to tell me you have a thing for my friend Greg?"

"Yes, because Daphne really likes Greg, and she has developed an enormous crush on him. You have no idea how much she talks about him. It is to the point where it's driving me crazy. Oh, and I need to warn you, Julio."

"Warn me about what?"

"Daphne intends to ask you all sorts of questions about Greg today."

"So, what you're telling me now is that you both have a crush on Greg?"

"What? No, I do not have a crush on Greg. I have a crush on you. Daphne's the only one that has a thing for Greg."

Julio's face lit up like a neon sign. His eyes were huge, and his smile was the biggest I have seen yet. "So, you have a crush on me, Sammy?"

"I didn't mean to say that Julio. I just cannot believe you had it so backward. When you asked if I had a thing for Greg, I meant Daphne was that thing."

"Samantha, you still haven't answered my question."

"Yes, I have a crush on you, Julio. However, this is downright embarrassing. I am just not used to feeling this way. It's all new to me, and hard for me to explain everything."

"Explain what?"

"How I'm feeling, Julio. I mean, I think it's a crush based on I like holding your hand, I like talking to you, and time often flies by whenever I'm alone with you."

"Do you want to kiss me, Samantha?"

A nervous giggle popped out before I could answer, "Yes, I'm pretty certain that I do. Why are you asking me that question, Julio?"

"Because I definitely want to kiss you, Samantha."

Feeling nervous, I blurted out, "Let's not talk about this anymore. My girlfriends are on their way over here, so I need to get back inside. I will meet you at the pool in a few minutes. Bye, Julio." I ran back inside and leaned my back up against the door a minute. All I could think of was how much I wanted to kiss him, but not now. The timing is not right. He just thought I had a crush on his best friend.

While I was in my room getting changed, I heard a knock on the backdoor. I grabbed my sunscreen, a towel, and the sunglasses off my bed. By the time I opened my bedroom door, Daphne, Maria, and Denise were standing in front of me. "Hi, girls."

Daphne had a smirk on her face when she asked, "Have you been down to the pool yet, Sammy?"

"No, I haven't, but I'm ready to go now."

My mom was in the kitchen with Daisy pouring herself a cup of coffee when I hugged her from behind.

"Where are you going, Sam?"

"To the pool, Mom."

"Sam, I thought we were going to the forest this afternoon to find out how much they increased the price of admission."

"Mom, thanks for reminding me. I forgot all about that."

"Sammy, seriously. What could be more important than the forest?"

"I don't know, Denise, I just forgot."

Then I heard Daphne giggle before saying, "I know why she forgot."

"Daphne, stop, you don't know anything." I was panicked by what she would say next and tried to rush her out the door.

"My mom gave me a strange look before saying, Okay, girls, have fun at the pool, and I will take you by the forest later."

We were standing outside at the foot of the stairs when I replied, "That sounds great, mom, thank you." I waved bye and ran down the stairs with Daphne.

When we were walking over to the pool, Daphne asked, "Do you know who's going to be there, Sammy?"

"No, I'm not really sure. Why?"

"Sammy, I have a lot of questions to ask Julio today, and they all pertain to Greg. I don't want everyone to hear our discussion."

"Oh, Daphne, please don't drive Julio crazy by asking him a ton of questions about Greg."

"Why? Are you afraid I'm going to chase Julio away?" I mouthed the word 'yes,' and Daphne broke out laughing.

When we arrived at the pool, everybody was here except for Eddie. We laid our towels out on the lawn chairs beside Tonya, and that's when I noticed the boys waving to someone. At the same time, Daphne was tapping me on the arm to get my attention.

"Daphne, what is it?"

"Look over there, Sammy?" I stood up to see what Daphne was pointing to, and that is when I saw Greg and Eddie. They were walking on the stone path that leads to the pool. I looked over at Julio and mouthed the words, 'Thank you,' and he smiled before Daphne went to tapping me on the arm again. I turned around, facing Daphne, and she was pointing at Greg.

Together we watched him enter the pool, take off his shirt, and dive in. Daphne jumped up from her chair, so I grabbed the back of her suit and asked, "Where are you going?"

"Sammy, I just want to make sure he's not drowning."

Tonya lifted her sunglasses up and asked, "Why? Are you a lifeguard, Daphne?"

"No, I'm not," Daphne admitted as she crossed her arms over her chest, pouting, and the four of us started to laugh.

"Daphne, you're so crazy. You need to calm down. You're going to chase that boy away."

"Denise, that man has done something to my brain, and I can't think straight. Just let me go see if he has it in his back pocket or something."

"Who has what of yours, in their back-pocket, Daphne?"

"Maria, she wants to see if Greg is holding her brain captive in his back pocket."

"Sammy, that's what I thought she said, and the answer is yes. Ever since Daphne laid eyes on Greg, she has lost her marbles."

That is when Alex yelled out, "Girls, are you going to join us in the pool to play Marco Polo?"

"Yes, of course, I love Marco Polo," Daphne answered.

Tonya told Daphne, "Listen, I don't want to get my hair wet, so I'm not playing."

"Yeah, I do not want to get my hair wet either, Denise added, if we're going to the forest tonight.

"Tonight?"

"Yes, I thought that is what we decided on yesterday, Sammy. I just had to wait for permission from my parents to sleep over your house."

"Cool, Denise, I just didn't know you were permitted to spend the night tonight."

"You can't be serious? I called Daphne this morning and told her that I could spend the night at your house. She told me that she would call to let you know before we came over. That's why I brought my overnight bag."

"Daphne called, but she failed to mention anything about this. Instead, she asked about Greg and wanted to know if he was coming to the pool."

"Hmmm, that figures."

"Tonya, since everyone is here now, why don't you ask the boys if they want to go with us to the forest tonight?"

"Denise is right everybody's here, so that makes sense."

"Shouldn't we wait for Monica?"

"Your right Denise. Where is she?"

"Julio, where is your sister?"

"Monica went grocery shopping with my mom. She will be back in a little while. Besides, she doesn't like the pool."

"I wish she would've told me that when I spoke to her on the phone."

"Samantha, she didn't want you to change your mind about going to the pool. My sister knows how much I was looking forward to hanging out with you."

"Whaaaaat, Julio, and Sammy?" Maria asked teasing.

"Did anyone else know about this?"

"Yes, Denise, everyone in my house knows how Julio feels about Sammy."

"Lewis, how does your cousin feel about my friend Sammy or should I say, Samantha?"

Julio smiled at me before answering for himself. "Sammy knows how I feel about her, Denise, and she's the only one that needs to know."

"Wow, I had no idea something developed between you two."

"Well, now you know, Denise," Julio replied, and he winked at me.

"Okay, enough of that, let's play Marco Polo.

"Are you serious, Alex?"
"Yes, Tonya, get in the pool." We all got up from the lawn chairs and jumped into the deep side of the swimming pool. Alex was Marco, so he covered his eyes with his hands and began to count.

"Oh no, we're not falling for that again, Alex. You are not going to cheat this time. We're using this." Lewis pulled out a black blindfold and tied it over Alex's eyes. We played three rounds of Marco Polo, and everyone decided they wanted to have chicken fights instead.

"Fine, who's going to fight first?" Tonya asked. All the girls stood in a circle with their dukes up, and we did one potato two potato, until the last two girls remained — that ended up being Daphne verse, Tonya. The boys had already selected among themselves who they were going to carry. Lewis will carry Tonya, and Greg will carry Daphne. Greg is much taller than Lewis, so that presented a problem. Alex is almost the same height as Greg and offered to carry Tonya, but Lewis told him no.

Then the boys decided Eddie would carry Daphne since he is the same height as Lewis. She climbed up onto Eddie's shoulders, and on the count of three, the fight began. It quickly ended with two big pushes and a pull sideways. Daphne and Tonya both went flying off the boys' shoulders and into the pool. After seeing the first fight, we decided not to play that anymore. Eddie asked, "Who is up for a challenge?

"What type of challenge, Eddie?"

"We can have pool races, Lewis. The guys verse the ladies, and we can do all four races freestyle, backstroke, butterfly, and of course, the underwater race."

"Did you really say the underwater race, Eddie?"

"Yes, of course. It's the one where you hold your breath as long as you can trying to make it to the other side of the pool. You had to have seen it on TV, Lewis. It's a big part of the Olympics."

"I'm sorry, what is it called again, Eddie?"

"It's called the underwater race, bro. What are you trying to say? You didn't see that one. I thought you watched the Olympics?"

I did watch the Olympics, and no, I didn't see that one, Eddie."

Lewis was cracking up, laughing until Eddie asked, "Well, what did you see, bro?"

"Eddie, I saw them compete in the breaststroke, butterfly, freestyle, and the backstroke."

"Oh, so you missed the best one, where they don't freaking breathe." Everybody was laughing, and Eddie went on to say, "Don't worry about it, Lewis. I will remind you to watch it next year when the Olympics is back on again."

"Okay, Eddie. You do that. I can't wait," Lewis told him, and everybody was still laughing.

That is when my mom drove by the swimming pool and called me over. "Sam, you need to get back to the house and walk Daisy. She has not been outside since early this morning. I would also like you to get showered and dressed now so that I can run you by the forest to find out the price of admission."

"Sure, Mom. Let me just tell everybody bye, and I'll head back to the house now."

"Alright, Sam, I'll be back in a half-hour. I'm just going to pick something up from the store."

When I walked back inside the pool area, I told everybody that I had to go as I wrapped my towel around my waist and slid my feet into my chancletas.

"Sammy will head back to your house in an hour."

"Sounds good, Daphne. I will see you then."
When I arrived home, Daisy was waiting for me at the door. I raced inside, put her leash on, and ran her back outside. We were at the foot of the stairs when I heard, "Do you mind if I go with you girls?" Julio bent down and pet Daisy on her head. She was stomping her paws up and down while wagging her tail. Daisy was extremely happy to see him.

"No, we don't mind at all if you join us, Julio, but don't you want to be at the pool with everybody."

He stood up and said, "No, I was only at the pool to spend time with you."

"Okay, then come with us." As I urged Daisy forward, she backed up instead and pulled me down the hall over to the back staircase. Daisy practically ran down the stairs and out to the field. The minute we reached the grass, she was already doing her business. "I guess my mom was right; she needed to go outside."

"Then, we should take her for a long walk, Samantha."

"Are you sure you can handle it, Julio? I mean, a long walk for Daisy can be up to a mile or two."

Julio took her leash from me with a grin on his face and said, "I think I can handle it; after all, I'm a soccer player." Then he reached for my hand. As soon as our hands touched, I felt this sort of nervous energy running through me. I wanted to ignore it and decided to talk about the first thing that popped into my head.

"Thank you for inviting Greg over to the pool today."

"The truth is I didn't invite him, Samantha. My cousin Eddie was hanging out with Greg at the video store. That's where he works part-time, and it was slow, so his boss told him he could go home. My cousin was there and offered to give him a ride. They arrived at our place, saw us all in the pool, and joined us. I was just as surprised as you were when Greg showed up."

"Now that's called great timing. Greg saved you from Daphne's long list of questions."

"Do you think her list is longer than mine?"

"I don't know, Julio, how many questions do you have for me this time?"

"Just enough to know everything about you."

"In that case, I think your list is about the same size."

We both laughed when I noticed we were walking into the complex next door. "Julio, what are we doing here?"

"Samantha, there is a park in here that I want to take you to."

"Okay, just as long as you know where you are going. I haven't been inside this complex before." We walked down this trail of patchy grass, and in the middle of the lawn, isolated away from the complex, was a set of three swings.

"Julio, what is this doing here? It's not even inside the complex."

"I think they moved the swing set over here to make room for the new playground that's inside the complex now."

"That's so weird."

"It is, but they are building another set of buildings right in front of this play area. Can you see the sign?" Julio pointed to a sign that read coming soon with a picture of some buildings on it.

"Oh, yeah, I guess you're right."

He grabbed the chains on one of the swings and said, "Come sit down." I took a seat on the swing and laid my head back against Julio, looking up at him.

"Now what?" Julio leaned down and kissed me on the cheek. Then he pulled me back in the swing and set me free. I felt like I was flying, and my heart was soaring through the air each time he pushed me.

"Samantha, I can see that big smile on your face. I knew you would like this."

"Julio, I do."

"Do you know that I can still remember you riding on the swings in our complex. Your smile would get bigger and bigger as you got higher and higher."

"I'm surprised you remember that, Julio? The playground was removed from our complex when we were around ten years old after someone was hurt."

"Well, I suddenly remembered that when I found this swing set here."

I yelled out, "Thank you for bringing me here, Julio."

"The pleasure was all mine, Samantha. I just wanted to see that big smile of yours again. Have you had enough?"

"Yes, I guess so." Julio grabbed the chains on the swing as I was coming in and slowed me down to a stop.

"There you go. I hope you enjoyed that."

"Thank you again, Julio. I did maybe a bit too much."

He took my hand to help me off the swing, and when I stood up, I hugged Julio then kissed him on the cheek. Julio wrapped his arms around me, and I pulled my head back to look up into his eyes. "Julio, I love this place." He didn't say a word, yet I felt his arms tense up around me. Then I noticed his breathing had become ragged, and his lips were parted. His eyes were big and bright, but they were staring off into the distance. I did not want this to lead up to our first kiss, so I grabbed Daisy's leash from him and took off.

Julio jogged past us then stopped a few feet ahead of me. I slowly walked up to him, and he placed his hands upon my shoulders and said: "You just set me on fire."

"What?"

"Samantha, my chest is pounding right now, and my head is spinning. I just thought you should know how you are making me feel at this very moment."

"How do you know I'm the one making you feel like this, Julio? Maybe you're just sick."

He started grinning at my comment as he placed his hands up on his hips, keeping his eyes on me the whole time, and said, "That's definitely not the case, Samantha. This only happens to me when I'm around you."

"Well, then I'm sorry that I make you feel that way."

"Are you kidding me? I love it when you make me feel like this, and when you kissed me on the cheek, my adrenaline was pumping so hard that I felt like I was on fire."

"Whoa, I'm glad that you explained that to me because your reaction sort of surprised me, and I wasn't sure how to respond to it, or what comes next, so I took off."

"Did you like it when I kissed you on the cheek, Samantha?"

"I did, and that's why I can relate to the way it made you feel since I experienced something similar."

"Now, I do not know if I should ever kiss you again, Julio. I mean, could you imagine what your reaction would be if I ever kissed you on the lips?"

"The thing is I can imagine that Samantha and I want you to pop kiss me."

"Is that what they call it? A pop kiss?"

"Yes, and I promise my reaction will be better. You just caught me off guard, is all."

"Maybe, I will one day, Julio. Right now, it is not the right time. I need to get back home. My mom and the girls are waiting for me." Julio walked us back to my doorstep, and he patted Daisy on her head then waved bye to me. I walked inside to find the girls in my room, and Monica was there too, which made me happy.

"Oh, finally, it's about time, Sammy. Where have you been?"

"Denise, I had to take Daisy outside for a walk."

"Who went with you? I'm only asking because after you left, Julio left the pool too."

"Daphne, you can stop your investigation. Julio went along with me on Daisy's walk, and we had a wonderful time."

"Why? What did you do?"

"We went to the park next door, and I rode on a swing while Julio pushed me."

"Now, that sounds romantic."

"Yes, it kind of was Daphne."

"Look, what's happening, girls. Sammy is falling for Julio."

"Whatever, Daphne."

"Yes, well, after the comments made at the pool today by Lewis, we all know Julio has already fallen for Sammy."

"Gee, thanks, Maria."

"You two would make a nice couple."

"Thank you, Monica. Now that means a lot to me that you approve since Julio is your little brother, but honestly, I don't think we're there yet."

"Where did Denise go?"

"Denise left to take a shower. She should be back in your room any minute now, Muñeca."

"Well, that's good. If everyone takes their shower right away, we should be able to leave here on time. Tonya, did you invite the boys to join us at the forest tonight?"

"Of course, I did, Muñeca."

"And is everybody going?"

"Muñeca, that's not what you should be asking me about."

"What do you mean? What should I be asking you about Tonya?"

A lot of things happened after you left the pool today."

"Yeah, right, like what?"

"Like Denise and Maria decided they wanted to have a chicken fight."

"No way, they were totally against it when I was at the pool."

"Well, that all changed after you left Muñeca. Denise climbed up on Eddie's shoulders, and Maria sat up on Alex's shoulders. They were about to start the chicken fight when Eddie challenged Alex to a wrestling match. Alex refused, and that's when Eddie splashed Alex in the face with water. That caused Alex to lose his balance, and Maria flew off his shoulders, but Alex caught her.

"Maria, do you want to explain the rest?"

"Yes, I wrapped my arms around Alex to hug him before I thanked him and–"

"Oh, is that what you call it, Maria?"

"I don't know what you are talking about, Daphne."

"Tell her about the kiss Maria."

"Well, I was about to, but you interrupted me, Daphne."

"Sammy, I told Alex thank you, and he pulled me in closer and kissed me. Just a peck on the lips, not a big deal."

"What are you talking about, Maria? It was totally amazing, and you missed it, Muñeca."

"Then what happened?"

"We remained in each other's arms until we left the pool."

"Maria, that's cool. I'm so happy for you. I had no idea you had a thing for Alex."

"Truthfully, I didn't, Sammy. This all happened unexpectedly."

"Muñeca, there's more. When I looked over across the pool after Maria fell into Alex's arms, do you know what else I saw?"

"No, because you haven't told me yet, Tonya."

"You're never going to believe this, Muñeca. Denise was on the deep side of the pool, sitting down on the ladder, holding hands, and talking to Eddie."

"What?"

"Exactly, Muñeca."

"Did anything happen between you and Greg, Daphne?"

"When Julio left the pool Lewis and Greg left shortly afterward to get something to eat."

"Oh, that sucks. I'm sorry, Daphne."

"Yeah, that sucked big time, but Greg is going to the forest, so who knows, maybe tonight I will get a chance to speak to him."

"Is everybody going to the forest tonight?"

"Well, the Sanchez boys are meeting us there with Greg."

"What about your brother Alvaro? Did you remember to invite him, Maria?"

"Yes, I invited Alvaro, but he already has other plans tonight."

"That's too bad. I was hoping to see him there."

"Me too, Monica, but maybe we can invite my brother to go out with us next time."

That is when Monica stood up and said, "I'm going to my house to get ready. I'll be back in a little bit." I noticed she was disappointed that Alvaro would not be joining us tonight. Therefore, I didn't believe she would be back, and I just waved bye to Monica as she left my room.

Then Denise walked in wrapped in a bathrobe. "Did you girls know that Monica just left?"

Tonya stood up and said, "Yes, she told us she was going home to get ready, and I'm leaving too so I can do the same. Just pick me up on your way out of the complex, okay, Muñeca?"

"Okay, see ya in a little bit." I took a shower, put on a pair of tight jeans, a tank top, and a cotton button-down shirt over the tank top. I rolled up the sleeves and buttoned up the first four buttons from the bottom. I put on a thick black belt with a huge buckle, spiked up my bangs, and left my hair down. Daphne applied my makeup, which consisted of blue eyeliner and lip gloss. Daphne, Denise, and I were ready to go.

"Daphne, did you remember to invite your brother and Michael to go to the forest tonight?"

"Yes, Sammy, I did, and I was told they would meet us there."

"Why do you suddenly sound annoyed, Daphne?"

"Sammy, now that Greg's going for sure. I kind of don't want my brother to go anymore, and I hope he cancels out."

"Oh, that's bad, Daphne, but I can completely understand that. I think that I would feel the same way as you do if I was in your shoes. I'm sure my brother Tommy would make my life a living nightmare."

My mom popped her head into my bedroom and asked, "Girls are you almost ready?"

I pulled my bedroom door open and told her, "Yes, Mom, we're all ready to go."

"Wow, you girls are all dressed up."

"Mom, I'm sorry I forgot to tell you that we're going to the forest tonight."

"That's alright. Tonya's grandmother already told me, and we are going to be your chaperones."

"Really, Mom, do you think we need chaperones? We're 14 now-"

"Actually, Sammy, I'm 15."

"Sorry, Denise."

"You see, mom. Monica, Denise, and Maria are 15 years old, so I don't think we need chaperones?"

"Sam, I'm not comfortable with allowing you to hang out at an amusement park at night unsupervised. What if something bad were to happen?"

"But mom, I went to this same fair at night last year, and the year before, and you didn't have a problem with me going."

"Your right Sam because Tommy went with you. Now your brother is away in college, so I will be the one going with you tonight."

"Fine, I get it."

"Listen, Sam, maybe next year I will feel differently about this but not tonight. Tonya's grandmother and I will not embarrass you girls if that's what you are so worried about. We will allow you your own space to run around the park, but we will be there in case you need us." Then my mom hugged me and told me she would be back when it is time to go. I reached over and shut my bedroom door and turned around to face the girls.

"Everybody better be on their best behavior tonight. Daphne that goes especially for you."

"Sammy, don't worry about me. You are the one who should be worried. Since you will not be able to flirt, hold, or kiss on your boy Julio tonight."

"Well, Daphne, I will try to do the best I can to control myself."

The three of us laughed, and Daphne replied, "I'm glad I don't have a chaperone."

"That is what you think, Daphne. I know my mom; she will keep a close eye on you and report everything back to your mom.

"She's right, Daphne, so you better give up on the whole Greg encounter unless you want Carmen to know about Greg."

Chapter 5 The Magical Forest

At six o'clock, my mom came knocking on my bedroom door again. "Girls, we need to leave now." Tonya and her grandmother are already downstairs waiting for us. We walked out to the kitchen, and my mom told us to head downstairs.

The four of us ran down to the van and climbed inside while my mom remained upstairs to lock the door. "Tonya, where's Monica? Isn't she riding with us?"

That is when my mom slid open the back door. "Ms. Harris, you don't have to sit back there. You can sit up here in the passenger seat next to Abuela."

"Are you sure, Tonya? I don't mind sitting in the backseat."

"I'm positive, Ms. Harris." Tonya climbed into the backseat, and my mom sat down in the passenger seat beside Abuela.

Tonya asked Abuela to turn on the radio, and we listened to nothing but freestyle songs back to back. Which was mine and Tonya's favorite, so we sang along to every song. By the time we arrived at the forest, the parking was so bad that Abuela was told to park the van on a grass field.

It must have taken us about ten minutes to walk from the field to the entrance, but it was fun. There was Christmas music playing on large speakers above us, and we all held onto each other's arm as we sang along with Christmas songs. By the time we reached the entrance, we could not wait to get inside. Daphne's brother was sitting down on a bench, waiting for us in front of the ticket booth.

We all ran up to Arturo when we saw him. Daphne hugged her brother, and I asked him if his best friend Michael was coming.

"No, he couldn't make it tonight, Sammy."

"That's okay, Arturo. You can hang out with our chaperones."

My mom hugged Arturo and told him, "Sam's right, you can hang out with us tonight, Arturo."

"Ms. Harris, are we chaperoning the kids today?"

"Yes, we are," my mom replied, sounding entirely cheerful.

Denise turned around to Daphne and said, "I'm glad I don't have a chaperone." I immediately reached over and high-fived Denise. Daphne crossed her arms over her chest as she turned her eyes away from us, shaking her head.

Then Arturo leaned over Daphne to tell her, "Look at how lucky you are. Mom could have been your chaperone tonight."

After hearing that, Denise and I were cracking up, and Daphne gave us another dirty look before saying, "I invited you here, Arturo as my brother. You're not my chaperone."

"Daphne, if Ms. Harris didn't come with you tonight. Mom would have sent me here to be your chaperone."

"Fine, Arturo, you're right."

"I know I am. Now, where is your friend Greg?"

"He's not my friend Arturo; he doesn't even know that I exist."

"Hopefully, it will remain that way, Daphne, for your sake."

"Arturo, please don't embarrass me. He's coming here tonight."

"I won't embarrass you, Daphne, but he better not try anything."

"What if he wants to hold my hand? Can he hold my hand?"

"No, absolutely not."

Daphne turned to Tonya and asked, "When are the boys getting here? Where are we supposed to be meeting them?"

"I spoke to Lewis before I left the house to get you girls. He said they were already leaving for the forest then. So, I think they're already here."

"Where Tonya?"

"Somewhere inside the forest, Daphne."

"Oh, and Monica's not coming tonight, girls. She called to tell me she doesn't feel good."

"Well, now I'm a little disappointed."

"Why, Sammy?"

"Denise, I just wanted all of us girls to be together tonight."

"Aw, Sammy," Daphne said as all the girls gathered around me in a group hug.

My mom walked up to us and announced, "We have everybody's ticket. I think it is time we go inside now. Abuela is already in line, waiting on us to join her." Once we were inside and past the gate, we were on this path lined with enormous trees. They were all lit up with lights, and in front of the trees were Christmas displays. The Christmas music was still playing from the speakers on the ground and above us on the light poles. Each display has a different theme, and you feel the joy

of Christmas in Miami. We were holding onto one another's arm, looking, and pointing at all the displays. There was Rudolph, Frosty the Snowman, and of course, elves, but my favorite display was of a bunch kids sledding in the snow.

Then all of a sudden, I smelled the cinnamon donuts; they were calling my name. "Mom, do you smell that? We're almost to the halfway point of the forest."

My mom lifted her head up and sniffed once before facing me, saying, "Yup, I think your right. I can smell them already."

"Sammy, we have to stop there and pick up some donuts. That's the whole reason I look forward to coming to this place."

"We will, Maria, for sure."

"I don't know if I can eat."

"Seriously, Daphne, it's a mini donut, not a meal."

"I know that Maria, but I'm nervous."

"That's not nerves that you're feeling, Daphne."

"Oh no, then what is it?" Tonya.

"It's excitement; you are just excited to see Greg, that's all."

"Yeah, I agree. You'll be fine, Daphne."

"I'm not so sure, Sammy, my stomach has been flipping out since we walked past the gate." Tonya looked over at me, and I looked over at Maria, and she looked over at Denise. Then we all looked back at Daphne and rolled our eyes at her.

"Whatever, eat your stupid donuts."

Arturo walked up behind us and said, "I'm sure Daphne feels just fine. She just doesn't want to stop for donuts because she would rather find this guy Greg instead."

"Shut up, Arturo, that's not true."

"Yes, it is Daphne, your obsessed with this guy. You haven't stopped talking about him since school started."

"Wow, I think Arturo's right, sorry, Daphne, we're still stopping to get donuts."

"You know what? At this point, I don't care anymore, Sammy."

There was an extensive line at the donut stand, and my mom asked us to sit down at one of the picnic tables. Arturo remained in line with my mom. We quickly found an available table and sat down. Tonya asked Abuela what she thought of the forest. Abuela told her that the forest was a magical place. She enjoyed the displays, but she loves the trees with all of the lights. Abuela even said that she would like to come back here again with her husband because the forest also seemed very romantic. Tonya started to blush and told her, "Abuela, that's so embarrassing. You can't be romantic with Abuelo."

"Why not? Do you think we're too old to be romantic? Romance is looking into the eyes of each other, then feeling and appreciating the beauty you see inside one another."

"Aw," we all said at the same time, "That's so beautiful, Abuela."

"Tonya, she's right. Abuela deserves romance, and at least she's old enough. My brother won't even allow me to hold hands with a boy." Tonya rolled her eyes at that comment from Daphne just as my mom joined us at the table with a bag of mini donuts.

"Mom, where's Arturo?"

"I'm right here, Sammy." I turned my head to look behind me and saw Arturo walking up to the table with another bag of donuts in his hand.

"Oh, I can't wait to see him," Daphne said, and she laid her head back and closed her eyes.

My mom asked, "Who does she want to see?"

"Just ignore her, Mom. Daphne is just being Daphne right now." Tonya and I looked across the table at one another, and we rolled our eyes again.

Tonya told Daphne, "You need to stop freaking out. You're making Ms. Harris and my Abuela worried now."

"Sorry, where are those donuts?" Daphne asked.

My mom handed Daphne the bag and told her to take one. Daphne reached in and grabbed out a donut from the bag and stared at it for a second before taking a bite.

"Well, what do you think, Daphne?"

"Ms. Harris, I can't believe how good these are."

"I told you so," I said with a smirk on my face.

"Yes, you did, Sammy, but man, they're delicious."

"Okay, girls, do you want any more donuts?"

"No," we all said that the same time.

"Okay, then let's get up from this table and start walking."

We all stood up and walked back into the magical forest. Tonya was now holding onto her Abuela's arm, pointing out the different displays to her. We all stopped when we saw the Nativity scene. Abuela and my mom said a prayer. When we walked a bit further down, we saw a banner that read, 'He's Here.' It was for Santa Claus. The stand was set up like one of the displays, except we could enter this one. We crossed a little bridge that was lined with a red-carpet. On the other end was an elf standing beside a polaroid camera that was up on a stand. "Can we take a picture with Santa," Denise asked.

"Can we, Ms. Harris?" I heard Daphne asking my mom before Tonya waved me over, and I followed her back over the bridge.

"Where are we going, Tonya?"

She stopped walking and pointed to a red velvet curtain that was hanging like a drape. "Muñeca, I just saw Arturo walk behind this curtain.

"So, what?"

"I want to check it out, Muñeca."

"Why are you so nosey?"

Tonya ignored my comment and ran over to the curtain. I joined her, and we could hear Arturo speaking in a very low tone of voice. The only problem was that we couldn't make out what he was saying. Then the curtain was pulled open, and Arturo walked out. Tonya and I jumped away from the curtain, and we smiled at one another. Arturo didn't catch us eavesdropping or attempting to. He walked up the ramp, and we followed. "Finally, girls, where have you two been?"

"We were just standing by the red curtain downstairs," Tonya answered.

"Okay, as long as you two didn't wander off." Arturo turned around with his hand on his hip and a surprised expression on his face.

Tonya rolled her eyes at Arturo before saying, "Don't worry. You were whispering; therefore, we couldn't hear what was said."

"Yeah, we tried to be nosey Arturo, but nothing came of it." Tonya rolled her eyes at me while Arturo shook his head, and he started laughing.

"Sammy, sometimes you girls are so honest that it's funny."

"I'm glad you see it that way, Arturo."

"Okay, guys, so who's taking a picture with the big guy?"

All three of us turned around at the same time when we heard that high-pitched childlike voice. It came from the elf standing beside the camera.

"They all are," my mom answered.

"That is great, you can all stand around Santa's chair, and when he comes out, he will take a seat. Then we can take the picture on the count of three."

"Sounds good," Denise replied with a big toothy grin as we walked over to the chair. It was a big gold chair with red velvet on the armrests.

"Now, is everybody ready to take the picture?"

Arturo said, "Excuse me, Miss Elf. I think somebody's still missing."

"Oh yeah, I almost forgot," the elf responded and started to giggle. Then in an incredibly soft, almost child-like voice said, "Santa, oh Santa."

"Yes, my dear," a deep husky male voice replied from behind a wall covered with another red velvet curtain.

"Santa, there are some people here who are filled with holiday cheer and would like to take a photo with you."

"This might sound silly girls, but now I'm excited to see Santa," Daphne told us while laughing.

"Yeah, me, too," Tonya admitted. We all looked at one another and started to laugh. We were all feeling excited and could not wait to see the big guy himself — Santa Claus.

Then we heard, "Ho Ho Ho" and bells jingling as Santa Claus appeared from behind the red curtain and he walked over to his chair. Santa shook everyone's hand while saying, "I must tell you that I have enjoyed reading all of your letters. It's just so wonderful to see all of you awake."

That was sort of funny—an unexpected, which made all of us laugh. When he finally sat down in his chair, he said, "Now, I think it's time to take that picture."

"Okay, girls, you heard Santa on the count of three, everybody smile or say cheese. We took the first picture, and the elf said, "Mom, you can buy the picture in five minutes from the table downstairs."

"That was only one picture, right?"

"Yes, mam."

"We need five pictures in total."

"Okay, get ready, girls, on the count of three, we will be taking the picture four more times." Each time a picture was taken, we stood in a different pose. For the last picture, I asked my mom, Abuela, and Arturo, to join us in the photo.

"Now, I can tell you that the last picture is my favorite Muñeca."

"This one's mine, Tonya, but you will be able to see it every day on my nightstand beside my bed."

Then suddenly, we heard someone yelling down at us. "Is anybody going to rate my performance?" Santa Claus was standing above us with both of his hands on his hips. Daphne took off, running back up the ramp and hugged Santa before pulling his beard down off his chin.

"Look, everybody, it's Michael."

Daphne walked back down the ramp with Michael beside her, and we all took turns hugging him. "Michael, you're Jewish. How can you be Santa?"

"Tonya, I'm an actor, sweetie. I can play anything, including Santa Claus."

We all started to laugh, and Daphne said: "You fooled me. I didn't even know it was you, Michael."
"Well, that's what a great actor should be capable of doing, Daphne."

"I have to get going, but thank you all for stopping by, and hopefully I will see you all again on your way out." Arturo watched as Michael walked back up the ramp.

My mom turned to Arturo and said, "If you want to stay here to hang out with Michael, you should. Abuela and I are with the girls, and you can join us again later if you want."

"If you really don't mind, then I would like to stay here for a little while. Besides, did you see that elf?"

My mom laughed before telling him I do not mind at all. After we picked up our pictures, my mom offered to hold on to them. She did not want them to get damaged or lost when we went on the rides. We were now standing at the end of the forest, where all of the amusement rides are located. My adrenaline was pumping with excitement. I wanted to ride everything that I saw.

Tonya asked, "Who wants to go on the zipper?"

"No, let's go on the Gravitron first," Daphne replied.

"Can we just eat something cause I'm only here to eat?"

"Denise, can we go on at least one ride before you eat something?"

"Girls, we are here for two more hours," my mom said.

"Where are you and Abuela going to hang out?"

"We will be sitting over at the picnic tables, Tonya."

"Now there are about 15 rides here, and that's including the children's rides. I think it is safe to say that you girls should have enough time to ride everything. When you are done, come get us."

"Okay, Mom, we will," I told her, and I gave her a hug.
My mom whispered, "Sam, try to find a ride that all the girls would like to go on and make that the first ride."

"That's a good idea, mom; I'll try that." She patted me on the back as I pulled away, smiling, and I ran back over to the girls.

"Let's take a vote. Who wants to go on the bumper cars? Raise your hand. Denise, Maria, and I raised our hands. "Okay, so it's the bumper cars first."

Denise and Maria took off toward the ride to get in line. When Daphne pulled me aside and said, "I don't get it, Sammy. The bumper cars are you serious for the first ride?"

"Yes, because I know it's the one ride Denise will go on."

Tonya looked at me before saying, "Daphne, Muñeca's right. Denise won't ride on anything except for the bumper cars and the Ferris wheel."

Daphne shook her head before telling us, "Alright then, I guess we're going on the bumper cars first."

We jogged over to Denise and Maria right on time. How many are in your party? I heard the woman ask Maria that was standing at the entrance of the bumper cars.

"Five," Denise answered.

"Okay, so you girls will need to wait for the next one." She then called out, "I need two riders, only two riders." A boy and a girl ran up the ramp together, and we leaned back to let them pass in front of us. First, the music came on, then sparks ignited on the ceiling, and the cars came alive. I suddenly felt extremely excited to ride on the bumper cars. I could hardly wait for it to be our turn.

"I'm going after you first, Denise, so you better watch out for me."

"Will see Sammy. Now that I know your plan, I will be sure to keep your car pinned up against the nearest wall. That way, you won't be able to move or get me."

The cars were all coasting to a stop, and the music turned off before everybody left through the exit door. Once everybody was gone, the same lady came back to the gate.

"Now, you said that there were five of you?"

"Yes," Maria answered.

The lady waved us in as she pulled open the gate.

"Look over there," Denise pointed to a row of five cars parked against the wall. The five of us ran over to the cars and climbed in. While looking for my seat belt, I found a rope instead. It was an actual dog leash with the same blue and white braid.

It even had the snap hook on the end to attach to a dog's collar. That is when I said, "Don't forget to put on your dog leash, girls."

"Muñeca, does that mean there's no seat belt?"

I was losing it laughing when I heard Denise say, "The dog leash is your seat belt, Tonya."

"Ohhh, okay, I guess I'm safe now I already put the leash on."

That is when everyone broke out laughing. Then we heard someone whistle, and I listened to the gate open again, realizing it was probably Tonya who left the ride upset with us.

"Muñeca, what's going on? Is there something wrong with this ride?"

"Tonya, you're still here."

"Yes, of course, I'm still here. Can you see what's going on from your car?"

"No, it's pretty hard to do with our back to the entrance Tonya. I am sure the ride is fine. It's only bumper cars." Then I heard footsteps running across the floor before Denise screamed. I panicked and tried to jump out of the car to get to Denise, but the dog leash held me up. I managed to remove the leash and stood up, right as Denise began to laugh, that is when I knew she was okay and sat back down. The music came on, as the sparks ignited, and my car was alive. My adrenaline was revved up, and I was ready to go. Before I could back up, I was bumped in the rear end by Denise. Afterward, she drove alongside me, waving to rub it in my face that she got me first. Now I had to get her back, so I quickly pulled out in front of her attempting to cut her off but completely missed. The driver in the car behind Denise waved to me as he rammed into her. It took me a moment to realize that the driver was Greg, and the passenger was Julio. A sudden burst of excitement filled me, and I was thrilled to see them until someone bumped into the back of me again. It was Daphne, although I could not see her, I could hear her laughing. Finally, I stomped on the gas and pulled out of that spot for a total of five seconds. That is how long it took Eddie to catch up to me and bump me back into the same place.

"Denise, how long do you want Sammy to remain in this spot?" It was Eddie, speaking to Denise. Now I realized what was happening. Denise meant what she said earlier, and she's keeping me against this wall.

Then I heard Alex say, "Don't worry Sammy, I'll move him for you." Driving full speed past me was Alex with Maria beside him.

"All clear," I heard Maria say, and I took off in search of the car with Greg and Julio. I could not see them anywhere at first until I drove along the other side of the bumper cars. Now they were right in front of me. I stomped on the pedal and was hit on the side.

"Hola, Muñeca," Tonya said, laughing sitting beside Lewis, who happens to be driving her around.

"Sorry, Sammy, I had to stop you."

"Tell me something, Lewis, who's around to stop me from hitting you?"

"What?"

That is when I turned my wheel and hit him head-on. "Oh, I get what you meant now, Sammy."

"Somehow, I thought you would, Lewis." The three of us were laughing as our vehicles turned off and we coasted to a stop. Then I heard a bunch of booing and complaining because the ride was over.

The woman replied, "Alright, everybody, it's time to go, please use the exit door and don't climb over the gate. If you want to ride again, just get back in line."

When I removed the dog leash and stood up, Julio appeared. He offered me his hand, and I took it before climbing out of the car. I was so happy to see him that I wrapped my arms around him. "I'm glad you're here, Julio."

"Me too, Samantha." He wrapped his arms around me and squeezed me. Then he took my hand as we left the ride.

Everyone was standing around, waiting for us at the exit. When Tonya saw us, she crossed her arms over her chest before saying, "Let me be the one to ask the question that's on everyone's mind right now."

"Okay, what is it?"

"Muñeca, when did you two become official?" Julio looked over at me, and I looked back at him.

"Tonya, we're not official. Julio hasn't asked me yet."

That's when Lewis blurted out, "Bro, are you serious? When are you going to ask Sammy out?" Julio just looked back at me, grinning.

"Okay, guys, who would like to go on the bumper cars again?"

We all turned around to see the woman operating the ride facing us waiting. "Listen, I still have four cars available, and once they're filled, I'm starting the ride."

"Let's go," Daphne said, and we all followed her back up the ramp to the entrance. I looked around and could not see Maria or Alex anywhere, but I saw Lewis standing beside Tonya, and Eddie was with Denise. Then I felt Julio tug on my hand, and when I turned around, he was climbing into the car beside us. He helped me into the car, and before I sat down, Daphne waved to me.

She climbed into the car in front of us, and a moment later, I heard Greg's voice." Sorry, Daphne, I guess you're going to have to put up with me." I remained standing to watch Greg climb into the car with Daphne, and when I saw her smile, I felt ecstatic.

Then I sat down, and Julio reached across my lap to clip on the dog leash. As he leaned back across my lap, he gently kissed my lips, and ultimately took me by surprise. I just sat back. Thinking I can't believe it, Julio pop kissed me. I instantly felt my heart beating faster, and I whispered, "I think I'm the one on fire now."

Julio squeezed my hand, and I looked down at our hands intertwined with one another and said, "Life is filled with unexpected moments, and this one is mine." I looked up at Julio and continued to tell him, "That was my first kiss, and you totally took me by surprise." Julio smiled at me and our eyes locked on one another. Then the sparks ignited above us. The music came on, and our bumper car came back to life. Julio released my hand and grabbed the steering wheel, heading straight for Eddie, who was riding with Denise.

"Samantha, did you know Eddie was the one attacking your car?"

"Yes, I sort of figured that it was him and Denise."

"Well, I think it's time for a little payback."

"Yes, I agree, get em, Julio."
Their car was right in front of us, and Julio was headed for them until Lewis and Tonya bumped us on the right side.

Lewis laughed before saying, "Primo, I knew you would go after my brother."

"This again, Lewis, how many people are you protecting?"

"Sammy, I love to pick sides, and they are forever changing."

"Good then, let's team up, Lewis, and we can both get Eddie. How does that sound?"

Julio gave me a strange look until Lewis replied, "Okay, let's do it." Now he had an enormous smile on his face and took off headed for Eddie. In a matter of seconds, we had them surrounded, and Julio bumped Eddie's car on the left side. At the same time, Lewis bumped him on the right side. Eddie tried to pull forward until Greg appeared with Daphne in their car, and he bumped Eddie head-on. We were all laughing so hard that you could hear us over the music playing through the speakers above us.

Then Eddie yelled, "This is war, Amigos, and I'm coming after all of you." Eddie turned his wheel, and his car started to push Lewis and Tonya's bumper car backward.

He succeeded and was out of the attack zone when all of the cars turned off. "Eddie yelled out, "No, turn my car back on. I must retaliate. Please, por favor, I'm begging you." Everybody was laughing hysterically, even the lady that operates the ride was laughing.

We were headed toward the exit when the woman running the ride said, "Okay, little man, if you want to continue your warpath, get back in your car."

Eddie was surprised and asked, "Are you serious?"

"Yes, go ahead."

"Wait. Can my family come too? They are the ones I need to attack."

The woman started laughing again and told him, "Sure. Why not? There's plenty of cars available."

"Alright then, it's wartime," Eddie replied. He ran back to his original car and climbed inside. The rest of us climbed into separate cars, and we told Denise that we plan on attacking Eddie first before he can attack us. That is when she decided to jump into her own bumper car by herself. This time when the sparks ignited and the cars came on. We all surrounded Eddie, then Lewis went around the back of us and bumped his brother first.

Daphne yelled out, "On the count of three girls, attack." We all turned our wheels and bumped into Eddie's car. When he began to yell, we quickly pulled away from Eddie, and he was able to escape. Then I noticed Julio was driving straight towards me, but he turned the wheel and plowed into Eddie at the last minute.

Greg was headed for Eddie too, and he missed Eddie and bumped Julio instead. Eddie pointed and laughed while

saying, "Look at that, folks. No loyalty in war. Julio, you were just ambushed by your best friend." That statement was just one of many that had us laughing the entire ride. Eddie is such a blast to be around that even his laugh is contagious. When the sparks were gone, and the cars slowly came to a rolling stop. Everybody climbed out of their car, still laughing.

Julio ran over to me to take my hand before I reached the exit, and Tonya pointed to Alex and Maria. "Look, Muñeca, everybody's hooking up, and it's all coming out in the open at the forest."

"You're one to talk, Tonya. You are always with Lewis, and I've seen you two holding hands walking down the halls at school together. Why don't you come clean with me and tell me how long you have been dating Lewis?"

Lewis and Tonya looked at one another before she finally answered, "Three months."
"You have been together for three months, and you didn't tell anyone?"

"No, I didn't, Maria."

"Why did you keep it a secret, Tonya?"

"I don't know, Maria. I have never had a boyfriend before, and everything is just really new to me. Now you all know, so can we move on from this?"

"Well, I think you guys are adorable together," Eddie told Tonya in a falsetto tone of voice. Then he went on to say, "I too want a boyfriend like you, Tonya." Julio, Lewis, Greg, and Alex were shaking their heads, laughing along with Eddie.

They didn't stop until Tonya turned to Eddie with her arms crossed over her chest and said, "Great, Eddie, you're mocking me now. Thank you for proving my point."

That's when the boys stopped laughing, and Eddie asked, "What point T-"

Alex interrupted and asked, "Where do you girls want to go now?"

Maria told him, "The Polar Express."

"Terrific, let's go," Alex said, and he took Maria's hand before walking off towards the ride.

"Sammy, I thought you said Maria doesn't ride anything except for the Ferris wheel and bumper cars."

Denise replied, "No, that would be me. Maria does not ride anything at the fair period. That is why I was shocked that she even agreed to go on the bumper cars in the first place."

"Well, Maria wants to go on the Polar express now, so we should get going."

After Lewis said that, we all turned around, and Maria and Alex were nowhere in sight. "Girls, we better start running or were gonna miss out on seeing Maria's reaction to this ride."

"Daphne, what about us? We want to see Maria's reaction too."

"Great, then you guys should start running Lewis." We all took off running behind Daphne, and I felt Julio take hold of my hand as he ran beside me.

"Tonya, where is this ride?"

"It's in the corner all the way in the back, Denise." Just follow me." Tonya and Lewis took the lead running side by side. We all followed behind them since they seemed to know where we were going.

There it was the Polar Express. It was a ride made up of all these chairs in the shape of a sleigh. The chairs were all attached to a track on the bottom, and it spun around in a circle. The ride had just come to a stop when we arrived, and Maria was standing beside Alex in line. A man at the entrance told us, "When you climb up the ramp, remember it's two

people per sleigh. No single riders. If you do not have someone to ride with, let me know." Julio helped me up onto the ride's platform. We walked up the ramp to the back of the ride until we found an empty sleigh and climbed in.

"Julio, did you notice the DJ booth?"

"Yes."

"Have you been on this ride before?"

"Yes, I have, but not with a girl." Then he placed his arm over my shoulders. The sleigh was leaning a bit toward Julio's side. Now with Julio's arm around me, my head was resting against his chest, and I could hear his heart beating.

I lifted my head to ask, "Do I make you nervous, Julio?"

 "No, you make me feel happy, Samantha." I laid my head back down just as a metal bar was brought down in front of us then locked into place. I looked up and realized it was the same man I saw at the entrance.

Less than a minute later, a DJ's voice came on over the speakers and said, "Give me the signal when we're ready to go." The house music started playing, and the ride was moving. I was so excited, and we were spinning around in a circle backward. It felt like we were rocking back and forth slightly. Then a DJ came on over the speaker and said, "Yell, if you want to go faster."

Everyone yelled out faster. Then all of a sudden, a siren sounded off while two red and blue strobe lights came on. The ride picked up speed, and we were spinning around in this circle very fast. I wrapped my arms around Julio when I first heard the siren, and I didn't let him go until the ride came to a complete stop.

As I removed my arms and took in a deep breath, Julio asked, "What did you think?"

"That was awesome."

He hugged me and said, "Yeah, for me too, Samantha."

We walked off the ride and joined Alex and Maria on the grass. Once everyone was together, Eddie asked, "Who wants to win some prizes for the ladies."

"What are you talking about, Eddie?"

"Lewis, I want to play a few of the carnival games and win a prize for my lady." Eddie grabbed Denise's hand, and he took off. We all quickly followed him over to the Ring Toss. All the guys handed the man at the booth a dollar. Then each one of them was given ten rings. There must have been about a hundred bottles in the center of the booth. The guys all took turns throwing their rings towards the neck of these bottles. Lewis was the best at it, with five rings around the necks of five bottles. Eddie did pretty well with three of his rings, and they were each given a choice of a stuffed animal. That is when Denise and Tonya were called over to pick a prize while the others walked over to the next booth, which had a wall covered in balloons in assorted colors. For a dollar, you were given three darts, and you had to pop three balloons. Alex went first and popped two balloons one after the other and with his last dart in his hand. He quickly glanced over at Maria before throwing it to puncture his third balloon.

"Maria, pick out your prize whatever you want."

"I want this one, Alex." Maria picked out a giant Saint Bernard.

The man running the booth grinned before saying, "For that one, your boyfriend will need to pop nine balloons."

Lewis replied, that is no problem, and he handed Alex his darts and Julio's. Then he began to clap and told Alex, "Get Maria, her dog."

"Thanks, primo," Alex said with a smile as he looked over at Maria.

Alex popped six more balloons, and the man behind the booth said, "That's incredibly good. You only need to pop three more."

"Wait! I popped a total of nine balloons. You said I needed to pop nine balloons to get the stuffed animal."

"Yes, nine more balloons. It takes a total of 12 balloons to get that stuffed animal."

"No problem," Eddie told the man as he handed Alex his three darts. Alex popped three more balloons, and Maria had her dog. Maria hugged and kissed Alex on the cheek while she told him thank you over and over again. When she was about to walk away to grab her dog off the counter, Alex caught Maria's hand and pulled her back over to him. He wrapped his arms around her and picked her up off the floor. He spun her around and gently kissed her on the lips before setting her back down on the ground.

"Wow, now that's the most romantic thing I've seen in a long time," the man behind the counter said. Alex and Maria smiled at one another as Maria grabbed her dog.

Lewis shook his head at Alex and said, "Bro, what was that?"

"I don't know," Alex replied with a grin, "But it feels great, Lewis." Alex didn't take his eyes off Maria once as he stood there, smiling back at her."

"Julio, seriously, do something about your brother. If you wait too long, Alex will be dancing and swinging on light poles in here."

"Yeah, isn't that awesome, Lewis?"

Lewis turned around to find his brother Eddie standing behind him. "No, Eddie, I don't think that's awesome."

"Of course, not Lewis, because this is your first relationship. Instead of enjoying it, you are too busy worrying about who is going to embarrass you. That is okay, though. You will learn one day."

"What will I learn, Eddie?"

"Bro, you're wasting so much of your time worrying about what other people think that you're not able to enjoy your life anymore. That is being superficial, and those people are miserable. Do you want to spend the rest of your life being miserable?"

"No."

"Great, because those people are boring. Now it's time for Skee ball."

Eddie turned to Julio and me and smiled before asking, "Did you two hear everything I said?" We both nodded our heads, yes.

"Good, then I won't have to repeat this to Julio later on in life. Being superficial is stupid. Be genuine and live from the heart."

Julio squeezed my hand and smiled at me before telling Eddie, "That's exactly what I plan to do."

"Come on, let's get everyone to play."

"Eddie walked over to everybody clapping his hands together. Let's get going. We're wasting time, and we have a few more games to play yet."

When we arrived in front of the Skee ball booth, I told Eddie that I would play. Eddie handed the man at the booth three dollars. There were three Skee ball machines, so Eddie, Julio, and I went first.

The man asked, "Is everybody ready?"

When we said yes, nine balls were released beside each machine. I grabbed my first ball and tossed it into the five hundred spot.

"A hole in one," Alex yelled. "Excellent job, Sammy."

"Beat these boys, Sammy. If anyone can do it, you can."

"Thanks, Daphne." I threw my next ball aiming for the five hundred, and missed. The ball did land in the one hundred spot, so I did get something. Halfway through the game, I looked over at Julio and noticed he was making it in the four hundred spot every time. That got me thinking, and I grabbed my next ball aiming for the four hundred, missed, and made it into the five hundred goal instead. I looked back at Julio and told him, "I just made it into the five hundred spot for a second time. It looks like I'm going to win this game after all." Julio looked back at me with one eyebrow raised. I looked back at him and asked, "Do you doubt that I'm able to beat you?"

"Something like that."

"Are you challenging me, Julio?"

Now he was grinning while nodding his head yes. He raised his ball up to show it to me before he tossed it into the four hundred goal once again.

"Fine, challenge accepted, Julio." I heard Julio laughing after saying that, and I ignored him as I grabbed my last ball. This time I missed the four hundred and five hundred spot. It was a wasted ball, no points given on that toss. It landed right down into the gutter. That's when I heard the bells ring and looked up to see Eddie's grand total of 1,800 points, followed by my overall score of 2,300 points.

"Muñeca, you beat Eddie."

Julio turned around to tell me, "You did very well, Samantha, but did you do well enough to beat me?" Then he winked at me before saying, "I guess we will find out soon enough." Julio bent down to grab his last two balls. He tossed the first ball into the four hundred spot. Then Julio looked over his shoulder at me and said, "I need to win this challenge so I can get you a prize." I stood up on my tiptoes and kissed him on the cheek.

"You are my prize, Julio, and you already gave me something I will never forget." His whole face lit up, and his lips parted.

"Do you really feel that way, Samantha?"

"Yes, I do."

He shook his head while saying, "You still need a prize to take home to remember this night."

"Fine, all you have to do is beat me, Julio, good luck."

He bent down to throw his last ball. It landed in the four hundred goal, and the bell rang. Julio won with a total score of 3,600 points. The man running the game called Julio over and told him, "Congratulations, you won, which prize can I get you?" He pointed to the stuffed animals hanging from the ceiling in the booth."

Julio smiled at the man before he replied, "I'm with the redhead, and she's my prize, so I want her to choose something to remember this night." I picked out a teddy bear beating a drum. I showed the bear to Julio and thanked him. He gently tugged on my hand and led me over to a bench and sat down.

Then he pulled me onto his lap to sit and wait for Greg and Eddie. They were at another booth with Daphne and Denise.

"When you pop kissed me, Julio, you made this a magical night for me. One that I won't ever forget, so I honestly didn't need anything else."

"Samantha, I just want you to have something to remember it."

"No one has ever touched my lips before tonight, so I doubt that I will ever forget it."

Julio picked up my bear and kissed it. I laughed, and he told me, "Now, you can take my kiss home with you too."

"Thank you, Julio, for the kiss and the bear."

"Your welcome, Samantha." Julio leaned in and closed his eyes, and I leaned in closer before closing mine and heard someone calling my name. My eyes instantly popped open as I pulled away and jumped off Julio's lap.

It was Arturo, and I saw him headed this way, so I tried to cut him off by running up to him instead. "Sammy, I have been going crazy looking for you girls everywhere."

"I'm so sorry, Arturo. Where is my mom and Abuela?"

"They are at the picnic tables by the concession stand still waiting for you girls to return. Your mom sent me to look for you when you didn't return on time, and that was over an hour ago."

"I'm so sorry, Arturo. I lost track of time. Can you just let my mom know that you found me, and we're heading over there now?"

Arturo raised his eyebrows at me with both of his hands on his hips. Arturo waved to Julio, and Julio waved back. I knew that was a warning, and I had to find Daphne along with the girls right now. "Fine, Arturo, give me a second to get the girls, and we will walk back together."

"Now that will work," Arturo said. "I'm giving you one minute, Sammy." I ran over to the booth where everybody was at.

"Girls, we have to leave now."

"Sammy, can't you wait a second? Greg just won, and Daphne hasn't picked out her prize yet."

I looked over at Daphne and replied, "Eddie, that's up to Daphne. Her brother has been looking for us over an hour,

and he only gave me a minute to locate Daphne and the other girls."

Daphne stopped speaking to Greg midsentence. She ran up to me and told the girls, "Let's go before Arturo gets even."

That is when all the girls left the booth, and we ran over to Arturo. I looked back at Julio, and he waved bye to me. I suddenly felt disappointed that our night together had come to an end while I stood there, staring at him. Arturo patted me on the back, saying, "I hope you all had fun, but we need to get going now." That is when I turned around, and we left.

My mom and Abuela had a look of relief when they saw us. "Thank you, Arturo, for finding the girls.

"No problem, Ms. Harris. I'm just one of the chaperones tonight."

"Maria, where did you get that enormous dog from?"

"Alex won it for me, Ms. Harris, at the carnival booth with all the balloons."

"Well, it's adorable, and boy is it big. Girls, let's all grab an end and help Maria carry her dog back to the car."

"I love dogs, and my mom won't allow me to have one."

"So, you chose the biggest one you could find at the fair, Maria?"

"Exactly, and I already named him."

"Let me guess you named the dog Alex."

"Denise, how did you know that?"

"That was an obvious choice, Maria."

"Perhaps it was come to think of it."

As we walked through the forest of lights, I could see what Abuela saw. The lights are romantic, and I wished I could walk through this magical forest holding Julio's hand. We walked past Santa's photo studio on the way out, and it was already closed. When we reached the exit, we each hugged Arturo and told him goodbye.

"What? No hugs for Santa?"

We turned around to see Michael standing behind us, wearing blue jeans and a t-shirt with his arms out for a hug. Everyone hugged Michael, including my mom and Abuela.

By the time we arrived home, I was exhausted and ready for bed. My mom must have known this and reminded me to walk Daisy before going to sleep."

As soon as Daphne heard my mom say that, she stood up and offered to go with me. Denise was tired and did not feel like going anywhere except to my room to lay down. I walked into the kitchen to put the leash on Daisy, and my mom gave me a strange look. "I'm just taking Daisy outside for her walk."

"Sam, I realize that just be careful and stay close to the building."

"Sure, Mom, I will." We walked out of my building and headed over to the clubhouse behind the pool. Daisy was sniffing around, but she was not doing anything but sniffing.

"Daphne, we have to walk Daisy over to her spot. She's not going to do anything here."

"That's fine with me. I will just follow you, Sammy." We walked out to the sidewalk, and I spotted a van pulling into the entrance of my complex. Greg and Julio climbed out of the van and stood out on the sidewalk a couple of yards away. I took off, running toward Julio with Daisy right behind me.

By the time I reached Julio, he had bent down and scooped me up into his arms. He closed his eyes and kissed me gently on the lips. I opened my eyes when I heard him say, "I had to wait a while for that second kiss, Samantha." Oh, and you forgot something."

"I did?"

Julio nodded his head yes as set me down and handed me my teddy bear. "Thank you, Julio; you made this night so much fun for me."

"You made it fun for me too, Samantha. I'm only glad you don't have a problem with boys going to the forest with you." I looked up at him, and he was grinning.

I started to giggle before saying, "Yes, I'm awfully glad too because you boys made it a lot of fun for us tonight."

"Can I go for a walk with you and Daisy?"

"Yes, we would like that."

Julio took Daisy's leash from me, and he took my hand. We were walking down the sidewalk when Daphne asked, "Do you guys mind if Greg and I head over to the picnic tables to talk for a little bit?"

"No, of course not, Daphne. I'll leave the door unlocked for you at home, so you can just walk inside when you're done."

"That's great, see you in a few minutes, Sammy."

Julio and I watched Daphne and Greg head toward the pool. "Not yet holding hands."

"They will, Samantha. Trust me." I lifted my head up and found a brilliant smile on Julio's face.

"How can you be so sure, Julio?"

"Greg is my best friend, and he tells me everything."

"So, what has he told you?"

"Samantha, I would much rather talk about you."

"What do you want to know?"

"Well, Samantha, you have kissed a boy now."

"Yes, I have."

"How did it make you feel?"

"I was shocked because it was unexpected, but it made me feel incredible."

"Okay, my turn to ask a question. Julio, did you finally kiss the girl that you wanted to kiss?"

"Yes, I finally did."

"How did it make you feel?"

"Alive."

"What do you mean by alive?"

"Just that, Samantha. I felt my heart racing, my blood flowing, and it was a rush — just the best feeling ever flowing through me."

Julio stopped walking and looked into my eyes. Then he said, "Sammy, you make me feel alive." I smiled up at Julio, and he continued to say, "And you make me happy." He closed his eyes and gently kissed me for the third time tonight. Like the bumper cars, I felt the sparks from that kiss, and it felt like he ignited something inside of me. It was an incredible feeling like nothing I had ever felt before. He walked me back to my door and handed me Daisy's leash. Julio said bye to Daisy, and he kissed me on the cheek. I walked inside and went straight to my room and sat down in my bean bag chair, looking out the window. I caught a glimpse of Julio walking in the parking lot over to his building. I even stood up to get a better view of him. Once he was out of sight, I sat back down in the bean bag.

"Is everything alright? Did you get into a fight with Julio?" I turned around to see Daphne standing next to my bed.

"No, everything's fine. Why do you ask?"

"Oh, because I have been standing here for like 20 minutes, and you completely ignored me. Do you want to talk about it, Sammy?"

"Not really."

"Sammy, maybe if you talk about it, you will feel better."

"I feel fine, really, but thank you."

"Okay then, I guess I will go to your brother's room and get some sleep. Good night, Sammy."

"Good night." Daphne walked out of my bedroom, and I cupped my hands around my mouth like a megaphone before saying, "I have a crush on Julio."

Daphne walked back into my room and shut the door, smiling. "Everyone knows you have a crush on Julio."

"He kissed me on the lips tonight. It's the first time I've ever kissed a boy."

"How was it?"

"Unexpected, thrilling, and magical."

"Sammy, you will need to do a little bit better than that."

"When Julio kissed me for the first time, it was unexpected. It was such a thrill feeling his lips pressed up against mine, and it left me feeling amazed afterward."

"I think I need more details, Sammy."

"Like what?"

"Like how many times have you kissed him tonight? A total of three times on the lips."

"So, it was a pop kiss?"

"Exactly, but even before we kissed, every time I am alone with Julio, I feel extraordinary. It's like we formed some sort of connection when we got to know each other better through our intimate conversations."

"When does this happen? You haven't told me about this before, Sammy."

"When we are walking Daisy, we talk about everything. Yet Julio still hasn't asked me to be his girlfriend."

"Is that what's bothering you?"

"It kind of bothers me now that we've kissed. I don't want Julio to kiss anyone other than me."

Daphne started to laugh.

"How is that funny?"

"I don't think you have to worry about that, Sammy. Julio is really into you."

"How do you know that for sure?"

"Greg and I spoke for about thirty minutes tonight. He told me that Julio is crazy about you, and he has been into you for a while. He always becomes distracted whenever they are playing soccer on Sundays. Julio has been seen looking over at your building instead of paying attention to the game. He has even left the field during a game a couple of times. Once to help your mom with groceries, and another time to go for a walk with you and Daisy."

I started to laugh. "Wow, I didn't know Julio left a game to go on a walk with Daisy and me."

"A guy is not going to tell you everything."

"Why not?"

"Because guys don't do that, Sammy."

"What if I ask him?"

"You can't ask a guy that, Sammy."

"Why not? Julio always asks me questions, and I answer them truthfully. When it is my turn to ask a question, he tells me the truth."

"Not about things like this, Sammy."

"Daphne, he has asked me if I had ever kissed a boy, and at the time, I hadn't. He asked me if I ever had a boyfriend. He asked me tonight how it felt to be kissed. I always answer all of his questions, truthfully."

"He asked you all of those questions?"

"Yes!"

"Wow, what did you ask him?"

"I asked Julio the same questions, and he answered all of them honestly as far as I know. We have agreed to be open and honest with one another about everything."

"What do you mean about everything? What is everything?"

"Come on. You know what I'm talking about, Daphne."

"No, I have no idea. What else have you spoken to Julio about?"

"How we make each other feel."

"And how does Julio make you feel?

"I told you this already. Julio makes me feel amazing every second that I am with him. Right now, I'm not with Julio, but I'm thinking of him and looking forward to the next time I'm going to see him again."

"You have it bad for him, Sammy."

"What are you talking about? You're the same way about Greg."

"Oh, and I almost forgot. The boys are playing soccer tomorrow. Greg and Julio invited us to watch them play."

"Daphne, when did they tell you that?"

"When they walked me back to your doorstep."

"Julio came with you back here?"

"Yes, when Julio left here, he went back to the picnic tables at the pool. To remind Greg that my stuffed prize was still inside Alex's van."

"Wait, he gave you the stuffed animal he won tonight?"

"Well, he gave me the stuffed prize he won for me tonight."

"Really, where is it?"

"In the living room." We both ran out to the living room. I had to see her prize from Greg. "Here it is, Sammy." Daphne held up a stuffed electric guitar. I started to laugh. "As you can obviously see, it's a guitar, and he's a rocker."

"Daphne, you won't ever question where this guitar came from. In fact, I think you will always remember this gift and Greg. If you ever forget, I will be there to remind you.

We were both laughing when Daphne stopped and said,

"I must admit, I've never had a guitar before.

"Neither have I, Daphne."

"Did you know that Greg plays in a band with his cousin?"

"No, I didn't know that."

"Yeah, Greg plays lead guitar in his band."

"Oh, that's cool."

"Yeah, Greg plays at the bonfire all the time too."

"I've heard of that place, but I haven't been there before. Daphne, have you been to the bonfire before?"

"Nope, but one of these days, Greg will take me. Sammy, I'm going to bed now, so I can watch Greg play soccer tomorrow."

"Okay, goodnight, Daphne. See you in the morning."

Chapter 6 The Girls 1st Soccer Game

The following morning Denise came into my room and woke me up. "Why is Daphne in bed with me? It's a twin bed, and she snores. Daphne already agreed to sleep on the top bunk. I'm afraid of heights, and I can't sleep up there."

"Come sleep in here with me. I do not snore, and there's plenty of room. It's a queen-size bed."

"Okay, just keep to your side."

"Fine!" Denise climbed into bed, and we went back to sleep. We woke up a couple of hours later, to Tonya and Maria squirting us in the face with squirt guns.

"Stop it! I thought I was drowning," Denise screamed.

A couple of seconds later, Daphne came running into my room, asking, "What happened? Who's drowning?"

Tonya yelled out, "Put away your squirt guns. It's the lifeguard," and everyone laughed, including Denise.

"Thank you, Daphne, for coming to my rescue. Tonya tried to drown me."

"How did she try to do that, Denise?"

"It's not a big deal, Daphne. I just sprayed Denise in the face with this," Tonya held up a squirt gun, and Daphne grabbed it out of her hand. That's when Denise pinned Tonya down to my bed, and I helped.

"Daphne, spray her in the face for me."

"You got it, Denise." Daphne sprayed Tonya in the face right as my mom walked into my room.

"I want to know what's going on in here right now."

"We were attacking Tonya with a squirt gun."

"Tonya, are you alright?"

"Yes, Ms. Harris, I'm fine. Can I use your hairdryer?"

"Of course, Tonya, you know where it is."

"Thank you, Ms. Harris."

"Now, the rest of you follow me into the kitchen. We need to make breakfast.

Once everyone was in the kitchen, my mom asked what everyone felt like eating.

"Ms. Harris, I love your pancakes."

"Now that sounds good, but I really want bacon."

"Well, since Maria wants pancakes and Sam wants bacon, we can make both.

"Ms. Harris, I don't know how to make pancakes."

"It's easy, Maria. The key to making pancakes is all in the ingredients."

My mom, Maria, and Daphne made breakfast for everyone. I just made a pot of coffee for my mom and a pitcher of orange juice for everybody else. While we were eating, my mom could not stop talking about the pancakes. She complimented Maria and Daphne on cooking them precisely right.

"Thank you, Ms. Harris. That's the first time I have ever made anything."

"Since you know the ingredients, Maria, you should surprise your mom by cooking them for her."

"You're right. My mom would love that."

"What do you girls have planned today?"

"Actually, we have been invited to watch the boys play soccer this afternoon Ms. Harris."

"What boys, Daphne?"

"Greg and the Sanchez boys."

"Are all the boys playing?"

Tonya smiled and answered for Daphne, saying, "Yes, Ms. Harris, the whole family, will be playing today, including Monica."

"How do you know that, Tonya?"

"Maria, while you were sleeping at five o'clock this morning, I was outside jogging with Lewis, and he told me."

"Oh yeah, the morning jog is something they do together every day. I've run into them when I've been outside walking Daisy."

"Sam, when did you start walking Daisy at five o'clock in the morning?"

"To be totally honest, it only happened once, mom."

"Yeah, Muñeca is not much of a morning person Ms. Harris."

"Well, that explains what's been happening to you, Tonya."

"Explains what Daphne?"

"Why you're losing your Cuban booty, Tonya."

"What? No, I'm not." Tonya jumped out of her seat, panicking, and she tried to look at her backside.

"It's still there. I am not losing it. I'm just making it tighter."

"Don't worry, Tonya, if you lose your Cuban booty. We'll just call you flat booty," and everyone laughed.

"Muñeca, you are the only one who should be called flat booty."

"Oh, burn," Daphne said.

"Yeah, it is flat, but so is my belly. Which means I don't need pliers to pull up the zipper on my jeans."

"Now, that's an even bigger burn," Denise added.

"Okay, you win, flat booty. I mean, Muñeca."

"Thanks, Tonya. Can you help me clear the table and clean the kitchen?" Denise stood up and offered to help instead. By the time we were finished in the kitchen, Daisy was standing at the backdoor.

"Denise, I have to take Daisy outside for her morning walk. Do you want to come with us?"

"That sounds good. I'm up for some exercise."

"Great, could you do me a favor first?

"Well, that depends on the favor."

"I just need you to run into my room and let everyone know where I'm going while I put the leash on Daisy?"

"Sure, Sammy, just don't leave without me."

As I was heading out the door with Daisy, everyone had decided to come with us. We walked past the clubhouse, and Tonya noticed a light on inside the weight room, so she walked up to the sliding glass doors.

"What do you see, Tonya?"

"I haven't looked inside yet, Daphne."

"Move out of the way. Let me take a look."

Tonya backed up as Daphne said, "Tonya, come back here. Lewis is inside lifting weights with Greg and Julio."

That's when we all ran up to the sliding glass doors to have a look inside." Maria, look, it's Alex."

"I see him, Daphne."

"What is that thing, Alex is twirling around over his head?"

"It looks like a towel Tonya."

Then Eddie ran out of the bathroom door into the weight room butt naked. He was chasing Alex down for the towel, and all we saw was Eddie's bottom, but it was enough to make us laugh. That was until we heard Daphne say, "Oh, crap, we've been spotted everybody run."

We took off running back to my building. By the time we reached my front door, we were all out of breath. Even

Daisy plopped herself down onto the floor, and Daphne started to laugh again before saying, "Now that was funny."

"Yeah, I think so too." We all jumped when we heard Alex's voice and turned around to see Alex, Lewis, Greg, and Julio, staring back at us from the staircase.

"Hi, guys. What have you been up to?"

"Oh, you know the usual Daphne, chasing girls who were spying on us at the gym."

"Alex, we weren't spying on you. Well, we were, but it was an accident."

The boys looked back at one another, and Alex said: "Well, that explains it. Thank you, Maria." I just put my head down and started to laugh.

Julio asked, "What happened, Samantha? Why are you laughing?" I lifted my head to see Julio smiling at me with a toothy grin.

"I'm laughing because we got caught, and it wouldn't have been that bad if Eddie had his towel."

"Sammy's right, and we wouldn't have been caught spying because we wouldn't have been laughing."

"So, Daphne, you admit that you were spying?"

"Only on you, Greg. I didn't expect to see Eddie like that." Daphne stood there, proud of herself. She admitted the truth to Greg while the rest of us could not keep it together, and we all dissolved into laughter.

"Well, don't you guys have a soccer game today?"

"Yes, we do, Daphne, and it starts in about thirty minutes."

"Good, I was just checking Alex since we have been invited to watch you guys play."

Alex instantly had his eyes on Maria when he replied, "That's fantastic. Are you all coming out to the field to watch us play?"

"Yes, and we're looking forward to it," Maria answered with a grin."

"Samantha, did you even get a chance to walk Daisy? You know, before you took off running back to your building." I turned my head away from Julio to laugh again while looking over at the girls. I slowly turned my head back to Julio after I found my composure and told him no. Julio's mouth dropped open, and he laughed before asking, "Samantha, do you think you should take Daisy for a walk?"

"Yes, I think that's a great idea." Julio bent down and grabbed Daisy's leash. Then he took my hand.

"Bye, guys," Julio said as we began to walk down the hall.
"Wait, where are you two going?"

"Tonya, we have to take Daisy for a walk. We will be back in a few minutes."

"Okay, if you say so, Julio."

We went down the backstairs and out to the sidewalk when Julio stopped. He wrapped his arms around me and kissed me gently on the lips.

"Wow, that was wonderful, Julio."

"For me too, Samantha. He smiled at me, then bent down and hugged Daisy. She became so excited by wagging her tail and barking a happy bark at him. Then she took off down the sidewalk smelling everything in sight. We did not stop walking until we were back at my doorstep.

"Samantha, will you watch me play today?"

"I will be there with the girls in a little bit."

"I'll be waiting for you until then." Julio pop kissed me for a second time before he bent down and hugged Daisy again. When he stood up, he handed me her leash and took off down the stairs. I walked inside and found Daphne sitting down at the kitchen counter.

"Were you waiting for me?"

"Yes, of course, Sammy, we have to get going, or we're going to be late."

"Ummm, Daphne, there just playing the game out on the field, not an arena." Daphne crossed her arms over her chest as she stood there, rolling her eyes at me. Then she turned and faced the living room. I was not the only one she was annoyed with. The rest of the girls were sitting down in the living room with my mom laughing and having a good time.

Realizing the problem, I decided to say, "Mom, we're leaving now to watch the boys play soccer." Daphne turned to me and smiled when the girls got up off the couch.

"Okay, Sam, just bring your beeper with you in case I need you for anything." The girls ran into the kitchen while I ran into my bedroom to grab my beeper.

"Got it, Mom. Love you." We walked out the backdoor with Tonya holding onto Daisy's leash while Maria and Daphne carried the beach blankets.

"Where are we going, Tonya?"

"To the field, Daphne. It's right beside the golf course, where the boys play soccer every Sunday."

When we walked out onto the field, the boys were all facing us with big smiles. Alex walked over to us with his eyes on Maria and said, "Ladies, we're glad you've come out to watch us play today."

"Thank you, Alex. Where should we sit?"

As Maria and Daphne set out the blankets, Julio ran up to me. He kissed me on the cheek and called Daisy over. Tonya dropped Daisy's leash, and she ran full speed ahead into Julio's arms.

Denise leaned over me and whispered, "Julio is going to be an excellent father one day."

Feeling sort of shocked by her comment, I replied, "Since I'm nowhere near that point in my relationship, I will only say that I hope your right for his children's sake."

"Sammy, you know what I meant by that."

"Yes, I do, you meant that he's a great prospect," and I began to laugh.

"Okay, I guess you do know what I mean, and now she was laughing too until Eddie appeared and kissed Denise on the cheek.

"It's so good to see you, honey. I'm going to be the soccer star on the field today." Then Eddie flexed his muscles to the boys on the field. The boys laughed, and one of them yelled out, "Eddie, you better get used to the idea of bringing your girlfriend every weekend if she's able to improve your skills that much."

"That's a great idea, I will," Eddie yelled back.

"Denise, baby, you're welcome to come to all my games every weekend." Denise turned her head to look at Eddie, and he leaned in and kissed her. As they pulled apart, Eddie said, "I meant to kiss your cheek, but those lips are amazing. All I can say is wow." He had everybody laughing like usual when Denise turned around, and pop kissed Eddie. This time when they pulled apart, it was different. They were blinking and staring back at one another instead of laughing.

"Thank you, baby," Eddie told Denise with a stunned expression on his face. When he turned around to walk back out to the field, Denise leaned over and pinched Eddie on the bum.

When Eddie spun around, Denise said, "It's for luck." Everyone was laughing, but Eddie and Denise were simply smiling at one another.

Lewis came over and spoke to everyone before walking up to Tonya and planting a kiss on her cheek. Then he told her, "I need to talk to you later about plans for tonight."

"Okay, when?"

Lewis looked over at me then Julio before telling Tonya, "After the game." He kissed her on the cheek again then ran back out to the field.

Alex clapped his hands together and said: "Let's play."

Julio pat Daisy on the head and stood up. "I have to go now, Samantha," and he handed me Daisy's leash. I pinched him on the bum as he was walking away, and he turned around, giving me an awful look.

I yelled out, "It's supposed to be for luck."

The game started, and we all took a seat and stared at Denise. "Why are you guys staring at me like that?"

"Denise, tell us everything."

"Daphne, what exactly do you want to know."

"Tell us about the kiss."

"Tonya, that happened by accident."

"What happened by accident?" Monica asked. We all turned around and saw Monica standing behind us.

"Hey, Monica, come join us on the blanket." I moved over so she could sit down with us.

"No, I'm going to stand. I'm fine. What happened by accident?" Monica asked again.

"Eddie leaned in to kiss me on the cheek and wound up kissing me on the lips when I turned my head. "

"Oh," Monica simply replied, and she kept her eyes out on the field. She appeared to be angry about something judging by the look on her face, and her arms crossed over her chest.

I looked up at Monica and asked, "Are you sure you don't want to sit down with us?"

"Yes, I'm positive, Sammy." Monica was squinting her eyes at Tonya or Maria when she answered me this time. I was not too sure which one since they were both sitting down on the same blanket beside one another.

Suddenly, Alvaro made a goal, and we could hear Eddie yelling. "You just got lucky, bro. That's not happening again."

"Denise, your boyfriend, doesn't appear to be doing his job as the goalkeeper."

"I wouldn't know much about that, Monica, since this is my first-time watching Eddie play, and he's not boyfriend, at least not yet anyway."

Now Monica had an evil smirk on her face as she stood there watching the game and said, "Look at Alvaro. He thinks he is the star on the field now."

Maria stood up and asked, "What's your problem, Monica? Everyone's out here to have a good time, and that's all. Why are you attempting to ruin it for us with your comments?"

She kept her eyes on Alvaro the whole time as she told Maria, "My problem is that Eddie just let Alvaro score. Your brother Alvaro is my replacement in today's game. I'm afraid if he continues to play well, they won't need me anymore."

Maria shook her head as she sat back down beside Tonya and replied, "You have nothing to worry about there, Monica. I know for a fact that my brother has no intention of playing soccer full time." Monica turned her head around, and I saw both girls jump. I leaned my head back to look up at Monica, and I saw that penetrating stare of hers fixed on Maria. No

words were exchanged, and eventually, Monica walked off the field with that angry look still on her face.

At first, everyone remained quiet until a few minutes later, when Denise sat up, asking, "What's up with Monica?"

"I don't know Denise, but she was acting creepy from the get-go."

"Daphne, I completely agree with you. I mean, where did Monica even come from? She just popped up out of nowhere, asking me what happened by accident."

"That is nothing, Denise. Monica was staring me down so hard that I felt her eyeballs touching me."

"Ugh, Maria, that's disgusting."

"Denise, Maria is not exaggerating when I looked up and saw Monica staring down at Maria. I jumped."

"Actually, Tonya, you and Maria both jumped."

"Muñeca, did you see the look on Monica's face when she was looking at Maria?"

"I did, Tonya, and it was frightening."

"Well, obviously, Monica's having a bad day."

"Monica's not having a bad day, maybe a week or a month, but definitely not just a day, Daphne."

"Denise, I don't want to talk about Monica anymore?"

"Then what do you want to talk about, Daphne?"

"Let's get back to discussing that kiss you had with Eddie."

Tonya sat up, rubbing her hands together before saying, "I want to know more about that kiss too, Denise."

"Fine girls, Eddie leaned in to kiss me on the cheek. He said something about me having to come to the field to watch him play every weekend. When I turned my head to ask him what he meant by that, Eddie kissed me on my lips instead of the cheek."

"Yes, but what about the second time when you kissed Eddie again?"

"Daphne, when we kissed the first time, I was stunned, and I liked it so much that I went in for a second kiss."

"Wait, I thought you kissed him at the pool, Denise, after the chicken fights."

"Who told you that, Sammy?"

"Oh, I told her that because I saw him kiss you on the cheek at the pool Denise."

"That's right. I did kiss him back on the cheek, Tonya. I forgot all about that."

"Do you want to make-out with him?"

"I'm not sure about that, Maria? Maybe."

"Denise, which kiss did you like better, the first or second kiss?"

"Tonya, the first kiss was the best because it was a surprise."

"Well, it was exciting for all of us who watched you kiss Eddie for a second time."

"Yeah, I agree with Tonya. It was exciting, and I can't believe you pinched his bum."

"Sammy, men love it when you pinch their backsides."

"No, they don't, Denise. Julio looked terrified when I pinched him." We all started to laugh when Julio looked over at me. Everyone was running past Julio across the field while he stood there staring at me.

Alex yelled, "Julio, what are you waiting for?" He took his eyes off me long enough to wave bye to Alex before he jogged up to me.

I stood up on the blanket, asking, "What are you doing, Julio? You're in the middle of a game. Shouldn't you be out there playing?"

Julio was staring at me intently with his piercing brown eyes when he replied, "No, I would rather go for a walk with you and Daisy." He grabbed Daisy's leash and put his arm around me.

Alex yelled out, "Julio, where are you going?"

"To walk Daisy. We'll be back."

Julio and I walked Daisy over to the lake on the golf course. I sat down on Julio's lap under a tree.

"I can hear your heart beating, Julio."

"You are Mi Corazón Samantha, which means my heart in Spanish."

"How can I be your heart? You haven't even asked me to be your girlfriend."

"Samantha, I just assumed we were already a couple."

"No, we're not anything until you ask me out."

"Are you serious, Samantha?"

"I'm very serious."

"Okay, fine. May I ask you a question?

"Yes, what is it, Julio."

"Do you like watching me play soccer?"

"That's not the question I was expecting you to ask me, Julio."

"Oh, I'm sorry, what was the question you were expecting?"

Now he was teasing me, so I told him nevermind, and I grabbed a rock to toss in the lake. Julio wrapped his arms around my waist and said, "Tell me, Samantha."

"No," I replied, and I started to laugh. Julio kissed my neck, and I instantly had chills.

"Julio, I know what you're doing, and that's not going to work."

"Then tell me, Samantha," and he kissed me again on the back of my neck.

"You have to stop doing that."

"I will as soon as you answer my question, Samantha."

"What question, Julio? I cannot even think straight. My head is so foggy right now." This time Julio kissed my earlobe, and I felt my hair stand up before the goosebumps appeared.

"Be honest, you know what your kisses are doing to me, Julio, and that's why your grinning."

Suddenly, I heard Alex say, "There you are." We both turned around and saw Alex standing about a yard away from us. Daisy ran up to Alex barking, and he paid her no mind, so she began to bite on his shoelaces. Alex was hopping from one foot to the other while saying, "Julio, you don't just walk off the field in the middle of a game."

"Can I just have a few minutes with my girlfriend, please, Alex?"

That is when I sat up, facing Julio, and told him, "I'm not your girlfriend. You have not asked me out yet. We're just some kissing bandits." Alex covered his mouth while shaking his head, looking as if he was trying not to laugh.

It took Alex a second, but he regained his composure and said, "Julio, talk to Sammy, and when you're done, come back to the field." Julio called Daisy over to him. She let go of Alex's shoelaces and ran up to Julio, smothering him with kisses. Julio grabbed her leash, then kissed the top of Daisy's head.

"Okay, Alex, I will be there in a few minutes."

Alex left, and Daisy sat down beside us. As soon as I laid my head back, Julio asked, "Did you enjoy watching me play today?"

"Yes, after all, you are my little soccer player Julio." I tilted my head up to see him smiling down at me and his eyes locked onto mine.

"Samantha, would you be my girlfriend?"

Instantly an explosion of happiness went off inside me as I nodded my head yes while I was saying yes. Julio leaned down and gently kissed me, then he slowly pulled away, staring into my eyes.

"Hmmm, nice kiss, Mi Corazón."

"Yes, it was Soccer Player, and now we need to get you back to the field." I stood up, and Daisy stood up beside me, waiting on Julio. He picked up Daisy's leash and reached out for my hand before we left.

We were almost back at the field when Julio stopped walking. He placed his left hand under my chin before telling me, "Now this is for luck Mi Corazón," and kissed me.

Just as we were pulling apart, I heard Eddie yell out, "Look what I found the Kissing Bandits." I turned around and saw everyone staring back at us. I felt embarrassed and hid my face against Julio's chest. Everyone started to clap, and I could hear Eddie and Alex laughing.

Julio put his arms around me as he called out to his brother Alex saying, "Really, the Kissing Bandits."

"Payback, little brother; I had to say something for you just taking off like that." Before Julio went back out to the field, he walked us back over to the blanket, and he kissed me then Daisy.

"Where did you guys go?"

"Tonya, we just took Daisy for a walk by the lake."

"What happened beside the lake?"

"Not much, Daphne, he just asked me to be his girlfriend." All the girls squealed and told me congratulations.

"So, Julio is officially your boyfriend now?"

"Yes, Tonya, it's official."

The girls squealed again before saying, "Finally" in unison. I felt as though Julio was staring at me, so I looked across the field, and I caught him and his magnificent smile facing me.

"Okay, girls, it's time to go. We have to get ready for tonight. Tonya bent down and picked up the blanket off the ground.

"Daphne, what's going on tonight?"

Before Daphne could answer my question, Tonya walked up and told us she was going back to her place with Maria, and she handed Daphne the blanket. As we were walking off the field, I heard, "Samantha, wait." I turned around and saw Julio jogging up to me. He took my hand, asking, "Will you go out on a date with me tonight, Samantha?"

"Julio, she can't. It's a girls' night, and were going to the arcade."

"Daphne, maybe the guys could meet us there."

"Muñeca's right, speak to your cousin Lewis. He knows the place were going to Julio, and you guys can meet us there."

"Now, let's get going, Muñeca." I kissed Julio on the cheek and quickly left the field with Tonya tugging on my arm.

Once we were completely off the field, I heard Daphne telling Tonya, "I will speak to Sammy. You and Maria, just go back to your place and get ready."

When we walked inside, Denise said, "I still haven't called my parents yet, Sammy, and I need to ask if I can stay another night."

"You should call them now from the kitchen phone. You do not want to use the phone in my room. It's messed up with tons of static."

"Sammy, you still haven't replaced your phone?"

"Nope, I keep spending my allowance at the arcade, mall, and video store with you, Daphne."

"Do you ever intend to get a new phone?"

"Yes, one day, I will, but not today, so you should still use the phone here in the kitchen Denise."

Denise walked over to the phone, hanging on the kitchen wall, while I walked into my room with Daphne.

"So, have you made out with Julio yet?"

"No, I haven't done that, and I'm not in a rush to do that either.

"Why not? What's the big deal?"

"I'm not in a rush to do anything, Daphne. As it is, Julio kissed me today on my neck and earlobe, causing my mind to go hazy. I can't even imagine what will happen and how my body will react to making out."

Daphne started laughing.

"Hey, why is that funny?"

"Sammy, if you ever get to first base, tell me what happens."

"Wow, Daphne, that was rude."

"No, it wasn't Sammy. It was honest."

"Okay, well, I would ask you to do the same, Daphne, but you haven't even kissed a boy yet."

"Well, I would if I could, and that boy would be Greg."

"Did you enjoy watching Greg out on the field today?"

"I always enjoy seeing Greg, live, and in-person."

"What does that mean, Daphne?"

"I always see him in my dreams."

"And do you make-out with him in these dreams?"

"Yes, we kiss all the time."

"Oh, I see. That explains why you're so fascinated with the idea of making out."

"Yeah, I guess you're right, Sammy. I just wonder what it's like."

"It might be disgusting, Daphne, but I will let you know if I ever find out, and you have to do the same."

"You have a deal."

"Daphne, why don't you make the first move?"

"How do I do that?"

"Just walk up to Greg and pinch his bottom."

"No, don't ever do that, Daphne, not to Greg."

"Why not Denise? Guys love that, were your exact words?"

"Sammy, a guy like Greg, would take offense to that. Do you remember the look on Julio's face after you did that to him?"

"Of course, Julio was not offended at all, Denise. He was petrified."

We both laughed, and afterward, I asked, "Does anyone know what time we're going to the arcade?"

Denise looked over at Daphne with a frown on her face. "Why are you looking at me like that, Denise?"

"Why haven't you told Sammy where we're going?"

"Well, I could ask you the same question, Denise. You're here too, so why haven't you told, Sammy?"

"You know what, Daphne? I'm going to take my shower now." Denise grabbed her bathrobe and left my room.

"Tell me what, Daphne? Where are we going?"

"Oh, Sammy, Greg is so fine that I get butterflies just being near him."

"Really, what does that feel like?"

"It feels like a bunch of bees flying around in my stomach."

"Wow, I get that feeling too, every time Julio kisses me, or stares into my eyes. Or even when he starts to ask me a bunch of questions."

"What type of questions does he ask?"

"Are you serious, Daphne? We talked about this already last night."

"Sammy, I was exhausted last night, and I don't remember."

"Fine, Julio once asked me if I had ever kissed a boy. It was awkward because my answer was no."

"Did you ask him the same question?"

"Yes."

"And what was his answer?"

"He said yes, but it wasn't with a girl he wanted to kiss. What's funny is that it made me jealous."

"When did he start asking you these types of questions?"

"Before we went back to school. Julio once told me that he wants to know everything about me."

"Man, Sammy, he has been into you for a while then."

"Yes, since the end of summer. We talk all the time, and we've had a lot of questions since then."

"What type of questions?"

"Daphne, come on, we talked about this already."

"I know, but just give me an example, Sammy."

"Okay, so Julio kissed my earlobe, and it affected my ability to think clearly, and I told him."

Daphne's mouth dropped open, and she grabbed her pillow and screamed, "No way" into the pillow.

"What happened? Why is Daphne yelling into her pillow like that?"

"Hey Denise, how was your shower?"

"It was great, but answer my question. Why are you yelling into your pillow?"

"Oh, it was nothing, Denise. I'm going to take my shower now." Daphne waved bye to us before leaving my room.

"Do you mind if I grab the dress out of your closet now?"

"No, not at all. Help yourself."

"Did Daphne ever bother to tell you where we're going tonight?"

"No, Daphne just kept stalling for some reason and tried to keep me occupied by getting me to talk about the same thing we discussed last night."

"I knew Daphne would do something like that just to prove a point."

"Well, can you finally tell me where we're going?"

"Of course, you're the one who should know most of all. Julio's birthday is on Wednesday, so his family is having a surprise party for him tonight at the clubhouse."

"Denise, I am officially the worst girlfriend already. I did not even know it was Julio's birthday on Wednesday, and I don't have a birthday present for him. Maybe I shouldn't go. I can pretend to be sick or something. Besides, I don't have anything to wear."

"Listen, Sammy, no one knew about this party until this afternoon, which means none of us are bringing a gift. I will go in your closet and pick out an outfit for you to wear tonight, and Daphne can braid your hair. Oh, and I actually know the perfect guy to do your makeup."

"What guy?

"Michael."

"Why would he be willing to do my makeup?"

"Well, he's one of my closest friends, and he's Arturo's best friend?"

"Are you sure he knows how to apply makeup, Denise?"

"Oh yeah, Michael learned everything in LA. He performs in local shows up there during the summer, and theatre performances require makeup, so he learned to do his own."

"How are you going to convince him to come over here?"

"That's simple. I will just give Michael a call, but don't tell Daphne."

"Denise, I don't want Daphne mad at us."

"Sammy, that's why we're not going to tell Daphne anything about Michael. She will throw a tantrum and try to stop us."

"But Denise, why would Daphne react that way?"

"Simple Michael is best friends with her brother Arturo, and Daphne doesn't want either one of them around when Greg's near."

"Are you going to invite Michael to the party?"

"Well, I was thinking about it. Since Arturo is friends with everyone and he used to play soccer with them."

"I think that would make Daphne angry."

"You're right. I'm going to do it."

"Do what, Denise."

"Call Michael right now and tell him to bring Arturo."

Denise left my room to use the phone in the kitchen. When she came back, I told her I didn't know that Arturo used to play soccer with the Sanchez boys."

"Did you know that one of the relatives of the Sanchez boys is coming to town from California?"

"No, obviously not if I didn't even know about the party until you told me, Denise."

"Well, apparently, this person has some news to share with the family?"

"Is it good news or bad news?"

"That I am not aware of, Sammy. I just overheard bits and pieces of the conversation Lewis was having with Tonya after the game."

Daphne walked into my room, abruptly telling me to take a shower. Then she turned to Denise and told her, "I can't believe you're still sitting in here in your bathrobe."

"Are you serious, Daphne, because I can't believe you didn't tell Sammy about the party tonight."

"Did you girls know that the only reason Greg is even going to the party tonight is that Julio happens to be Greg's best friend? Otherwise, he would be at work right now."

"Why do you make everything about Greg? You didn't even answer my question, Daphne."

"What question, Denise?"

"Forget it. I already took care of it like usual."

"How did Greg get out of going to work tonight, Daphne?"

"You won't believe it. Greg's cousin is Mig, and he was one of the players on the field today playing soccer."

"I've never met Greg's cousin, so I don't know who that is."

"Well, it doesn't matter, Sammy, since his cousin won't be at the party. The point is Mig offered to work for Greg tonight at the video store so that Greg can attend the party."

"Where is Greg now?"

"He went back to his cousin Mig's house to get showered and dressed for tonight. Alex will leave here shortly to pick Greg up, and I'm going with him."

"Wait, how are you going with Alex to get Greg?"

"Denise, Maria invited me to go with her and Alex. Maria is one of my best friends. I can't let her down."

"I can't believe it, Daphne. You are so selfless, making such a sacrifice for a friend."

"Sammy, I can hear the sarcasm in your voice."

"Good, it was well deserved." I stood up and chucked a pillow at Daphne; she caught it and grinned.

"So, where are you going, Sammy?"

"I'm going to hop in the shower." I opened my closet door and grabbed my robe before leaving my room. After my shower, Daphne braided my hair, and I found the clothes Denise picked out for me lying on my bed, so I quickly got dressed. Afterward, I left my room in search of the girls and found Denise working on Daphne's makeup in the dining room. Daphne was already dressed wearing black jeans with a black net shirt over a gold sparkly tank top, and she had on her sparkly gold flats to match. She looked adorable and was almost ready to go when Tonya walked into the kitchen through the backdoor.

"Maria and Alex are downstairs in the van waiting for you, Daphne."

"Tonya, can you tell them to wait? Denise is nearly finished."

"No, I'm not going back downstairs. I have to get ready myself." Daphne jumped up, and waved bye to us before she ran out the door. I walked into the kitchen with Denise to get something to drink, and Tonya was already in the linen closet, grabbing a towel.

"Hi, Ms. Harris."

"Hi Tonya, what are you up to?"

"Oh, I'm about to take a shower, and I need to get ready here."

"Sounds good. Your bathrobe is on the top shelf in the linen closet." Tonya grinned and thanked my mom."

Denise turned to me and asked, "Does Tonya still live here?"

"Yup, part-time since we were five years old," and we both laughed.

"I can't believe you don't have the bunk beds in your room anymore."

"My mom wanted them in my brother's room now that Tommy is away in college. So, if my brother wants to bring a friend home, he can. Of course, that has to be a male friend. My mom already told Tommy no girls allowed."

"How is Tonya holding up with that? I mean, does Tonya still come over to spend the night whenever she wants?"

"Yes, that hasn't changed."

"Does she go into your brother's room while he's not home to sleep on the bunk beds?"

"Are you kidding?" I asked, laughing. "No, Tonya just climbs into bed beside me, and she orders me to stay on my side of the bed."

"Oh, speaking of Tonya, you better grab the dress and shoes you want to wear now. Tonya is like a hurricane, and she will try on several things in my closet before she ends up wearing the first outfit she put on." Denise reached in my closet and grabbed the dress.

"Sammy, I'm headed to your brother's room to get dressed. I'll be back shortly."

Tonya was back a couple of minutes later, wrapped in her bathrobe, and she headed straight for my closet. "I like what you're wearing, Muñeca. When did you get that outfit?"

"It belongs to Denise. She's letting me borrow it."

"Well, you look super cute."

"What are you going to wear tonight, Tonya?"

"Jeans for sure," and she found an outfit to put on. All was good until Tonya tried to get the zipper up.

"Don't just stand there, help me, Muñeca."

That's when Denise walked back into my room, asking, "What's wrong with Tonya?"

"Nothing serious, although Tonya thinks it's the end of the world, and she is about to cry over it."

Tonya stood up and said, "Look, Denise, my Cuban booty looks good in these jeans."

"Yes, the jeans look great, Tonya. I agree with you, so what's the problem?"

She sat back down on the foot of my bed with her arms over her chest, saying, "I can't wear them because I can't get the zipper to move up."

"Standup, Tonya, and let me help you." I sat back watching Denise and Tonya tug on the zipper, and like she said, it wasn't moving.

"Muñeca, please have some compassion and get the pliers. You know I didn't mean it when I called you flat booty."

"Oh, alright, Tonya. Lay down on the floor." I reached into my nightstand and grabbed out the needle nose vice grip. I grabbed the flap of the zipper, and on the count of three, I pulled it up.

A couple of minutes later, there was a knock at the door. "Oh, that must be Michael," Denise said, and she headed out the bedroom door.

"Who is Michael?" Tonya asked.

"You know Michael, Tonya. He is Arturo's best friend." Tonya stared back at me with a blank look on her face.

"Daphne's brother is Arturo. His best friend is a blonde guy with blue eyes. He's always with Arturo whenever we go to Daphne's house." Tonya kept shaking her head no at me.

"Tonya, he played Santa Claus."

"Oh yeah, Jewish Santa, I remember him."

"Great, now he's at the door waiting to be let in." Tonya and I walked out to the living room to answer the door when we found Michael already sitting down on the couch. My mom and Denise were with him discussing the surprise party for Julio.

"I remember Alex telling me something about a party when he came by here this afternoon."

"Alex came over here today?"

"Yes, Sam, he was looking for you and Julio. Is it true the two off you wandered off today during the game?"

"Alex told you all of that, mom?"

"No, Sam, his mother, Pilar, told me that part." Now I felt a touch of anxiety, but I answered truthfully and told her yes. "Why would you two wander off in the middle of a game like that, Sam, and why didn't you tell me about the party?"

"Mom, we just left for a few minutes to walk, Daisy, and I didn't know anything about the party until about an hour ago."

"Well, that's because it's supposed to be a surprise party, Ms. Harris, and nobody was invited to the party until today. It's a big deal because Lewis's father is even coming to the party from California."

"Oh, I know about Juan coming to town. Pilar has been looking forward to seeing her brother for some time now, and since she was keeping it a surprise, I'm the only person she could tell."

"Did you know about the party for Julio, mom?"

"Of course, Sam, Pilar wanted me to go, but I'm not going. I have a lot to do around here, and I'm expecting your brother to call me back tonight.

"So, you knew about the party before me, mom."

"Yes, I did, and I'm very proud of Pilar and Monica. They managed to put this celebration together at the very last minute, and you should have a lot of fun tonight."

"Why didn't you tell me about the party, mom?"

"Because it was a surprise, Sam." Everyone laughed, including me. Then my mom stood up and handed me a shiny blue wrapped box with a silver bow.

"Mom, what is this?"

"A gift for Julio for his birthday from all of us."

I stood up and hugged my mom while staring at the present in my right hand. "Thanks, mom, you thought of everything."

"Be sure to thank your brother Sam. He's the one who told me this afternoon to run out and pick up a gift for Julio. It's just a bottle of cologne that your brother suggested I buy."

"Where's Arturo? I saw him for a minute standing at the door, yet he never came inside."

"Arturo just ran back downstairs to park the car. He should be back any minute now."

"Thank you, Denise. I was starting to assume he went off somewhere with Daphne."

Michael smiled before saying, "That's right, Daphne's here."

"Yes, she is, Sammy, go tell Daphne her brother and Michael are here? I'm sure she would like to see them."

Immediately I stood up, about to tell my mom where Daphne went until I noticed the look on Denise and Tonya. Both of them had a worried expression on their face. They didn't want me to say anything in front of Michael. Luckily that's when there was a knock at the front door, and I ran to answer it.

"Oh, hi, Arturo." My anxiety heightened as he bent over, kissed me on the cheek, and walked past me inside.

"I just asked about you, Arturo."

"Hello again, Ms. Harris, I just moved my car into a parking space since we'll be here for a little while. Oh, and before I forget, my mom told me to remind you about a lunch date you two have planned for tomorrow."

"I'm looking forward to that. I won't forget. Just be sure to remind your mom we're meeting up at one o'clock, not two." Arturo grinned, knowing exactly what my mom meant. Carmen is horrible at being on time for anything.

"Okay, so who am I doing makeup for first?"

"That will be Sammy," Denise replied, smiling at Michael.

"One thing I do need is the best lighting."

"Michael, you will find that in the dining room."

"Do you mind, Ms. Harris, if I use your dining room as a makeup station?"

"Not at all, Michael. Be my guest, and where is Daphne?"

Michael and Arturo stood up and walked over to the dining room, as Tonya leaned over to speak to my mom. "Ms.

Harris, Daphne left with Alex and Maria to pick up Julio's best friend, Greg. They should be back soon. Then when everything is ready, Lewis will call me here at your house. That way, we can all walk over to the clubhouse together and hide before Julio arrives."

"Wow, that sounds like everything has been perfectly planned out, Tonya."

The three of us whipped our heads around to see Arturo standing behind us. Tonya swallowed so hard it looked as though she tried to swallow a golf ball, and Denise stood up. "I'm so glad you feel that way because I want you and Michael to come with us."

My mom smiled and said, "That's a wonderful idea, Arturo. You and Michael should go to the party. I know Pilar would love to see you along with her boys and Monica."

"What do you think Michael should we go?" I don't know, let me think about it while I'm doing Sammy's makeup." Michael called me over and patted the chair in front of him, telling me to have a seat.

Less than five minutes later, Michael handed me a mirror, asking, "What do you think, Sammy?"

Before I could answer, my mom said, "Michael, I think Sam looks beautiful — not too much makeup."

"All I did was use light pink on her cheeks and a neutral pink lip gloss on her lips. Then a tiny bit of mascara to make her eyes appear brighter."

"Thank you, Michael. I like what you did."

"My pleasure, Sammy. Now, who is up next?"

"I am," Tonya said, and she walked right up to Michael and sat down.

When Tonya was finished, Michael turned to Denise and asked, "Do you still want what you told me over the phone?"

"Yes, I do, go ahead. I trust you."

"You got it, Denise. You're getting the works." Michael stood up, brushed her hair, and made a braid using only the top of her hair. Next, he parted out her hair and started making tight curls throughout the back. He put those curls into a ponytail. Then wrapped the braid around the ponytail. He used blue eyeshadow on her lower eyelid with a white and pink on the top. He arched her eyebrows with the black eyebrow pencil. Then he used a silver eyeliner to give her cats' eyes. He highlighted her cheeks in a plum color with a matching plum lipstick. When Michael was finished with Denise, she looked like a runway model.

"Sammy, do you mind if I run back into your room? I want to borrow your black boots with the three-inch heel."

"No, not at all, go ahead, Denise."

"Michael, if I ever have plans to go anywhere special, you must do my makeup. Your incredible, and I want the works."

"Yes, of course, call me anytime, Ms. Harris."

"Thank you so much, Jewish Santa," Tonya told Michael batting her eyelashes at him. Just then, there was another knock at the door, and Tonya got up to answer it. She walked back into the living room with Daphne, Maria, and Greg.

"Hi, guys, welcome back,"

"Hey, Denise, you look great. Who did your makeup?"

"Daphne, it was Michael. He's here." That's when Daphne finally noticed Michael and Arturo sitting there beside my mom on the couch. She stepped back from Greg with a shocked expression on her face.

"Is everything alright, Daphne?"

She closed her mouth and blinked a couple of times before she replied, "Yes, everything's fine, Greg. I'm just surprised to see my brother here, that's all." Somehow Daphne held it together, and she introduced Greg to her brother and Michael. That's when I left the living room to feed Daisy, and Daphne, along with Arturo, followed me into the kitchen.

"Daphne, there's something I need to tell you."

"Oh no, what is it now?"

"Michael and I have been invited to the party."

"Wait, are you going as my chaperone or my overprotective brother?"

"No, I'm just going as your brother, and I will always be around to protect you, Daphne, but I won't embarrass you."

"Really, Arturo. He nodded his head, yes, and she flew into his arms for a hug. "We're going to have so much fun tonight."

"So, you don't mind if I come to the party?"

"Absolutely not. I would love it, Arturo."

"Okay, then I will speak to Michael about it again. I just didn't want to intrude, Daphne."

"Thank you, Arturo."

"So, that's Greg."

"Yup, that's him."

"Are you dating him now?"

"Nope, he still doesn't know that I exist."

I laughed. "What is it, Sammy?" Arturo asked.

"Greg and Daphne both have a crush on each other, but they are both extremely shy, so no one has made a move yet."

"Wow, thank you, Sammy, for telling my brother everything."

"Sorry, Daphne. I did not mean to jump into your conversation. I'm leaving now to give you two some privacy."

As I walked out of the kitchen, Greg was there and asked, "When are we supposed to walk over to the clubhouse?"

"We're just waiting for Lewis to call Tonya. Then we'll run over to the clubhouse and hide."

Greg chuckled before saying, "Sammy, you're the only one who needs to run and hide. Julio won't even notice the rest of us."

"Why would you say something like that, Greg?"

"Maria, it's like I told you after you picked me up. I spoke to Julio over the phone barely an hour ago. He sounded distraught because he wanted to go out on a date with Sammy tonight, and Sammy told him no." Now I felt my cheeks turning bright pink, and I had instant butterflies just hearing that Julio had a conversation about me. Greg brought me back out of my own thoughts with his question. "How are they keeping Julio away from Sammy?"

"What?"

"Sammy, when I spoke with Julio, the last thing he told me was that he was going to take a shower and head over to your house. To go for a walk with you and Daisy."

"Really, Greg?"

"Yes, really, Sammy."

"Greg, you have to stop talking to me about Julio."

"Why should I? He's my best friend, and he adores you."

"I know Greg. Only I need you to understand that I'm anxious to see Julio and that feeling I have is becoming more intense because I'm beginning to miss him."

"Oh, then I'll stop Sammy, but you two are meant for each other. There is no doubt about how you make Julio feel. I haven't ever seen Julio so crazy infatuated with anyone before. Soccer has always been his infatuation until now."

"Excellent, Greg, thank you for helping me with my little problem."

"It's no problem for me, Sammy. Just consider it retribution for the phone call I had to endure with Julio before I came over here." I rolled my eyes, and Greg just laughed.

A few minutes later, there was a knock at the door. Tonya looked through the peephole. Then ran into the living room and said, "It's Julio and Lewis."

"No way what are we going to do?"

"Yes, way, Daphne," Greg replied while grinning at me.

"Is this your way of saying I told you so, Greg?"

"Sammy, take it whatever way you want. I told you Julio had his mindset on coming over here to go for a walk with you and Daisy. The dude is totally infatuated, and you shot him down when he asked you out on a date tonight."

Now I felt this tingling of excitement stirred up inside me, and I wanted to see Julio right now. Greg must have seen the look in my eyes, and he mouthed the word 'no' to me while he shook his head.

Greg was right, so I turned to my mom and asked, "Can you answer the door while we hide in the hallway?"

"Sure, I can, honey, but what do you want me to say?"

"Mom, when Julio asks for me, tell him that I'm busy getting dressed and that you will let me know he passed by."

We all ran into the hallway, and my mom answered the door. I could hear his voice, but I couldn't make out what he was saying. Just hearing his voice sent my heart soaring. My mom finally shut the door and walked up to me.

"Sam, I told Julio you were getting dressed, and he asked if he could take Daisy for a walk."

I looked up at Greg, and he shrugged his shoulders before saying, "I told you so." I started to giggle as I walked into the kitchen and hooked Daisy's leash to her collar. Then I ran back over to the hallway to hide.

Ten minutes later, the boys were back with Daisy. Lewis said, "Ms. Harris, could you tell Tonya that I know she will be leaving here in five minutes, and I just passed by to inform her that I'm running late, but I will meet up with her at the arcade."

"Not a problem, I will tell her. Have a good night." My mom shut and locked the door up again, and Tonya turned to everyone and said, we're leaving here in five minutes.

The minute we arrived at the clubhouse and pulled the door open, the fragrant smell of Pilar's delicious cooking was all I could smell. Monica, Alex, and Mr. Sanchez were setting up the food on a table toward the back. The table had two huge trays loaded with Columbian style arepas stuffed with melted cheese, and tamales wrapped in banana leaves. These were both a favorite of Julio's. I could smell his grandma's old recipe of Colombian Arroz con pollo. It's a smell I have enjoyed every single Sunday for a while now. I walked over to Monica and asked if I could help with anything.

"No, I've got everything covered, Sammy, thank you."

Then Alex called me over, "Sammy, can you find out if Arturo and his friend would be willing to take over the music tonight? The stereo is in that wood cabinet beside them."

"Okay, will do, Alex. Oh, and get everyone ready to hide in front of the sofas. As soon as I get the beep, saying they are coming, I will let you know."

"Sounds good, Alex. By the way, where are you hiding the Arroz con pollo?"

Alex laughed before asking, "You can smell it?"

"Yup, and it smells delicious."

"Sorry, Sammy. That's why I had to hide it from that big guy over there." Alex was pointing to Greg.

Monica was finally smiling when she said, "Yeah, we can't let Greg see it. He will eat it all. Oh and Sammy, I'm sorry that I didn't go with you to the forest last night. My mom and I started planning my brother's birthday party after I left your place. It was a last-minute thing, and I would have told you why sooner, but of course, I couldn't."

"No, you couldn't, and I totally get it. You were planning a surprise party, and in order to keep it a surprise, you have to keep it quiet."

"Exactly."

"I'm happy you did it this way Monica since it ended up being a surprise for all of us."

"Well, I honestly could have used your help. I spent nearly the whole afternoon decorating this place. While my mom was at the airport picking up my uncle. That's why I didn't play in today's game."

"Oh, Monica, I'm sorry. That explains why you were so unhappy out on the field today."

"Yeah, I guess. Do you remember my uncle Sammy?"

"Of course, I do. Hello, Mr. Sanchez."

"Hi, Sammy, how is your mother and your brother doing?"

"Everyone's good. Do you miss living in Miami, Mr. Sanchez?"

"Yes, very much, nevertheless I'm glad that I did not pass up on the opportunities that were made to me." Monica looked upset after her uncle made that statement, but she didn't say anything.

Alex announced, "They are on their way now. Turn off the lights, and everyone duck behind the couch." Mr. Sanchez headed for the back room when he saw Alex and Monica squat down in front of the table, and I ran behind a sofa just as the door opened.

Someone said, "It's just us. Don't jump out."

Monica asked, "Alvaro, is that you?"

"Yes," he whispered, and he bent down behind one of the couches.

The door opened again, and this time I could hear Lewis saying, "Julio, come in here."

"No, I'm not walking in there. That's trespassing."

"Seriously, Bro, I have to check if I left my sunglasses inside here."

"Lewis, I don't even know why you were in there, to begin with. You have no business being in that place."

"I'm telling you, the door was unlocked, Julio. The same as it is now, so I came in here to relax on the couch and listen to some music."

"Okay, so if the door is unlocked at someone's house, do you just walk inside, have a seat, then put your feet up, and watch a little TV?"

"No, Julio, of course not."

"This is no different, Lewis; we don't belong in there."

"Julio, do you want to see Sammy?"

"Of course, I want to see her."

"I'm not leaving until I have my sunglasses."

"You don't need your sunglasses. Lewis, it's nighttime."

"Bro, we're going to an arcade. A lot of people wear sunglasses in the arcade to avoid the glare of the machines."

"Lewis, I haven't ever seen you wear sunglasses at an arcade."

"Well, I do now, and they're somewhere in that room. Eddie is waiting for us, and if you keep him waiting, we won't be going anywhere."

"You're the one keeping him waiting, Lewis."

"I guess you don't want to see Sammy that bad."

"Fine, where did you leave your stupid glasses?" Julio asked as he walked inside the clubhouse.

"Surprise," everyone yelled as they jumped out from behind the couches. Monica turned on the lights, and Arturo put on the stereo. Julio stood there looking around the room with his hand on his chest, grinning. While everyone walked up to Julio, wishing him a happy birthday. I noticed he was just standing there, searching the room with his eyes. Therefore, I snuck up on Julio and was about to take him by surprise when Greg walked up.

"Julio, who are you looking for?"

"Samantha, is she here?"

Julio continued to scan the room when Greg turned his eyes to me and said, "Yeah, man, Sammy's here somewhere," then he gave me a smug look.

"Trying not to laugh, I shook my head at Greg before I stood up on my tiptoes and covered Julio's eyes. Julio exhaled with the sound of relief.

"Mi Corazón." Then I felt his cheeks rise up into a smile underneath my hands.

"Surprise, Soccer Player." He grabbed my hands and pulled them up over his head as he turned around. He was now facing me as he lowered my arms down around his neck and kissed the top of my nose.

"Samantha, I don't want to smear your lipstick, and you look beautiful."

"Thank you, Julio. You always look handsome."

Julio smiled broader as he began to sway back and forth to the song playing it was by REO Speedwagon 'Can't Fight This Feeling.' I danced in his arms while staring up into Julio's incredible brown eyes.

"You missed your walk with Daisy and me tonight."

"Yes, I know. Thank you for taking Daisy out on her walk for me, Julio."

"I just wanted to make sure Daisy went out before you went out, Samantha."

"Well, I was sort of busy trying to get beautiful for you."

"You're always beautiful, Sammy, inside and out, so you can't become something you already are."

"Julio, you make me feel wonderful all the time."

Eddie walked up to Julio just as the song ended. He tapped him on the shoulder, saying, "Hey, Primo, are we going to the arcade or what?" Julio turned and hugged his cousin.

"Thank you, Eddie. You guys did it. You surprised me."

"Yeah, I know Julio, but the best surprise is standing right in front of you." Now I was grinning, and Eddie said, "Sammy, I'm not kidding, all Julio wanted to do was get to the arcade to spend time with you." Julio squeezed my hand, so I picked my head up, and he winked at me with a brilliant smile.

That alone ignited an intense feeling of joy inside me and made my heart beat rapidly. "Eddie's right, I just wanted to spend the evening with you, Samantha."

"Hey Alex, where is my dad?" I heard Lewis ask from behind us.

"Crap, I left him in the back room."

Alex walked around the wall, and I heard him yell, "Tio, no." That's when Julio and I ran over to Alex, and what we saw made us laugh. Mr. Sanchez was sitting down on a fold-out chair, eating from the party tray with a serving spoon while drinking a beer.

"Is that what I think it is, Alex?"

"Yes, it is Sammy."

"Samantha, what is it?"

"Julio, that was your Arroz con Pollo."

"Tio, don't eat it all. Save me a bite."

Now Mr. Sanchez was laughing before he replied, "Aye, Julio, I got hungry. I'm sorry, but your mother's cooking is hard to resist."

Alex was cracking up, and Julio told his uncle, "It's so good to see you," as he leaned down to give him a hug.

"Aye, *Sobrino,* it's so good to see you too and happy birthday."

"Why are you hiding back here by yourself, Tio?"

"Because this is where we were keeping the Arroz con Pollo safe, Julio." Now they all started to laugh again, and that's when I left.

"Hey, Sammy, have you seen my dad?"

"Yes, Lewis, your dad is in the back room."

"Where is that exactly?" I pointed out the area and told him to bring four spoons.

"Why spoons, Sammy?"

"Just bring them with you, Lewis. Trust me."

I joined Greg and Daphne on the sofa beside the dance floor. After I sat down, I turned to Daphne and asked, "Have you danced with anyone yet?"

"No, not yet, Sammy. I'm waiting for the right person to ask me."

"What if I ask you? Will you dance with me, Daphne, and the rest of the girls?"

"Yes, but I'm only dancing to a song I like, Sammy."

"Fair enough, Daphne. Let me know when a song comes on that you like." Arturo put on 'Break my Stride' by Matthew Wilder, and Daphne smiled.

"Excuse me; I'll be right back."

"Where are you going, Daphne?"

"This song is mine and my brother's favorite song."

"Since when?"

"Since we were little kids, Sammy."

Daphne walked up to her brother, and they started to dance. I noticed Michael headed in my direction, and I sat up. Before he could grab my hand, I grabbed his instead and told him, "Let's dance, Michael." While out on the dance floor, I spotted Monica. Then promptly felt the weight of her evil glare from across the room. She was blatantly staring at Alvaro, Maria, and Tonya. Feeling the need to protect Tonya from whatever is going on, I reached out and tugged on her arm, telling her to join us. When the song ended, Michael walked back over to Arturo, beside the stereo, and went back to being the DJ's helper. Arturo played the next three songs by Prince and the Revolution, so there was no way either of us would be leaving the floor now. When the fourth song came on, I felt Julio's arms wrap around my waist from behind. 'Is This Love' by Whitesnake was playing. At the same time, Greg was walking up to Daphne, and I was excited for her until Julio spun me around to face him.

Now I was staring up into his stunning brown eyes, feeling wholly captivated with him. Julio leaned in to kiss me, and I closed my eyes as I felt his lips brush up against my cheek before he whispered, "I just want to spend this evening with you." I placed my head down on his shoulder, and he held me close to him in his arms. It was so romantic that I had chills, the good kind from head to toe. I lifted my head and saw Daphne dancing with Greg beside us. I felt ecstatic knowing how much this moment meant to her too. The next song playing was 'Love Me Tomorrow' by Chicago. I looked over and saw Greg wrap his arms tighter around Daphne.

"Julio, what are the odds they will keep on playing slow songs that Greg can tolerate enough to continue dancing with Daphne?"

He laughed before saying, "I just thought that very same thing, but don't worry, Greg is into Daphne."

"Do you know that for sure, Julio?"

"Yes, he is my best friend, and he tells me everything."

"Like what has he told you about Daphne?"

"She makes Greg happy whenever she's around him. Daphne's honesty took him by surprise, and now Greg finds her intriguing."

"Really, Julio intriguing?"

"Yes, Samantha. Those are his exact words, not mine."

When the song was over, Monica announced it was time to cut the cake. The four of us stood there on the dance floor, looking back at one another. You could see the disappointment on our faces. We knew that once the cake is cut, the party is coming to an end. Pilar called Julio over, and he reached down to take my hand prior to leaving the dance floor. When we walked up to the table, Pilar asked Julio to walk around to the other side. Julio sucked his teeth, and it made a sound before he released my hand. "Sammy, you can come with Julio and stand next to him."

"It's time for you, Julio, to do the most crucial job of the evening."

"What job is that, mom?"

"To make a wish and blow out your candles." I quickly ran around the table to join Julio while his mom lit the candles. We all sang Happy Birthday and Julio leaned down about to blow out the candles on his cake when his mom said, "Wait; did you make a wish?"

Julio closed his eyes, and Eddie yelled out, "Primo, wish for the arcade." Everybody was laughing except for Julio. He opened his eyes and blew out the candles. Then he wrapped his arms around me and kissed me gently on the cheek. Pilar moved the birthday cake over and placed another dish in front of Julio filled with whipped cream and cherries.

"Okay, Julio, tell me honestly, which cake do you prefer?"

"Mom, I can't believe it. You made me Tres Leche?" She nodded her head yes as Julio reached over and hugged his mother. He left Pilar with a beaming smile.

"Let me cut the first piece for you, mom." Julio cut into the Tres Leche and prepared three plates. He handed his mom the first plate, and Julio gave me the second plate.

When Julio took his first bite from the third plate, he smiled at his mom and told her it's delicious.

Maria walked up behind us and said, "I can serve the rest. You three should have a seat over there," she pointed to the table in front of us with three chairs." Then Alex walked up behind Maria and kissed her on the cheek.

Pilar smiled and told her, "Yes, I think we will have a seat over there. Thank you, Maria."

Once the three of us sat down. Pilar turned to me, asking, "Do you think something is going on between Alex and Maria?"

Julio and I laughed before I replied, "Yes, I think they are keen on one another."

"She would be good for Alex. I like her."

"Mom, what are you talking about? Who's good for Alex?" I turned my head and saw Monica standing beside us. Her sharp eyes set off an alarm inside me, and I stood up.

"Here, take my seat, Monica." She quickly sat down just as I left the table.

Daphne waved me over, and I just sat down when I heard Julio say, "May I have everyone's attention for a minute." Greg stood up first. Then Daphne joined him. I stayed on the couch and just turned my head around to face Julio. His eyes locked on mine, and he was already smiling. "I want to apologize to all of you for walking off the field earlier today. I'm just so crazy about Samantha that I haven't been able to think straight. I finally asked her out this afternoon, so it's official. Samantha is my girlfriend, and we are a couple." Everyone was clapping, and I noticed Greg was staring at me with that same smug look on his face again. As I shook my head, grinning back at him, Greg began to laugh.

Eddie walked up to Julio while making an announcement. "This Primo is a sad moment for all of us, and let me tell you why. Everyone out on that field today enjoyed your original title.

"What title, Eddie?"

"The Kissing Bandits, Primo." Everyone broke out laughing, including Julio and me.

"Hey, Julio, happy birthday, man." Julio had just made his way over to me when Alvaro stopped him. While they were discussing the game, two more guys joined them. Then all of a sudden, I felt a chill and jumped off the couch. Julio reached out for my hand while he whispered, "Where are you going?"

"Nowhere, I'm just cold from sitting under the ac vent." Julio pulled me against him, and he wrapped his arms around me. That's when I saw Monica over Julio's shoulder with a vexed look on her face. She was staring at us from across the room. This made me feel uncomfortable, so I leaned back and told Julio I would be back in a few minutes after speaking to Tonya. Since I didn't whisper this time, Alvaro heard me.

"Sammy, do you mind if I walk with you? I still need to say bye to Tonya."

"No, of course not, Alvaro, come with me." When I was walking across the room, I felt Julio's eyes on me the entire time. Tonya was standing in a corner, speaking to Daphne and Greg.

"Hey, Tonya, Alvaro was just coming over to say bye to everyone."

"Are you leaving now, Alvaro?"

"Yes, I have to get home to do a few things."

"Okay, well, don't be a stranger." Tonya leaned over to hug Alvaro, and he jerked his head away and took a step back.

"Alvaro, are you alright."

"He's fine, Tonya, where's Lewis?"

Tonya, along with the rest of us, jumped the minute we heard Monica's hostile tone of voice. Everybody slowly turned around and what we saw was a very angry girl standing behind us. Then Tonya replied, "I don't know where Lewis went off to Monica. He left here with your brother Alex." Now I knew from the sound of Tonya's voice she was mad. Alvaro still appeared to be nervous, and he was looking around the room, probably for an exit.

I noticed he was staring at the sliding glass doors when he quickly said, "I have to go now tell Lewis bye for me." Then Alvaro took off, behind us through one of the many sliding glass doors, and Monica didn't say another word.

"Monica, I'm worried about you, is everything alright?" She never answered me. Instead, she stood there in silence with her mouth gaping open, and her arms crossed over her chest while she watched Alvaro run down the stairs. When Alvaro was no longer in sight, she took off behind him out the same sliding glass doors.

"Muñeca, she's freaking me out."

"You're not the only one, Tonya. Today has been a very strange day." Monica left the sliding glass doors open, so Tonya and I walked outside. We walked up to the railing and stared down at the pool while talking about what just happened.

"Hey, it's getting late, and I have to go jogging in the morning."

"Alright, let's go back inside, Tonya, and will say goodbye to everyone before we leave?"

"Okay, but do it fast, Muñeca."

We walked up to Maria, Daphne, and Denise to tell them we're ready to leave. At the same time, Michael walked up and asked, "Girls, where did everybody go?" It wasn't until Michael asked that question that I realized everyone's gone.

"Yeah, the Sanchez boys left a few minutes ago, and I guess Greg went with them. Do you think I can wait for Greg to come back, Sammy?"

"Not if your sleeping at my house tonight, Daphne, we're leaving now."

"Fine, Sammy, let's go then."

Arturo and Michael walked us back to my doorstep, and they realized it was late, so they decided to head home. We all said our goodbyes then walked inside. While watching TV in the living room, Tonya passed out washcloths and told us to wash our face, or we will have clogged pores in the morning. Denise replied, "Okay, Tonya, thank you," and she went back to watching TV. Tonya came back out to the living room again after washing her face to tell us she was going to bed.

A few minutes later, I turned to Daphne and asked, "Did you kiss Greg tonight?"

"No, of course not, Sammy. Greg makes me feel shy and a bit nervous."

"That's exactly how I felt when I first started talking to Julio."

"Really, Sammy?"

Denise smiled before adding, "It's exciting to feel that way, and we've all felt like that before, so enjoy it, Daphne."

"Just try to be yourself, Daphne, but don't get too crazy."

"Me crazy? Of course not, Maria," and we all laughed.

"Wait, what was that?"

"What was what, Denise?"

"That sound Maria."

"Shhhh, I heard it again." We all remained quiet until Denise jumped up, saying, "That sounded like a rock," and we all followed Denise into my bedroom.

Tonya was standing up in front of my bedroom window when we walked into my room. "Tonya, who is it?"

"It's the boys' Denise, their downstairs." Tonya pointed to the window, and Daphne ran up to take a look.

"Girls, come over here. Maria, Denise, and I walked up to the window, and we took a look outside. There standing below my window was Greg and the Sanchez boys. They were all smiling and waving up at us.

When I backed away from the window, I asked, "Girls, what are we going to do?"

"Sammy, I want to go outside and see them."

"Okay, Daphne, let's go see them."

"How are we going to do that, Tonya?"

"You'll see, Muñeca."

"Daisy, do you want to go outside for a walk with Auntie Tonya?"

Instantly I had the biggest smile on my face. I hugged Tonya and said, "You're a genius." We all ran into the kitchen, and Tonya grabbed Daisy's leash.

"Your mom is sleeping right now, Sammy, and we don't want to wake her up. At the same time, we don't want her to worry if she does wake up, and we're not here."

"So, what do you have in mind, Denise?"

"I think we should leave her a note and place it on the refrigerator."

"That's a great idea, Denise. Hand me a piece of paper and a pen."

"No, Sammy, I think Maria should write the note because her handwriting is more legible."

"Okay, Denise, I'll just write. 'We're out for a walk with Daisy.'"

"Sounds perfect, Maria."

"Denise placed the note on the refrigerator under a refrigerator magnet."

"Let's go," Daphne whispered, and we followed her out the door. By the time we arrived downstairs, the boys were nowhere around. "They left. We took too long," Daphne whined with her usual pouty face."

"Disappointment is just a part of life, Daphne. Now since we're outside, let's walk Daisy over to her favorite spot."

"Fine, Tonya, we will just follow you," Daphne replied, sounding depressed. We walked over by the pool, and the boys were all there standing under the clubhouse.

Daphne turned to us and whispered, "We found them."

As we got closer, we saw them standing in a huddle around Julio's mom and Uncle Sanchez. They all turned and faced us at the same time, appearing to be upset. Julio said something to his mom before he ran up to me.

"You didn't say good night to me before you left."

"No, Julio, I didn't. You and your family were nowhere around when we left."

"I'm sorry about that, Mi Corazón. Something happened, and we had to leave immediately to address it. By the time we came back, everybody was gone except for Greg."

"Greg wasn't even there when we left the clubhouse."

"I think he was there you just didn't see him because he was in the back eating what was left of the Arroz con Pollo."

"Did he eat all of it?"

"Well, Greg finished off whatever was left behind." Now we were both grinning at one another when Denise walked up to us.

"Guys, I don't want to interrupt you, but Alex is calling you, Julio."

"Give me a second, Samantha. Please don't leave." Denise stood by me as we looked over at the family huddle.

"What's going on?"

"I don't know yet. Julio only said something happened, and they had to leave to deal with it." Tonya, Daphne, and Maria walked up shortly after I said that.

"Girls, did you notice, someone is missing from the family circle?"

We all whispered, "Monica."

"Oh no, we should go," Daphne said, sounding nervous.

"I can't, Daphne. Julio asked me to wait for him."

"Fine Sammy, let's take a seat over there, at the picnic tables, I'm tired of standing."

As soon as we started to walk over to the picnic tables, I could feel Julio following me with his eyes. We all took a seat at the first table, and Tonya whispered, "You know this has something to do with Monica if she's the only one missing. Plus, she has been acting crazy all–;

Tonya stopped speaking midsentence after noticing something behind me, and she looked frightened. I instantly had chills on the back of my neck that made my hair stand up. This was definitely not a good feeling. I took in a deep breath and turned around to see Alvaro standing behind me. His clothes were covered in dirt along with his face. His hair was a mess, and he was visibly upset. Maria jumped up from her chair and asked, "Alvaro, what happened to you?"

He didn't answer his sister. Instead, he looked over at the clubhouse and took off running. Maria ran after her brother, yelling, "Alvaro, Alvaro, come back here."

Then as if things weren't chaotic enough, I hear Alex yelling," Guys stop, Eddie, grab them." I turned my head to look toward the clubhouse when Lewis and Julio ran past us.

"Oh crap," Eddie yelled out, with both of his hands cupping the sides of his head.

While Alex yelled, "Let's go. What are you waiting for?" Eddie and Alex took off, running down the same path toward the parking lot just like everyone else before them.

I sat there, shaking my head, wondering what in the world was going on. When Daphne said, "Look, Uncle

Sanchez and Pilar are speaking to Greg." We all turned and faced the clubhouse again to see Pilar and Mr. Sanchez waving bye to Greg as they were walking away.

Greg had a mischievous grin on his face as he walked over to us. He grabbed a chair from a nearby table and joined us. "Wow, I can't believe how this night turned out."

"Tell us what happened."

"Wait, Tonya. Maybe he's not allowed to tell us. Then Denise turned to Greg and asked, "Are you allowed to tell us what happened?"

"I'm sure he can tell us something, Denise. Come on, Greg, tell us what did Monica do?"

Greg smiled at Tonya before saying, "I don't even know how to explain what happened, but I'm sure you will hear all about it when the guys return."

"What if they don't come back, Greg?"

"Why wouldn't they come back, Daphne? Are they going to be abducted by aliens?"

"Gee, I hope not. That would be terrible. Who would you play soccer with next Sunday?"

Everyone laughed except for Greg, who openly started to stare at Daphne with a smile on his face.

"Hey, Daphne, do you want to go for a walk with me?"

Daphne looked stunned, and it took her almost a minute before she answered, "Sure, Greg, that'll be great." They both stood up and headed out to the sidewalk.

Once they were gone, Tonya sat back in her chair, saying, "That was amazing."

"Yeah, finally, now where's Eddie?"

"I don't know Denise, and I'm too tired to care. Can we just leave now?"

"No, Tonya, we can't go anywhere."

"Why not, Muñeca?"

"Maria is still missing. Remember, she ran after her brother Alvaro."

Tonya sat back down, saying, "You're right, Denise. I forgot all about that because I'm so tired, and obviously, I need some sleep."

"Obviously," Denise replied."

The three of us sat quietly at the picnic table. We had our arms crossed in front of us, trying our best to stay awake. At one point, it felt like we were having a yawning competition. Then Tonya jumped up to her feet and yelled, "Finally, they're back." All of the Sanchez boys walked up to the table and sat down except for Alex.

"I'm taking Maria and Alvaro home. Tonya, can you make sure to get Maria's overnight bag to her sometime this week?"

"Of course, Alex, I'll make sure she gets it."

"Thank you, Tonya. Now I have to get going." Alex jogged out toward the parking lot and was gone.

Tonya turned to the boys at the table and asked, "What in the world is going on here?" None of them said a word, and they all came back scuffed up with dirt and grass stains all over their clothes.

"Look, you abandoned us at the party. Then you guys throw rocks at Sammy's window. We come downstairs to find you here, but then you all take off again. We deserve some sort of explanation."

Julio looked at Lewis, and Lewis looked back at Julio before they both turned to Eddie.

"What? Do you want me to tell them?"

"No, Eddie," Julio said, shaking his head.

"Lewis, you need to tell them what happened. Denise is right; they deserve an explanation."

"Are you sure?" Julio nodded his head, yes. Then he looked down toward the ground.

"Alex and I walked down to the van to get something for my dad."

"Yeah, a beer," Eddie said, laughing. Julio and Lewis both sat up and gave Eddie an angry look.

"Okay, guys, "Sorry."

Lewis continued with the story. "Alex opened the side door, and we caught Monica in there with Alvaro."

"You caught Alvaro and Monica doing what exactly, Lewis?"

Julio stood up and said, "Alvaro was having sex with my sister inside the van."

"No way," Tonya replied, "I thought Monica hated him."

"Monica couldn't have hated Alvaro that much if she's having sex with him."

"That's pretty obvious, Denise."

"Lewis, what happened after that?"

"Tonya, that's when things went a little crazy. My cousin Alex climbed into his van to go after Alvaro. He saw red when he realized what was going on in his van. Alvaro luckily ran out of the van through the back doors and straight into the golf course. We came back up to the party to tell Julio and Eddie what happened. My father heard everything, and he told my aunt Pilar what was going on. A few minutes later, my father and Pilar were standing beside the van, waiting for us when we walked out of the golf course."

"Julio, what happened right now when you ran after Alvaro?"

"Samantha, I caught up to Alvaro, and Alex pulled us apart." Julio stood up and asked, "Can we go for a walk, Samantha? Are you up for a walk?"

"Whatever you want, Julio."

"That's all I want. To go for a walk with you and Daisy."

"Alright, we can go now." I handed him Daisy's leash, and Julio took my hand as I stood up.

"Girls, I'll be back."

"That's fine, Sammy, go with Julio. Take your time. Don't rush back. I'll be fine here alone with these two beautiful ladies."

"Eddie, I'm still here, bro."

"Aye, Lewis, why do you ruin my dreams? I want to think I'm alone conversing with these two beautiful girls."

"But Eddie, you're not alone. I'm sitting right here beside you, and Tonya's my girlfriend."

"You know what, Lewis? You have been messing crap up for me since you were born. Do you know I was once an only child? It was awesome. Everybody spoiled me. Yeah, and then this guy right here was born," Eddie pointed to Lewis.

We all started laughing, and Lewis yelled, "Eddie, how do you remember being an only child? You were two years old when I was born." Everyone broke out laughing again.

"Listen, Lewis, a person no matter what age does not forget being the prince of the family." Lewis shook his head, trying to back away as Eddie hugged him. Eddie had poor Lewis locked in an embrace when he told him, "I love you, Lewis, even if you are a little shit."

Lewis shoved Eddie before telling him, "Okay, enough, bro. Get off me."

Julio squeezed my hand to get my attention and bobbed his head to the side twice, indicating he was ready to go. I waved bye to the girls as Julio, and I walked out to the sidewalk with Daisy. We walked right past my building when we came up to a bus bench, and Julio sat down. He pulled me onto his lap. Then I felt his arms wrap around me as he placed his head down on my shoulder. "Julio, talk to me. Tell me what you're feeling."

"I'm feeling betrayed by one of my friends. I'm angry about it, and I'm disappointed with my sister."

"What were you going to do, to Alvaro, if Alex didn't stop you?"

"I don't know, Samantha. I'm angry and want to know why he had sex with my sister?"

"Well, I always thought your sister hated Alvaro."

"No, my sister has had a crush on Alvaro since she was 11 years old."

"Did Alvaro have a crush on Monica?"

"No, he didn't. He thought my sister was very annoying. Remember, at the time, they were just 11years old."

"Has he changed his feelings toward your sister recently?"

"Well, I think it's safe to say yes since he was caught having sex with my sister."

"You have a point there, Julio. I'm sorry. That was a stupid question. It's late, and I'm exhausted."

"Samantha, I'm sorry for keeping you up so late and talking to you about all this stuff."

"Julio, don't be silly. I'm glad that you feel comfortable enough to speak to me about it, and I hope you feel better."

"Before we go, I want to thank you, Samantha, for waiting on me to come back to the picnic tables tonight. I've been wanting to kiss you the whole night. During my party, I had to tell myself to wait for the goodnight kiss. Then after we danced together, I just wanted to steal you away from the party."

"To do what with me, Julio?"

He placed his hand on my cheek and kissed my lips. When he pulled away, I tilted my head to the side to kiss him down his neck. He squeezed me, and I noticed his breathing had accelerated. I loved that I was getting to him, so I kissed him behind his earlobe.

Julio yelled out, "Samantha," right before he pulled his head away. Then he stared into my eyes and cupped my chin before covering my lips with his again. This time he kissed me over and over again feverishly until his tongue brushed up against mine. This caused me to feel instantly lightheaded, but it also set off a burst of energy inside me. It was interrupted by Daisy when she started to bark. We pulled apart, and I bent down to pet Daisy. She was already standing up, facing the sidewalk. "Julio, Daisy is ready to go. We need to start walking back over to the pool." As we were walking back down the sidewalk, I saw Lewis and Tonya headed in our direction.

"Hey guys, Greg is back at the picnic tables with Daphne so, we came looking for you. It's really late, and I need to get some sleep, Muñeca."

"Tonya, I'm tired too. Let's tell Daphne and Denise it's time to go." Together the four of us, along with Daisy, walked back over to the picnic tables. Denise and Eddie were gone by the time we arrived. I asked Daphne where they were, and she said they would be right back. Tonya rolled her eyes and stomped her foot as she crossed her arms over her chest.

"If you want to go to bed now, you can, Tonya."

"Yes, Muñeca, I'm tired, and I still have to get up to go jogging."

"Here, take the key and just leave the door unlocked for me, and I'll be up in a few minutes."

"Good, see you in the morning, Muñeca." Lewis left with Tonya to walk her back to my apartment.

"How are you doing, man? Are you feeling alright, Julio?"

"Yeah, I feel great now," Julio told Greg while smiling at me.

"Sammy, are you blushing."

"Absolutely not, Daphne."

"What exactly have you two been doing?"

"Nothing, Daphne."

"You two were up to something I can tell, Sammy. You can't lie to me."

"Daphne, have you kissed Greg yet?"

"No, she hasn't kissed me yet," Greg answered.

"So why don't you just kiss her?" Julio asked. Greg leaned in and kissed Daphne on the lips. My mouth dropped open, and I looked over at Julio. He was covering his mouth, and his eyes were huge. When they pulled apart, Daphne was smiling. Greg sat back in his chair and locked his fingers behind his head while grinning at us.

"Wow, guys, that was really something," I said, laughing. "How was that, Daphne?"

"What, Sammy?"

"How was that kiss, Daphne?"

"What, kiss?"

"The one you just got from Greg."

"I don't remember Sammy."

Daphne leaned over Greg, and she kissed him right on the lips. When they pulled apart, Greg just leaned back in his chair again, grinning at us.

"Oh, I get it. They're messing with us, Samantha."

"When did you guys first kiss? Since this is obviously not the first time."

Greg and Daphne started cracking up laughing.

"Come on, Daphne, tell me."

"If you stop pouting, Sammy, I will tell you."

"I'm not pouting. I'm just exhausted. Now tell me, Daphne."

"On our walk earlier, Sammy. Greg kissed me on the lips, and I liked it so much that I kissed him back."

"Yeah, and I enjoy kissing Daphne so much that we've been kissing pretty much non stop ever since.

"Wow, Greg, I never thought I would hear you say something like that."

"Hey, neither did I, Julio."

"Do you think Denise and Eddie are off making out somewhere?"

"I don't really know Daphne, but Julio and I just made out on the bus bench."

"For real?"

"Yes, when I looked up at Julio to see his expression, he was simply smiling.

"Primo," We heard Eddie say as he walked back over to the picnic tables holding Denise's hand.

"So, what have you two been doing?"

"We were just talking, Daphne."

"Yeah, with our lips."

"Eddie, you're not supposed to kiss and tell, dude."

"Greg, do you honestly think I'm going to kiss this beautiful girl and not brag about it. No way, Jose, I'm going to tell everybody."

Now everyone was laughing until Eddied asked, "Where did Lewis go?"

"He walked Tonya back home, and I guess he went home."

"Listen, I love you and Lewis, you hear me. But the next time you guys have me chasing you around in the golf course when I catch you, I'm kicking your butt."

"Okay, Eddie," Julio told him, laughing and shaking his head.

Then Eddie clapped his hands together and announced, "It's time to stand up and walk the girls home."

Chapter 8 What's Really Going On

"Muñeca, are you still sleeping?"

"Yes, Tonya, isn't that obvious."

"When are you going to get up?"

"In a little bit, Tonya. Let me go back to sleep to finish my dream."

"Why? Are you dreaming about Julio?"

"What?"

"Are you dreaming about your boyfriend, Muñeca?"

"I was until you woke me up. Now go away."

"Wouldn't you rather see Julio for real?"

"Tonya, what is that supposed to mean?"

"It means if you get up right this minute, you can see Julio in person."

"No, I went to bed late last night, Tonya, so I want to sleep for another hour."

"Okay, then I'm not going to tell you what happened."

"That's fine with me. I don't really care."

"Muñeca, I'm hungry."

"Go into the kitchen and make yourself something to eat."

"Do you want me to make you something?"

"No, Tonya, I just want you to go away."

"Why? You're awake now."

"That's only because you won't stop talking to me."

The phone rang, and Tonya answered it. "Here, Muñeca, it's for you," and she placed the phone to my ear. I heard someone say hello, hello, Sammy, are you there? I sat up, still half asleep.

"Here, Tonya, hold the phone for me. I need to pick up the phone in the kitchen. This one is broken."

"No problem, Muñeca," Tonya said with a smirk on her face as she batted her eyelashes at me. I just rolled my eyes at her before leaving my room to head into the kitchen.

"Hello."

"Sammy, it's Maria. I have to talk to you about last night."

"Yeah, what happened?"

"Let me just tell you that I am mad at Alex and his entire family."

"Okay, tell me why?"

"Is Tonya listening?"

"No."

"Go get Tonya and share the phone."

"Okay, hold on."

"Tonya, come into the kitchen with me. She wants to tell us what happened last night."

"Who does?"

"Maria."

"Is that who is on the phone?"

"Tonya, I thought you spoke to her when you answered the phone?"

"No, the phone in your room is broken, remember?"

"Then how did you know the call was for me?"

"Duh, because you live here, Muñeca."

"Whatever. Come sit beside me and share the phone." Tonya rolled her eyes but sat down beside me on the floor. Tonya put her shoulder against mine, and we placed the phone between us to rest between our shoulders.

"Tonya said wait," and turned the volume up to max.

"Okay, Maria, go ahead. We're both listening."

"Several times yesterday, Monica asked my brother to leave the exercise room to join her upstairs at the clubhouse before the game, and my brother declined her invitation."

"When the game was over, my brother and a few of the guys decided to get showered and dressed inside the exercise room instead of going home. It made sense because Julio's surprise party was happening a few hours later. After everyone was showered and dressed, one of the guys suggested they go upstairs to help Monica. Everyone left the exercise room except for my brother. Alvaro decided to remain downstairs to avoid seeing Monica again before the party. Now Alvaro had all this free time, so he got undressed, wrapped himself in a towel, and went into the sauna."

"It's not safe for Alvaro to go into the sauna by himself."

"Tonya, it can be relaxing, and Monica has Alvaro totally stressed out."

"Well, I don't think Alvaro is going to feel any better if he suffers from heatstroke, Muñeca."

"Whoa, Tonya, you're totally exaggerating."

Maria yelled, "That's not the point. Can you two please let me finish telling you what happened?"

We jumped and dropped the phone on the floor. As Tonya reached out to grab it, Daphne opened my brother's bedroom door. "Get back on the phone. Maria's still talking."

"Daphne, are you eavesdropping again?" She giggled and quickly shut the bedroom door.

I picked the phone up off the floor and handed it over to Tonya. "Maria, hold on, Muñeca will be back in a second." I walked into my brother's room to find Denise and Daphne sitting on the bottom bunk, holding the phone between them. I turned around and walked back out to the kitchen. I joined Tonya back on the floor, and she placed the phone between us.

"Okay, Maria, everyone is on the phone now, including Denise and Daphne.

"That's great. Can I finish what I was saying now?"

"All four of us replied in unison," Yes, Maria."

"Alright, so where was I?"

"Alvaro was in the sauna."

"That's right, thank you, Daphne."

"My brother went into the sauna. He was in there for about ten minutes when Monica walked in. Alvaro was totally shocked to see her. First of all, she's in the men's locker room, and second, Alvaro was only wearing a towel. He asked Monica, what are you doing in here? That's when she sits down on the bench, completely ignoring Alvaro. A couple of minutes later, Monica starts to complain that it's too hot. Alvaro responds, it's supposed to be hot. It's a sauna.' Monica stood up, and Alvaro felt relieved, thinking finally she's leaving, but that's not what happened."

"Maria, what happened?"

"Monica stood up and began removing her clothes while staring down my brother. Alvaro told her to stop playing around or get out, but she didn't. Wearing just a bra and panties, Monica tried to climb on top of Alvaro's lap. He pushed her away and jumped up off the bench. Then Alvaro headed for the door, but Monica got there first, and she shoved my brother after she snatched his towel off. Alvaro fell backward onto the bench, and Monica ran out the door. My brother tried to leave, but he couldn't get out because Monica was leaning up against the door. Alvaro gave up and sat down until the timer went off. When Alvaro tried opening the door this time, Monica was nowhere around. He walked out of the sauna and went straight to the bathroom to put on his gym clothes before lifting weights for another hour. Afterward, while taking a shower, Monica suddenly pops up naked and joins him in the shower. Alvaro tells her to get out before someone catches her in there, and she informs him that she locked the door."

"Then what happened?"

"I don't know all the details Daphne except I do know they were interrupted."

"What? By Who?"

"You see, Muñeca, I told you last night Monica is freaking crazy."

"Oh my gosh, Tonya, don't interrupt Maria."

That's when Tonya got mad, and she ran into my brother's room, yelling at Daphne. "How dare you say anything to me? You weren't even supposed to be on this call. You're lucky that Muñeca tolerates your nonsense because I would've kicked you out of my house for listening in on my phone calls." I walked into the room, asking Tonya to follow me back out to the kitchen. We both sat back down on the floor, and I picked up the phone again, asking Maria to continue.

"Girls, Eddie knocked on the men's door. The intrusion scared Monica so bad that she ran into the women's locker room. My brother answered the door, and Eddie asked my brother to go with him to the airport to pick up his dad. My brother threw on his clothes, grabbed his duffel bag, and left."

"Wait, I thought Pilar picked up Mr. Sanchez."

"No, who told you that, Sammy?"

"Monica told me last night at the party."

"Surprise, Monica lied."

"Yeah, obviously, but why was Monica so mad at Alvaro last night. I mean, did something else happen in the bathroom."

"Alvaro never bothered to tell Monica that he was leaving with Eddie."

Now we were all cracking up until I asked, "How long do you think Monica waited in the women's locker room for Alvaro?"

"Not long enough because she still made it to the party."

"That's mean, Maria."

"Is it, though? I don't think so, and you haven't heard the rest of the story yet, Denise."

"You're right, Maria, finish telling us what happened."

"Okay, during the party, Alvaro noticed Monica was angry, so he decided to avoid her. When my brother left the party, Monica ran up to Alvaro in the parking lot, asking him to follow her back to the van so they could finish where they left off. A few minutes later, Alex showed up and caught them in the middle of having sex. Now I understand that Alex was mad. However, my brother had to run into the golf course in order to get away from Alex."

"Maria, that's his little sister, so I don't blame Alex for going after your brother. He doesn't know Monica seduced him."

"Denise, my brother, hid in the golf course for almost two hours until he showed up at the picnic tables, and the reason he took off running again was that he saw Alex standing underneath the clubhouse."

"Okay, Maria, so call your boyfriend Alex and tell him how Monica instigated the whole thing."

"Tonya, Alex took us home last night."

"Did Alvaro tell Alex what happened?"

"Yes, my brother told Alex everything that occurred, and he apologized, saying what he did was wrong. Then he reminded Alex that I'm his sister, and if he caught someone getting intimate like that with me, he would want to harm that person too. After that discussion, Alex apologized to Alvaro, and they parted on good terms. However, things are still nasty between Julio, Lewis, and my brother. When Alvaro took off running from the table last night, Julio ran after him and tackled my brother in the parking lot. They were both on the ground, and Lewis stood over them, yelling something about Monica. Then Alex showed up and pulled Julio off of my brother."

"I don't blame Julio for that. Monica is his sister, and Julio's not aware of what his sister did."

"Sammy, my brother, tried to speak to your boyfriend about what happened, and Julio punched him in the face. Luckily, Alex was able to separate them before it went any further."

"Maria, I'm sorry this happened to Alvaro."

"Thank you, Sammy. Can I ask you and Tonya to do me a favor?"

"What's the favor?"

"All I want is for you and Tonya to speak to Julio and Lewis. Explain to them what happened, and maybe they will realize it wasn't entirely my brother's fault."

Tonya and I agreed to do it, and Maria told us she would give us a call back later. As I hung up the phone, Daphne walked out of my brother's room, and Tonya apologized to her. "Oh, nevermind that, Tonya, you were right. I'm too nosey for my own good, but that phone call was interesting, and I'm glad I listened in on it."

"Your right, it was Daphne, but I'm not talking about anything until I eat breakfast. That's partly the reason why I lost my temper in the first place. I'm hungry."

"Okay, then let's get you fed. What do you feel like eating, Tonya?"

"Denise, you're going to laugh when I tell you this, but I want pancakes and apple juice again. It's sort of becoming my favorite weekend breakfast.

"Tonya, it's Monday."

"I know, Denise, but it feels like the weekend with you here and no school. By the way, how did you get your parents to allow you to sleepover on a Sunday night?"

"My mom is off today, Tonya. Now, do you remember the recipe to make the pancakes?"

"Are you kidding? Denise, I have been making pancakes with Ms. Harris since I was like six or seven years old."

"That's great, you can prepare the batter, Tonya, and I'll cook the pancakes."

"What do you want me to do, Denise?"

"Daphne, you can make the apple juice and set the table."

By the time we all sat down to eat. Tonya was already munching on her bacon. Then all of a sudden, Tonya told us, "Put down your forks; we need to say grace." We all held hands as Tonya said the blessing. We were all eating in silence until Daphne began to talk about her favorite subject Greg.

"Girls, did you know Greg is working today at the video store? His cousin Mig is coming by to pick him up in an hour.

"No, I didn't know that," Tonya replied, rolling her eyes."

"Well, he does. Oh, and tomorrow Julio and Lewis start their new job at the Pro shop. Does anyone know where that is?"

"Yes, it's just a couple of blocks from here, Daphne. Why?"

"Tonya, maybe you don't know this, but Alvaro was supposed to start working there tomorrow with Julio and Lewis."

"Gee Daphne, you're talking nonstop this morning."

"Denise, I'm just so amped up after that phone call. Do you think Alvaro will still want to work there?"

"I don't think so, Daphne."

"When will you speak to Julio, Muñeca?"

"I'm planning to speak to him today. We have our best conversations when we're out on our walks with Daisy, so perhaps I'll do it then."

"When are you going to speak to Lewis?"

"To tell you the truth, I have no idea, Muñeca."

"Tonya, you told Maria you would speak to him about Alvaro?"

"Eventually, I guess I'll have to. The problem is today would not be the right time. I went jogging with Lewis this morning, and he was all excited about spending the rest of the day with his father before he heads back to Anaheim tomorrow. A conversation like this could ruin his day, and I don't want to do that."

Daphne stood up from the table and announced she was leaving to go next door to visit Greg before he goes to work. Then Denise got up and told us she's going with Daphne. Tonya and I cleared the table when there was a knock on the front door. I ran to answer it, leaving Tonya in the kitchen to start on the dishes. It was Lewis, and he asked to speak to Tonya. I told Lewis to come inside, and I pointed to the kitchen. Right as I was about to shut the door, Julio appeared in front of it. "Good morning, Samantha."

"Good morning, Soccer Player," we both stood there, grinning at one another until Julio said, "Daphne told me to run over here."

"Did she tell you why?"

Julio's grin got wider before he answered, "Yes, she told me that you were going for a walk with Daisy, and you wanted me to go." I just shook my head thinking; Daphne is such a busybody.

"She's right. I need to take Daisy out for her morning walk, and I would love it if you came with us."

Julio bent down and called Daisy over. She ran into Julio's arms, nearly knocking him over, giving him kisses. He began to pet her behind the ears looking up at me. "What's that look for, Julio?"

"Samantha, I wasn't sure at first if Daphne was right because you were shaking your head no."

"Oh, I just thought it was amusing that Daphne sent you over here. Now let me run inside to tell Tonya where I'm going, and I'll be right back with Daisy's leash."

We were walking out toward the field beside the golf course. When Julio asked, "What's on your mind, Mi Corazón?"

"Maria called me this morning to tell me about her brother's side of the story." Julio stopped walking and turned to me.

"What was Alvaro's side of the story?" I told Julio word for word what Maria told me over the phone. By the time I was finished, Julio had a troubled look on his face, and we continued our walk in silence.

As we reached the end of the path, I turned around, facing Julio, and said, "I know Monica is your sister, but she has been acting a bit crazy lately. You should have seen how rude she was to Maria and Tonya yesterday."

"Yes, well, I think that's due to Monica's jealousy."

"Who is Monica jealous of?"

"I think she's a little bit jealous of you and Tonya."

"Why would your sister be jealous of us?"

"Lewis and I have been spending a lot of time with you and Tonya lately, which is making my sister feel excluded."

"Julio, that not it."

"Samantha, you don't understand how close Monica, Lewis, and I have been our whole lives."

"Okay, if that's the case. Then can you explain to me why Monica treated Maria so poorly yesterday?"

"No, I can't explain that, Samantha."

"Exactly, because there is no explanation for Monica's behavior. Julio, I am going to be completely honest with you. For the past two days, your sister has been thoughtless, rude, and creepy."

"Well, I haven't seen her be rude to anyone."

"How fortunate for you, Julio. I can only tell you that I have witnessed it for myself several times, and I have decided that I don't want to be around your sister until she starts treating people with some respect."

"I see, Sammy. You're taking Alvaro's side."

"I'm not taking anyone's side, Julio."

"If you're blaming my sister, then you're taking Alvaro's side."

"First of all, I'm simply pointing out to you how your sister has been behaving. It's all based on my own observation, not what someone has told me."

"Samantha, you were friends with my sister until you received that phone call from Maria this morning, but oh no, you're not taking sides at all."

"Julio, you can believe whatever you want. I'm not here to convince you of anything. I just told you how I feel and what I have decided to do about it. If you feel the need to blame someone, then blame Monica. Hold her accountable for her reckless behavior instead of blaming Alvaro and Maria."

"Thank you for telling me how you feel about my sister Samantha. I've already made plans to go to the movies this afternoon with my family. Since Monica will be there, I won't bother to invite you."

"That's fine with me, Julio."

He was looking down at his wristwatch when he said, "I have to go home to get ready."

"Okay, bye."

"Samantha, what do you mean, 'bye?'"

"You just said that you have to go home, so go."

"Do you think I'm going to leave you out here alone on the golf course?"

"It's daylight, Julio."

"That's not the point, Samantha. I'm not leaving you out here alone, and I don't approve of you walking around out here without me. I don't care what time of day it is."

"Sometimes, Julio, you're impossible to deal with." He lifted his chin, then put out his hand. I took it, and he walked me back to my doorstep in complete silence. Julio kissed me on the cheek before asking me to tell Lewis to head home now. I walked inside to find Tonya out in the living room with Daphne and Denise.

"Is Lewis still here?"

"No, Muñeca, he left about five minutes ago. He's taking his father to the movies. I thought you were going with them."

"I'm not going anywhere because Monica is going."

"Are you going, Tonya?"

"Absolutely not, for the same reason."

"How did Lewis feel about that?"

"Listen, I just told Lewis how Monica has been treating me, and that was enough for him to understand why I don't want to go."

"Well, aren't you lucky? I just had more or less the same conversation with Julio, and he accused me of taking Alvaro's side." I sat down beside Tonya with tears in my eyes, and she wrapped her arms around me.

"Muñeca, you need to calm down. It can't be that bad."

"Tonya, we got into a disagreement, and now Julio's mad at me."

"How can Julio be mad at you? He adores you?"

"My conversation with Julio didn't go very well. I was brutally honest about how I'm feeling."

"Muñeca, I'm sure everything will be fine in a day or two."

"I'm not so sure, Tonya. Julio told me that Monica is jealous."

"Jealous of what?"

"Of us. Julio told me that Monica feels left out because of the amount of time Lewis and Julio spend with us."

"That's ridiculous, Muñeca."

"Well, I think Monica is jealous of Tonya, and it has something to do with Alvaro because she hasn't been rude to Sammy, Daphne, or myself."

"Denise, I think you might be right. However, jealousy does not excuse her behavior."

"Sammy, I totally agree with you, and I'm not actually looking for an excuse. I'm just trying to put the puzzle pieces together to understand her actions. I've been close to Monica for over three years, but it's like she changed overnight, and I want to know why. Can you tell me the excuse Julio gave you for Monica's behavior with Alvaro?"

"He didn't give me one, Denise. Why don't you give Monica a call?"

"I have Sammy several times."

"And what did she say?"

"Nothing, she won't come to the phone."

Daphne sat up, saying, "Well, I didn't see Monica at the apartment this morning, or I would have spoken to her about it."

"What were you going to say to her, Daphne?"

"I don't really know, Denise. I just wanted to hear Monica's side of the story, but she never came out of her room."

"Do you girls want to go down to the pool for a little bit?"

"Sammy, I called my brother, and he's already on his way over here to pick us up."

"Daphne, do you intend to tell your brother Arturo what happened last night?"

"Yes, of course, Sammy, I tell my brother everything."

"You most certainly do, and don't forget Michael, too," Denise added.

"None of us can forget Michael," Tonya replied, laughing. Then there was a knock on the door, and Daphne quickly jumped up to answer it.

"Can you come to the door for a minute, Sammy?"

"Sure, give me a second." I stood up from the couch, and Tonya had a worried look on her face.

It was Julio standing at the door, so I walked outside and shut the door behind me. "Samantha, sometimes, I become overly protective of my family. Especially my sister. I know you didn't mean those things that you said earlier, and I understand that you were upset after speaking with Maria."

"Julio, I have no intention of hurting you or your sister. I have seen your loyalty, compassion, respect, and love for her. Which is awesome because she is your sister, and I even understand why you protect her. Nonetheless, it doesn't change the way I feel. I meant what I said earlier, and if you can't understand that, then we should take a break too. Perhaps you can use this time to get the whole jealous thing sorted out with your sister."

"Samantha, come on, I don't want what happened between Alvaro and my sister to come between us. Please let this go, and let's get back to normal."

"Why are you here, Julio?"

"What do you mean? I came over here to speak to you."

"No, I mean, why aren't you at the movies?"

"I couldn't go to the movies without you."

I hate to admit this but hearing him say that made me feel incredibly happy. The minute a smile appeared on my face, Julio wrapped his arms around me. When I looked up at him grinning, he kissed me.

"Hi, guys, what are you up to?"

Julio and I jumped back to see Michael standing beside the staircase, grinning at us.

"Hey, Michael, we were just talking."

"Yeah, uh-huh, if you say so, Sammy."

"I'll just go inside now to get Daphne and Denise for you."

"Okay, great, Sammy, I will just wait out here with your boyfriend."

When I ran back inside, Daphne and Denise were hanging out in my room, listening to the stereo with Tonya. "You girls need to hurry up and get going. Michael is outside right now with Julio, and I don't want Michael to hear about last night from my boyfriend."

Once I said that, the girls ran into my brother's room and grabbed their stuff. They hugged Tonya then me as they headed out the door. Daphne ran up to Julio, asking, "Where's my brother?" Julio pointed to the parking lot then offered to carry the girls' bags down to the car.

"Samantha, I will be back later," Julio said while he followed Daphne down the stairs carrying the girls overnight bags. Tonya and I walked back inside and went straight to my room. I spun the dial on the stereo until I heard 'Here I go Again' by Whitesnake.

"Muñeca, what happened now?"

"Julio couldn't go to the movies without me, and he doesn't want the situation between Alvaro and Monica to come between us."

"He's right, Muñeca. It's not your problem."

"At least I kept my word to Maria, and I spoke to Julio."

"Good, now let's go get ready for the arcade."

"What?"

"Lewis is going to meet up with us at the arcade after the movie lets out."

"I need to call Julio to let him know where I'm going. I also want to invite him to go with us."

"Muñeca, he's already going to the arcade. Everybody is going to be there."

"How is everybody going to be there?"

"Greg gets out of work at six, and the movie is at four o'clock, so everybody will head to the arcade after six. Now Muñeca, we need to figure out what we're going to wear." Tonya ran into my bedroom. By the time I walked into my room, Tonya was already in my walk-in closet, going through all my clothes.

"Tonya, what about Daphne and Denise?"

"What about them?"

"Do they know about the arcade, Tonya?"

"Of course, they do. I told Daphne about it when we were cooking breakfast this morning. That's why she wanted to go and see Greg after breakfast. Just to make sure he would be able to join us."

"When did you find out about the arcade?"

"Lewis and I talked about it while out on our jog this morning. I tried to wake you up to discuss it, but you wanted to sleep for another hour so you could dream about Julio."

"Tonya, you never let me go back to sleep.

"That's not exactly true. I was about to go cook something to eat when the phone rang."

"Oh, that's right, but you told Daphne while you were making breakfast this morning, so why didn't you tell me, Tonya?"

"She was driving me nuts, Muñeca. Daphne wouldn't stop talking about Greg almost the entire time we were making breakfast. All I heard was Greg this, and Greg that, Greg, Greg, Greg. Finally, I told Daphne if she would stop talking about Greg, we will make plans to see him tonight at the arcade. Honestly, that's all I said, and it was like magic. Daphne didn't mention his name again until we sat down to eat."

"What should we wear tonight, Tonya?" I held up the needle nose vice grips, and we were both laughing. At six o'clock, we were still getting ready, and Daisy was barking at the front door. My mom walked in my room, and Tonya followed her out into the kitchen. I remained in my room, blow-drying my hair. As soon as I turned it off, I heard a knock on my bedroom door. I yelled out, "Come in," as I tried to find my hairbrush that was somewhere on my bed, but nobody came in.

A few minutes later, Tonya walked back into my room.

"Muñeca, why didn't you answer your bedroom door?"

"I said, come in, didn't you hear me?"

"No, but that's not the point you didn't actually open the door?"

"Tonya, I've been busy trying to get ready. Look at the time. We're going to be late."

"Let me help you, Muñeca." Tonya spiked and sprayed my bangs into place while I applied my mascara and lip gloss.

"Perfect, we're done. Let's go, Muñeca." I grabbed my beeper and headed out the door when I ran into Julio. He was standing on the opposite side of my bedroom door with a hand full of balloons in fluorescent colors of pink, blue, yellow, and purple.

"Wow, the balloons are so beautiful."

Julio smiled before asking, "Will you be my date tonight to the arcade?"

"Yes, I would love that." Julio smiled as he handed me the bundle of balloons. On the yellow balloon, he wrote, "I'm sorry, Mi Corazón." I saw he signed it in cursive. The signature didn't look like his name, though. "Julio, what did you write there?" I pointed to the yellow balloon.

He grinned before asking, "Are you pointing to my signature."

"Well, as a matter of fact, I am."

"It's my nickname given to me by my girlfriend, Samantha."

He wrote Soccer Player as a signature. "That's perfect, Julio. I love it." I wanted to kiss him badly after seeing that, but I wouldn't dare, not in my house and not with my mom around, so I hugged Julio and thanked him instead.

"Are you ready to go, Samantha?"

"Definitely, just give me a second to place the balloons in my room."

"I'll be waiting for you in the living room, Mi Corazón."

After I tied the balloons to my closet door, I ran back out to the living room and found everyone waiting for me except for Tonya.

"Does anyone know where Tonya wandered off to?"

"She's probably in your brother's room on the phone, Sam." I walked into my brother's room, and Tonya was up on the top bunk on the phone as usual.

"Tonya, we're ready to go now."

"Coming, Muñeca." Tonya jumped down and slid her feet into her clogs before joining everyone out in the living room.

"Well, girls, I don't think you will need that ride from me after all."

"No, but thank you, Mom, for offering to take us."

Alex stood up and said, "We're running late, so if everybody's ready, we should leave now."

"You must be home by curfew, Sam. You have a big day tomorrow." I nodded my head yes as I hugged my mom. Everyone else waved bye as they walked out the door.

Julio, Tonya, and I climbed into the back of the van. "Do you two think it was a good idea to leave Alex alone with the radio?"

"If you're worried about it, Tonya, you should sit up front beside him."

"Oh, and what, leave you alone back here with Sammy? I don't think so, Julio." Tonya started to laugh then yelled out, "Psych" before she walked up front to sit beside Alex.

"Wow, Alex, now I know why they are called Captain chairs. They are spacious and even have armrests."

"If you want to remain in that seat, Tonya, you need to be the DJ."

"No problem, Alex. Where are your cassette tapes?"

"The cassette case is in the back behind Sammy, I think."

"I'll get it," Julio replied before he climbed in the back behind me. That's when I looked around and remembered when Alex and Eddie would spend their weekends working on this van, and boy, is it awesome. The whole van is lined with shag carpet, and the ceiling has wood paneling with lots of lights. Alex and Eddie installed the sofa I'm sitting on, which is in the shape of a J. There is one bench seat but only holds two people, and it's right behind the passenger seat.

As we pulled up into a driveway, Tonya climbed into the backseat with a somber look. Julio smiled at her and said, "Here you go, Tonya, I just found it."

He handed her the cassette case, but she didn't take it. Tonya sat down beside me and announced, "Were at Maria's house." Julio's smile was gone and replaced with a stone-cold expression on his face. I stood up to reach for Julio's hand to help him climb over the sofa and noticed his hand was trembling.

At the same time, Maria opened the passenger door and sat down. "Hello, everybody," Maria said, smiling and sounding happy as if nothing ever happened.

Tonya squinted up her face saying, "Maria, I'm confused, aren't you mad at Alex?"

"I was, until this afternoon, when Alex showed up to my house. He took me out to lunch, and we have decided to let Monica and Alvaro sort this mess out themselves."

"What about your feelings toward Julio, Lewis, and Alvaro?"

"The same thing." Then Maria turned around and looked directly at Julio and said, "Unless you touch my brother, Julio. If you touch my brother again, then you're going to have a problem with me."

Julio hopped over the sofa and sat down beside me before he replied, "Maria, I don't want a problem with anybody. There are lines drawn in the sand that you don't see, but you know not to cross them, and that line was dating my sister. He should have valued our friendship more instead of sleeping with her. He made that decision, not me."

"How do you think my brother feels, Julio?"

"What do you mean, Maria?"

"I mean, how do you think my brother should react now that I'm dating your brother?"

"He shouldn't react to anything. You're just dating."

"Yes, but I'm Alvaro's sister, and if I kiss your brother, how is it any different?"

"You're not sleeping with my brother Maria. That's the difference."

"No, not yet, but maybe one day, I will, Julio. Should Alex ask Alvaro for permission, or should we reconsider our relationship?"

Alex turned around in his chair before saying, "She's right, Julio. What's the difference? I've been friends with Alvaro for years, and now I'm suddenly dating his sister. The only thing I'm having a tough time forgiving is that the act took place in my van."

"You have every right to be angry about that, Alex. It was very disrespectful."

"Yes, it was Maria, and I plan on speaking to Monica about it tomorrow."

"Are you only holding Monica accountable for what happened in your van?"

"Absolutely, Julio, she is the one who had the keys to my van, not Alvaro."

"Alright, I see your point, Alex. I will speak to Alvaro the next time I see him and apologize."

"I'm glad to hear that, Julio."

"Me too," I said, smiling at Julio.

"Maria, honestly, I didn't give any thought to how Alvaro would feel about you dating Alex."

"No, of course not Sammy, because it's Alex, and he has been like everybody's big brother in your neighborhood for years."

"Your right Maria." Julio's trembling stopped, and the look on his face remained serious but was no longer so severe.

"I know I am Sammy, and I'm going to be very candid with you because I think you deserve to know the truth."

"Okay, go for it, Maria."

"On Saturday, when I called Alvaro to invite him to go with us to the Forest, I told him that I have a crush on Alex. My brother immediately freaked out, declined the invite, and hung up on me."

"Yesterday was the first time my brother witnessed Alex and me together as a couple."

"So, Alvaro had to accept your dating my brother and deal with Monica?"

"Exactly, and don't forget you punched my brother in the face Julio, so he really had a horrible day."

"Poor Alvaro, I feel so bad for him. Alex, can we go back to Maria's house for a second? I want to speak to Alvaro."

"Not tonight, Tonya. My brother doesn't want to see anybody right now."

"Maria, I just feel bad for your brother, and I think we all owe him an apology."

"Fine, come to my house on Thursday or Friday. I just want to give Alvaro time to calm down."

"I don't think we will be able to see him this week. Maybe when Muñeca gets back."

Julio turned to me with a horrified look on his face when he asked, "Where are you going, Samantha?"

"I'm going to my dad's for Christmas."

"Why didn't you tell me?"

"Julio, I forgot. The last couple of days have been so crazy."

"When are you leaving?"

"December 22nd, oh crap, I didn't realize this before now, but that's tomorrow, and I will be back on Saturday, January 2nd."

"You won't be here for Christmas, your birthday, or New Year's?"

"No, I am spending those all with my dad like I do every year since my parents' divorce. I'm sorry, Julio, please don't be mad at me for not saying anything. I simply forgot, and I will miss you."

Julio was disappointed, and I felt terrible until he wrapped his arms around me and told me, "I want you to go and have a great time with your father. You are lucky he's still part of your life. I will be here waiting for you when you get back."

Tonya reached over and hugged me from behind. "I'm going to miss you, Muñeca, and don't worry about your clothes or your bed. I will take care of them for you while you are gone."

"Wait, how much will I owe you for babysitting my stuff?" We both started laughing, and Julio sat back, shaking his head.

Alex pulled up to the entrance of the mall and told us he would meet us inside with Maria after he parks the van. The three of us walked inside and went straight to the arcade. Tonya spotted Lewis playing pinball and walked up to him. Julio and I continued walking to the token machine. He loaded the machine up with dollar bills, and we filled our pockets with tokens. Then Julio pointed to a race car that was a few feet away from us. When I looked inside, I saw Greg and Daphne. I turned to Julio, grinning, and we took off running up to the car. Julio got there first and was standing behind the car, and I joined him. Julio whispered on the count of three, and at three, we banged on the plexiglass window. They were clearly startled, and Greg jumped up and smacked his head on the roof inside the car. We could hear him asking, "What the heck was that?" Julio and I were cracking up, and Greg climbed out, laughing. "Dude, you scared me so bad that I smacked my head, and I probably have a concussion. I turned my head toward Daphne, and she was still in the car, looking up at me with a scowl on her face.

"Gee Daphne, that's a lovely shade of rose on your cheeks. My blush comes in a compact, and it's usually pink."

"You blush all the time, Sammy, so you don't need a compact."

"Whoa, you burned me, Daphne."

She climbed out of the car, grinning, and said, "I sure did."

"Hey, man, I spotted a foosball table around the corner. You want to play?"

"You know it, Greg. Let's go," Julio replied. Then he grabbed my hand before we took off for the foosball table. I watched Greg place his two tokens on the machine. Julio asked, "Did you reserve the table for the next game?"

"Yup," Greg answered."

"Look over there," Julio said, and he pointed to the skee ball machines. "There are four machines, so we can all play at the same time."

"That's one I like to play — whack a mole," Daphne told Greg, and she pointed out the machine.

"Okay, baby, we can play that next."

Daphne clapped her hands together, saying, "Yay." I turned my head and noticed that the foosball table was now available, so I took Julio's hand and walked over to the table.

"Greg, come over here, the tables open." Julio waved Greg over, and Daphne followed.

"Girls, those two handles are yours, and these two handles are mine and Greg's."

"Got it. Let's play, Julio! Daphne was standing across the table in front of me when I asked her, "Are you ready for this?"

"I'm ready, Sammy."

"Just wait, once my baby gets the hang of this game, were going to crush you and Julio."

"He's dreaming, Mi Corazón. I think we need to wake Greg up."

"Okay, Julio, let's do this."

"You can't intimidate us guys," Greg said before leaning down to kiss Daphne. At the same time, Julio shot the ball across the board.

"Oh, so you want to play dirty now?"

"Let's play girls against boys," I whispered to daphne, but she gave me a puzzled look, so I kicked the ball into my own goal.

Julio looked over at me, confused. "Ooops, sorry, Soccer Player." Greg tossed the ball back onto the table, and Daphne kicked the ball over to Julio. He kicked the ball into the goal and scored.

Greg looked over at Daphne and told her, "Look, baby, you have to turn the handle this way. You turned the players in reverse and kicked the ball to Julio."

"I'm sorry, Greg," Daphne told him, smiling. We continued to play this way until the boys gave up and told us they didn't want to play anymore.

I high-fived Daphne before saying, "Okay, that was fun; let's play for real." Daphne inserted two more tokens into the foosball table, and we started to play again. The boys came back to the table, and Julio asked, "Mi Corazón, did you do that on purpose?"

"Of course, not Julio," I told him, grinning.

Julio picked me up and set me down behind him then grabbed the handles on the foosball table. Greg did the same thing with Daphne, and we were left to watch the boys play. Then I heard someone say, "What is this crap?" All four of us turned around to find Eddie, Denise, Michael, and Arturo staring back at us, cracking up. "How do you play a game without these two beautiful girls?" "Let's go, girls. Come on, hang out with Eddie. We will all play together." I simply smiled as I waved bye to Julio. We followed Eddie over to the Skee ball machine.

"Come on, Sammy. I know this is your favorite game. Now tell us how to play, Sammy." After explaining the game to everyone, we slid our tokens into the slots, and I threw out my first ball. It landed in the four hundred spot, which brought back the memory of playing skeeball with Julio at the Forest.

By the time we were all on our last ball, Julio had walked up to me and placed his token onto the coin box. "I have the next game, Samantha."

"Sure, when I'm done, the machine is all yours, Julio."

Greg walked up to Daphne and said the same thing. "That's fine, Greg. I'm still going to beat your score with my last ball right now."

Eddie walked up to Greg and Julio, smiling. He placed his arms over their shoulders and told them, "I'm so proud of you two Penibles. You two finally realized you came to have fun with the girls."

"Yes, Eddie, we realized that now get off me."

"Okay, Greg, I have to get back to the game anyway, and I plan on beating your girlfriends with my last ball."

"Whatever you say, Eddie," Julio replied as he shook his head laughing.

When Eddie tossed his ball, Julio yelled, "Watch out." Eddie missed his goal, and it left him with no additional points.

"Now that was a dirty trick, Primo."

"Oh, I'm sorry, Eddie, did I mess up your game?" Eddie turned around and gave Julio a dirty look. "I'm sorry, but I can't allow you to beat the girls."

"Julio, I'm not beating anyone. Have you taken a look at the board?" I had 3,200 points, Denise had 3,300 points, and Daphne had 3,400 points. Eddie was in the last place with a total score of 2,800 points. Now it was just us girls, and we all had one ball left. Denise tossed her final ball, and her overall score was 3,500. Daphne threw her ball, and she ended the game with 3,800 points.

Everyone was saying, "I think you won, Daphne."

"No, I won't win. Sammy will beat me if her ball lands in the 1,000 spot." I tossed my ball, and it landed in the one hundred spot."

"You did it, Daphne. You won," Greg told her while Daphne jumped up and down from being so excited.

While Arturo hugged his sister, Michael walked up and said, "Okay, move over. It's our turn now." Then he laughed and hugged Daphne.

The three of us girls moved out of the way, and the game began. Greg made it into the three hundred spot. Michael made it into the five hundred place, and he was beaming with pride from his first throw. By the time they were down to their last ball, Julio had the highest score. He leaned over to toss his ball when Eddie yelled out, "Foul ball." The buzzer went off, and we looked up at the board.

Arturo turned to Julio smiling, and said, "You won!

Greg was smiling when he announced, "I like this game. I never thought this game would be so much fun."

"You like anything that's competitive, Greg." We all turned around to find a guy standing there, smiling, dressed like a rocker. I felt Julio take my hand and squeeze it.

"Hey, you're here already, Mig."

"Yeah, I just got through closing the inventory, and Lupe sent me home. It's a slow night, so they only need one person at the video store."

"Great, do you want to play a couple of games with us, Mig?"

Mig looked at me, and then he looked back at Julio and answered, "Yeah, we can do that, Julio."

Greg pulled Daphne to the side, and they had a quick discussion. While Julio and I stood beside the skeeball machine waiting, with Mig staring at us. When Greg returned, he asked, "Is everybody ready?"

Daphne replied, "No, why don't you hang out with your cousin and Julio for a little bit? I would like to spend some time with just the girls and my brother."

"Are you sure, Daphne?"

"I'm positive."

Daphne latched onto my free arm and said, "You're coming with me, Sammy." I looked up at Julio, and he was already staring down at me.

He kissed me then told me, "I'll come looking for you in a few minutes.

We quickly found Eddie and Denise playing air hockey. Another table was open beside them, so Daphne inserted two tokens, and we began to play. That's when Lewis and Tonya showed up. "Well, where have you two been?"

"We were over there, Eddie." Tonya pointed to the race car.

"Oh, the make-out car," Eddie said. "Yes, I'm fond of that game. Come on, Denise. Let's go for a car ride." He tossed Lewis his paddle and told him, "Here, Hermano, play some air hockey with Tonya."

We all went back to our game when Lewis asked Tonya, "Have you seen my cousin Alex?"

"Alex drove us here, Lewis, but he dropped us off in front of the mall and took off with Maria to park the van."

"Maria's here?"

"Yes," she's here with Alex."

"How did they make up already?"

"Simple, today, Alex went over to Maria's house, and they talked things out, Lewis."

"What about Alvaro? Is Alex okay with Alvaro too?"

"Yeah, Alex and Alvaro are fine now, Lewis."

"Tonya, how is Alex good with everything after what Alvaro did with Monica?"

"It's no different than what Alex is doing with Maria."

"What are you talking about, Tonya?

"Remember, your cousin Alex, is dating Alvaro's sister Maria. It's the same thing, Lewis."

"No, it's not the same thing, Tonya. Alex is not sleeping with Maria."

"First of all, Lewis, stop yelling, and secondly, they have been in the van for a very long time, so anything is possible."

"Tonya, I doubt it."

"Lewis, the point is that it's not fair to hold Alvaro responsible for something Monica wanted to do."

"Okay, Tonya, but Alvaro has been friends with my family for years. It's just disrespectful."

"Oh, but it's not disrespectful to Alvaro for Alex to date his sister? Is that what you're saying, Lewis?"

"You're right, Tonya. It's the same thing. I will apologize to Alvaro when we go back to school."

"Or whenever you see him," Tonya said. "Now, let's play, Lewis."

"Fine, you are going to lose, either way, Tonya."

"No, you're only one point ahead of me, Lewis."

"Babe, one point means I'm winning."

"No, babe, it means I still have to score two points, and I win the game," Tonya told him with a grin. My game was over, so Daphne and I watched Tonya and Lewis play this out.

"Okay, let's see you kick his butt, Cuban booty,"

Tonya smacked the puck to goal, but Lewis blocked it. Lewis slapped the puck to goal, and Tonya stopped it. Then Julio, Greg, and Mig walked up. Lewis reached over to high-five Greg's cousin Mig, and Tonya smacked the puck.

All the girls yelled out, "Score," and Lewis shook his head.

"Now this is it, Tonya. Get ready. Game over," Lewis told her. He smacked the puck, but Tonya blocked it and screamed, ouch.

"Hold on. Time out, you hit my fingernail with the puck."

"Babe, I'm sorry," Lewis said, and he ran over to Tonya's side of the table. As he held her hand to look at her finger, Tonya was pouting up until Lewis kissed her boo-boo, then she pulled her hand away.

"Game on, Lewis." She smacked the puck, and there was not enough time for Lewis to run back to his side of the table. The scoreboard was flashing, and Tonya won. Lewis was in the middle of calling her a cheater when Alex and Maria walked into the arcade. Alex announced it was time to get going, and that's when Denise reappeared with Eddie, Arturo, and Michael. We said our goodbyes and walked to the van.

On the way home, everyone was laughing and joking around until we pulled into Maria's driveway. That's when the van went silent, and Maria kissed Alex on the cheek before she told everyone bye and climbed out. Eddie pulled his head away from the window and asked, "What do you guys want to do?"

"What are you talking about, Eddie?"

"Lewis, I want to know if you and Julio want to be men today? Alvaro is standing outside right now, so here is your opportunity to own up to your mistake and apologize."

"Bro, are you serious?"

"Yes, Lewis, go apologize to Alvaro for overreacting and take Julio with you. Or you two can stay in here feeling like a couple of cowards and continue to blame Alvaro for doing the same thing as Alex is doing right now. What's it going to be?"

"Eddie, we were all shocked and overreacted yesterday. Give them some time to make up their own minds on how to deal with Alvaro."

"Okay then, I won't say another word, Alex." Eddie stopped talking and moved to the passenger's seat and sat down.

Alex was looking at his rear-view mirror while backing out of the driveway. When Julio turned to me and said, "Alex, wait." Alex stopped the van, and Julio kissed me on the cheek before climbing out along with Lewis. Together they walked up to Alvaro, and we could see them speaking to him for about ten minutes. Then all three of them walked back over to the van. When Julio opened the side door, Alvaro popped his head inside, and he said hi to everyone. Eddie opened the passenger door and climbed out.

He walked up to Alvaro and told him, "Bro, we're like family, so like every family, we get into disagreements. But that's family. I better see you on the field this Sunday, or I'll be back to kick your butt."

Eddie hugged him, and Alvaro went to laughing before telling him, "Okay, Eddie, I'll be there."

"I'm not joking, Alvaro, I will give your Arroz con Pollo to the dog."

"We don't have a dog."

"Did I say dog, Lewis?"

"Yes, Eddie, you did."

"Sorry, I meant to say, Greg, which is pretty much the same thing." Now everyone was laughing, and Alex told Eddie to get back in the van so we could get going. We all waved to Alvaro as we pulled away.

"Tonight, you two little Penible people have become," Eddie paused for a moment before finishing his sentence and saying, "Big Penible people."

Everyone was laughing when Alex replied, "Come on, Eddie, cut them a break already."

"Alright, you two seriously made me proud tonight when you apologized. A real man will always apologize when he is wrong. He won't blame other people; that is for weak men. A real strong man will own up to his mistakes, and he will apologize because that man has integrity. Now we are human after all, so get ready to make many mistakes but learn from them and don't continue to repeat them. A man who continues to apologize and then does the same thing repeatedly is not sincere, and his apology is worthless. Eddie put his hands together as if he were praying and went on to say, "Therefore, he is a worthless man not to be trusted very sad, don't become this man," and we all started laughing. "Okay, let me get back to being serious, and this is the final thing I'm going to say. Life is not easy, and I have been lucky to have my father and our Uncle Gio. Together they have taught me to be a man. You must learn to forgive, apologize, and own your mistakes. Now I will continue to watch over the two of you and guide you because I love you both, and we are forever family."

Julio and Lewis thanked Eddie, and they each gave him a one-armed hug while Eddie pat them on the back.

Eddie smiled at them both before saying, "Now go walk your girlfriends home."

When we arrived at the foot of my staircase, Tonya ran up and hugged me. "I'm going to miss you, Muñeca."

"I'm going to miss you too, Tonya."

"Wait, where are you going, Sammy?"

"Lewis, I'm going to see my dad for the holidays. I will be back on January 2nd."

Tonya turned around and hugged me again, saying, "I'm not going to see you again until 1988."

"I'm only going away for ten days, Tonya it's not that long."

Lewis started shaking his head and said, "Well, take Julio with you, Sammy. Don't leave him here miserable without you. It's not fair to the rest of my family."

I looked up at Julio and smiled before telling Lewis, "I wish I could." Julio bit his bottom lip, and now I could see the frustration building up in his eyes. "I should go now. I have to get upstairs and pack."

Julio walked upstairs with me, and I was not looking forward to saying goodbye to him, but I knew I had to. When we arrived in front of my door, he told me, "I'll wait out here for you and Daisy." I instantly felt elated and must have had the biggest smile on my face as I walked inside.

"Sam, is that you?"

"Yes, Mom."

"Okay, honey, don't forget to take Daisy out for a walk!"

"I'm going to walk her right now, Mom."

"Good, and be sure to tell Julio I said to have a goodnight."

"Okay, I will."

"Oh, and Sam, let Julio know if he wants to walk Daisy while you're gone, he can."

"I will let him know now."

Julio bent down, saying, "There you are, Daisy. I have been waiting to see you." He picked her up in his arms, and she went to giving him kisses. "I'm going to miss you, girl, while our Samantha is gone."

"You don't have to go without seeing Daisy while I'm gone. My mom just told me that you could come over here and walk her whenever you want."

"Really? I would like to do that."

We walked down the sidewalk, and Julio took my hand along with Daisy's leash. "Will you call me while you're gone, Samantha?"

"Yes, I can do that."

"I start my job tomorrow at the Pro Shop, so that should keep me busy during the day."

"That's right. What will you be doing, Julio?"

"I'll be picking up golf balls from the driving range. Washing down the golf carts and charging them. Alvaro has another job at a mechanic shop, and he loves cars, so I don't blame him for accepting the other job. Plus, I think he will be making more money."

"I'm happy for Alvaro."

"Yeah, me too, and I'm glad I apologized. Eddie was right. It felt good to apologize and own my mistake."

"You're a man now, according to Eddie."

"No, not yet, but I'm working on it, Mi Corazón, and I'm going to miss you like crazy."

"I'm going to miss you too, Julio." He wrapped his arms around me and kissed me at last before we headed back to my building. When we reached my doorstep, he hugged me again, and I quickly pop kissed him then ran inside.

Chapter 9 Separated over the Holidays

My mom came into my room and woke me up at half-past four. I had to take a shower and get dressed, then take Daisy outside. As I was walking Daisy, I saw Tonya and Lewis. They were on their morning jog, and they stopped long enough to wish me a pleasant trip. When I arrived back home, my mom told me to grab my bags and put them beside the backdoor. I quickly ran into my room to grab my suitcase and purse. I carried everything out to the kitchen and set my case down beside the door. That's when my mom walked into the kitchen, asking, "Do you have everything you need?"

"Yes."

"Then let's get going, Sam."

When I opened the door, Julio was standing there waiting for us. "Good morning, Ms. Harris, Samantha."

"Good morning, Julio," my mom said, smiling at me.

"Samantha, can I help you with your suitcase?"

"Of course, Julio, I would appreciate that, thank you." We walked down the stairs, and Julio didn't seem to have a problem carrying my hefty suitcase.

My mom told us, "You two wait here while I pull up the car."

"Julio, how did you know I was leaving now?"

"Lewis and Tonya came and got me. They said they saw you walking, Daisy."

"Yes, I ran into them out on the sidewalk."

"I'm sorry I missed out on that walk with you and Daisy this morning."

"Well, you will have a few without me too, Julio."

"Samantha, I will miss you."

"I will miss you too, Soccer Player."

He wrapped his arms around me and held me until my mom pulled up to the building with the car.

On Wednesday, December 23rd, I called Julio to wish him a Happy Birthday, and we spoke for a couple of minutes. On Friday, it was Christmas, so my mom called to wish me a Merry Christmas along with my brother, but later on that night, my mom called me again, and this time she put Julio on the phone. He was over the house to walk Daisy. A few days later, it was my birthday. My mom called and had a choir of people singing "Happy Birthday" to me over the phone. Tonya, Lewis, Julio, and my brother all took turns speaking to me afterward. It was the best gift, and I truly loved hearing from everybody. On my last day with my dad, we went out to breakfast before driving to the airport. My plane was delayed for over two hours, and I was anxious to get home. When I finally arrived at MIA International airport, I was starving. My brother came along with my mom to pick me up from the airport.

"Are you hungry, Sam?"

"Yes, Mom."

"Good, do you want to go to your burger place?"

"Mom, I would love that."

"How was your trip, Sam?"

"Okay."

"How was your dad?"

"Okay, I guess. I spent most of the time with Auntie Beth."

"Are you glad to be back?"

"Yes, Mom, I missed you, and thank you for the phone calls."

"I would have called more often, but it's expensive to speak long distance."

"Mom, I'm totally aware of that. Dad told me make your call but make it fast. It's long-distance, which stands for it's expensive." My brother and my mom laughed. My dad is always complaining about how expensive everything is all the time. When we arrived at my favorite burger place, I practically jumped out of the car and headed for the entrance.

"Sam, please wait for us, honey."

"I'm sorry, Mom, I didn't realize that I was walking so fast. I'm just hungry. Dad took me out to breakfast, but the waitress handed me a kids' menu, and I was still half asleep, so I ended up ordering from it. You should have seen dad's face when my smiley face pancake arrived."

Now my mom was cracking up before saying, "That's alright, Sam. I completely understand you've never been much of a morning person." Tommy grabbed the door and held it open for us. We walked inside and put in our order with the cashier. My brother grabbed the cups, and we walked over to the beverage station. Tommy handed me a cup, and I turned around to speak to my mom, but she was gone.

"Tommy, where's Mom?"

"Sam, I'm not sure, maybe she went to the bathroom. I'm going to find us a table beside the atrium." Tommy led through the double doors, and I heard, "Surprise." Daphne, Denise, Tonya, and Maria were all sitting down at a table with my mom. I hugged each of the girls before I sat down with them.

"So, how's your dad?"

"Maria, he's the same as usual, always working."

"What was the weather like?"

"Cold, and it was starting to get to me the last couple of days."

"Did you miss us?"

"Tonya, I missed everybody, and I can't wait to get home to see —"

"Let me guess... Julio," Daphne said, teasing.

"Well, I was going to say Daisy, but yes, I want to see Julio too."

"I'm glad to hear that, Samantha." I turned my head around, and Julio was standing right behind me with a gorgeous smile and a bouquet of flowers. My heart was racing the minute I heard his voice. I just wanted to wrap my arms around him and kiss him for days.

"Julio, I missed you so much."

"Samantha, I missed you too."

"What nobody missed me?" Eddie asked. I looked behind Julio and saw Eddie.

"Of course, I missed you, Eddie. Now come join us at the table."

Just then, our names were called over the intercom. Everyone left the room to go pick up their food except Julio and me. He handed me the flowers he was carrying.

"Are these daisies?"

"No, they are called Narcissus. They are the December flower. I thought they would be perfect since we are both born in December.

"That's cool. I didn't realize you were born in December too, until the day of your birthday party, Julio. I guess I need to get in the habit of asking you more questions."

"I'm willing to tell you anything you want to know. All you have to do is ask, Samantha."

"Okay, Julio, get ready because I have a lot of questions."

"Good, I look forward to hearing all of them, Mi Corazón. Now let's go get your food." Julio took my hand before we walked over to the counter to collect my tray, loaded with a burger and fries.

"Where did Eddie and Denise go?"

"They are in the arcade room, Sammy."

"Uh-oh, Daphne, is there a race car in the game room?"

"Gee, I hope not, Tonya. We may not ever see them again." The three of us laughed the whole way back to the table. By the time we sat down, they had called Eddie's name over the intercom.

Julio walked back in the room with Tommy asking, "Has anyone seen my cousin?"

"We think Eddie went for a car ride." After Tonya said that, we all broke out laughing again.

Julio shook his head and asked, "The arcade room?"

"He went in there with Denise."

"Oh, nevermind. I guess I will go get our food without Eddie. Do you want to go with me to pick up the trays, Samantha?"

"Sure, I'll go with you, Julio." We left the table and headed for the counter. Halfway there, Julio took my hand, and we stepped outside instead.

"Samantha, I missed you so much, and the one thing I regretted not giving you before you left was a kiss. I would like to give you that kiss now."

"Then what are you waiting for?" Julio pulled me into his arms and kissed me gently on my lips. I had instant chills and was left feeling incredibly happy."

As we pulled apart, Eddie popped his head out the door to tell us to come eat. We ran back inside, and Julio grabbed his tray from the counter.

"What do you want to do tonight, Muñeca?"

"Tonya, I don't even know yet. Right now, I'm just enjoying spending my afternoon with all of you."

"Sammy, the reason that I'm asking this question is that we want to spend the night at your house."

"Well, Daphne, I need to run that by my mom first."

"Mom, is that alright with you?"

"Yes, that's fine, but your brother's home, which means there are no bunk beds. Where are the girls going to sleep?

"Two of the girls can sleep on the sofa bed in the living room, and someone can sleep in the room with me. Unless everyone wants to sleep in my room in sleeping bags."

"That's not a problem, Sammy we can figure that all out later on. In the meantime, Ms. Harris, I want you to know that we intend to wake up early tomorrow to make you breakfast in bed."

"Now that sounds very nice, Daphne, thank you."

"Wait," tomorrow's Sunday. Now I know why you want to spend the night at my house."

"Why would that matter, Sam?"

"Tommy, the Sanchez boys hold a soccer game on the field every Sunday."

"But, we also want to hang out with your sister Tommy."

Daphne's right, we've missed you so much. You have been gone for ten days, Sammy."

"Denise, you and Daphne will still need to go home after we leave here to pick up your clothes. Will Eddie be okay with that?"

Eddie laughed before saying, "Sammy, they already have their clothes in the Sanchez van."

Now everybody erupted into laughter, but I felt mortified.

"Sammy, I'm just teasing you."

"Eddie, I don't mean to insult you or any of your family by calling you the Sanchez boys."

"Julio, do you feel insulted?"

"Nope, I actually like it."

"Yeah, me too because we are the Sanchez boys. When did you start calling us that?"

Actually, Eddie, I'm not the only one who calls you that. All the girls refer to your family as the Sanchez boys since the Forest when everyone coupled up."

"Sam, who coupled up?"

"Tommy, we all met up at the Forest one night and..." I suddenly felt a tap on my knee. It was Julio looking directly across the table at me. Once my eyes met up with his, Julio looked over at my mom.

"And what, Sam?"

"Oh, it's not important, Tommy we can talk about this later."

"Yeah, well, you forgot to mention Greg was at the Forest too, Sammy."

"Your right Daphne so you should be the one to tell my brother all about it once we get home."

Julio was grinning when he whispered, "What did your brother do now to deserve that?" Tonya obviously heard Julio's question and busted out laughing along with us.

"Guys, what's so funny."

"Nothing, mom, thank you so much for taking me to lunch and surprising me with everyone here."

"Honestly, Sam, I can't take credit for this one. Your brother came up with the lunch idea, and Tonya invited everyone."

Tonya whispered, "You feel like crap now, don't you?" I nodded my head, yes, and she laughed again along with Julio.

"What's so funny now?"

"Mom, I was just thanking Tonya."

"Okay, but don't forget to thank your brother too, Sam."

"Tommy, thank you for doing this for me. I mean it, I really appreciate it, so when you get home, hide in your room. At least until I tell you that it's safe to come out."

The entire table erupted into laughter from Denise, Eddie, Tonya, and Julio. While my mom and Daphne had a confused look on their face.

My brother was staring me down before he asked, "Sam, what exactly do you have waiting for me when I get home?"

Denise stopped laughing long enough to reply, "Just stay in your room Tommy when you get home, or you'll regret it."

"That's for sure," Eddie added as he rolled his eyes.

My mom stood up and thanked everyone for joining us for lunch.

She asked Julio if he would like to ride back with us. We rode in the backseat and held hands the whole ride home. Julio offered to carry my suitcase, but my brother wouldn't allow him to. Tommy just asked Julio to take Daisy outside for a walk instead. Julio's face lit up as he told Tommy he had a deal. When I unlocked the door, I could hear Daisy whimpering on the other side, so I began to open the door slowly. Daisy was impatient and yanked the door wide open. She jumped up on her hind legs and sent me sailing right into Julio. We both were headed for the ground when I felt Julio pull me forward. He fell first, and I landed on top of him with big girl Daisy standing over us, giving kisses. My brother and my mother got off the elevator and came running down the hall when they saw us on the floor.

"Are you two, alright?"

"Yes, mom, we're fine, I answered, laughing."

Tommy helped me up. Then I helped up Julio. We followed my mom inside, and she asked what happened. I told her and Tommy everything with Julio standing beside me. When Daisy jumped up on Julio again, everyone panicked, but he didn't lose his balance this time. Which made me think maybe Julio fell on purpose to break my fall.

"Daisy appears to be crazy about you, Julio."

He was grinning and replied, "Well, that's good, Ms. Harris, because I'm crazy about her too."

"I'm glad to hear that, Julio, and don't forget you agreed to take her outside for a walk."

"Why are you so rude, Tommy."

"Sam, I'm not rude. I was just reminding Julio of our conversation in the parking lot before I have to lock myself up in my room to avoid the retribution my little sister has planned for me today."

Julio and I started laughing when a smirk appeared on Tommy's face before he said, "All I can say is beware of what you start because payback can be rough."

"Maybe you should have remembered that Tommy before you flushed the toilet on me several times when I was taking a shower on your last day home."

"Sam, that was over a month ago when I was in town for Thanksgiving."

"Revenge has no time limit, Tommy, but after what you did for me today, I forgive you."

"Good, then call off your attack Sam."

"Listen, just go in your room, and after I've spoken to Daphne, it should be safe for you to come out."

"She's in on your attack?"

"No, dude, Daphne is the attack, so you should listen to your sister and stay in your room."

"Well, in that case, thanks for the heads-up, Julio, and don't forget to tell me when it's safe to come out, Sam."

Tommy walked into his room, and Julio was looking at me, shaking his head, grinning as I latched the leash to Daisy's collar. We walked down by the lake where Julio sat down first under the tree. He leaned his back against it, and I sat down on his lap. Daisy was running around the lake, barking at the ducks.

"Did I disappoint you, Julio?"

"You impressed me."

"Impressed you, really?"

Julio wrapped his arms around me, and he kissed the top of my head before saying, "Yes, I can only imagine what it must be like to sit down with Daphne to talk about Greg for an hour."

"Well, then you better not upset me, Julio, or you could be next."

"Oh, I don't think I can handle Daphne too. I already have Greg to deal with, and it's Daphne this and Daphne that all the time."

"Look at Daisy barking and running around nonstop, even her tongue is hanging out."

"Daisy's just happy you're home, Samantha, and I'm happy too." Julio leaned in and kissed me. I looked up into his big brown eyes, smiling back at him.

"I'm glad to be back. I missed you so much that I thought about you every day, and I often thought about what I was missing being away from you like kissing you."

I turned around on his lap so that I was facing him. Julio leaned in and kissed me slowly repeatedly until I felt his tongue brush up to mine. Then our kissing was constant and rapid. I surprised myself by my impulse to want to kiss him back just as vigorously. It was crazy the overwhelming desire I had to kiss him all day if I could. When I felt my head growing light, I pulled away, realizing that I was out of breath. I leaned back and noticed Julio's breathing was heavy.

"Julio, did I leave you breathless?"

"Yes, and I'm not ashamed to admit it." He pulled me closer, lifted my chin, and kissed me again."

When we pulled apart this time, I could see the stars above us. "Julio, do you realize it's nighttime already? We must have been out here for hours."

He chuckled and said, "I lost track of time, Mi Corazón. I'm sorry, let's grab Daisy and get you home." Daisy was asleep on the grass beside us. I stood up, and Daisy barked.

"It's time to go, big girl," I told Daisy as I bent down and grabbed her leash. Julio was holding my hand and Daisy's leash as we walked back to my doorstep.

"Samantha, I will see you in a little while. Don't forget to speak to Daphne and rescue your brother from his room."

"Oh yeah, I totally forgot about that. Look what your kisses are doing to me."

"Then Julio smiled, and pop kissed me again before taking off down the stairs.

As soon as I walked inside, Tonya asked, "Where have you been, Muñeca? We've all been waiting for you." That's when I saw Denise, Daphne, and Maria, sitting on the couch across from her staring back at me.

"I was outside walking, Daisy."

"Yeah, for over two hours, Sammy." My cheeks started burning, so I knew I was beginning to blush. "I see your blush comes in a lovely shade of pink. I guess that I was right, and you don't need your blush compact after all."

"Touché Daphne."

"So, what have you and Julio been up to?"

"Nothing Denise, I don't kiss and tell." I walked into my mom's bedroom, and she wasn't in there, so I walked into my brother's room, and he was gone too. When I walked back out to the living room, I asked the girls, "Where did my mom and brother go?"

Tonya looked at the girls before saying, "They're at the video store renting a movie."

"Oh, cool. What movie?"

"Tommy didn't say."

"Why didn't you go with them, Daphne? Is Greg off today?"

"No, he had to work, but he should be getting off work any minute." Something was up, but apparently, no one has any intentions of telling me about it. I'm just hoping it's not my brother's payback.

The girls were all wearing jean shorts and t-shirts, which means we're not going out anywhere. "What do you girls want to do for dinner?"

"I'm not hungry yet after eating lunch so late. What about you, Muñeca? Are you already hungry?"

"Yes, I'm starving, Tonya."

"That must have been some walk you were out on with Julio if you worked yourself up an appetite like that."

"It was amazing, Daphne."

Daphne's mouth dropped open as she asked, "What happened exactly?"

"Nothing happened. Like I said before, I don't kiss and tell."

"Unless you want to tell me what's going on tonight."

"We can't tell her anything, Daphne."

"Why not Tonya? What's the big deal?" Tonya didn't answer me; instead, she just sat there, shaking her head no.

"Nevermind, forget I asked Daphne. Tell me this, though, what time is Greg coming over?"

"He'll be here at —"

Tonya interrupted, "Daphne, no." Daphne stopped talking and looked up at the girls.

I stood up and asked, "Does anyone want to tell me what's going on?"

"No," the four of them said in unison.

"Fine, be that way. Someone turn on the TV. Or I'm going into my bedroom to listen to the stereo."

"Let's go in your room Muñeca." Tonya stood up and took off into my room.

By the time the rest of us walked in, Tonya already had the stereo on. 'Kiss on my list' was playing by Hall and Oates. My mind immediately raced back to my time spent with Julio earlier but was short-lived when interrupted by Tonya.

"Muñeca, I'm working on a mixed tape. If a song comes on, I like, get ready to press the record button on the cassette player."

"Why me? You're sitting beside the stereo, Tonya."

"Fine, I just saw you were daydreaming, and I wondered what you could be thinking about."

"Well, you can keep on wondering, because I'm not telling you anything, Tonya."

"That's fine. While I do that, you should put on your bathing suit along with a pair of shorts and a t-shirt."

"For what, Tonya?"

"Keep wondering, Muñeca."

Five minutes later, my mom walked in my room.

"Girls, everything is ready. Let's go downstairs."

We followed my mom down to the picnic tables beside the pool. My brother was standing in front of a barbecue grill.

"Welcome to your luau party, Sam."

Feeling completely shocked, I turned to my mom and asked, "Seriously?"

As my mom nodded her head yes with a beaming smile, the girls all yelled out, "Surprise." My mom placed a lei over my head and handed me a grass skirt to put on. Tonya's grandparents showed up right as we all put on the grass skirts. They had brought with them two trays loaded with white rice and black beans.

My brother was barbecuing steak and hotdogs. My mom set out a big bowl of salad. She also had an appetizer tray on each table. It was spam cut into squares with pineapple on top and held together with a toothpick topped with a cherry.

"Mom, why do you have spam as an appetizer?"

"Sam, it's what your father and I ate a lot on our honeymoon in Hawaii. Try it. You might like it."

I grabbed one spam square as my mother watched, and reluctantly took a bite.

"Well, what do you think, Sam?"

"I'm shocked, mom, it's delicious."

"Thank you, Sam, I cooked it while you were out on your walk with Daisy and Julio. I wanted everything to be a surprise."

"Believe me, Mom. I'm stunned by everything you've done for me." As I hugged my mother, the Sanchez boys arrived along with Greg wearing shorts and no shirts. My mom handed out a lei to each of them.

As my mom was placing a lei over Eddie's head, he told her, "Ms. Harris, I am the one who came up with all the men going shirtless tonight. I wanted us to become authentic Hawaiian men. I learned that from watching a luau on TV."

"Are you joking, Eddie?"

"No, Lewis, we needed to look authentic if we're going to attend a luau."

"Eddie, you told me you went to a luau, and they made you take your shirt off."

"Lewis, I can explain that."

"Go ahead, tell me."

"Sure, I lied, but you look authentic, and that's the whole point."

Everybody was laughing, watching Lewis chase Eddie around the picnic table. They only stopped when Monica arrived holding hands with Alvaro. The fact is that everyone stopped speaking midsentence, including my brother, who looked lost staring at Monica. My mom was the first one to greet them. "I'm so glad you two could make it to the luau.

Your mother told me you were dating Alvaro. I hope you don't mind, Monica."

"No, I don't mind. I know you and my mom are like sisters, and you tell each other everything, Ms. Harris." That is when I reached over my mom to hug Monica before sliding a lei over her head. Then I hugged Alvaro before handing him a lei too.

Eddie clapped his hands together and said, "Everybody's here now, so it's time to put some music on." Just as Michael and Arturo walked up to me wishing me a happy belated birthday. I hugged them, and Michael handed me a present. "Thank you, Michael."

"Open it up, Sammy. You might want it right now." It was a cassette tape.

"You made this for me?"

"Yes, well, Arturo, Daphne, and I made it for you. It has all your favorite songs."

"Thank you," I walked over to Eddie to hand him the tape.

"Sammy, what is this?"

"What does it look like, Eddie?" We both started laughing as he slid the cassette into the boom box and pressed play. 'Into the Groove' by Madonna was playing, and all the girls stood up. They started dancing with Arturo, Michael, and Eddie. When I spotted Daphne's mom, Carmen, walking up to the picnic tables carrying a cake box. My mom simply smiled at Carmen, and Daphne came running over to me at the table.

"Oh, I hope my mom likes Greg, or I don't know what I'll do, Sammy."

"Don't worry about that, Daphne. I'm sure she will."

"Tommy asked, "Who is ready to eat? Grab a paper plate off the table and let us get this moving off the grill. I have hotdogs and steak. If you prefer curry chicken, it is in the pot over there on the table. "Denise, can you pass out the chicken?"

"Of course, Tommy. I just need tongs and a serving spoon."

"Denise, is this your mom's Jamaican curry chicken?"

"It most certainly is Sammy. I asked her to make it for you since I know how much you love it, and Michael passed by my house to pick it up on his way over here."

"Wow, thank you so much, and please be sure to thank your mother for me." I hugged Denise before handing her my plate and the tongs along with a serving spoon.

"Tommy, don't forget to mention we also have Colombian tamales." Julio's mother, Pilar, yelled out as she was carrying a tray over to the picnic tables. Julio ran over to his mom and took the tray from her. He was smiling at me when he returned, carrying the tamales.

"I know these are your favorite, Samantha and I even went shopping with my mom to pick up all the ingredients."

"Really?

"Yes, and I helped my mom make them for you."

"In the banana leaves and everything, Julio?"

"Yes, of course, Sammy," Pilar answered.

"Thank you both so much. I can't believe you went through so much trouble, Pilar. I mean, because Julio doesn't cook, that must have been hectic."

Pilar was smiling as she reached out and hugged me while saying, "They were made with love from both of us."

"Your tamales look delicious, do you mind if I have one now?"

"Not at all, help yourself, Lori. I made them with my son for everyone to enjoy."

My mom and Carmen reached in the tray, and they each pulled out a tamale. Then Tonya's grandparents also grabbed a tamale. I handed Julio my plate loaded with curry chicken and asked for a tamale.

"Are you happy with the curry chicken and tamales?"

"Honestly, they are the best birthday presents ever, and everyone can enjoy them with me."

"Did you know that your brother Tommy called everyone on your birthday."

"No, what for?"

"For this, your luau and instead of buying a present, Tommy suggested we bring something that you would like to eat instead."

My mom called Pilar over to the table, and we stopped talking. "I just want to tell you both that the tamales are fantastic."

"Yes," Tonya's grandparents said, "Delicioso."

Carmen stood up and told them they are wonderful as she reached in the tray for another tamale. Julio and Pilar were smiling, and Pilar thanked everyone for the compliments.

My brother walked up to Pilar, handing her a paper plate, asking her which steak she would like from the grill. Pilar loves Tommy, and in her eyes, he can do nothing wrong. She was grinning the minute he spoke to her. Pilar followed Tommy over to the grill, and I could hear her talking to him about Monica as usual.

All five tables were full, and everyone was eating until Eddie popped in another cassette tape. 'Oye Como Va' was playing by Santana. When Eddie stood up and took my mom's hand, and Alex took his mom's hand. Together, the four of them walked over to the center and began dancing. Tonya's grandparents joined them, and before I knew it, everyone was dancing except for Julio and me because I was still eating.

"Look how happy our moms are, Julio."

"My mom definitely needed this, Samantha." He kissed me on the cheek and smiled at something he spotted behind me as he pulled his head away.

"What is it, Julio?"

"Mi Corazón, did you notice even Greg is dancing?"

"Well, that makes sense. It's sort of a rock song, I guess, and Greg's a rocker."

"I should have known that's exactly what it is," and we were both laughing.

The next song to come on was 'All of You' by Diana Ross and Julio Iglesias." The minute the song came on, Julio stood up with his eyes on me. He took my hand and led me to the center where everyone was already dancing. I noticed our moms suddenly stopped dancing, and they walked back over to the picnic table. Pilar and my mom were smiling at us as they turned their chairs around before sitting back down now facing us. As we danced to this song, Julio held me in his arms. I placed my head down on his shoulder, and that's when Julio sung the song to me word for word. By the time the song was over, I felt as if we had drifted off into our own little world for a few minutes.

'Modern Love' by David Bowie came on, and that is when I noticed everyone was back to dancing beside us. This time even my brother was dancing with my mom.

How she got him to leave the barbeque grill was beyond me, but I was happy to see him out here dancing beside us. When the song was over, Carmen announced it was time to cut the cake. I followed Carmen and my mom over to the picnic table, where I spotted the cake box. Carmen lifted the cake out of the box and was about to light the candles. When I said, "Wait, Mom, before Carmen lights the candles, can you take a picture of the cake? It's so beautiful."

Carmen had the biggest smile on her face and told me, "I'm glad you like it, Sammy. Arturo and I made the cake, and Michael came up with the luau theme that we used to decorate your cake."

Michael added, "On the cake, you will notice a big ocean wave, with six Hawaiian girls dancing under the palm trees beside the ocean. The girls are there to represent each of you. There's one for Tonya, Denise, Maria, Monica, Daphne, and of course, you, Sammy." I immediately looked up at Monica, who was standing beside the table, and I smiled at her. She looked back at me than the cake, and I saw a big smile appear on her face.

"Thank you so much, guys. I can't believe how much work went into decorating my cake, and that's why I must take a picture of it to have as a memory." My mom handed me the polaroid camera, and I took a picture of the cake. Right after I gave the camera back to my mom, Carmen had the candles lit. Everyone sang "Happy Birthday," and I made my wish before blowing out the candles. My mom snapped a few more pictures while I cut the cake.

The party was over when my mom stood up to tell me that it was time to walk Daisy. I went back home with Julio, and everyone else stayed behind to clean up. Daisy was waiting for us at the door, so I walked inside long enough to grab her leash off the wall. We took her for a walk on the dog trail. "I had such a wonderful time tonight. I always wanted to go to a luau since I was around seven years old.

My mom has the most amazing pictures at a luau with my dad. Ever since I saw those pictures, I have wanted to attend one, so having a luau-themed birthday party was superb.

"Julio, did you like it?"

"I most certainly did, and now I know why it was a luau party. He kissed me on the cheek and said, "I learned something new about you today."

Did you see the incredible cake Carmen and Arturo decorated for me?"

"Yes, I did."

"The cake had six Hawaiian girls?"

"How do you know it was six girls and not seven?"

"Each of the girls represents us — Tonya, Daphne, Denise, Maria, Me, and your sister Monica so yes, it was six, not seven girls on the cake."

Julio was smiling at me, and I went on to say, "I don't know if your sister is done being mad at the world. I'm hoping she has gotten over whatever upset her because I miss her, and I want to go back to being friends with her again."

"That would be nice, Samantha, but it makes no difference to me on how I feel about you. Julio stopped walking and turned around, facing me. "You mean the world to me. I felt so lost and miserable while you were gone."

"I missed you too, Julio, and I can't wait to see you playing soccer tomorrow." Julio picked me up in his arms before he spun me around. Daisy started barking her happy bark, and Julio set me back down. He pop kissed me then gave me that sexy wink of his as he retook my hand. Julio reached down to grab Daisy's leash off the ground, but she took off running. He released my hand and ran after Daisy.

He caught up to her right before she could jump in the lake. I was so relieved, and I thanked Julio profusely.

"We better go. People are waiting for me, Julio."

"Are you sure you want to go now? You don't want to sit here for a minute?" I looked up at him, and he was pointing to our tree.

"Okay, just for a minute." Julio led me over to the tree, and we sat down.

"Mi Corazón, I love it when you come to watch me play."

"Soccer Player, I will come and watch you play tomorrow, only if you promise not to get up and leave in the middle of the game."

"In that case, I promise," and he kissed me. I stood up, telling him I think it's time to go. Julio tugged on my hand, pulling me back down on his lap, but this time I was facing him.

"Kiss me one more time, then will go, Mi Corazón."

"Do you promise, Julio?"

He nodded his head yes with a smile as I leaned in toward him and kissed his lips again. What started off as a pop kiss quickly turned into a passionate make-out session until I heard him moan and something poked me. I was startled and screamed as I jumped off his lap. Julio quickly placed his hand over his zipper.

"I'm sorry, Samantha." I looked down at Julio's face and noticed he looked flushed.

"It's alright. I'm sorry, I screamed, Julio. It just surprised me." Now we both had a silly grin on our face as we stood there staring at one another.

"Are you okay now, Samantha?"

"Yes, I'm okay. How about you?"

"I'm good, everything's good." I could tell by the expression on Julio's face that Julio was still feeling a bit embarrassed.

"Maybe we should head back now."

"Yeah, let's do that, Samantha."

When we arrived at my building, Julio stopped walking at the foot of the stairs.

"Will you come upstairs with me to say good night?"

"Do you want me to, Samantha?"

"I do."

We walked inside the back door and were standing in the kitchen when I heard my mom say, "They're back." I took Daisy's leash off her, and Julio gave Daisy a biscuit. My mom and Carmen were standing at the kitchen counter, filling up their wine glasses.

"Sam, you will find everyone in the living room waiting for the two of you. I will be in my room with Carmen if you need me."

"Thank you, Mom." We walked out to the living room, and everyone was there.

"Finally, you're back, Sam, and right on time too. We're about to watch a movie."

"What movie Tommy?"

"One, you're going to enjoy Sam." I was instantly nervous after he said that, and I looked around the room. My mom was right everyone was in the living room. Tonya, Daphne, Denise, Maria, and Monica were on one couch. Lewis, Greg, Eddie, Alex, and Alvaro were sitting on the floor in front of them.

Michael and Arturo were sitting on the other couch. Julio sat on the floor, and I sat in front of him beside Arturo and Michael.

My brother had his eyes on me when he said, "Alright, now is everybody ready?"

"Yes, we're ready," Daphne and Tonya answered simultaneously, sounding annoyed, which made me think my brother had everybody wait until I got here to play the movie. My heart was pounding as I watched him insert the tape into the VCR.

As soon as the tape began to play, I realized it was our home movies. I ran after my brother as the video was playing, and he ran straight into my mom's room. "Mom, your daughter wants to hurt me."

"Yes, I do because your stupid son is playing our home movies and showing them to all of our friends." My mom didn't say a word. She just looked over at Carmen with a worrisome look on her face.

"What happened?"

"Nothing, Sam. You and your brother go watch your movie, and we'll be out in a little bit." I looked at my brother, and he looked back at me with a stunned expression. We both walked out of my mom's room together.

"Sam, what do you think happened?"

"I have no idea, Tommy."

"Whatever it is, Sam, remember I'm always here for you and mom, and we will get through it together." Tommy hugged me, and all the worry was gone for now. "Come on, let's go back out to the living room and watch a real movie."

Tommy found a comedy to put in the VCR, which I was only able to watch half of before I fell asleep. I woke up to the sound of my mom and Carmen telling everyone to wake up.

My brother stood up and said, "Okay, then, let's go camping." All the boys stood up and followed my brother into his room. My mom and Carmen looked shocked, judging by their expression.

"Sam, take all the girls into your room now and shut the door."

"Going right now, mom." We all stood up and walked into my room, and once my door was shut, the show began.

We could hear my mom ask, "What's going on in here, Tommy?"

My brother replied, "Sam invited all her friends to stay over before discussing it with me."

"Tommy, I'm sorry, you know the rules. I do not allow you and Sam to have friends over at the same time to spend the night.

"But Mom, this is my last night home. I go back to school tomorrow. Can you just make an exception this one time?"

"Fine, Tommy, but every single one of your friends' better stay in your room tonight."

"No problem, mom, they can do that. Right, guys?"

"You have nothing to worry about, Ms. Harris. We will stay in here. You have my word on that."

"Thank you, Alex, and good night boys."

"Next, I heard Carmen ask, "Where are you going?"

"Home," Arturo answered.

"Oh, no, you are staying here tonight. Lori is going to need our help to make sure everyone stays in the right room."

"Mom, you can't be serious."

"Yes, I am very serious, Arturo. That is what's happening tonight. I will sleep on the pull-out sofa bed in Lori's room, and you can sleep on the sofa in the living room."

Suddenly there was a knock on my bedroom door. I stood up to answer it, and my mom was standing in front of my door looking very angry. "Your brother has invited the boys to stay the night in his room. Which means no living room or walks with Daisy tonight."

"Okay, Mom."

"In the morning, we can all make breakfast together, just like we talked about doing earlier today during lunch."

"That sounds good, mom I will see you in the morning."

After I shut the bedroom door, I whispered, "Did anyone know my brother was doing this?"

Tonya was the first one to say, "No, I had no idea, and he tells me just about everything."

Denise stood up and turned on the stereo before saying, "Sam, we didn't know anything about it, but if we're going to discuss it, we should have some sort of background noise, so the boys don't hear us."

"How is your mom letting your brother get away with this?"

"Daphne, I think it's a combination of two things. One, my mom doesn't want to make a scene and two because he's going back to school tomorrow."

"Yeah, but honestly speaking, your brother should be allowed to have his friends over to spend the night. It's only fair."

"My brother is always allowed to have friends over to spend the night, Tonya."

"Then what's the problem, Muñeca?"

"Do you even realize that everyone in my room has a boyfriend, including you, Tonya?"

"Yes, I do."

"Great, and do you realize that everyone's boyfriend is spending the night tonight next door in my brother's room because my mom did, and so did I."

"For some reason, I didn't realize that Muñeca. I am guessing it has to do with it being past my bedtime. Please turn off the lights and the stereo. It's time for bed." I grabbed two sleeping bags from my closet and two comforters and blankets. I handed them over to Maria and Monica.

"These will be perfect, thank you, Sammy."

"I wish at least two of you could have slept out in the living room on the sofa bed, Maria."

"Don't be silly. This is perfect, Sammy."

"Tonya, do you realize nobody wants to sleep beside you on the bed?"

" Muñeca, I don't care. I just want to go to sleep. I'm tired."

"Fine. Is everybody okay with the sleeping arrangements?"

"Yes, we're fine," Denise answered.

"Yeah, nobody wants to sleep beside Tonya, so you're stuck with her, Sammy."

"Whatever, Daphne, turn off the lights, good night."

Chapter 10 The Decision

I woke up the next morning to the sound of Tonya's voice. "Get up, Muñeca. Come on, wake up. It's time to make breakfast."

"Tonya, let me sleep."

"No, get up now. Do you want Julio to see you like this?"

"What?"

"Julio, remember him? He spent the night in your brother's room."

"Crap, that's right." I sat up and climbed out of bed. "Let me take a shower." I grabbed my robe and ran into the bathroom. I came back into my room, and Tonya was ready to braid my hair. I just put on a t-shirt and shorts when my mom walked in.

"Girls, I want you to take your showers and get dressed in my room this morning."

"Mom, I already took a shower."

"That's fine, Sam. The rest of the girls can take their shower in my room." The girls all stood up and followed my mom into her room. I walked into my mom's room a couple of minutes later to hand Monica a pair of shorts and a purple t-shirt.

Monica hugged me before saying, "Thank you, Sammy. You know purple's my favorite color."

"Yes, of course, I remembered that, Monica. Now I will see you in the kitchen after your showered and dressed. I better get going before my mom starts looking for me."

I walked into the kitchen and grabbed the pancake mix. Luckily, we had a big box, so I don't have to make the batter from scratch. Tonya saw the box and asked, "Is that box going to make enough batter for everyone.

"Yes, it should and don't judge me for not making the batter from scratch, Tonya. I'm just trying to jump on things before everyone wakes up. As I prepared the batter, Daphne joined us in the kitchen, and she grabbed two cans of apple juice out of the freezer.

"Do you have two pitchers?"

"You will find several under the counter in that cupboard," Tonya told Daphne, as she pointed to the cabinet.

Daphne went to work on making two pitchers of apple juice, and Denise walked into the kitchen. Is the batter ready, Sammy?"

"Yes, here you go, Denise."

Tonya already had the frying pan up on the stove, and I handed Denise the cooking spray along with a mixing bowl filled with pancake batter. Denise used a ladle to pour the pancakes onto the pan. She was using two different frying pans for cooking the pancakes. My brother walked into the kitchen and saw the empty box up on the counter.

"Sam, is there any more of that mix left?"

"Yes, there is another whole box of it in the closet."

"Cool, where is the waffle iron? I want to make some waffles." I opened the bottom drawer on the oven to grab out the waffle iron for my brother. Tommy watched me and said, "Thanks, Sam, I wouldn't ever have looked for the waffle iron in there. Since mom used to use that bottom drawer to keep food warm while she's cooking."

"Is that what the bottom drawer on the oven is used for?"

"Yeah, it keeps food warm while you're still cooking. But it only works if you're using the oven."

"How do you know that, Tommy?"

"Home economics in the eighth grade."

"Just so you know, Tommy, I'm the one who placed the waffle iron in the drawer, not mom. I didn't think it was used for anything other than storage."

"Well, now you know Sam, and I need to start cooking." Tommy hopped off the stool he was sitting on at the counter and walked back into the kitchen.

"Hey girls, I'm plugging in the waffle iron on this counter beside the coffee pot. Be careful. I don't want you to burn yourselves."

"Do you want me to make the batter for you?"

"No, I got it, Sammy. Besides, I want to be able to say I made the waffles. I'm already using a mix instead of making the actual batter."

"Who are you making the waffles for, Tommy?"

"The guys, of course, Denise. They are in my room asleep, but when they wake up, they are going to want some grub."

"Tommy, that's why I'm making pancakes."

"Men prefer waffles, Denise."

"Oh, whatever. You're so annoying, Tommy."

"You won't think I'm annoying for long, Tonya, when you realize that I'm helping you out."

"Really, how are you doing that, Tommy?"

"Tonya, do you even realize how long it would take to make enough pancakes to feed everybody?"

"Tommy's right, Tonya. I've only made four pancakes so far."

"See, told you, Tonya," my brother said as he stuck his tongue out at her. Tonya rolled her eyes at my brother and stormed off toward the dining room. Monica walked into the kitchen, and she immediately ran out.

"Is Monica okay?"

"I'm not sure, Denise. She ran into the restroom and shut the door."

"One of us should check on her, Sammy." I nodded my head yes as I left the kitchen. When I reached the bathroom door, I could hear Monica on the other side, barfing.

"Monica, can I get you anything?"

"No, I will be out in a minute, Sammy."

"Okay, let me know if you need anything."

Arturo ran into me as I was walking away from the bathroom door. We could hear Monica throwing up from the hallway. "What's going on? Who's in there?"

"It's Monica. She's not feeling well this morning."

"Does she need anything?"

"I just asked her that, and she said no."

Arturo followed me into the kitchen, and Maria was in there preparing a breakfast tray.

"Sammy, can I take one of your flowers for the tray?"

"Of course, you can. My mom will love that."

"Great," Maria said. "I just want the tray to look pretty." She placed a clear juice glass on the tray. It had just the head of the flower floating on top of the glass.

"That really looks pretty, Maria."

"Thank you, Sammy. I just wanted to add a simple elegance to the tray."

Denise placed two plates on the tray, loaded with pancakes and bacon. "Wait up," Tommy said, and he put a triangle waffle piece on each plate. "In case they want to try my bonging waffles."

We headed into my mom's room with Daphne carrying two glasses of apple juice. Tonya had two cups of coffee, and Maria was holding the tray. "Good morning, we brought you some breakfast."

Maria set the tray down on the coffee table in front of Carmen. "What do we have here?" Carmen asked. She looked at the plate of food before saying, "Lori, come join me. The girls really made us a wonderful breakfast."

"Thank you so much, girls. I meant to join you in the kitchen to assist with breakfast. I just got caught up talking to Carmen, and I guess you didn't need me after all."

"Mom, we were able to handle making breakfast, and Tommy made the waffles." My mom stood up and joined Carmen on the couch. Daphne handed my mom and her mom each a glass of apple juice. Then Tonya handed them each a cup of coffee.

"Wow," Carmen said as we left the room, trying not to laugh. Once we arrived back in the kitchen, we thanked my brother for making the coffee and waffles.

"They are so bonging that I know you want to try one, Sam."

"Yes, I will admit your waffles smell yummy, so if you have enough, I wouldn't mind sharing one with the girls."

"Well, I have four waffles made and another one on the iron. How many pancakes do you have, Denise?"

"Right now, I have six pancakes Tommy, with another two cooking."

"So, I will need nine waffles, and you need 12 more pancakes. You know what that means?"

"Yes, that it's a cook-off. How do you know what Arturo and Michael want?"

"They might want both Denise, so I'm making extra,

"Then me too."

Eddie walked into the kitchen, grinning while he asked Denise, "What's going on in here? The aroma coming out of this kitchen is driving me crazy."

"Good morning, Eddie."

"Awe my beautiful Denise, good morning. What are you making over there?"

"Pancakes."

"They smell wonderful I can't wait to try them."

Daphne walked past Eddie and told him, "The guys are all having waffles."

"Okay, Daphne, no problem. Denise, save me a pancake, and I will eat both."

"It's okay, Daphne. I'm making extra pancakes.

"Really, why, Denise?"

"Because I knew people would want both."

When my brother was finished making his waffles, he headed straight to the dining room table and called the guys over. I placed the butter and syrup on the table while Daphne set a pitcher of apple juice down. Julio was smiling at me when he said, "Good morning Samantha. Will you and Daphne be joining us for breakfast?"

To see Julio's smile and to hear his voice first thing in the morning had me feeling both elated and lightheaded. All I could do was smile at him; I couldn't speak. "No, Julio, we still have some work to do in the kitchen."

"Come on, Sammy, we need to help Denise with the pancakes." Daphne tugged on my arm, and I followed her back into the kitchen.

"Sammy, what's wrong with you? Are you okay?"

"I'm fine, Denise. Why do you ask?"

"It's just that you have a silly grin on your face."

"Oh, I can explain that."

"Daphne, no, I can tell Denise about that myself."

"Are you sure, Sammy?"

I rolled my eyes at Daphne, and she put her hands up, saying, "Okay, I was just trying to help."

"Tell me what happened, Sammy."

"Julio was sitting down at the dining room table, and when he spoke to me, for some reason, I became tongue-tied. Daphne had to save me, and it was totally embarrassing."

"Has this ever happened to you before, Sammy?"

"No, and I hope it doesn't ever happen again."

"Well, I wouldn't worry about it, Sammy. I imagine seeing Julio first thing in the morning sitting down at your dining room table just had you a bit frazzled. I have to admit when Eddie walked into your kitchen asking about breakfast, I was caught off guard for a moment myself."

"Your right Denise, I was. Now, tell me what can I do to help you with breakfast?"

"I don't think we need anything at the moment —" Just then, Eddie ran into the kitchen and interrupted, asking Denise for some pancakes. She turned to me, grinning before handing Eddie the plate of seven pancakes. "Ummm, Sammy."

"Yes, Denise."

"Can you make more pancake batter?"

"Absolutely," and we were both laughing.

As we walked out of the kitchen to the dining room table to have our breakfast, we overheard Lewis saying the games canceled. Daphne set her plate down on the table before walking over to the living room. We could hear her asking Lewis, "Why is the game canceled?"

Julio answered instead of Lewis and said, "It's raining Daphne. That's the only time we don't play soccer." I turned my head around to face Julio, and his eyes were already on me. Then Monica walked past the dining room table without saying a word to any of us and headed straight into the living room. I saw Alex stand up the minute he saw his sister Monica.

"Monica, are you alright?"

"Alex, I think I'm pregnant."

We all heard that and stood up from the table just in time to watch Monica walk out the front door. Alex turned to Eddie, and I witnessed the confused look on both of them before they ran out the door behind Monica.

Lewis and Julio were staring down Alvaro. Tonya looked at me and said, "I'm grabbing Lewis, grab Julio before something happens." Tonya and I managed to get the boys to follow us into Tommy's room. In there, the four of us sat down on the sleeping bags that were still on the floor.

"Listen, you two can't get in the middle of this. Whatever's happening now is between Alvaro and Monica. It takes two to make a baby, so please don't take on Alvaro."

"Muñeca's right, and who knows she might not even be pregnant. Monica has assumed the worst-case scenario when it could be that she simply ate something yesterday at the luau that made her sick."

"Tonya's right. After all, there was a lot of food at the party last night." Julio had his eyes locked on me the whole time, and he hadn't said a word. In a way, he didn't have to say anything. The look on his face was enough to let me know that he was boiling mad.

Someone said knock-knock before opening the bedroom door. It was Greg, and he walked up to Julio and told him, "Hey, I have some good news for you." Julio remained quiet with his eyes on me.

Greg cleared his throat before saying, 'It stopped raining so we can play after all."

Julio put his arm around me and told Greg, "I don't think that would be a good idea. Can you call your cousin and ask him to give Alvaro a ride home? I don't want him around my family anymore today."

He was frowning when he replied, "Sure, man, I'll call him now." That's when Tonya handed Greg the phone. Around twenty minutes later, Daphne came into my brother's room to tell us she was leaving. Mig showed up shortly afterward and picked up Greg and Alvaro.

Maria knocked on my brother's door and said, "Everyone's gone now. It's safe to come out."

The four of us walked back out to the living room. My brother and my mom were sitting on the couch beside Maria.

"Guys, I heard what happened. Try not to get upset about anything because Monica is not certain of her condition yet."

Tonya replied, "Muñeca and I just got through saying the same thing."

"Yes, well, I'm pretty sure that this situation with Monica has only contributed towards Pilar's decision to move to California."

"Mom, what are you talking about?"

My mom sat up with tear-filled eyes before saying, "I spoke with Pilar last night during your party, and she told me that she has decided to move to Anaheim, California."

"Why does she want to move away?"

"Sam, she has been offered an amazing job opportunity in California."

Lewis stood up and replied, "Yeah, it's the same opportunity my dad accepted, and that's why he's living in California now. The job is to help manage and run one of the businesses my uncle Guillermo owns. My father and my Uncle want the whole family to move to California. That was the big surprise my father had to share with us on Julio's birthday."

"Julio, when does your mom plan to do this?"

"Samantha, my mom originally turned down the job on the day of my birthday. She had no intention of leaving Miami until my sister was found inside the van with Alvaro later that night. My mom changed her mind instantly and decided were moving to Anaheim at the end of the school year. She said that it would be better for the family if we lived by one another. When she announced her decision, we were standing under the clubhouse, and that's when Alvaro appeared at the picnic tables. I was furious, and I blamed him for everything."

"Sorry, Maria, your brother has terrible timing."

"I know, Julio. Alex told me everything, and I'm sorry."

"You're leaving me, Julio?"

He nodded his head yes as a tear slid down his face. I wrapped my arms around him and held him tight. Then I started to cry, and once I started, I was unable to stop.

Tonya stood up, yelling at Lewis, "Why didn't you tell me the truth? You told me you were going to stay here. You lied to me. Why did you lie to me, Lewis?"

"I never lied to you, Tonya. My aunt Pilar had no problem with me staying here to attend high school as long as I kept my grades up. I had no idea Monica would do something like this."

"But Lewis, it's not fair." Lewis placed his arms around Tonya, and now she was crying too.

"I've changed my mind, Julio. I don't want to be friends with your sister anymore."

"You don't have to be, Samantha. It makes no difference to me. I told you this before, and I mean it."

My mom walked back into the living room and asked, "Are you still going with me to take your brother to the airport?"

"Yes, I'm going with you, Mom."

"Okay, we're leaving here in five minutes." I looked up at Julio, and his eyes were watery and red.

"I need to go to the airport with my family. When I get back, if you want to go for a walk with Daisy and me, we can talk about everything then." Julio kissed me on the cheek, then wiped his eyes before he stood up and walked to the front door. Everyone followed, and I waved bye to Maria, Tonya, Lewis, and Julio. When I shut the door, I stayed there with my back pressed up against it crying.

Daisy ran over to me, barking as I slid down the door and held her. She licked my face and made me smile. "I love you too, big girl." Five minutes later, my mom and Tommy found me lying against the door, holding Daisy.

"Please go wash your face and meet us down at the car, Sam."

"Okay, Mom. I will be down in a second." I ran into my bathroom, and the puke smell was still present. I sprayed the room with deodorizer before running into my mom's bathroom to wash my face. On the way to the airport, my brother mentioned that he was happy because I came along to drop him off, which made me feel good. When we arrived at the airport terminal, my mom hugged my brother, and she was already crying.

By the time I hugged Tommy, I was in tears, too, until my brother told me, "Cheer up, Sam, I'm only a phone call away whenever you need me. Now I need you to take care of mom and Daisy for me while I'm gone." When Tommy walked inside, my mom pulled away from the terminal, and she cried the whole way home.

The moment we walked inside, and I saw Daisy, the flood gates opened again. My mom placed her arms around me before saying, "Sam, your brother will be back again over the summer."

"I know, Mom, and Julio will be gone." I cried even harder, and my mom held me tighter.

"I'm sorry, honey. That is rough. I was upset when Pilar told me she has decided to move to California. Please don't take it out on Julio. It's not his fault."

"I realize that, Mom."

"Besides, you know Julio will be back. He wants to attend school here at UM."

"That would be like years from now, mom. We're only in the ninth grade."

"Sam, I was just trying to help you find a light at the end of the tunnel by letting you know that he will be back."

"Thank you, Mom. I appreciate it, and I loved my luau party. It was the best party yet. I think everyone had a lot of fun last night."

"Yes, I think so too, and the breakfast you girls made this morning was terrific. Carmen and I couldn't believe it. We ate everything. Even the coffee was perfect.

"Your son made the coffee and the waffles. Denise and I made the pancakes. Actually, I prepared the batter, and Denise cooked them."

"Well, everything was wonderful, so thank you, Sam."

"Mom, I know you're trying to change the subject, but I have to get something off my chest."

"Okay, what is it."

"I'm feeling extremely frustrated because, after every party or even get together, Monica has found a way to mess it up."

"Monica didn't mean to mess up anything this morning, Sam."

"Trust me, Monica has been real spiteful lately."

"Sam, if Monica is pregnant, then she can use a friend. Life is going to be very rough on her, and I feel bad for Pilar."

"How can you feel bad for Pilar when she has decided to move away?"

"Pilar is my best friend, and I want her to be happy, Sam."

"Well, I don't agree with Pilar's decision, and I'm mad at her."

"Please don't be mad at her, Sam. She loves you very much, and that would only hurt Pilar more to know that."

"I don't care, mom, she hurt me when she decided to move away."

"Since you feel that way, Sam, you need to be told the truth, but it's not to be repeated to anyone."

"Fine, tell me the truth, mom. I'm listening."

"Monica has been fighting with Pilar every day since her brother Juan moved to California. The fighting became worse when she began to date a boy named Rick. Do you know him, Sammy?"

"No, I haven't even heard of him."

"Well, that's good because Monica started dating this boy right after Juan moved to California, and Pilar caught them in bed together."

"When was this?"

"Months ago, Sam, but it happened in Pilar's own home, and that's the first time she spoke to me about moving to California."

"Wait, mom, how is that even possible? The Sanchez boys would never allow Monica to bring a guy home."

"She was sick and stayed home from school, so Pilar left work early to check on her. When she arrived home, she found

Monica in bed with this boy. The boy ran out of her house, wearing only his boxers. Pilar chased him down and told him if he ever comes near Monica again, she will have him arrested."

"And Pilar never told the boys?"

"No, not to my knowledge."

"Mom, why doesn't Pilar just send Monica away to live in California with Mr. Sanchez? Why does everybody have to go?"

"I don't know the answer to that, Sam. All I can tell you is that I understand Pilar's decision. Her exact words to me have been that she just wants to get her daughter back on the right track."
"I'm sorry, mom, but I still don't think it's fair that everyone should be made to move to California because of Monica." I started to cry again, and my mom held me.

"Just enjoy the time you have left with Julio. Don't spend it worrying about what's going to happen." I pulled my head away to tell my mom she's right when there was a knock on the kitchen door. My mom answered the door, and it was Julio. I ran out the door hugging him and kissing him.

"Hi, Soccer Player."

Julio had a big smile on his face, and I had my hands up on his shoulders when he replied, "I missed you, Mi Corazón."

"Do you want to go for a walk with me, Julio?"

"Can we bring Daisy?"

"Yes, she can come too," I told him, laughing.

"Okay then, I'll go."

"Great, give me a second to get her." I walked back inside, and I grabbed Daisy's leash. I opened the door to hand the leash to Julio. Then I shut the door before walking to my mom's room to get Daisy.

"Sam, please don't mention what we talked about with Julio."

"No problem, Mom, and thank you for telling me the truth."

"I only told you so you could understand what Pilar has had to deal with Sam. Her decision was not easily made, and she just wants the best for her children."

"Mom, I don't think Monica and the Sanchez boys are children anymore."

"Samantha, they will always be Pilar's children no matter how old they get, and that goes for you and Tommy too. You two will always be my children, and I'm going to miss her if she leaves." My mom had tears in her eyes, and it was breaking my heart.

"Please don't cry, Mom." I gave her a hug and told her, "You're going to make me cry again."

"Well, I don't want that, so go walk Daisy, and I'll be fine by the time you get back."

We walked Daisy down the backstairs, and I headed for the golf course. "Samantha, we're just skipping the sidewalk altogether and going straight to the golf course?"

"Yes, I think we need to talk." I continued to walk at a fast pace all the way to the lake. Julio arrived seconds later with Daisy behind me. "Julio, have a seat so that I can sit down."

He gave me a strange look and replied, "Okay, Mi Corazón, but I want you to know that you're very demanding today. You didn't even hold my hand when we walked out here."

All I could do was laugh before saying, "I'm sorry about that, Julio. I just have to say what's on my mind."

Julio sat down and said, "Good, I want to hear what you have to say."

"Look, I know that moving away to California is not something you want to do, but you don't have a choice. You must do whatever your mom decides, which means we only have five months left. I don't want to spend our time together, crying every day. Instead, I want us to enjoy every minute we have left.

"I agree with you, Samantha, and that's what I want too."

"Good, now here comes the hard part Julio. I don't believe in long-distance relationships. We are only 15 years old, and we have our whole lives ahead of us. That means while you are here in Miami, we can remain boyfriend and girlfriend, but once you leave, it's over."

"Samantha, I don't want to move away from you. When you were away visiting your dad, I was miserable. At least I was able to spend time with Daisy, and she lifted my spirits. However, this time when I leave, I won't have either one of you. I will be lost and alone without you and Daisy."

Julio wrapped his arms around me, and I could feel him shaking. I couldn't see his tears, but I felt his teardrops. They landed on my right cheek as I held him in my arms. We rocked back and forth, holding one another until the tears subsided from both of us. Now Julio was doing all the talking. "I know I'm in love with you, Samantha, and I disagree with us breaking up. We have to figure this out but breaking up is not the answer."

"How do you know that you're in love with me, Julio?"

"Mi Corazón, I have known that I'm in love with you since the day you left to see your father. For ten days, I was completely miserable, with no appetite or ambition. Then there came the point where I didn't want to leave my bed except to walk Daisy. You took my heart and happiness with you."

"Have you ever been in love before, Julio?"

"No, I have not ever felt this way in my entire life."

"Neither have I until I fell in love with you."

"Really, Mi Corazón?"

"Yes, I Love you, Julio. You are the first thing I think of when I wake up and the last before I sleep. It's going to be rough on both of us when you leave."

"It will be, Samantha, I agree with you, but for now, let's enjoy the time we have."

"Well, we have school tomorrow Julio, so we ought to start kissing."

Within days we fell back into our regular routine, and on Saturdays, the girls spent the night at my house. We spent Sundays watching the boys play soccer and afterward had lunch together at the picnic tables. When everybody was done eating, we all went our separate ways. That's when Julio and I would take Daisy out by the lake for an hour. He would play fetch with her, and she would chase him around the lake until they became tired enough to join me under our tree. That's when Julio would hold me in his arms while Daisy laid her head down on my lap to take a nap. For the most part, we have been happy and didn't let anything bother us anymore.

Two months later, on a Sunday, it was pouring outside, so the soccer game was canceled due to rain. Daphne, Greg, Julio, and I were sitting down in my living room watching a movie when there was a knock on the kitchen door. I answered the door, and it was Monica. I haven't seen her since the day she left my house after she announced that she might be pregnant. Now here she is standing in front of my door wearing an oversized sweatshirt and shorts. I could tell she was pregnant, even with her arms crossed in front of her. "Is my brother here?"

"Yes, Julio's here watching a movie in the living room. You can come in if you want." Monica walked inside without saying another word to me and headed straight for the

living room. Daphne jumped when she saw Monica, who was now standing directly in front of Julio. I sort of felt bad for not announcing Monica was here until she pointed at Julio, saying, "I know you're going to the fair, and I want to go with you."

Julio looked over at Greg and rolled his eyes before he replied, "Thanks a lot, Monica, that was a surprise for Samantha and Daphne." Now Julio had an annoyed look on his face, and he sounded aggravated.

"Well, they know now, so it doesn't make a difference. The point is that I'm going with you, Julio."

"No, you're pregnant, Monica. You're not going anywhere, especially to the fair. That's ridiculous."

"I have to go, Julio. I just won't ride anything, okay?"

"Tell me why you have to go to the fair, Monica."

"Alvaro is going to be there, and I haven't spoken to him in almost a month."

"Monica, I don't blame him. Leave Alvaro alone already. What's wrong with you?"

Julio stood up and walked to the front door. "Monica, leave now."

"No," Monica yelled back. "Not until you agree to take me."

That's when I stood up and told her, "If Julio asks you to leave my house, Monica, then you need to leave right now." She turned her head to me, and she began fidgeting with the strings on her sweatshirt. "I'm sorry, Monica, but I don't want to be a part of whatever's going on between you and Julio, so please leave." I walked to the front door and stood beside Julio. He opened the door again, and Monica kept her eyes on Julio shaking her head as she walked out the door. He shut the door behind her and locked it. I took in

a deep breath and let it out slowly to the count of ten. Then we joined Greg and Daphne on the couch.

"What was that all about, Julio?"

"Daphne, that's called crazy, and I deal with it every day. Just ask your boyfriend."

"Is that true, Greg?"

Greg had a smirk on his face when he replied, "Yup."

"What I'm about to tell you does not leave this room."

"Fine, say it already, Julio."

"Samantha, what's wrong with you?"

"I'm sorry, Julio, your sister just gets to me. I feel bad for her one minute, but then her attitude sucks, so then I'm mad her the next minute for treating you like garbage. Now that I've thought about it, maybe I'm better off not knowing anything that has to do with your sister."

"Julio, don't listen to Sammy. I want to know what's going on, so tell us."

"Daphne, you don't want to know anything that has to do with Monica. She is a world of doom and brings everyone down with her."

"You're right, Samantha, and I'm sorry that you've had to deal with this nonsense." I looked over at Julio, and he was sulking. Now I felt terrible and told Julio that I was sorry for overreacting.

Daphne sat up and said, "Great, now go ahead and tell us what's going on, Julio."

"Alright, last month my sister went to the doctor with Alvaro. The doctor felt around her abdomen and said she must be further along. My sister called the doctor a liar and kept telling him he was wrong. He told her, 'Let me show you with an ultrasound.' When the doctor did the ultrasound, the

baby appeared to be closer to four months based on the development and size, which meant Alvaro is not the father.

"What you have got to be kidding."

"No, I'm not Daphne."

"Anyway, back to the story, Alvaro drove my sister home and told her it was over, and that was about a month ago."

"Wow, that's horrible poor Alvaro."

"I agree with you, Samantha, and that's why I have no intention of taking my sister to the Fair."

"Julio, I don't understand why Monica wants to see Alvaro. I mean, obviously, that relationship is over with."

"My sister keeps calling Alvaro's house all hours of the night. She blows up his beeper. Monica even stole my mom's car and my brother's van to drive over to Alvaro's house on two separate occasions."

"Well, what I want to know is who's baby is it?"

Before Julio could answer Daphne, I blurted out, "It's Rick's baby, isn't it? Your sister tried to trap Alvaro with Rick's baby? Didn't she?" Julio snapped his head around and stared at me with his mouth gaping open, appearing utterly shocked by my question.

"How do you know about Rick?" I placed my hand over my mouth. "Samantha, tell me how you know about Rick."

"Can I speak to you alone, Julio?"

"Of course, whatever you want." I took Julio out to the balcony and shut the sliding glass door.

"Your mom was upset, Julio, and she spoke to my mom about Rick."

"What did she tell your mom?" I told Julio what I knew that his mom walked in on Monica and Rick.

"Here is what you don't know, Sammy. Monica already knew she was pregnant for a couple of months before she got with Alvaro. Rick wants nothing to do with Monica since she became pregnant because he doesn't want her to have the baby."

"What Alvaro said about my sister seducing him was true. For some reason, Monica thought she could just replace the father, and her mind was set on Alvaro."

"Now, of course, Alvaro wants absolutely nothing to do with Monica. No one can blame him. Everyone in my family agrees with Alvaro. What she tried to do was completely messed up."

"Your sister is really crazy. I'm sorry that you and your family are having to deal with this."

"As you can see, Monica's mood is very unpleasant. My mom told us it's her hormones from being pregnant. Either way, I can't stand to be around her anymore."

"Did you know that Alvaro was even considering marriage because he thought Monica was pregnant with his child. The same day he found out the baby was clearly not his, Alvaro beeped Alex, and we all met up with him at the Pro shop. He told us what the doctor said and about the ultrasound. Alvaro wanted us to know the truth because he knew Monica would never tell us the truth. Alvaro was right when we arrived home that evening. Monica was waiting for us in the living room so that she could tell us how Alvaro no longer wants to be a father. She told us that we needed to speak to him about his family obligations. My brother Alex was the one that told her we knew the truth. That we spoke with Alvaro after he dropped her off at home. That didn't stop Monica. She kept trying to convince us that Alvaro was lying and that he was the father."

"My mom still believed Alvaro was the father, and that Monica was telling the truth until my mom went to the doctor, with my sister. The doctor told my mom that Monica was at least four months pregnant. When my mom arrived home after the visit to the doctor, she had a meeting with us. To tell us precisely what the doctor said and about catching my sister in bed with Rick. Then, of course, that's when Monica confessed to everything, and she told us she didn't want the baby to grow up without a father. She's suffering from abandonment issues again, and it all started back when my father left us. It went away soon after moving into my grandmother's house because my uncles moved into her home shortly after we did. The thing is after my father left us, my uncles filled that void and became our father figures in our household. Even though they live in California, and we're here, they are still our male role models. Monica clearly needs them in her life now more than ever before."

Instantly tears filled my eyes after hearing that last sentence. Now feeling upset, frustrated, and angry, I blurted out, "Julio, why doesn't your mom just send Monica to live in California? It doesn't make sense to me why you should all have to go."

"We have all asked my mom that question many times."

"What does your mom say?"

"My mom said we're family, and we all go together. When we are eighteen, we can go off to college wherever we want and choose to do what we want, but until then, we stick together. Alex turns eighteen in May, so he said that he's staying here in Miami."

"Is Eddie going to stay too?"

"I'm not sure, but he will be eighteen in August, so he could go up for the summer and come back here."

"At least I find comfort in knowing Alex will remain here with Maria."

"Samantha, when I leave here, I will have nothing just a broken heart. Is there any way you will reconsider a long-distance relationship?"

"No, Julio, because we're only 15 years old with our whole lives ahead of us."

"So, what does that mean? Please explain this to me because I don't understand what you are trying to say."

"Please don't talk about this anymore, Julio."

"How else am I going to get you to change your mind if we don't discuss this?" Then I felt my eyes burning before the tears came, and I was crying again uncontrollably for about an hour. Julio tried to calm me down initially, but it was no use, so he held me until I let it all out. When I finally stopped, we walked back inside. Arturo and Michael were here now to pick up Daphne and Greg. I hugged everyone before they left out the door.

"Hey, it stopped raining. Do you want to go for a walk, Daisy?" She came running up to me, wagging her tail when she heard the word walk. I attached her leash, and we headed out the door. Julio reminded me that we had to stop off at his place on the way home. His mom made Arros con Pollo for everyone to have after the game, but the game never happened today. Which meant Pilar had tons of food leftover, and she'll want us to take some back to my mom. On the way back to my place, we stopped off at Julio's. Daisy and I stayed outside, but when Julio came back out, he appeared to be upset.

"What's wrong, Julio?"

"Monica has been fighting with everyone in the house today."

"About what?"

"She's still demanding to go to the Dade County Fair next week, and the constant arguing is getting on my mom's nerves. Alex told me that my mom has been crying most of the day."

"Listen, we don't have to go to the fair. The whole reason Monica wants to go there is to see Alvaro. How did Monica find out that Alvaro was working at the fair?"

"Alex told my mom yesterday that he was leaving to give Alvaro a ride to work. My mom laughed and said he must not be a good mechanic yet. I said no, the mechanic shop moved to Fort Lauderdale. Alvaro is working at the fair. Monica overheard us talking, and you know the rest."

"Let's go somewhere else, Julio."

"Where else do you want to go?"

"I would love to go roller skating. I have a pair of speed skates with pink neon laces and wheels."

"That sounds good, and I have a pair of speed skates too, but I have neon yellow laces and green neon wheels."

"Great, then we can go next week on Saturday. We just have to tell Daphne about it, and she will invite everybody else."

When my mom arrived home from work, I told her about the situation at Julio's place and that his mom made us dinner. My mom called Pilar and asked her to join us. She came over thirty minutes later, and my mom was ready for her with a bottle of wine. The four of us enjoyed a lovely dinner, and afterward, Julio helped me clear the table. While we were in the kitchen washing the dishes, I could hear Pilar and my mom talking. Pilar kept telling my mom that she has to meet her brother Gio.

"No, thank you. I'm fine, Pilar, no more men for me. Besides, that's the one brother you have that has never even been to Miami. He has only lived on the west coast in

California since he has moved to the States. I live here in Florida, so what's the point?"

"Yes, I guess you're right. A long-distance relationship is impossible," Pilar replied. I wanted to cry at that very moment realizing even Pilar knows that a long-distance relationship won't ever work out. I tried to forget what I just heard Pilar say, but it was no use. I was about to cry, and Julio noticed. He stopped drying the counter and held me.

"Samantha, what's wrong?"

"Nothing, I'm just tired. It's been sort of a long day, Julio."

"Go lay down and get some rest. I can take Daisy outside for her last walk."

"Thank you, Julio." I hugged him and kissed him on the cheek before I walked into my room. I was so upset that I cried myself to sleep that night.

It was Friday night, and everyone was finally all together at the picnic tables. Daphne asked what everyone was doing tomorrow, and I told her that Julio and I are going roller skating. Then I invited everyone to come along with us.

"Thank you for inviting me, Sammy, but I would rather do something else."

"Are you sure, Denise?"

After Denise nodded her head, yes, Daphne stood up and said, "Well, let's think of something we could do as a group." Three places were mentioned leaving us to decide between the arcade, movies at a theatre, or the drive-in.

As we were trying to decide, Denise stood up and announced I got it," Let's go to makeout beach."

"Why do you want to go to Hobie Beach?"

"During the day, it's Hobie Beach, but at night it's known as makeout beach because that's where everybody goes parking. It's really cool, Greg, if you would just give it a chance."

"What's so cool about it, Denise?"

"For starters, you can park your car right on the beach Greg."

"I don't have a car, Denise."

Daphne shook her head at Greg before saying, "Denise tell us what else we can do at makeout beach."

"Listen to the waves and look at the stars with Greg. Go for a romantic walk with Daphne on the beach and feel the sand between your toes."

"How is that romantic, Denise, when we are going there as a group?"

"Look, Greg, everyone goes there at night to make-out and hang out. A lot of people go there in groups and wander off on the beach. That's what we can do, and it will be so much fun."

"Denise, don't take it personally, it's just not something I'm interested in doing."

"Have you ever seen the city all lit up at night from Hobie Beach?"

"No, I haven't."

"Well, it's the most incredible view of Miami you will ever see. You have to experience this with us, Greg."

He stood up, facing the Sanchez boys, and asked, "What do you guys think?" After a couple of minutes, he turned back around and told Denise the guys are leaving it all up to the ladies to decide where we're going.

"Well, I haven't ever been to Hobie Beach at night."

"You are going to love it, Sammy."

"We're not going in the water, right?"

"No, Tonya, you don't ever go for a swim at night. That's very dangerous. That's when the sharks are out."

"Is it really romantic and fun, Denise?"

"Yes, Daphne, you're going to love it."

"Then, let's go to makeout beach."

"Wow, Daphne, so you are sold on the location-based on it being romantic?"

"If that's the case, let me tell you about the skating rink. They have a couples-only skate, which usually happens at least two different times during the two-hour session. Where they play two back to back love songs with the lights turned down low. There are also these twinkle lights that shine down on you in the shape of little circles and different colors as you skate around the rink holding your boyfriend's hand. It's all very romantic. In fact, it's the same exact thing as dancing to a slow song with your boyfriend except for your wearing roller skates."

"Let's go skating then!" Maria and I started laughing.

"What's so funny?"

"You are, Daphne."

"Can I tell you the truth, Maria?"

"Of course, Daphne."

"The truth is that I wanted to go to the fair, but I don't want Monica to go with us and ruin it."

"Why don't you just go to the fair then?"

"Sammy, I didn't mean for you to hear that."

"Well, I did, and I think you should go. Monica won't go with you guys. She only wants to go with someone from her family."

"Greg, take Daphne to the fair, bro," Lewis said.

"How am I going to sleep at your house then, Sammy?"

"Daphne, I will be home by ten o'clock, so just come back to my place by eleven o'clock."

Then Denise chimed in, saying, "I have an even better idea. Let's all go to makeout beach. Come on, Sammy. If you and Julio go, everyone else will go too, including Greg."

"Julio, do they have an afternoon session at the skating rink?"

"Yes, Mi Corazón, from 2 pm-4 pm. Why?"

"Can we go to the afternoon session instead, Julio? That way, we can go to makeout beach tomorrow night with Denise, Eddie, Maria, Alex, Lewis, and Tonya."

"Hey, wait. What about Greg and me?"

"What do you mean, Daphne? I thought you were going to the fair."

"No, if you guys are going to makeout beach, then I want to go too and make-out with Greg on the beach."

Everyone's mouth dropped to the floor before we all broke out laughing. Daphne just sat there with her arms crossed over her chest, saying, "Isn't that what everyone's going there for?"

"No one openly admits to that, Daphne."

"Tonya, as long as I can get a bit of romance and make-out with Greg on the beach, I will be satisfied."

Greg and Julio shouted out, "Daphne, please stop."

Daphne spun around to see them laughing, and her eyes nearly popped out of her head. She turned to Tonya and said, "Maybe I shouldn't have blurted that out after all."

"Julio, would you like to go to makeout beach? It's going to be extremely romantic. Everybody we know will be there, including Daphne and Greg."

"Oh yeah, that sounds romantic, Sammy. Going to makeout beach with eight of your closest friends."

"Greg's right Samantha, there's nothing more romantic than that." Then Julio and Greg, along with the rest of the Sanchez boys, all broke out laughing again.

Then Eddie walked up to the picnic table with Monica. Suddenly, everyone became quiet. He took a deep breath before saying, "Monica has decided that she will be going to the fair with us tomorrow."

"We're not going to the fair anymore."

"Oh no, then where are you going, Denise?"

Monica was standing in front of us with her arms crossed over her chest, looking menacing as ever, waiting for an answer.

Tonya stood up and asked, "Why? You have not been invited, Monica?"

"Listen, if I want to go somewhere, I'm going. I don't need you to invite me. You're just a jealous person, Tonya, and you are jealous of me because I'm with Alvaro now. He is off the market, and I'm having his baby."

"You're right, Monica. I am jealous of you. Not because you're with Alvaro or having a baby."

"I'm having Alvaro's baby," Monica yelled at Tonya.

"Monica, that still has nothing to do with why I'm jealous of you. I'm jealous of you because you have two brothers and two cousins who were willing to fight for your honor. Yet you take them for granted and treat them like garbage. You yell at them constantly, and you don't even realize how lucky you are. I would love to have a cousin or a brother who would do that for me. Heck, I would love to have my mom live with me. I don't have any of that, so yeah, I might be a little bit jealous of you.

As far as you and Alvaro are concerned, I wish you both total and complete happiness, especially with a child involved."

"Thank you, Tonya."
"You don't have to thank me, Monica. That's how I honestly feel. Tomorrow we're going roller skating in the afternoon and to Hobie beach tomorrow night. It's supposed to be romantic, so I'm inviting you and Alvaro if you want to join us."

Monica looked over at Eddie and Julio before saying, "Thank you, Tonya, for the invitation, but I won't be able to make it." Then Monica turned around and took off. Nobody spoke for a few minutes.

Finally, Denise turned to Tonya and asked, "What was that?"

"Look, I invited Monica, and she's not going, so what's the big deal?"

"What if she would have said yes, Tonya?"

"Denise, she's pregnant feeling lost, confused, and I'm sure she's scared. Monica is only sixteen years old with a baby on the way. Alvaro wants nothing to do with her. No offense, Maria, I know Monica is nuts right now, but that sucks."

Julio, Greg, Daphne, and I all turned our heads to look at Maria. We were just waiting for Maria to tell Tonya the truth about the baby, but she didn't say anything. Instead, Maria remained quiet, staring at the ground in front of her.

Eddie was the one to speak up and say, "Tonya, those were very kind words. I appreciate the respect and understanding you have shown my cousin. However, I don't know if she deserves it. Her hormones have made her a little bit moody lately."

"Just a little," Lewis said, laughing, and that's when Julio and Eddie began to laugh with him.

"Tonya, my sister Monica is over five months pregnant. Alvaro is not the baby's father. The baby is from another guy Monica saw before Alvaro was ever in the picture. Please don't discuss this with anyone else. Were all very close, so I'm trusting all of you to keep this to yourselves."

"I won't tell anyone, and I'm sorry."

"Sorry for what, Tonya? You didn't do anything wrong. Monica is the one who has been disrespectful to you for months now. I should be thanking you for being so polite when you speak to her."

"Eddie, how can you even say that? I was so direct and bold when I spoke with her?"

"You were respectful when you spoke to her, and you invited her to go out with us. That's more than I can manage to do nowadays. Please, Tonya, tell me your secret."

"What secret, Eddie?"

"Your secret to maintaining your patience, Tonya. You see, in our household, we wake up to Monica yelling about everything. A few times, I found myself yelling back at her, and you know what I was yelling?"

"No, what were you yelling, Eddie?"

"I was yelling at her 'stop yelling' or 'calm down.' That's my other favorite thing to yell every day, but it never works; Monica only becomes angrier." We all started laughing while Eddie was telling us, "That's fine, laugh, but I'm telling you it's rough."

"Eddie, how can you yell calm down? If you are yelling, then you are not calm yourself."

"Exactly, that's my point, Denise. It's ridiculous, Monica is making me crazy. All I know is it's her hormones, or she really hates me. We will know for sure in about four months."

Everyone continued to laugh, but Eddie looked like he was serious. Alex stood up and asked, "Are you girls ready to go?"

"Yes, let's get going," Tonya answered.

Give me like two minutes, Alex. I left the table and ran back home to grab my overnight bag. I met up with everyone again at the van. When I climbed inside, I was surprised to see Julio sitting in the back, waiting for me. I sat down beside him and took hold of his hand. "What are you doing here, Julio?"

"I'm going for a car ride with my brother Alex to drop off my girlfriend," and he winked at me."

When we arrived at Daphne's house, Julio climbed out behind me, carrying my bag. Arturo and Michael were in the front yard working on Arturo's car as usual.

"Daphne, do they ever do anything else besides work on that car?"

"Tonya, it's one of those things that men like to do. I'm no different. I work on my van every chance that I get."

"If you say so, Alex," and Tonya turned her head to me, rolling her eyes.

"It's hot out here, Daphne. We need to go in the house."

"You're right let's go. We followed Denise and Daphne to the doorstep. Julio handed me my duffel bag, and I kissed him on the cheek.

"Thank you for coming with Alex to drop me off. I will be home tomorrow by noon so that we can go out on our date to the skating rink."

"I'm looking forward to it, Samantha." Julio wrapped his arms around me and hugged me one more time. Then he kissed me gently on the lips before releasing me.

I was taken by surprise with that kiss and had instant butterflies. I stood there, on the doorstep, just watching Julio walk back to the van.

"Julio just swept you off your feet, huh, Sammy?"

"He often does that to me, Maria." Then I looked behind her and saw Alex standing there, smiling back at me.

As soon as I walked inside, Tonya told me we forgot to bring the sleeping bags again. "That's not a problem, Tonya. I have lots of comforters, and you can use them to sleep on and cover up with tonight."

"Thank you, Carmen."

"Oh, and Sammy, your mom, will be here in an hour."

"My mom?"

"Yes, Sammy, your mom is coming over with Pilar so we can have a ladies' night tonight."

"Well, that sounds great, Mom," Daphne said with a smirk on her face.

"Oh, Daphne, stop it. You can go one Friday night without your boyfriend." Carmen stood up to leave the minute Daphne started whining.

"Mom, it's not fair. Greg's off tonight, so I don't understand why you won't allow him to pass by for a little bit."

"Daphne, I said no, and I mean it, you can see Greg tomorrow." Carmen left the living room, looking very perturbed.

"Your mom's right Daphne. It's a girls night tonight, so why don't you try to enjoy the evening with all of us. Tomorrow, you will spend the entire day with Greg."

"I know, Sammy. I just miss him."

"Stop pouting, Daphne, and give Greg a chance to miss you."

"Do you think he'll miss me, Denise?"

"Yes, Daphne, I'm sure Greg misses you, but you need to allow him to experience that feeling in order to appreciate you more when you do spend time together."

"Denise, I didn't look at it that way, thank you."

"Where are you going, Daphne?"

"I'm going to apologize to my mom."

When Daphne left, we all took turns thanking Denise for speaking to Daphne. Then Arturo walked inside with Michael.

"Sammy, where are my mom and sister?"

"They are in your mom's room."

"Okay, thanks."

"Do you girls mind if I join you all on the sofa?"

"No, not at all, Michael. Have a seat.

"Thank you, Denise, now what have you girls been up to?"

"Nothing yet, how come you're not dirty?"

"I don't tinker with cars, Denise. That's Arturo's thing, not mine."

"Hey, Michael, do you plan to be Jewish Santa again?"

"That's not until the end of the year, so I don't know yet maybe. Why are you going back to the forest again, Tonya, to take pictures with Santa?"

Before Tonya could reply, there was a knock at the front door. Daphne and Carmen came running down the hall to answer the door. It was my mom and Pilar. I stood up and walked over to hug them. When I sat back down, Michael asked, "Is that Julio's mom?"

"Yes, Pilar is Julio's mom and my mom's best friend."

"How interesting. Excuse me a second, Sammy. I will be right back."

Michael stood up and walked over to Carmen, Pilar, and my mom just as Arturo walked back into the living room. Arturo nodded his head toward the front door, and Michael announced, "I've got to go, girls." He waved bye to the moms before following Arturo out the door.

"Daphne, where is your older brother Javier?"

"Maria, he moved out after he finished school to live with his girlfriend."

Carmen said, "Okay, girls, let's go."

"Where are we going, Mom?"

"Someplace Daphne. You'll see soon enough."

Tonya and I climbed into the car with my mom and Pilar. Daphne, Denise, and Maria jumped in the car with Carmen. We arrived in front of a Mexican restaurant.

"Mom, what's going on?"

"Sammy, you will know soon enough."

"That's the same thing Carmen said earlier, Mom."

"Well, whatever it is, I hope it involves Greg."

"Why?"

"Ms. Harris, everything revolves around Greg in Daphne's world."

"Tonya, I want you to know that Greg feels the same way about Daphne. While Greg is at my house, all we hear is Daphne, Daphne, Daphne."

"That's so cute, Pilar. I had no idea Greg was capable of sharing his feelings."

"Oh yes, Lori, Greg is very expressive."

"Good, that means their perfect for one another, Tonya said, smiling at me."

Once Carmen arrived, we all walked inside together. Daphne kept asking, "Why are we here?"

A hostess greeted us at the entrance and told us to follow her. The restaurant was beautiful. It had an atrium in the center that allowed in natural light from the skyline in the ceiling. There were big clay pots filled with plants scattered around the room, and I saw beautiful green vines on the back wall. We walked past the atrium to a place in the back of the restaurant. The Hostess finally stopped at a table set up to accommodate twelve people. The first thing I noticed was the large abstract mural painted on the back wall above our table. This room also had clay pots that were much smaller and sat up on the built-in shelves along the side of the walls. The hostess waited for all of us all to be seated before handing us each a menu. Then she left seven menus behind.

Daphne was smiling and said, "I know why we're here."

"That's great, Daphne, now can you tell us?"

"Denise, we are here to celebrate my birthday. It's in three weeks. My mom wanted me to have a big traditional Fifteens party, but I told her I'd rather go to a Mexican restaurant. My mom was disappointed until I told her why."

"And why did you want to come to a Mexican Restaurant, Daphne, instead of having a huge party?"

"To hear the Mariachis sing 'Happy Birthday' to me, Denise."

We all broke out laughing, and Daphne said, "Go ahead, laugh. It's my birthday, and that's what I want."

"Hey, did anyone see where my mom went off to?"

"Sammy, I saw your mom, my mom, and Pilar walk into the Cantina."

"What's that?"

"The bar," Daphne answered. "My mom loves margaritas."

"After we leave here, is everyone still sleeping at my house?"

"Yes, of course, Daphne."

"Okay, good Sammy. Now, where are those Mariachis?"

"I don't know, but the moms are back with their fishbowl margaritas."

Carmen walked up to Daphne and asked, "So. what do you think?"

"Mom, it's nearly perfect. Only one person is missing."

"Gee, I wonder who that could be, Daphne," Carmen replied with her eyebrows raised and in a tone of voice that sounded like a warning.

We all looked over at Daphne, and Denise told her, "Let Greg miss you for a change." Daphne exhaled while shaking her head and eventually sat back in her chair, with her arms crossed over her chest.

The waiter came over to take our drink orders. He also dropped off a couple of baskets of tortilla chips and bowls filled

with salsa. We all dove into the basket of chips. Then I looked up and saw Arturo, Greg, Michael, and Javier walking over to the table. I looked at Daphne, and she was still talking to her mom. Then Greg took a seat in front of Daphne without saying a word to her. He sat there, watching her smiling.

All of a sudden, Daphne stopped speaking midsentence and turned her head to see Greg sitting down in front of her.

"Happy Birthday, Daphne."

"Greg, you're here," Daphne said with excitement.
"Yes, I am," he replied with a huge smile on his face.

Daphne turned her head and told Carmen, "You're the best mom. I love you."

"I Love you too, kid."

Arturo, Javier, and Michael sat in the chairs directly in front of Tonya, Denise, and me. Daphne had not said one word to any of them yet when Arturo stood up and walked over to Greg to stand behind him.

"Hi Daphne, I just wanted to let you know that your brothers and Michael are here, too."

"Oh my gosh, when did you guys get here?" Daphne asked as she waved to Javier and Michael.

"We walked in with Greg since we picked him up from his house and drove him over here. I hope you don't mind, Daphne."

"You did that for me, Arturo?"

"Of course, I did that for you. Now I will let you go back to talking to Greg."

Arturo walked back to his seat and sat down in front of me. We all ordered our food and talked about our plans for tomorrow. When we finished eating, Carmen said, "Thank you, Daphne."

"For what, Mom?"

"For wanting Mexican food for your birthday. Everything was delicious."

That's when we all said, "Thank you, Daphne," in unison. Then the waiter came back to our table with a cup of ice cream and a lit candle on top. As we were about to sing happy birthday, The Mariachis walked in, and our waiter waved them over. Daphne got her birthday wish when they sang 'Happy Birthday' to her.

When we were about to leave the restaurant, Daphne hugged her mom and told her she was looking forward to her Quinceanera. The next day Tonya called Abuela and asked her to pick us up instead of my mom. She has a minivan, so all five of us will fit in her vehicle. When Abuela showed up, my mom was riding shotgun beside her. "Mom, I wasn't expecting to see you here."

"Sam, nobody bothered to give Tonya's grandmother the address to Carmen's house. When she called me to ask for it, I offered to ride with her and show her in person how to get here."

When we were about a block away from my complex, Daphne pointed to Julio and Greg walking Daisy on the sidewalk. "Mom, how does Julio have Daisy?"

"Julio came by the house before I left, asking to take Daisy out on her morning walk. I let Julio know that I wouldn't be back for about an hour, and he said that was fine."

"Daisy is such a lucky girl to be walking around outside with those two guys. " We all started laughing, and Daphne asked, "Was that funny?"

Denise told her, "Yes, but only because it came from you, Daphne, and we know that you meant that from deep down in your heart." Somehow we all ended up spending the afternoon

at the pool instead of the skating rink until four o'clock. At six o'clock, we met back up with the boys at Alex's van.

Alex was driving, and Maria was his copilot and DJ. We were traveling on US-1 when Alex said, "Let me know, guys when you see the revolving shark. That's where I need to turn right."

Daphne was the first one to spot something, and asked, "Does the shark look like it's trapped on a carousel?"

We all looked out the window, and Julio told Alex, "Get ready to make a right." Alex made a right then pulled up to a toll booth.

Greg handed Alex a dollar to pay the toll, and now we were traveling on the Rickenbacker Causeway Bridge. The sun was still shining over the bay as we crossed the first bridge.

"It's so beautiful here," Maria commented, sounding excited.

"Maria, have you been to Hobie Beach before?"

"No, Alex, this is my first time, and the view from here is astounding."

"Then Maria, allow me to be the first one to welcome you to the beautiful Biscayne Bay. This bridge that we are on connects Miami to the barrier islands of Virginia Key and Key

Biscayne. I haven't been over here in a couple of years, and I never realized just how magnificent the views are until now. Thank you for allowing me to see it through your eyes." Maria was blushing, and I could see Alex's grin from the backseat. I turned my eyes away from them and went back to looking out the window. The bay is so blue that some parts are a turquoise color. You can see water for miles and miles. As we drove over the second bridge, I saw people still fishing on the pier.

"Do you girls know where you want to park? We have two options to choose from we can park on the sandy beach side on the right. Or we can make a U-turn and park on the left side, which is the rocky side, but will have incredible views of downtown Miami after the sun goes down. It's up to you, girls, I'm all ears." Denise and Tonya talked it over and weighed the pros and cons of what they really wanted to see and do. Tonya and Denise agreed they wanted to lie on blankets on the beach. The rocky beach might be too uncomfortable. "Okay, so what have you girls decided?"

Daphne blurted out, "Sandy beach, Alex."

"Yes," I agree. We want to see the sunset."

"Muñeca, I was just about to say that."

"I know Tonya, but you were taking too long, so Daphne and I said it for you."

Denise smiled before saying, "Excellent choice, ladies, thank you." Alex pulled the van up onto the beach. He parked under a tree, and all the boys jumped out first. They stood in front of the doors helping the girls climb down from the van. I was the last one to exit the van. When I saw Julio with his arms up, I had a brilliant idea to jump into his arms. Which I did, and he fell backward onto the sand while holding me. We were both laughing when he said, "Somehow, I knew you were going to do that, Samantha," and he kissed me on my forehead.

"Okay, you two, at least use the beach towels."

After Eddie said that, I realized Julio was covered in sand, and I had it already in my shoes and some in my hair. I stood up and put out my hand to help Julio up. He took my hand and pulled me back onto his lap. I was already laughing before I landed on top of Julio. Then Julio started laughing again as soon as I landed on top of him. We were laughing so much that everyone came from behind the van over to where we were. Just to see what was going on.

"What are you guys doing?"

"Denise, it looks like they're having fun playing in the sand."

"Eddie, let's go for a walk on the beach just you and me."

"Okay, baby, but can we play in the sand too?"

We were all cracking up when Alex said, "I hope everyone has what they need because I'm shutting the doors on the van. It's time to go for a walk on the beach." We all found a spot on the beach a few yards away from one another. All of the girls brought a blanket to lay out on. Julio walked by the tree beside the van, and I laid our blanket out under the tree. Julio sat down first and held up his hands to me. I smacked them away and told him, "No, I'm not falling for that again."

"Falling for what, Mi Corazón?"
He sat up on his knees, then wrapped his arms around my waist and pressed his head against my hip. I leaned down to kiss the top of his head and told him that I would be right back.

"Where are you going, Samantha?"

"Just give me a second." I ran over to the cooler and grabbed a couple of ice cubes.

Alex saw me and smiled before saying, "Get him, Sammy." I looked back at Alex with a devilish grin.

When I walked back over to Julio, he sat up on the blanket with his back against the tree. I pulled on the back of his shorts, dropped the ice cubes down. Then Julio jumped up onto his feet. He was laughing and jumping up and down, trying to get the ice cubes to fall out. I was busy laughing hysterically until the ice cubes landed on the beach. Then I noticed Julio was staring back at me with a massive grin on his face. That was my cue to start running. I took off down the beach, and he was right behind me. Then I saw people in front of me walking on the beach, so I ran into the shallow water.

I felt the water splashing up and down my legs as I ran. When all of a sudden, Julio picked me up and fell backward onto the sand. I was safely wrapped in his arms, laughing and almost out of breath.

"You can't outrun a soccer player, Mi Corazón."

"I know, but I had to try Julio." I still sounded like I was out of breath.

"Try as much as you like. I will always catch you, Samantha."

"Wow, I hope that's true, Julio."

"It is, and you know what I should do now, Mi Corazón?"

"What?"

"I should take you to the pier and show you off to all the fishermen. I would be the envy of everyone, for the best catch of the day."

"You're so silly, Soccer Player."

"This, I already know, and that's why you love me."

"Oh, that's why," I said, laughing as I stood up, offering Julio my hand.

He pulled me back down on top of him again, and he slid his arms around my waist before asking, "Where's my trophy?"

"What are you talking about, Julio?"

"My trophy, my reward, you know, for the best catch of the day." I tried not to laugh as I closed my eyes and kissed him gently on the lips. When I pulled my head away, Julio was smiling and told me, "Yes, definitely the best catch."

We walked back over to our tree and sat down on our blanket to watch the sunset.

Julio held me in his arms, and I told him about Daphne's dinner at the Mexican restaurant. He didn't even know his mom was out with us last night. All Julio knew was that his mom went out with friends, and his mom mentioned how much she would miss everybody once she's gone.

"Your mom was talking about my mom and Daphne's mom Carmen. They had a ladies' night at the Mexican restaurant and drank fishbowl margaritas."

"Samantha, will you visit us in Anaheim?" I felt the tears building up inside me, and I was becoming upset.

I took in a deep breath before I was finally able to respond with, "Yeah, I guess so."

Eddie finally returned from his walk on the beach with Denise, and he asked everyone to join them.

"Where are we going, Eddie?"

"Alex, it's getting dark now, which means it's time to go for a walk on the beach." We all followed Eddie and Denise down the beach. Everyone was holding hands with their partner walking one couple behind the other. Eventually, I walked off with Julio toward the edge of the water. I just wanted to feel the combination of the water and the sand between my toes. Then I heard Daphne scream, shark behind us. I quickly spun around, kicking water at Daphne before I took off running down the beach again.

Julio yelled, "Get her," and about a second later, Julio, Daphne, and Greg ran after me. Julio caught up to me first and wrapped his arms around me before whispering, "I will always catch you, Mi Corazón." I turned my head to look up at him and saw Julio's piercing brown eyes on me. I leaned in and closed my eyes, about to kiss those sweet lips when Daphne caught up to us. She was splashing us with water by the time Greg arrived, and he kicked sand on our legs.

"Daphne, I was just about to kiss Julio."

"Oh, Mi Corazón, you have been tarred and feathered."

"What Julio?"

He pointed to my legs, and I looked down, realizing instantly what he meant. Our legs looked like we were wearing concrete pants. The four of us laughed, and Julio helped me rub

the sand off my legs. Then we rubbed the clumps of sand off his legs. "Awe, that sucks all that work has been wasted."

"Not necessarily, Daphne."

I looked up at Greg, then Julio shouted, "On the count of three." We tackled Greg to the ground, and Daphne kept him pinned down while I kicked water onto his legs, and Julio kicked the sand. Eddie and Lewis caught up to us right after we tarred and feathered Greg. Julio was still in attack mode when he tackled Lewis to the ground. I kicked water on his legs too, while Daphne kicked the sand, and Tonya ran up to help Daphne kick even more sand onto poor Lewis. The three of us were cracking up laughing when we noticed Greg and Julio standing off to the side, taking a look at the job we've done to Lewis.

Lewis yelled, "You two better stop laughing and come get these girls off me along with this sand before Alex and Eddie leave us here." That's when all five of us surrounded him, rapidly patting the sand off his legs.

Then I heard, "What are you guys trying to do?" The five of us turned around to see Eddie, Denise, Alex, and Maria, staring at us with a look of confusion.

"Nevermind that, Eddie, we are ready to walk down the beach with you guys."

"Okay, whatever you say, Lewis, but were you like the sand statue or something?"

'Yeah, Bro, something like that," and we started laughing.

It was dark, and the stars were out by the time we walked back to our blankets on the beach. Eddie suggested that we all hop back in the van to park on the opposite side. He wanted to see the lights of the city. Everybody thought that was a great idea, so we picked up the blankets and left. Alex drove down about a hundred yards and made a U-turn. He went over the bridge and parked on the rocky side. We all climbed out of the van to take a look at the view of the Miami skyline. Then Tonya mentioned that she was becoming hungry and felt tired.

That's when Alex announced it was time to go, and we left. This time the boys were discussing where they wanted to eat, and the girls stared out the window at the spectacular view of the Miami skyline. It's such a beautiful sight all lit up at night. By the time we reached Bird Road, everyone had decided on pizza. We all agreed the best pizza comes from a local Italian restaurant at the East Bird Shopping Plaza. Maria walked inside and ordered two large pizzas to go. Alex asked Lewis if there were enough drinks for everybody in the cooler. Lewis told him there was plenty but reminded him that we would need napkins and plates. Julio and Greg offered to walk over to the grocery store and pick some up. After they left out the side door, Alex turned around facing us before asking, "Did you all have fun tonight at Hobie Beach?"

Daphne sat up and replied, "It's nighttime, Alex, which means it's called makeout beach."

"Ignore her, Alex, the answer to your question is yes, I had a great time, and I didn't even make-out."

"You didn't make-out, Sammy?"

"No, Daphne, but we kissed a lot, and we had a wonderful time."

"Who didn't make-out?" Daphne asked. "Please raise your hand." I was the only one raising my hand.

"Wow, guys, I'm the only one, really?"

"I'm afraid so, Sammy. Don't worry about it. I will speak to my cousin tonight and make sure it doesn't happen again. You know he may not know how to do that yet?"

Everybody was laughing when I said, "No, Eddie, that's alright. He knows how to do that, so your conversation's not necessary."

"Are you sure about that because there is a movie that I can have him watch to learn how to do that, Sammy?"

'I'm positive, Eddie, but what type of movie were you going to have Julio watch?"

"Dracula, of course, that man gets all the chicks."

Now I was even losing it laughing before I told him, "Eddie, he doesn't kiss anyone. He bites them on the neck."

Then Julio and Greg climbed back into the van. "Why is everybody laughing? What did I miss?"

"Nothing much, Greg but Sammy might need to start wearing garlic on those walks with Daisy."

"What? I don't get it, Daphne, and why are you all laughing again?"

"Okay, so we just found out that Sammy and Julio are the only couple that didn't make-out tonight at makeout beach. Then we learned from Eddie that you could learn a lot about kissing from watching Dracula."

"That's not true, Daphne. Samantha and I kissed a bunch of times."

"Yeah, you kissed Julio, but you didn't make-out, and that's what you were supposed to do because you were at makeout beach."

Tonya tapped Julio on the hand and said, "Don't listen to Daphne. Your cousin has everything under control. Just go home and watch the movie with Eddie."

Everyone was laughing again, and I yelled out, "Gee, thanks, Tonya."

"Not a problem Muñeca and when we get home, we will watch Top Gun. The make-out scenes are amazing." I just shook my head laughing while Denise and Daphne agreed.

Julio sat up and ran his left hand through his hair before saying, "You girls enjoy your movie. Samantha and I will be outside on a walk with Daisy later."

"Oh, that's why you guys walk Daisy so much."

"Greg's right and I knew that because you're the Kissing Bandits."

"Alex, that's not all they do. They also have their Q and A sessions on those walks."

"Daphne, that was a secret."

"Oops, I forgot. I'm sorry, Sammy."

"Samantha, you told Daphne about our talks?"

"Julio, I didn't tell her everything, just a few things."

"Dude, don't give Sammy a hard time. Some of those questions were blunt."

"Greg, you weren't supposed to say anything."

"Julio, did you tell Greg what we talk about?"

"Yes, because I was afraid that some of my questions were too forward."

"They were Julio, but I answered them anyway, didn't I?"

"Yes, you did, Samantha."

"Well, I hope you didn't tell him everything."

"No, just my answers and the questions that I asked you, Samantha."

"Okay, good."

Maria showed up with the pizzas, and Alex drove us home. We all had dinner together beside the pool at the picnic tables. After I finished eating, I announced that I'm leaving to walk Daisy. Tonya teased me and asked, "Are you sure you don't need to watch the movie first, Muñeca?"

"I'm positive, Tonya. Enjoy your movie, especially the make-out scene, and I hope you learn something."

"Just for that, Muñeca, you should have to watch Dracula with Eddie." Now we were both laughing as Julio took my hand, and we left.

Chapter 12 The Quinceanera

It's been over three weeks now since we had dinner at the Mexican restaurant, and Daphne's mom has been busy planning everything for the Quinceanera. For starters, Carmen has six girls come over to her house every Saturday afternoon for dance class. The class consists of two of Daphne's cousins, Tonya, Denise, Maria, myself, and of course, Daphne. Carmen has turned her two-car garage into a temporary studio for these classes, where she has been teaching us two dances to perform at the party.

On top of that, Carmen is currently searching for the ideal banquet hall, a specific dress for Daphne to wear, and the perfect cake. Then there's Daphne's father, who is coming to town for the second time this year. Daphne's parents are still married, but Daphne tells us they shouldn't be. I think that's because he works in Peru and only comes to town once a year in January when the weather is the absolute best.

Today it is Saturday, so we are on our way to Daphne's house for our dance class. When we pulled into the driveway, Tonya asked, "Where's Arturo and Michael?

"I don't know why?"

"Muñeca, it's Saturday, shouldn't they be outside working on Arturo's car?" My mom looked back at Tonya shaking her head, laughing while the four of us hopped out of the car.

When we knocked on the door, Arturo answered, but he wasn't looking like his usual self. I looked over at Tonya, and she was already looking back at me with her eyebrows raised. (Which is code for what's that about?)

He told us to come inside and have a seat in the living room, which is odd because we usually go straight out to the garage.

"Are your cousins here yet?"

"No, they aren't coming today, Tonya, and I have to get back to my room. Just wait here for my mom and Daphne. They will join you in a couple of minutes."

It must have been at least twenty minutes before Carmen walked out to the living room. "Hi, Girls, I meant to call and let you know that practice is canceled for today."

"Okay, I can call my mom and ask her to pick us up."

"No, Sammy, I will have Arturo drop you off."

Carmen left the living room, and Daphne never appeared. We all just sat there, looking confused until Arturo grabbed his keys off the coffee table. "Are you all ready to go?" The four of us nodded our heads, yes, as we stood up to follow Arturo out the door. We got about two blocks from his house when Arturo pulled over.

"I'm sorry, but I need a minute to calm down." Arturo was looking out the car window with his left hand on his forehead.

"Arturo, your clearly upset. Can you tell me what's going on?" He faced me, shaking his head no with his lips trembling and tears in his eyes.

"Please tell me what's going on? I just want to help you."

"No one can help Sammy. My father is here in Miami. He arrived this afternoon, and he saw me working on my car outside with Michael."

"Wait, what do you mean? Michael doesn't work on cars."

"Tonya, not now."

"Sorry, Muñeca."

"No, he doesn't. You're right, Tonya. He stands outside with me while I work on my car. Michael knows that's what I love to do. He does it every day for me."

"Well, why does he do that? Isn't that boring?"

"Perhaps Michael finds it boring, but he hasn't ever told me. All I know is that we do everything together because we love one another and Michael is my boyfriend. Today when my father arrived, he yelled at Michael and forbade him to ever come to my house again. Michael asked why, and my father told him, 'because you destroyed my son.'" I covered my mouth as I felt the tears swell up in my eyes, feeling sick to my stomach and heartbroken. Arturo surprised me by wrapping his arms around me, and together we cried. A few minutes later, I noticed Denise, Maria, and Tonya were also crying in the backseat. That's when Arturo pulled away, wiping his face.

"Arturo, where is Michael now?"

"I don't know Sammy; I wish I did." Then I saw the tears forming in his eyes again, so I wrapped my arms around him and held him tight.

"I've got an idea. Let's go get some pizza and go to Michael's house."

"That's a great idea, Tonya. Can we do that, Arturo?"

"Really? You guys don't mind?"

"No, of course not Arturo. That's why I suggested we do that?"

We showed up to Michael's house with two pizzas and a 2-liter bottle of Jupina. When he answered the door, Michael was taken entirely by surprise. "What are you all doing here?"

"We're here to have dinner with you, Michael."

"Arturo, I wasn't expecting to see you here."

"Well, Arturo's here, and I'm hungry, so let us in so we can eat."

Michael laughed before saying, "Yes, mam, sorry, for the delay Tonya." He backed up, allowing us room to walk inside. Tonya set the pizza's down on the dining room table and asked if his mom will join us.

"No, my mom is at dinner with friends tonight. She won't be home for hours."

"Perfect. Can we hang out here and watch a movie?"

"Yes, Denise, I don't see why not."

"Great. Where are the plates, Michael?"

"In the kitchen cabinet, Maria, over the sink."

"Got em, thank you." We all sat down at the table, ready to eat.

When Michael said, "Sammy, can you say grace?"

While we were in the middle of eating, Arturo apologized to Michael for his father's behavior.

"Arturo, you can't apologize for your father. It's not your fault."

"He had no right to speak to you like that, Michael."

The dinner conversation became intense until Tonya said, "I just have to say that I didn't even know you guys were a couple."

"Neither did I, but I did hear about a family vacation with two Casanovas from Daphne." Michael and Arturo looked over at one another and snickered. "Wait, what's so funny?"

"Sammy, the family vacation was in Fort Myers. Arturo and I had been friends for about a year, but we were not that close. So, I was surprised when Arturo invited me on this trip. Now I already had a crush on Arturo at the time. I was 13 years old, and I didn't realize that I was gay. On our second day there, a couple of girls wearing bikinis hung out with us on the beach. Just try to picture that for a moment. Feeling sort of jealous and definitely confused, I decided that I would speak to as many girls as I could, and I did. However, Arturo did the same thing, yet it worked."

"What worked?"

"It turns out that we were both speaking to all of these girls to make each other jealous."

"Oh, got it."

"Anyways, it was during summer, so when the trip was over, I left for Los Angeles. I couldn't eat or sleep when I first arrived in LA because I missed Arturo. On the second week, Arturo called me to ask when I would be back in Miami. I told him in a month."

Arturo replied, "That long?"

I told him, "Yes. Why? Do you miss me?"

To my surprise, Arturo answered, "Yes, I do."

From that night on, we spoke to each other every night before bedtime. By the time I came back to Miami, we had revealed our true feelings for one another and have been together ever since."

"Does Daphne know?"

"Yes, of course, my sister knows, and so does my mother. My mom calls Michael her third son, and she loves him very much we all do. That's why today after my father said those things to Michael, my mother asked my father for a divorce before she kicked him out of the house."

"Arturo, does that mean your parents are getting a divorce?"

"Yes, Tonya, but they haven't been happily married for years. Why else would my father go back home to Peru and accept a job while he was there on vacation?"

"You have a good point there, Arturo."

"Thank you, Denise."

"My mother told us afterward that we're all better off without my father if he can't accept us for who we are. Then Daphne replied, your right, mom, Dad only comes to town to torture us for ten days anyway."

We all laughed, and Michael said, "I love that girl, Daphne. She always says whatever is on her mind."

Arturo smiled before saying, "You should also know that Daphne doesn't want the traditional Quinceanera anymore."

"No way, Arturo, how could your sister do that to Carmen?"

"It's simple, Sammy. My father is only in town because my sister is having a Quinceanera, so she has decided that she wants to have a formal party instead."

"I don't get it. What does that mean exactly?"

"Tonya, that means Daphne still wants the party and to see Greg in a tuxedo." We all went to laughing when we realized she just wants to change the name of her event."

"Arturo, where is your father now?"

"I don't know, and I don't care, Michael. I only cared about you and wanted to know that you were okay." Michael's eyes teared up as Arturo hugged him.

Michael pulled away from Arturo and told him, "Stop saying nice things to me. You're going to make me cry in front of the girls."

After watching a movie with Michael, Arturo dropped us off at my place. The girls went into the living room while I headed into my mom's room. I was about to tell my mom what happened at Daphne's house when she told me she already spoke to Carmen and is aware of what happened earlier today.

"All I want to know is where have you been?"

"Mom, we bought pizza and went to Michael's house."

"Did the girls come back here with you?"

"Yes, everyone except for Daphne."

"What do you girls have planned for tonight?"

"Nothing, I have to walk Daisy, and we plan on staying here."

"That sounds good. I will leave you to it."

"Okay, bye, mom."

I opened her bedroom door about to leave when my mom said, "Sam, the next time your plans change. Call me to let me know where you are."

"Mom, I'm sorry I should have called you. I didn't mean to make you worry."

"I would have been worried if you weren't with Arturo. Now go walk Daisy before she leaves a puddle in the house."

When I left my mom's room, I put Daisy on her leash and walked out to the living room.

"Do you girls want to go for a walk with us?"

"Sure, let's go, Sammy. Maria surprised me with her exuberant response.

We walked over by the clubhouse, and the Sanchez boys were sitting down at the picnic tables.

"You're here," Eddie exclaimed with excitement. Lewis ran up to Tonya and hugged her while Julio walked over to me with a bright smile. He didn't say a word as he took Daisy's leash from my hand and led us over to the picnic table.

Maria sat down and asked, "Is this what you guys do when we're not here?"

Alex smiled at Maria, then reached for her hand before he answered, "Yes, because we're miserable, so we sit here and console one another."

"Well, I'm feeling better now that my baby's here," Eddie said as he wrapped his arms around Denise.

"We're leaving. We will be back in a little bit."

"Julio, where are you going?"

"To walk Daisy, of course," Julio told Eddie with a beaming bright smile.

Tonya yelled out, "Enjoy Muñeca."

Julio replied, "Don't worry; we will." Now we were on the sidewalk, and he was talking and walking at a rapid pace.

"I thought you were sleeping over at Daphne's house."

"Yeah, me too."

"I'm happy you're not so you could be here with me tonight." Suddenly, he stopped walking and kissed me gently on the lips, then began walking again.

"I look forward to my evenings with you and Daisy."

When we reached the golf course, Julio dropped Daisy's leash. He bent down to pick it up and picked me up instead. "Julio, what are you doing?" He spun me around, and Daisy ran beside Julio in a circle barking happily. Julio kissed me again before he set me back down and picked up Daisy. She went crazy, whimpering and giving Julio kisses. He set her back down, holding onto her leash, and took my hand. "I'm not sure, Julio, but I think Daisy loves you more than anybody."

"Samantha, I'm just so happy to see you," and he kissed me again. He was looking into my eyes when he continued to say, "My day is only rewarding when it's spent with you, Mi Corazón." He placed his hands on either side of my cheeks. I closed my eyes as he tilted my head back and kissed me. This time I felt his tongue brush past mine, and I was instantly swept off my feet with this elated feeling. It was so intoxicating that I just wanted to remain out here, kissing this boy forever until Daisy started barking at us.

We pulled apart, and Julio was left with a goofy grin on his face that made me laugh. "What's so funny, Mi Corazón?"

"It's nothing, but I think someone is getting jealous, and I need to share you with her."

Julio said, "Come here, Daisy." He tapped on his chest, and Daisy stood up on her hind legs and placed her two front paws up on his shoulders, wagging her tail.

"Whoa, when did she learn to do that?"

"That's nothing. Look what else Daisy can do." Julio taught her to roll over, sit, speak, pick up her leash, and give paw.

"Aw, that's cute." I ran over to Daisy to hug her.

"Samantha, now we have a big problem. I don't have any treats for Daisy. Every time she follows a command, I reward her with a treat."

"You can give Daisy a biscuit. I have plenty upstairs."

"No, Sammy, those won't work. She wants the treats that I make for her."

"Daisy's not fussy. She loves any kind of treats."

"I disagree. Daisy refused to do any tricks for me until I gave her beef chunks."

"Julio, what is that?"

"You know, the chunks of beef your mom uses in her beef stew."

"What?"

"Allow me to explain, Samantha."

"Go ahead, Julio, you have my attention."

On the third day that you were gone, I went by your house to walk Daisy. Your mom made stew and asked me if I would like a cup. Of course, I said yes, her stew is fantastic. While I was eating, I decided to wave a piece of beef in front of Daisy. I put out my hand and told her to give me a paw, and she did it, so I gave her the beef chunk. Ever since then, I would go to the store and buy a small pack of beef chunks to cook up for Daisy as a reward."

"How long did it take you to teach her all these tricks?"

"A week, but if I don't have the beef chunks, she won't do the tricks."

"How did you get her to do the commands now?"

"Samantha, I just told her, and she did them."

"Well, it sounds to me like Daisy has graduated. Which means you don't need to bribe her anymore. Besides, we never give Daisy people food. If it makes you feel better when we get back to my apartment, you can give her a biscuit."

"Okay, I will give her a biscuit, but Mi Corazón, she loves the beef chunks." I just started laughing, and Daisy barked.

"You see, she wants the beef chunks."

"Julio, you're so silly. Daisy barked because she's happy."

"Samantha, do you want to sit by the lake and talk?"

"I would love that, Julio, but it's after my curfew."

"Come on, let's get you home then." We walked back to the picnic tables, and everybody was quiet.

"What's going on?"

Denise looked up at me with tears in her eyes and said, "The boys just told us they're leaving next month."

"Is that why you wanted to sit by the lake, Julio?

My eyes were watering up, and my nose was starting to run. When Julio squeezed my hand, I whispered, "Can we go back to the lake now?" Julio nodded his head, yes, with tears in his eyes as we left the picnic table. We sat down under our tree with Daisy beside us. "Now that we're here, please tell me everything I need to know, Julio. I don't need any more surprises."

"Samantha, we all assumed that we would be allowed to spend our summer here."

"But that's not the case, is it?"

"No, it's not."

"When are you leaving, Julio?"

"In 29 days. The day after school, let's out on a Saturday at seven o'clock in the morning. My uncle Gio bought the plane tickets today when he picked up my sister Monica from the airport."

"Your sister already left?"

"Yes, because she's pregnant. They don't want her traveling as it is so close to her due date."

"That makes a lot of sense."

"My uncle Gio has never had any kids of his own. He loves my sister as if she were his daughter. She will stay with him in Anaheim. My mom will leave in two weeks to be with my sister. Lewis, Eddie, and I will be the last ones to leave in 29 days."

"What about all of your furniture and belongings?"

"That will all stay here with Alex. He was hired to work at the post office, so he's definitely staying here."

"I wish you could stay with him, Julio."

"Me too, that's why I asked, but my mom said, no." His voice cracked when he said no. We both sat in silence, holding one another for what must have been hours. Alex showed up and told us it was late, and we need to go home.

"Alex, can we have five more minutes?"

"No, I'm sorry, Julio. Mom sent me out here to find you after she got off the phone with Ms. Harris. Sammy should have been home a long time ago."

That's when we stood up and walked back to my building in complete silence. When I walked inside with Daisy, the only light on was over the kitchen stove.

This meant my mom had been up to check on me. She always turns on the light above the stove when I'm outside late with Daisy. I gave Daisy her biscuit and told her it was from Julio. I walked inside my room and went straight to the window. Julio was standing downstairs below my window, looking up. I waved to him and blew him a kiss. He placed both hands over his heart and smiled. That's when I noticed Alex standing behind him, and they both waved bye to me as they walked away.

"Did he tell you everything, Muñeca?"

"I guess so, Tonya." She climbed out of bed and wrapped her arms around me. I laid my head down on her shoulder, and we both cried.

"At least we have each other, Muñeca." I nodded my head yes as I stood up and wiped away the tears. "Where are you going?"

"I'm headed to the bathroom to wash my face, then to bed."

"Okay, Muñeca, just be sure to turn off the lights when you come back and stay on your side of the bed."

Sunday morning, my mom came into my room to wake us up. "Girls, I need you to get up right away. I already made breakfast, and it's on the table. Remember today is Daphne's big day, so you girls have a long day ahead of you." Tonya climbed out of bed first and put on her bathrobe as she tossed my robe over to me.

"Hurry up, Muñeca; I'm starving, plus we still need to wake up, Denise and Maria." Immediately after breakfast, my mom drove us to the seamstress to pick up our dresses. Our second stop was to Carmen's hair salon. Everyone had their hair washed, blow-dried, then put up into a ponytail with tons of curls and bobby pins.

Our third stop was to Daphne's house, where we had our makeup session with Michael.

He applied a peach color to our eyelids and cheeks with brown mascara. My mom handed out a jewelry box to each of us with a set of pearl earrings inside for us to wear. We were allowed to sit on the couch to watch TV for thirty minutes before getting dressed. Our dresses were identical in baby blue satin with a navy blue velvet bow that ran around the waist and hung down in the back. The seamstress added the velvet bows to the dresses last night.

Carmen was thrilled to see us all dressed and ready for the party. It was her vision that we were wearing. She picked out everything from our hairstyles to the dresses and makeup.

"When can we see Daphne?"

"At the party, Denise, no one will be allowed to see Daphne beforehand."

"Well, that's sort of disappointing, Carmen. Since we have been anxiously looking forward to seeing Daphne in the dress, she talked about all week."

"And you will Tonya at the party tonight."

The day was flying by, and it was time to head to the banquet hall. When we walked inside, the first thing I saw was the dance floor with a DJ booth beside it. As I looked around the room, I noticed mirrors on the walls along with six round tables, each set for ten. Carmen told us each table had assigned seating but not to worry about it because we would all sit together beside Pilar's boys. Tonya picked up the name card in front of her and said, "Muñeca, look, I'm sitting in Julio's seat. I have his card."

I started to giggle before saying, "Tonya, I don't need to look at the card your always in his seat."

"That's true, but I promise to move once he gets here."

Tonya went back to reading all of the name cards on the table. When she was through, Tonya announced that Daphne and Greg wouldn't be sitting with us tonight.

"I don't care where they sit as long as I can see Daphne in her dress."

"Denise, I'm sure they will pull up two chairs and sit with us at some point."

"You think so, Sammy?"

"Yes, I do. By the end of the party, Greg will be sitting beside Julio, talking about guy stuff like they always do."

"Well, it's no secret that wherever Greg goes, so doesn't Daphne.

"Exactly."

My chair faced the entrance, so I watched the door waiting for Julio to arrive. I was feeling a bit excited to see him in a tuxedo. Especially after seeing how nice Michael, Arturo and Javier looked in theirs. Finally, Julio was here, and I couldn't take my eyes off him. He looked gorgeous in his tux with his hair gelled back and that handsome smile on his face. He leaned down with his piercing brown eyes staring back at me and whispered, "Mi Corazón, you look beautiful," as he kissed me. The minute I heard his voice and felt his lips brush up against my cheek, I had butterflies. Then I got a whiff of his cologne right before he pulled his head away, and that left me feeling surprised and lightheaded. Once everyone sat down, the photographer came over to our table to take pictures of us.

While the photographer took our picture, I whispered, "You look incredible, Julio, and you smell fantastic. He turned just his eyes to me as I saw the flash from the camera. "I have to be honest. I wasn't expecting you to smell so good." Now Julio was grinning when I pulled my head away from him after taking the final picture.

"Muñeca, where is your mom? I have not seen your mom or Carmen since we walked inside. Do you want to walk around the room? Maybe we can find out which table she has been assigned to."

"Okay, if you want, Tonya."

"I do, Muñeca," and she stood up.

Julio stood up when I did. "Where are you going?" he asked me with a look of concern.

"I'm going to look for my mom with Tonya."

"Do you want me to go with you?"

"No, that's alright. Stay here. I will be back in a second."

We said hi to several relatives of Daphne's that we had seen a few times. Then Tonya pointed out another table that was at the end of the dance floor.

It was set up like the rest of the tables with a white linen tablecloth and a flower arrangement in the center, except this table was rectangular and faced the dance floor. Then there was also a big chair in the middle with armrests covered in white satin with a navy-blue velvet bow tied in the back. Tonya pointed to the bow, and we agreed that had to be Daphne's chair. Before we could make it back to our table, the lights went dim. By the time we reached our table, there was music playing and a spotlight shining down on the dance floor. I kissed Julio on the cheek and whispered, "Te

Amo, Julio." He pulled his head back and looked at me with a startled expression.

He took my hand under the table then whispered, "Te Amo, Mi Corazón," and he kissed me softly on my temple. We were both staring at one another, grinning from ear to ear. Even when I was engaged in a conversation with Maria, I found myself looking back at Julio. It was like I could not keep my eyes off him.

He leaned in and asked, "Do I look nice enough for you, Samantha?"

"Julio, I would marry you just to see you in a tuxedo again."

Now he was smiling so big that his eyes were beaming before saying, "That will happen one day, Samantha," he squeezed my hand and searched my eyes.

"What?"

Just as Julio was about to explain, the spotlight on the dance floor started moving in a circular motion, and a drum roll began. Then out walked Daphne from behind a red velvet curtain looking stunning in a navy-blue satin ball gown with off the shoulder straps. She was wearing a silver tiara with her hair down in big flowing curls. Daphne was escorted by her mother and her oldest brother Javier. The DJ announced the first dance with Daphne would be with her brother Javier. Right before the music came on, Carmen left the floor.

We all watched Daphne dance in her gown, and it was mesmerizing. She looked as though she was floating around the dance floor. Prior to the next song, Carmen walked up to our table, asking, "Is everyone ready for the traditional waltz?" We all sat up with a puzzled expression.

Tonya said, "I thought we weren't doing this anymore." However, Carmen must not have heard her because she continued to tell us to line up with our partners beside the floor and wait until we have been announced. When the first dance was over, while everyone was applauding, Javier left, and out came Greg.

Then the DJ announced, "To reflect on elegance and grace, Daphne and her friends will be performing the waltz." I was trembling as we walked onto the dance floor.

Julio murmured, "Don't be nervous, Mi Corazón. I will guide you every step of the way," and he winked at me. From that moment on, I was no longer nervous and just allowed Julio to take the lead.

We flowed along with the music, and every move felt effortless, instead of calculated. When the dance was over, while everyone was clapping, we took turns hugging Daphne before walking back to our table.

The moment we reached our table, the DJ spoke again, saying, "The traditional salsa will now be performed."

In a state of panic, we all ran back over to the dance floor with Denise asking Tonya, "Did Carmen tell you we had to perform both dances?"

"No, she only mentioned the waltz."

All of a sudden, the velvet curtain pulled open, and my mom walked out escorted by Michael, followed by Pilar and Arturo. Finally, Carmen walked out onto the dance floor, accompanied by her eldest son Javier. They all stood in a circle around Greg and Daphne. When the music started to play, our moms began to dance.

As my jaw hit the ground, I looked back at everyone and saw the same shocked expression on everybody else. Obviously, this was always meant to be a surprise and took some planning because watching them dance was amazing. Carmen definitely held some sort of dance practice for the moms too, and they had on matching dresses and heels. Tonya smiled at me, saying, "Now, this is amazing."

Alex told Julio, "Look at Mom. She's finally happy."

When the dance was over, Alex walked up to Arturo to thank him for not only dancing with his mom but for bringing back her smile. "Oh, it has been a lot of fun, and we had a blast, Alex. No need to thank me. It was all my mom's idea anyway."

"Arturo, I still can't believe my mom was out there dancing the salsa. I have not seen my mom dance like that in many years.'"

"Did you know about this, Sammy?"

"No, I had no idea, Alex, but I loved it."

The minute we sat back down at our table; I noticed the table in front of the dance floor was occupied. Michael, Arturo, Javier, Carmen, Daphne, Greg, Pilar, and my mom were seated at this table. Daphne was sitting down in her satin chair, looking like a princess on her throne.

"Tonya, I know where my mom is sitting now."

"Yes, your mom is sitting at the married couple's table."

"What?"

"Muñeca, I feel like we're at Daphne and Greg's wedding."

"Does anyone else feel that way?"

"Yes," we all said at the same time, and everyone broke out laughing.

"Boy, you guys sure know how to dance. No wonder you guys didn't have to attend dance practice with us at Daphne's house."

"Denise, I would have loved to attend a practice with you."

"Thank you, Eddie, but you don't need it. Why do you and your family know how to dance so well?"

"We're Latin, baby. It's in our genes." We all started cracking up at Eddie's explanation. "Do you want to dance with me some more?"

"I would like to dance with you again." That's when Eddie stood up and led Denise back out to the dance floor. The food arrived at the table a few minutes later.

While we were eating, Julio began to tell everyone about his day with Greg. "Today, Greg asked me to come along with him to do everything."

"Everything like what Julio?"

"Well, for starters, Tonya, Greg had his hair cut at Carmen's salon."

"No way. How short is it?"

"His hair goes right past his shoulders now. You can't tell because Carmen slicked his hair back and put it into a ponytail. What is really funny is that Carmen tied a blue ribbon around the end of his ponytail. It looked genuinely nice until Greg lost the ribbon, and oh man, did he flip out."

"Oh, that's sweet. Greg just wanted to look perfect for Daphne's birthday."

"Yes, well, I also had my hair done there because I wanted to look my best for you, Samantha."

"Your hair looks nice, Julio, and I like your hair like that."

"Thank you, Mi Corazón."

Julio was smiling big time while he continued to tell us about his day with Greg. "When we left the salon, we had to pick up the tuxedos. Greg had to have his jacket altered and was asked to try it on one last time to make sure it fits properly. Greg put on the jacket and looks at himself in the mirror, and that's when he first noticed the ribbon was gone. We searched the store for an hour, but no ribbon was ever found. Finally, the man running the store asked Greg what's wrong, and it turns out they have plenty of ribbon. They cut a piece of blue ribbon for Greg, and it looks identical to what Carmen tied to his hair. When we leave the store, Greg climbs back into the car and finds the original ribbon."

We all broke out laughing, and Denise said, "Aww, that's sweet, and Greg looks great tonight, so Daphne must be ecstatic."

"They both look fantastic. Especially, Daphne, she looks like a princess."

"Yes, they both look like they belong on top of a cake, Mi Corazón."

"Julio, that's not nice."

"I agree with him, Muñeca."

"Oh, boy, I know you do, Tonya."

When Julio was finished eating, he placed his arm around the back of my chair, and I could smell his cologne. The smell was driving me crazy. "Julio, what is that cologne you're wearing?"

"It's the one you gave me for my birthday, and today is the first time I'm wearing it. Do you like the way it smells on me?"

"Yes, maybe a bit too much."

"I'm glad, Mi Corazón. I wanted to smell good for you."

"Then you succeeded, Julio, the smell on you is actually rather captivating."

Julio had a mischievous grin on his face when he turned to me and said, "That's good to know." Then he whispered, "You keep me captivated every day, and he kissed me on my temple."

I giggled and shook my head before asking, "How do I do that?"

"You're doing it right now."

"Doing what, Julio?"

"You're keeping me captivated with your beautiful smile and the sound of your laugh."

The music was back on, and Julio stood up and asked me to dance. As soon as I smiled, he held out his hand to help me up before walking me out to the dance floor.

Everybody from our table eventually joined us. While we danced to 'Open Your Heart' by Madonna. The next song was by Lionel Richie 'Say You Say Me,' and the whole room suddenly erupted with applause. I turned my head and saw Daphne with her arms wrapped around Greg dancing beside us. The DJ continued to play three more slow songs until he announced it was time to cut the cake. Then it was wheeled out on a cart. It was a three-tier cake, all white with blue bows and silver balls. After Daphne blew out her candles, everyone walked back to their table to sit down. While the cake was being served, Carmen, Javier, and Arturo thanked everyone for joining them to celebrate Daphne's birthday tonight.

"Maria, what about the religious ceremony and the changing of the shoes?"

"I don't know, Tonya, but I know Daphne just wanted to have a formal birthday party."

"Yeah, but we also had to dance the waltz tonight, and her cousins didn't even dance with us. It's supposed to be seven couples, not five."

"Tonya, look around the room. Her cousins are not here. They never showed up. That's because her cousins are from her father's side, and her father refused to attend his own daughter's birthday party."

"That should not matter, Maria. They're still her cousins, and they live here in Miami. I don't understand why they didn't come."

"You would have to ask Carmen about that, Tonya. I don't have all the answers to everything you're asking about."

When the party was over, my mom came over to our table. "Well, girls, are you ready to go now?"

"Yes, Ms. Harris," the girls answered in unison.

"Sam, are you alright?"

"Yes, Mom, I'm good."

"Okay, I guess you're just sleepy because you're the only one who didn't answer me."

"I'm sorry, mom, my mind was on something else."

"That's fine. We need to get going." I hugged Julio and kissed him on the cheek before I left. We all climbed into my mom's car to head home.

"Did you girls all have fun tonight?"

"Yes, we had a great time, Ms. Harris. Thank you for driving us around all day and helping us get dressed."

"It was my pleasure, Denise. I enjoyed every minute of it."

"Ms. Harris, I thought we weren't supposed to dance tonight."

"Tonya, after Carmen spent all that money on the dresses and makeup. Pilar and I convinced Carmen that everyone deserved to see the dance, especially her. We performed our dance too, for the same reason."

"That was incredible, Mom."

"Thank you, Sam."

"Yes, Ms. Harris, that was an awesome surprise."

"Now that's good to hear, thank you, Tonya.

"You all looked so beautiful."

"Do you really think so, Denise?"

"Definitely," we all answered at the same time.

"I have to be honest, girls, we practiced twice a week for about a month with Arturo, Michael, and Javier. Carmen is an excellent instructor. She was very patient with Michael and me. We had no idea what we were doing."

"It didn't look like that tonight. You were fantastic, Mom."

"Yeah, you were great," Maria said.

"We all enjoyed seeing you out there dancing."

"Thank you, girls. I have to admit tonight was a lot of fun. Pilar and I enjoyed watching all of you dance the waltz with her boys. Did you know they learned a lot of these types of dances by the time they were seven-years-old?"

"No, Eddie told us it was because he was Latin that he knows how to dance so well."

My mom laughed before telling us, "Tonight meant the world to Carmen and Daphne, so please be sure to thank Carmen for everything when you see her again."

"Ms. Harris, I will be sure to do that."

"I know you will, Maria, thank you."

"Okay, now that we're home, you girls better hurry up and get Daisy out for a walk. I'm sure those boys won't be at the picnic tables waiting forever."

"Mom, you know about that?"

"Oh, honey, like I've told you before, Pilar and I talk about everything. Just do me a favor and change out of those dresses first."

Chapter 13 Day Twenty-seven

"Muñeca, get up. We only have 27 days left."

"What?"

"You're wasting day 27."

"No, I'm not. Everyone is still sleeping at this time, Tonya. Only chickens, and you are up this early."

"Julio's up. I just saw him outside by the pool now."

"No, he's not. I'm not falling for that again, Tonya."

"Yes, he is Muñeca. I just saw him when I was jogging with Lewis."

"How long ago was that?"

"I just came back, so it was like five minutes ago, and Julio asked about you."

"Oh yeah, what did he want to know, Tonya?"

"Well, Julio asked...

"Uh-huh, go ahead. I'm listening?"

"If I tell you Muñeca, you have to promise you won't be mad at me."

"Wait. Why? What did you say?"

"Muñeca, you have to promise."

"Alright, I promise, tell me what you said, Tonya."

Tonya stood up and walked over to my window and said, "Julio wanted to know if you intend to waste day 27 by spending it in bed." Now she was giggling, and when she turned around to face me, I threw a pillow at her face.

"Hey, you promised not to get mad at me."

"Yeah, well, you told me that you spoke to Julio."

"Only because it's day 27, and I don't want you to waste a single day that you have left."

"Gee, thank you, Tonya, but if that's the case, then why are you here with me? Shouldn't you be with Lewis spending day 27 together?"

"I would be but...

"But what?"

"He's sleeping in this morning since we couldn't go jogging because it's raining." I took another pillow and threw it at her head just as she was about to sit down on the edge of my bed. Tonya tried to duck, but it was too late. The pillow struck her right in the face, and she fell off the bed. Tonya hit the floor, screaming, "Crap, what was that for?"

"You even lied about going jogging, Tonya."

"You're not thanking me now, but you'll thank me one-day, Muñeca, for not allowing you to waste the day in this bed." I just pulled the covers over my head and yelled at her to go away.

Right after that, my mom walked into my room. "I can hear you two from my bedroom. Since you're both up, who's going to help me make breakfast?"

We both replied, "Me." Then I hit Tonya one more time with a pillow before dropping it onto my bed. Tonya looked at the pillow then at me, shaking her head. We both walked into the kitchen to help my mom with breakfast. We made a spinach and cheese quiche along with a pitcher of orange juice. Tonya placed the pitcher in the fridge to stay cold while my mom put the quiche into the oven to bake. Then we stood there in the kitchen watching my mom take out three champagne flutes and the ice bucket. Tonya looked over at me with her quizzical brow.

I shrugged my shoulders, giving her a blank look when she pointed to my mom. I nodded my head, yes, before asking, "Mom, who is that for?"

"That's for Pilar and Carmen. We are going to have a mimosa with brunch."

Tonya's eyes were bulging out of her head, and her mouth dropped open. I ignored the impulse to laugh and asked, "When are they coming over?"

"Oh, the ladies should be here in about an hour. I'm going to make them another quiche with ham, cheese, green peppers, and onions."

"Ew, I hate green peppers."

"Who cares? It's not for you, Tonya."

"Duh, I know that, Muñeca. I was just making a statement."

"Yeah, one that doesn't matter because that's not what you're eating, Tonya."

"Muñeca, do you need more beauty sleep? Because right now, you are not very pretty with that attitude."

"I'm sorry, maybe that has something to do with the way I was woken up this morning."

"Or maybe the problem is that you're not entirely awake yet, Muñeca."

"I'm standing here making breakfast, aren't I?" When Tonya did not respond, I turned around to face her, and she sprayed me in the face with the dish sprayer from the sink. I reached over and snatched the spray gun out of her hand and slipped. I grabbed Tonya on the way down, and she ended up on the puddle of water on the floor beside me.

We were both laughing as my mom stood over us, frowning. "I hope the two of you have gotten everything out of your system.

Now I need this kitchen floor cleaned up, and you have 30 minutes to do it. If you need me, I will be in my room." When my mom left, Tonya smacked the puddle on the floor, splashing water on me, and I pulled away. "I don't think that bit of water even matters now since you already look like a wet rat Muñeca."

"You do too, Cuban Booty." Tonya stood up first and put out her hand to help me up. I grabbed the mop out of the closet, and Tonya grabbed the bucket. We had the floors clean and the counters dry in less than a minute. I looked over at Tonya, and she whispered, "It was worth it."

"Yeah, it was."

Tonya put her arm over my shoulders as we walked into my brother's room, yelling, "It's day 27. Get up before you sleep the day away."

Denise and Maria sat up startled. "Come on, girls, it's time to get out of bed."

"Okay, just don't yell anymore, and I will get up."

Tonya and Denise walked out of the room when Maria asked, "Why do we have to get up now? It's still early."

"Well, for starters, your mother-in-law will be here in less than an hour."

"Who?"

"Pilar, she will be here in less than an hour."

"Oh, Sammy, do you think Alex will marry me someday?"

"I don't know is that what you want?"

"It's hard to say for sure, but I think I'm falling in love with him, Sammy. It was devastating to think that Alex might move away."

"Yeah, I know how that feels, Maria."

"Sammy, I'm so sorry. I wasn't thinking."

"Don't worry about it, Maria. She hugged me, and I felt like I was about to cry. "Enough of this emotional stuff, there's no time for it. We need to get ready."

We stood up just as Denise walked back into the room, and Tonya was right behind her, saying, "I've changed my mind, Denise. I'm taking my shower first." When Tonya turned around to leave, Denise stopped her with a pillow to the back of her head. Maria and I ran past them to my room. I was in there long enough to grab my robe before I walked to the bathroom. The water was already running when I slid open the shower door. I jumped, surprised to find Tonya in there, already taking her shower. I quickly slid the door shut as she started to laugh.

"Muñeca, did you honestly think you were going to take a shower before me?"

"Of course not. Enjoy your shower, Ice Princess."

"You know I will because I beat you again, Muñeca," and she started to laugh.

"Yes, you did," I replied as I flushed the toilet before walking out, just in time to hear Tonya scream. My mom caught up to me as I was walking back to my room.

"Sam, did you turn the faucet on while Tonya was in the shower?"

"No, Mom, I flushed the toilet."

My mom was grinning, which meant she was trying not to laugh while she told me, "No more of this stuff when Pilar and Carmen arrive, please."

"Not a problem. I'm done, Mom."

"I hope so," I heard her say under her breath as she headed for the kitchen.

The minute I walked back into my room, Denise asked, "Why aren't you in the shower yet? Pilar will be here soon, and Maria was waiting for you to finish."

"Tonya beat me to the shower, so I flushed the toilet."

"Is that why Tonya screamed?"

"Yes, it is Maria." Denise covered her mouth, appearing shocked, and Maria broke out laughing.

Just then, Tonya walked into my room. "What's so funny?"

"Nothing, how was your shower, Ice Princess?"

"Very funny, Muñeca, that crap was cold."

Everyone laughed even harder, and I stopped laughing long enough to ask, "Does that mean I won?"

After everyone was showered and dressed, my mom asked me to take Daisy outside for her walk. The girls all decided to come with us, and that is when we saw Arturo's car pulling into the parking lot. We all ran down the stairs and up to Arturo's car as he climbed out.

"What are you doing here?"

Michael climbed out of the passenger seat and answered for Arturo, "Well, for starters, we dropped off Carmen."

"Where is she?"

"Carmen walked over to the pool with Daphne."

"Daphne's here already too?"

"Yes."

"Awesome," I looked down and realized Arturo was wearing shorts and a polo shirt.

"Arturo, are you playing in today's soccer game?"

"Yes, it's the last game, so everyone's coming. It should be like the old days on the field. It looks like we will have 11 players on each team for a change."

"Is Greg here yet?"

"No, I don't think so, Maria. He is coming with his cousin Mig. At least that's what Daphne told us about a hundred times on the ride over here." As soon as we laughed, Daisy barked.

"Girls, that means we have to go. Daisy needs to use the bathroom, but we'll see you in a little bit."

We walked over to an area beside my building, where there is a large patch of grass. Daisy loves this spot, and she did her business right away before tugging on her leash to return home.

Carmen and Daphne were sitting in the living room when we came back. We took turns hugging Carmen and thanking her for everything when there was a knock on the door. It was Pilar, and my mom asked me to set the table.

When it was time to take our seats, Tonya, Denise, and Maria sat at the counter, leaving Daphne and me to sit at the table with the moms. My mom brought a quiche to the table. I grabbed the other quiche out of the drawer and set it on the counter for the girls. Once everyone was seated, we held hands while my mom said grace. Afterward, I stood up to cut the quiche into slices.

"What did you think of our dancing girls?"

"It was awesome. Pilar, we couldn't believe our eyes."

Daphne smiled before saying, "Sammy's right, it was incredible. I loved it."

Pilar had the biggest smile I had ever seen on her face as she sat back and told us what happened after the party. "When I arrived home with my boys, Alex said, 'Mom, dance with me.' I looked up at him thinking he was crazy because it

was way past my bedtime until I saw that smile on his face. Then I thought he was just teasing. You have to understand Alex and Eddie are the pranksters in the family, so of course, I didn't believe him until he ran into the kitchen and turned the radio on.

Then I knew my boy was serious and wanted to dance with his mom. We danced to one song, and when it finished, all the boys had formed a line waiting to dance with me. It was a beautiful evening, and I didn't get to bed until I danced with all of them. We laughed so much and had so much fun that it took me forever to fall asleep."

"Those boys are wonderful. They really are Pilar. We are going to miss them and you so much."

"Lori, I will miss you too." My mom and Pilar hugged one another with tears in their eyes.

Pilar wiped away her tears before saying, "Carmen, I have to tell you. The best thing for me had to be dance practice this whole month. It was my outlet, my escape. I needed that break, from all the stress, the kids, everything. I looked forward to it every week." Pilar reached over and hugged Carmen.

"I wish you didn't have to go. I'm going to miss you so much, Pilar."

"I'm going to miss you too, Carmen."

"My eldest son Alex will stay here. I wanted all my children with me, but Alex has chosen to stay here in Miami. Where he will be starting a new job soon, but I am worried about him. Please watch over him for me, Lori."

My mom reached out her hand and held Pilar's. "You know, I will."

"You must promise to visit me once we're settled and in our new place."

"Of course, we will," my mom told Pilar while wiping at the tears that won't stop coming.

"When we first move up to California, we will stay at my eldest brother's house."

"That would be Guillermo, right?"

"Yes, Lori, the one I tried to set you up with."

"He is so handsome, Carmen, and has never been married. I wish you could help me to convince Lori to meet my brother."

"As I said before, I don't need another man in my life. Besides, I am too busy for romance. I work full time and take care of Sam and her brother."

"Your son is away in college, and Sammy will be in high school soon. You can find time now to have some fun too."

"My life is fulfilling enough without a man Pilar."

"I will leave it up to you, Lori. One day hopefully soon, you will change your mind. My house will be ready by the end of the summer. Or should I say it's supposed to be ready by then? My brother Guillermo keeps changing the remodeling plans for the house, so I hope it's ready before school starts. Then you should come to California to visit me, and you too, Carmen."

Carmen held up, her champagne flute and said, "Here's to Pilar and her new adventure in California." My mom, Pilar, and Carmen toasted their champagne glasses, and that is when the tears formed in my eyes. I got up from the table and ran into my room.

Denise, Maria, and Tonya were already in here on the verge of tears themselves. Denise held her arms out to me, and I dove in crying with my head on her shoulder. A few minutes later, Daphne came into my bedroom with Pilar. We all quickly sat up, wiping away our tears. "Girls, I'm so sorry.

It breaks my heart to separate you all from the boys. We have been so lucky to have all of you in our lives. It has torn me up inside, and I have cried many nights over it. We will miss all of you a great deal." When Pilar started to cry, we all hugged her. Daphne waved to the girls, and they all stood up and left the room. It was just Pilar and me alone in my room now.

"Pilar, I know your decision was not an easy one to make. I do realize you are doing what's best for your family.

It just hurts on account of how much I'm going to miss all of you, especially Julio."

"I'm going to miss you too, Sammy, and I know how Julio feels about you. For that reason, I have to admit... Pilar paused to wipe away her tears. "One of the things that have kept me up at night was knowing how this separation is going to hurt you both. Your hearts are one with one another, so I believe in time, everything will work out for the best. Sammy, I hope you will find a way to forgive me. You, Tommy, and your mother have been like family to me. I love you all very much, and I want you all to visit me in Anaheim." Pilar hugged me before she stood up and left my room. I moved to the beanbag chair to stare out the window. After a while, I saw Julio walking by my building with Greg and Lewis. He tapped Greg on the shoulder, then walked up to my window and waved to me. I waved back to him and blew him a kiss. When he left, I ran into the bathroom to wash my face before I grabbed the blankets out from the linen closet. Pilar, Carmen, and my mom were in the living room, talking when I walked in.

"Sammy, are you okay, sweetheart?"

"Yes, Carmen, thank you."

"It's the boys' last soccer game, and they are expecting a large turnout. I just wanted to know if you ladies would join us out on the field to watch the game. "

"Can we come? Would the boys mind?"

"Carmen, the boys would love it if you all attended their final game."

My mom was smiling at me when Pilar said, "Then we better get going, I wouldn't want to be late." We all walked out the door and down to the field together.

Maria and Denise carried the blankets while I held Daisy's leash. When the boys saw us, they were all smiles. Julio ran over to me and picked me up. He spun me around once before leaning his head down to kiss me. His lips were about to touch mine when he left me baffled with a kiss on the cheek and set me down. I looked up at him feeling perplexed until I noticed he was waving to someone behind me with a big smile, so I spun around and saw our moms. They were standing behind me, waving to Julio. I turned my head back around, facing Julio again, feeling a bit embarrassed that I was caught up in the moment and forgot all about our parents. Julio's eyes remained on our parents when he asked, "Are they here to watch us play?"

"Yes."

"Wow, this is the first time my mom has ever been out here."

"Well, then you better give it your all, Soccer Player." I kissed him on the cheek and told him that I had to get going to help layout the blankets for our moms. Julio looked down at me with the same big smile, but I also noticed he had a twinkle in his eyes.

"Okay, Mi Corazón, wish me luck. It's our last game."

"Good luck, Soccer Player, and remember you owe me a kiss on the lips, preferably by the lake later after the game." Julio was grinning, and he winked at me before running back out onto the field. I walked over to where all the girls were standing.

"Who wants to help me layout the blankets?" Daphne grabbed one blanket, and Tonya grabbed another one. We laid all three beach blankets out side by side.

Carmen called Michael over, and he walked up slowly.

"Come have a seat with us."

"Are you sure the girls won't mind, Carmen?"

"You've got to be kidding me. Of course, we don't mind. We want you to sit with us."

"Okay, then, I will Denise, thank you." Michael sat down beside Carmen on the very end of the blanket.

"Michael, are you sure you're comfy?"

"Yes, why, Sammy?"

"It's just that we have plenty of room, Michael, so I want you to relax and enjoy yourself."

Carmen hugged Michael and left him smiling instead of looking all uptight while Daphne ran up to Greg out on the field. Everyone was clapping except for Lewis. He ran up behind Tonya and startled her before kissing her on the cheek. All the boys on the field began yelling out things like "Woohoo" and whistling until Alex and Eddie walked over to the blankets. They spoke with Carmen, my mom, and Pilar first. Then they walked over to where the four of us girls were standing. Eddie grabbed Denise and dipped her back prior to kissing her while Alex picked up Maria in his arms and kissed her gently on the lips before setting her back down. When everybody started clapping, Alex and Eddie ran back out to the field. Then the game began, so everyone sat down to watch.

Every time one of the Sanchez boys ran past us, they would look over at Pilar to make sure she was watching. It was adorable; they were happy she was out here. Julio kicked the ball into the net and scored for his team first. He looked over at his mom immediately afterward, and Pilar

was already standing up, yelling, "Great job, Julio." He definitely heard that and had a vast smile on his face. The game was so much fun to watch, and I was surprised by how many people showed up to play. On the opposite side of the field, three boys were sitting down watching the game instead of playing because they had too many players. The real surprise, though, was Arturo and Alex. They teamed up and made it near impossible for anyone to get the ball away from them.

Nonetheless, my little Julio somehow managed to get the ball away from them on two occasions, and that's when his team took it to the net. Pilar told us, "Julio gets in and moves fast, so Alex is focused on keeping the ball away from him. In the past, he has spent entire games chasing Julio back and forth across that field."

"How do you know that, Pilar? I mean, isn't this your first time watching them play?"

"No, Sammy, I've been watching the boys play soccer since they were little. When they got a bit older, my brother Juan started coaching them out here on this field. I didn't want to interfere, so I stayed away, but my brother Juan spoke to me about what when on after every game."

Pilar stood back up, and I turned my eyes back to the field. Julio was running across the field, kicking the ball with Alex right behind him. Julio pulled his leg back before kicking the ball up and over to Lewis. Once Lewis had the ball, he ran the rest of the way across the field until he was standing in front of goalkeeper Eddie. Arturo caught up to Lewis, and he was able to kick the ball away from him and over to Alex. Now, Arturo and Alex ran side by side across the field, over to the goalkeeper who was Greg. This was becoming intense. We all stood up to see if Alex makes it in for the win when Julio arrived and went for the ball. Alex kicked the ball before Julio, aiming for the net, and came up short of the line.

No point was scored; then Lewis kicked the ball. He sent the ball flying across the field. Mig kicked the ball into the net past Eddie, the goalkeeper. It all happened so fast that everyone was shocked. Julio and Lewis ran up to Mig and hugged him.

They were not paying attention when the ball was tossed back in the game. Arturo and Alex took that soccer ball back across the field within seconds. Alex kicked the ball. Greg failed to block it, and they won. Pilar stood up, clapping while saying, "Great game, everyone!"

We all stood up, clapping along with her, and she cupped her hands around her mouth, yelling out toward the field, "Time to eat!"

"Everyone should have a seat at the picnic tables, and I will bring everything down."

"That sounds great, Pilar and I have a couple of 2 liters of soda upstairs that I can bring along with a bottle of fruit punch."

"That's perfect, Lori."

"I'll have a few of the boys help me bring down the food. I have paper plates and cups upstairs that I bought for today too."

"Okay, Pilar, I will meet you back at the picnic area within five minutes." My mom and Carmen headed back to my building. I bent down to pick up the blankets from the ground when Julio grabbed the end of the last blanket.

"What did you think of the game, Samantha?"

"I enjoyed it; we all did, including your mom." Julio was grinning after I mentioned his mom. "Oh, and your mom said I could have your tamale."

"She made tamales?"

"Yup, but she said I could have yours."

Julio laughed before saying, "If you really want it, it's yours. You can have it."

"What are you talking about over here?"

"Nothing much, Daphne, I just told Julio that his mom made tamales."

"Oh, really?" Greg asked, sounding super excited.

"Crap, you don't tell the garbage disposal about food. Especially my mom's cooking," Alex said from behind us.

Greg replied, "Too late. I already know that we're eating tamales and hmmm, Pilar's Arroz con Pollo.*"

"Okay, well, my mom needs help bringing the drinks down to the picnic tables, and Pilar needs help with the food."

"No problem, I got the food."

Lewis spoke up and told Greg, "No way, Bro. You can help Ms. Harris with drinks," and Alex laughed.

"Alright, you heard him, Greg, it's time to go." Julio took my hand, and the four of us headed back to my place. As we walked inside through the kitchen door, we saw everything set up already to go on the counter. There was a small cooler filled with ice cubes from the ice maker along with two bottles of soda and a bottle of fruit punch.

"Mom, do I take everything on the counter?"

"Yes!" she replied, then added, "I will be out in a minute."

Carmen walked out to tell me, "Your mom is on the phone with your brother. He went to see your dad this weekend, and he has a girlfriend. Your brother is not happy about it."

"If she can make my dad happy, then I'm happy for him. Tommy will be alright."

"Your brother left your father's house, and he's now back at school. When he was supposed to stay until Tuesday with you, dad."

"Don't worry, Carmen. My brother will be fine. Thomas just needs time to adjust to the idea of my dad dating. Please tell my mom that we took the drinks down to the pool."

Daphne walked back out to the kitchen, looking upset. "What's wrong?"

"Sammy, your mom, is on the phone with your brother, and he sounds agitated. I could hear your mom speaking to him over the phone from the bathroom, so I'm worried about you becoming upset too."

"Daphne, I'm okay with my dad having a girlfriend."

"You are, Sammy?"

"Yes, I hope someone can make my dad happy, and I hope my mom will meet someone someday too. My parents have been divorced for over two years, so it's time for them to move on."

"Is that what you're going to do when I'm gone, Sammy?"

"What are you talking about, Julio?"

"Are you going to move on and fall in love with someone else after I'm gone?"

"No, Julio, that's not what I'm expecting to happen, but I'm sure you will forget all about me once you've gone." I left the kitchen and walked into my bedroom.

I heard Daphne say, "Wow, that was a really stupid question." I was sitting on my beanbag chair, looking out the window when Daphne walked in.

"Are you okay?"

"Yeah, I'm great," I replied as I continued to stare out the window.

"Sammy, he didn't mean that. Julio's just upset."

"I'm upset too, and it's not my fault that he's moving away."

"Well, maybe if you weren't going to break up with him when he leaves Sammy."

"Do you think I want to break up with him, Daphne? Should I put off the fated breakup for a later date because it hurts now? Do you think it will hurt less if I wait a week or two?"

"No, I don't know what I'm saying, Sammy, except maybe the long-distance thing can work. I mean, you don't know until you've tried it. "

"Daphne, I can't believe that you of all people would be the one to tell me this. Your mom and dad have lived apart for five years. Your mom hoped the distance would give them time to work out their differences; instead, they grew even further apart. Now, after five years, she's filing for the unavoidable divorce."

"You're right, Sammy. I don't know what you should do." Daphne put her arms around me and hugged me.

I wiped my eyes on her shirt, then told her, "Sorry, they're wet."

She just rolled her eyes before saying, "You're lending me another t-shirt, Sammy." I laughed as I reached into my drawer to pull out another shirt for her to wear. That's when I heard my mom ask Carmen if she was ready.

"We better go, Daphne."

When we walked into the kitchen, Julio was still there, hanging his head down. "Greg was the one who noticed us walk into the kitchen and asked, "Are you ready to go girls?"

Julio lifted his head and stared back at me with a sad look in his eyes. I reached out for his hand, which he held out to me and used to pull me into his arms. "I'm sorry, Samantha. I shouldn't have said that."

"No, you shouldn't have, although I can understand why you did." We locked eyes, but before I could go on, my mom and Carmen walked into the kitchen.

"Oh, you're all still here. Great, we can all go down together."

Julio can carry the cooler, and Greg; you can help out by bringing down the soda. Sam, don't forget the fruit punch."

"I've got it right here, mom."

"Lori, I already have the wine, so everyone's ready to go."

"Carmen, I forgot all about the wine. What would I do without you?"

"You would have to make a second trip or remain sober." The moms laughed the whole way down the stairs. On the way over to the picnic tables, we spotted Pilar ahead of us with Lewis behind her carrying two trays of food. Alex had his van parked up on the grass with the side doors open and the stereo on.

"Muñeca, the boys just came back from the store with a cooler filled with ice and sodas."

"That's fine, Tonya. It's better to have plenty then not enough for everybody."

"Your right Sammy. Now, where's the food?"

"Greg, you're eating last, my friend," Eddie told him, grinning while patting him on the back.

"Don't worry, Greg, I will make sure to feed you. After all, you are my biggest fan."

"Thank you, Pilar." Greg stuck his tongue out at Eddie.

"Whatever, Bro, but keep in mind you won't be able to have seconds until after everyone else has eaten."

"Eddie, that's fine with me, dude, as long as I don't have to wait for the first plate." I looked back at Greg, and he was standing in line behind me with a big smile.

Once Julio had his plate of food, we joined Greg and Daphne at a picnic table. Greg's cousin Mig was sitting with them up until we joined them. It was so bizarre when I sat my plate down on the table Mig gave me a strange look before he stood up and told Greg, "Will talk later, I have to go."

"Okay later, Mig. I'll beep you when I'm done."

"You're leaving already, Mig?"

Mig looked over at me before answering Julio. "Yeah, man, I think so. If I do not see you again, have a safe trip, and good luck in California."

"Thanks, Mig. I appreciate that." Julio high-fived Mig, then he left. Greg was looking back at Mig shaking his head.

"What's up? Is something going on between you guys?".

Greg looked at me, then smiled at Julio before answering, "No, everything's all good, dude."

"You know if it's about you needing a ride home, my brother, Alex, can drop you off."

"Nah, Mig will be back for me later. I just need to beep him after we finish eating."

Julio stood up and told me he was going over to the mom's table to thank them for coming. I watched from my chair as Julio hugged Carmen, and I heard him thanking her for the party last night. Then Alex stood up and rushed over, saying, "Yes, thank you, Carmen. The best part was seeing my mom dancing and smiling. I haven't seen my mom that happy in a long time."

"You see? I told you," Pilar said, laughing. "Even my children know how happy it made me. Thank you again, Carmen. We will leave here with so many memories. That will be a memory that will remain on the top of our list."

One comment was all it took, and I felt the tears form again. I stood up and left the table before anyone could see me falling apart. Julio caught up to me in the parking lot. He did not say a word. He just took my hand as I continued to walk across the lot into my building. When I arrived at my apartment, I fumbled with Daisy's leash, and Julio took the leash from me and called Daisy over. He hooked the leash onto Daisy's collar and took my hand as we left out the door. We walked down to the golf course. A couple of tears were sliding down my cheeks when Julio turned around facing me. He lifted my chin and wiped away my tears with his thumb.

"Please don't forget about me when I'm gone."

Just hearing the word 'gone' triggered even more emotions inside me. I could not answer him. The heavyweight on my chest was too much for me to handle without crying again. I just stood there staring up at him feeling lost in a world of heartache. Julio turned around and bent down, telling me to climb up. Now this made me laugh, and I had to ask," What do you want me to do?"

"Climb on my back, Mi Corazón. There is someplace I want to take you to." I climbed up onto his back and laid my head against his shoulders. Julio stopped walking when we reached the other side of the lake. "I found this a couple of days ago, and I couldn't wait to show it to you."

In front of us was a tree with a tire swing. "You want to try it out? It will help you feel better."

"Why would a tire swing help me feel better?"

"It's going to help you relax. Just try it." Julio convinced me, so I climbed onto the tire. "See? Your feet aren't touching the ground, Samantha. It's just like a regular swing except your sitting on a tire, and soon I'll have you flying through the air." Julio pushed me, and I closed my eyes to focus on the feeling of the wind in my hair. When Julio stopped the swing, he said, "See, you're smiling now. I know what you like. You have to admit that you feel a little better."

"Yes, I do, and your right. It is relaxing. Thank you, Julio." He leaned in and kissed my lips gently before picking me up. Then he carried me back to the lake. "Where's Daisy?" I asked in a panic. Daisy barked at the sound of her name. She was walking right beside Julio. When we were back at the lake, Julio took a seat and pulled me onto his lap. "You know. I could have walked over here on my own."

"I do know that Mi Corazón, but I enjoy holding you as much as I can."

"There's something I want to tell you, but I haven't because I'm afraid it might sound a bit selfish."

"Tell me anyway, Samantha, I want to know everything."

"Okay, here it goes. I enjoy it when we're alone. I enjoy it when you carry me. I enjoy seeing you smile. I enjoy holding your hand. I enjoy kissing your lips and smelling your cologne. I'm going to miss everything about you, Julio."

"Samantha, I have something to admit to you too."

"What is it?"

"It's just that I go to bed every night, thinking that I can't wait to fall asleep because when I wake up, it'll be another day, and I get to see you again.

I can't wait to see your smile and hear your voice. It's music to my ears and my heart. Your laugh fills me with happiness. When you're sad, it tears me apart. My favorite moments have all been with you. My favorite conversations are with you. I love you, Samantha, and I don't want to leave." He wrapped his arm tighter around me and laid his head down on my shoulder.

"Julio, how do I go on every day from here without you? I don't know how to live without you, and I don't want to learn how. I don't want you to leave me." I started to cry as I held onto him tight with both of my hands wrapped around him.

"Mi Corazón, I don't want to be away from you either, and I don't want you to get used to living without me, so who sounds selfish now?"

"Nobody is being selfish, Julio, we're being honest. I'm scared that once you leave, you will stop loving me, and I will never see you again."

"Samantha, I fear the same thing, and it's tearing me apart." I heard his voice crack and felt his teardrops as they fell onto my cheeks and slid down my face. He suddenly pulled his head away from me and raised my chin. Looking into my tear-filled eyes, he said, "Samantha, I love you, and I have only felt this way for you. I can't go on without seeing you. We can visit one another and call each other." I tried to calm down and pay attention to what he was saying when Daisy climbed onto my lap. She went to licking away my tears then Julio's, and we both laughed. After all our tears were gone, she jumped off my lap and sat down beside us. Julio held me in his arms while rocking me back and forth. We sat like this for over an hour until Alex showed up. He was standing under our tree, across the lake.

"Hey, you two. Everyone is worried about both of you. It's getting late, and everybody is getting ready to go. The least you could do is come and say good-bye."

Julio frowned before saying, "Okay, Alex. We're coming now." Alex didn't move a muscle. He waited for us, and we walked back together.

"Look who I found," Alex announced when we arrived back at the picnic tables.

"I should have known the kids were out walking, Daisy," my mom replied with a smile.

Pilar looked back at us, smiling before tapping on her lap, saying, "Come here, Daisy." Julio released her leash, and Daisy took off running to Pilar. She had been petting Daisy for a few minutes when her tongue began to hang out the side of her mouth, which meant Daisy was utterly happy. Then I heard Pilar say, "Sit big girl and hand me your paw." To my surprise, Daisy did precisely what she was told.

"You had your mom help you train Daisy?"

"Oh yeah. She was the one who showed me how to cook the beef chunks. I don't know how to cook anything. Well, except for beef chunks. Oh, and I know how to prepare tamales."

"Yes, you do, Mi Hijo, and you need to learn how to cook."

Julio appeared to be blushing when he replied, "Okay, Mom. I will take a class or something."

"A class? No, you will learn by cooking with me in the kitchen. Did you show Lori all the tricks we taught Daisy?"

"No, Mom. I haven't."

"Oh, that's great. Let me show her."

"She knows tricks, Pilar?"

"Yes, Lori. My son Julio and I taught her a few things."

"Watch," Pilar said as she stopped rubbing Daisy's back. "Daisy, give Lori your paw. Lori put out your hand."

Daisy sat down in front of my mom and stuck out her paw. Then Pilar stood up and moved her index finger in a circle while telling Daisy to roll over. Daisy kneeled and rolled over; it was so cute.

"Wow, Thank you so much. Sammy said she tried to teach Daisy tricks with no success."

"Mom, I didn't have beef chunks."

"Can someone tell me about these beef chunks?"

"Ms. Harris, I used the beef chunks from your beef stew to train Daisy. She's stubborn; without the beef chunks, Daisy wouldn't do anything."

My mom and Carmen were laughing while Pilar nodded her head in agreeance with Julio.

"My mom even drove me to the store to buy a package of beef chunks a couple of times, and she showed me how to cook them. I would usually cook up to three pieces at a time every day until she learned everything."

"Pilar, I have to be honest with you. That's the cutest story I've ever heard."

"I agree with Lori, it's a cute story, and your mom is so kind for going along with this. I can't imagine anyone ever telling you no Julio with how sweet and polite you are."

Pilar grinned and replied, "Oh, it can be difficult at times, Carmen. However, I do manage to tell Julio no ever so often."

An hour later, we left the picnic tables to head back to my apartment with Daisy. Julio came with us, and he handed me Daisy's leash once we reached my front door.

My mom walked inside first, so I quickly pop kissed Julio and told him, "I'll see you tomorrow before school."

Julio was wearing a half-smile on his face when he pulled me into his arms and said, "I can't learn to live without you, Samantha, so I hope you will change your mind and give the long-distance thing a chance." He kissed me

again and waved bye to me with tears in his eyes. I walked inside, feeling horrible like I was on the verge of crying. I just kept thinking our hearts are already broken, and Julio has not even left yet on Day 27.

It is Sunday morning, and Julio just beeped me. That means he is headed over to my place to go for a morning walk with Daisy and me. The minute I opened the backdoor, Julio was standing there in front of the screen door smiling. I have not seen him smile like that in a while. He pulled open the screen door and took Daisy's leash from my hand while I shut the backdoor behind me.

"So, what's up, Julio? Why do you appear to be so happy?"

"The truth is that I'm incredibly happy. I am spending my morning with my two girls. What do you want to do today, Samantha?"

"I would like to spend my day with you, Julio."

"That's great because I want to spend my day with you too." Julio leaned in and kissed me on the cheek. Then he ran around the field with Daisy until they were both worn out. Afterward, we walked back to my place, and I opened the door to let Daisy inside. Julio got down on one knee beside Daisy to hug and kiss her. Daisy gave him in return a ton of kisses, and Julio's eyes became red as he teared up. "I'm going to miss you so much, Daisy." He squeezed her once more, and this time tears were running down his face. She pulled her head back and sat down in front of Julio. Daisy placed both of her paws up on his shoulders and tried to lick away his tears. Then he used his shirt to wipe away the tears and patted her on the head. Daisy suddenly stood up and walked inside. I shut the door behind her, and Julio was looking at me. He had an expression on his face that was breaking my heart.

"We can't do this today; we promised each other we wouldn't worry about what's going to happen." Julio turned his back to me.

"I know I'm the one who said that Samantha, two weeks ago. It's just that it's less than a week before I leave, and I keep hoping that my mom will change her mind."

"Julio, I feel the same way you do." I walked up to Julio and said, "Let's enjoy today and make a memory."

He turned around to face me with a slight smile on his face. I wrapped my arms around him and took in a deep breath. I let it out slowly to prevent myself from crying. Julio kissed me before saying, "You need to go put on a pair of jeans. Greg and Daphne will be here soon with Maria."

"Why? Where are we going?"

"We're going roller skating.

"Really? Oh, I can't wait, Julio."

"I'm glad you're excited, Mi Corazón. I am too. Now don't forget your skates. I will be back here in thirty minutes."

"Okay, see you then," I ran inside to get ready. I walked into my mom's room and asked if it was okay if I went skating.

"Who are you going with, Sam?"

"Julio."

"Wait. What time are you going?"

"I don't know."

"What about breakfast or brunch?"

"I'm not sure, Mom, but I'm not really hungry. I'm just excited that I'm finally going to the skating rink with Julio."

"Well, you can go after you eat. Remember it is a school night, and even though it's the last week of school, it's also the most important week for you.

The SATs start tomorrow and will continue until Wednesday. I want you to be well-rested. These assessments will decide where you will go to college."

"I know, Mom. I will make it back home early. I promise."

"Okay, go get ready; I'm sure Julio will be back here soon." I went to my room and put on a pair of thick socks and jeans. I put my hair up into a ponytail and sprayed some perfume. When I opened the front door, my mom was outside speaking to Julio. I walked out the door, and they stopped talking. Julio put out his hands, and I handed him my skates. My mom had a concerned look on her face. "Sam, do you have your beeper?"

I opened my purse and looked inside. "Yes, Mom. I have it."

"Great, I should see you again in a little bit."

"What do you mean, mom?" My mother rolled her eyes at me while shaking her head. Julio took my hand and told me we needed to head down to the pool. That grabbed my attention, so I waved bye to my mom and jogged down the stairs. When we reached the picnic tables, Julio picked me up and spun me around twice. He stopped to kiss my lips when our eyes locked on one another.

"You smell so good, Mi Corazón."

"I wanted to smell good for you. I'm glad you like it, Soccer Player. Now, do you ever plan on kissing me?"

Julio leaned in, and we closed our eyes when I heard, "Who are we still waiting for, Muñeca?"

Our eyes instantly popped open, and we were staring back at one another, grinning when I answered Tonya by saying, "I think we're still waiting on Greg and Daphne?" I was still looking at Julio with my eyebrows arched when I asked him, "Am I right?"

"Yes, you are Mi Corazón."

"Well, I can't wait to show you my moves at the skating rink, Tonya. I can skate. You can ask Julio."

"I believe you, Lewis, either way, you have to show me those moves today. We'll be at the skating rink by two o'clock, so the truth will be revealed."

"Wait. Two o'clock?" Julio suddenly had a frown on his face, and he set me down. We both had a seat at the picnic table beside Tonya and Lewis.

"Tonya, it's only nine o'clock. What are we doing until then?"

Lewis shook his head with a smirk on his face while Tonya stood up, asking Julio, "Did she forget?"

"Yes."

"And you didn't bother to remind her, Julio?"

"No, I didn't, Tonya."

"Why not? Is it because you didn't want her to get upset again?"

"Yup."

"Remind me about what, Tonya?"

"I have to tell her; I'm not going to wait until we're there, Julio."

Tonya retook her seat and said, "The farewell brunch that your mom and Carmen put together for the boys is today."

"Wow, I forgot all about that," I covered my mouth, feeling ashamed as I looked over at Julio.

"I'm so sorry, Julio." I stood up and wrapped my arms around him, whispering, "I'm sorry about this morning too."

"It's okay, Samantha. I honestly haven't been looking forward to this brunch. It just makes everything seem final and that I have to accept that I'm actually leaving. That's why I was upset this morning, and I was trying to spare you from becoming upset too."

"Oh, Julio," was all I was able to get out before the tears arrived. He pulled up the hem of his shirt and wiped away my tears then gently kissed me on the cheek. That's when Daphne and Greg showed up telling us that everybody was already at the van waiting for us. We pulled up to the restaurant, and it was the same place we celebrated Daphne's birthday at before her formal party.

"A Mexican restaurant for breakfast?" Julio asked, looking at me.

"Yes, they have a champagne brunch on Sundays, Julio. Which means our mothers are going to get toasted on mimosas instead of margaritas this time Sammy."

"Wow, I didn't know all that, but now that I do, I think you might be right, Daphne."

"That's okay. I brought my driver's license. If they get toasted, I can drive them home."

"Eddie, does that mean you are not going with us to the skating rink?"

"Yes, Daphne, today, I plan to spend the day at the pool with Denise."

Alex told the hostess we had a reservation, and I saw her look at the chart on the podium. She grabbed a stack of menus and told us to follow her. We were back in the same room from last time. Only this time, an additional four-seat table pushed up against the main table, making it a total of 16 seats.

Greg sat down, rubbing his hands together before saying, "I'm ready to eat."

Lewis and Eddie told him, "You eat last, bro!" We all broke out laughing.

"Man, where is Pilar when I need her? She is the only one who appreciates my appetite."

"Daphne, if you ever marry Greg, I hope you become a millionaire, so you can afford to feed him!"

The waiter came over to our table to take down everyone's drink order, and he told us to help ourselves to the food stations whenever we want. Greg stood up first, and we all followed him into the atrium. There were seven stations here, each with a silver dome filled with a variety of food. You could select from breakfast or lunch items or have both. All the boys grabbed a plate and filled it with eggs, sausage, and breakfast *burritos*. Tonya and I chose the Mexican casserole, which had sausage, egg, peppers, and cheese. I also found the dome with breakfast meats, where we picked up some bacon for Tonya. Daphne was in line waiting for the chef to prepare a breakfast *taco* for her filled with chorizo, eggs, and potato. At the same time, another chef was preparing huevos rancheros for Denise and Maria. Once everyone had their food, we all walked back to the table. Our mothers still had not arrived yet, and Greg was ready to eat. Julio told Greg that we had to wait to say grace. That is when Greg said, "Alright, everyone needs to hold hands. Is everyone holding hands?"

"Yes," we all answered in unison.

Then Greg lowered his head to say grace. When he was finished, Denise told him that was amazing. We all broke out laughing, and Greg was smiling as he thanked Denise for the compliment. After we finished eating, Carmen and my mom showed up with Tonya's grandparents. A few minutes later, Michael and Arturo also made it to brunch.

"Did you kids eat already?"

"Yes, Ms. Harris," Greg answered, "But don't worry. I said grace first. I can repeat it for all of you since that was only my first plate, and I plan on eating again."

Carmen smiled before telling Greg, "I can believe that," and we all started laughing again.

"Greg, why don't you say grace for us in Spanish?"

"Oh, I speak Spanglish, Ms. Harris. Now Julio speaks fluent Spanish; he can say grace for you. Go ahead, Julio." Julio looked over at Greg with a shocked expression. Even his mouth was gaping open.

"Okay then, Julio, would you do us the honor, please?"

"Of course, Ms. Harris." After Julio said grace, our parents thanked Julio, and Abuela said, "Oh, I'm going to miss you boys so much. It breaks my heart that you're all leaving." I looked across the table at Julio, and he was already looking at me. I could see the tears in his eyes as I felt the tears building up inside me.

"Oh, look!" Carmen called out to Daphne. "It's the Mariachis!" They came over to the table and played 'Cielito Lindo.' As they began to sing each word in the song, we all paid attention to the lyrics. There could not have been a more perfect song at this moment. When the song was over, the whole room erupted with applause. Everyone at our table was now smiling instead of on the edge of tears.

Alex stood up, asking, "Who's ready for round two?" All of the boys headed out toward the atrium for a second-round except for Michael. He remained seated beside Carmen.

"Michael, you don't want seconds?"

"No, I can't do it, Carmen. Summer is coming, and I'll be in LA soon, which means auditions."

"Oh, that's right. How long will you be gone?"

"The entire summer. I don't get back to Miami until three days before school starts up again."

"Are you excited about attending high school this year Michael?"

"Yes, and yes, definitely, Carmen. My favorite elective is, of course, drama. It should be so much better in high school."

The boys returned with nothing that resembled breakfast on their plates. They had bean burritos, taquitos, and enchiladas. While the boys were eating, Greg was the one smiling between bites. Tonya announced, "It's 12:30, which means we should leave her within the next half-hour."

"Thanks, Tonya, that means I only have enough time for one more plate." Greg stood up and headed back for round three. He returned with two plates filled with pastries. He offered one to each of the parents and all of the girls.

"Hey, where's our dessert, man?"

"Oh, Lewis, I left yours over there, man." Greg was grinning while pointing to the exit door.

The boys all stood up, and Lewis stuck out his chin before saying, "I'm going to get my own dessert."

Greg finished off his dessert and pushed his plate away before telling Lewis, "Okay, but hurry up, man. I'm ready to go." When the boys came back, Greg announced, "It's one o'clock, Lewis. You need to hurry up and eat that flan before you get yourself into trouble with Tonya."

Now Lewis was grinning, and he turned to Greg, saying, "Bro, calm down, we have plenty of time. Do you want some flan?"

"No, dude, I'm good."

"Are you sure, bro?"

"Okay, give me some of that flan, Lewis."

"Oh, wait, bro. I forgot about you and left your plate at the table over there," and he pointed toward the same exit door.

Everyone laughed, except for Greg, who said, "Whatever, Lewis. I'm full anyway." We all stood up and thanked the parents for brunch. Denise and Eddie stayed behind, but I invited them one more time in case they changed their mind. Denise shook her head no, and Eddie declined again, mentioning how they still have plans to spend the day at the pool.

When we arrived at the skating rink, the boys stood in line for us to buy our tickets. As soon as the doors opened, Julio and I rushed inside to put on our skates. Then he found a locker for us and put our shoes inside along with my purse. He dropped in a quarter, pulled out the orange key, and I was glad to see the safety pin was still attached to the key. Julio clipped the key to his laces, and we joined everyone at the skate rental. Alex, Tonya, and Lewis had their speed skates on already, so we were just waiting for Daphne, Greg, and Maria. They were in line at the skate rental. The music came on, and Julio grabbed my hand. "Alex, we'll be on the rink."

"Okay, Julio, I will let everybody know."

As we were skating around the rink, I spotted the arcade and pointed it out to Julio. He led us off the floor and into the arcade. I placed two dollars in the change machine.

"What do you want to play first, Samantha?"

It was hard to decide the arcade was incredible with so many machines to choose from, and all of them available. Finally, I chose an air hockey game to play first. Julio won, and we skated around the arcade until I spotted a car in the corner. It was covered in blue Plexiglass and had an opening on either side of the machine. Julio climbed into the car through the left side, and I jumped in from the right side. We were sitting on a bench seat with a big screen in front of us.

Julio had the steering wheel in front of him, along with a shifter on the dashboard. There was a red button blinking that, and that was the start button. The floor had three pedals; the clutch pedal, brake pedal, and of course, the gas pedal. When the game began, it was so loud, blaring a countdown from three to one through the speakers. Julio was on the first course, driving against all these other race cars on the screen. Halfway through the game, he lost interest and told me to play instead. I attempted to climb over Julio's lap until I felt his hands on my waist. He was trying to help me over his lap, but I leaned down to kiss him instead. As our lips touched, we jumped after hearing a loud smack against the window. Immediately after, we heard Greg and Daphne laughing hysterically, and I looked back at Julio. He was already smiling and giving Greg the bird until he realized I saw what he was doing. Then Julio quickly put his hand down, grinning at me. He whispered, "Mi Corazón," with his hand on my cheek and kissed me while Daphne knocked on the roof non-stop until we climbed out.

"Hey, it's too bad Eddie didn't come with us. He would have loved this car."

"You're right about that, Daphne. Now let's play some pinball." I took Julio's hand while we skated over to the machines with Daphne and Greg behind us.

There were five pinball machines all lined up against the wall. "Here, you each need to take a quarter and play whichever pinball machine you want." I waited for everyone to pick their machine before I chose between the last two.

Finally, I settled on the KISS pinball machine, and I just released my first ball when I heard Tonya say, "Muñeca, is this what you came here to do?"

"Crap, Tonya. I just lost my ball. Now I only have three balls left."

"Who cares about that? We came here to skate."

"Your right, I will be out there right after this game."

"Sammy, are there any more games you would like to play in here first?"

"No, Greg, you're actually going to have to skate while we're here."

"Okay, but Tonya, if it doesn't work out for me, I'm coming back here to the arcade, and you can come to get me when it's time to go."

"I will keep that in mind, Greg, now Muñeca, hurry up."

"I'm not leaving until I've finished playing this game." Tonya went back out to the rink, and we soon followed.

The four of us were standing at the entrance to the skating floor, and Greg kept saying, "I don't know about this."

"I'll help you, Greg. Hold my hand."

"What if you fall, Daphne?"

"Then will fall together, Greg. Don't think about that right now. Just give me your hand, babe."

Daphne put out her hand, and Greg took it right before he stepped out onto the floor. "What is wrong with you, Greg? You skate just fine."

"She's right, you're not wobbly or anything."

"That is because I know how to skate, Julio. I'm just scared of falling. You know because that's a long way down."

Julio and I started laughing while Daphne was shaking her head at Greg. At the same time, Tonya came up behind me, and she took my hand. I released Julio's hand before I left with Tonya to the middle of the rink. Together we held our hands crisscross while we spun around in a circle. Then Tonya took off, and I was right behind her while we did the shuffle, which is synchronized skating one behind the other.

On every turn, we did our taps to the right before crossing our right foot over our left foot. Then the rest of the time, it was footwork and dance moves. We were having so much fun, and I put my hair down to enjoy the feeling of the wind blowing through my hair. Daphne and Maria joined us, and the four of us did the shuffle to 'Let's Dance' by David Bowie." This time it was a little bit harder around the turns to remain synchronized, being that there are four of us. When the song came to an end, the DJ announced it was time to clear the floor to start the races. Lewis clapped his hands together and said, "Finally, it's on."

All of us sat down to wait for our age group to be called out onto the rink. The first race was for the girls' ages five to nine years old, followed by the boys the same age range for the next race. One little boy caught my attention. He had on these tiny little speed skates with fluorescent wheels and laces. He was sucking on his lower lip with his eyes fixed on the finish line. The Floor guard said, ready set go, and the boy fell right where he was standing. Of course, another boy won the race, but his parents were sitting right beside us, cheering the boy on the whole time. He stood up from the floor with a look of disappointment on his face. When he was exiting the floor, I told him, "You'll get them next time."

The little boy smiled at me before saying, "Yes, I will," and he held up four fingers before saying, "I'm four years old." His mom bent down, and he ran into her arms, smiling.

We watched two more races, and Lewis was growing impatient by the minute. Greg noticed and told him, "Dude, chill out. It's not like you are going to win anyways."

"Oh, I'm going to win big time. Just watch me, Bro."

Greg was grinning when he replied, "Okay, we'll see what happens, dude." The DJ announced that all male racers ages 14 and older should come out onto the floor. Alex, Julio, Greg, and Lewis all stepped out onto the rink. The floor guard yelled out, "On your mark." Everyone bent down. "Get set." Lewis, Alex, and Julio bent their right leg back. "Go!"

The three of them pushed off on that back leg and were at the finish line in a matter of seconds. Then the DJ announced, "Let's give a round of applause for the winner." Lewis shot both of his arms straight up in the air above his head. He had a huge smile on his face, and Tonya was literally jumping up and down with excitement.

When Lewis came off the floor, Tonya grabbed hold of him in a tight embrace. "I'm so proud of you, baby. You did it. You beat everyone." She kissed him and praised him some more until the DJ announced it was time for the female racers. Tonya, Daphne, Maria, and I joined the rest of the racers at the starting line. "On your mark." I placed my right foot behind me. "Get set." I leaned all the way back. "Go!" I pushed off my right leg and was at the finish line in the blink of an eye. Tonya was right behind me, and she put her arm over my shoulder.

"As long as it was one of us that won, I'm happy."

I looked back at Tonya and told her, "You came in second place. That's excellent, considering we were way in the back behind ten girls."

"Yeah, I guess so, Muñeca, but first is better."

"Oh, stop it. You win half as many times as I do." We cleared the floor watching the guards skate around the rink picking up the cones.

"Look, Muñeca, they're picking up the cones. You know what that means?"

"Not really. What does that mean, Tonya?"

"It means the couples-only skate is up next."

"Really? Daphne asked, sounding immensely excited until she turned her head in search of Greg, then with a frown on her face, she asked, "Where are the boys? Did they even watch us race?"

"No, I don't think they did," Maria replied, sounding disappointed. "I bet they're at the arcade lets go check it out."

Maria tugged on Daphne's arm when the boys jumped out, saying, "Surprise!" The boys had been hiding behind a big blue carpeted beam beside us.

"Of course, we watched the race, and we saw you come in first place, Mi Corazón."

"Yes, she did," Maria told Julio with a bright smile on her face, and her arms slung over his brother's shoulders. Alex turned Maria's head as he leaned in to kiss her. Julio and I turned around to face the rink. When I felt him place his arm over my shoulder and whisper, "I always watch you. I can't help it. I'm in love with you." I kept my eyes on the rink, but I could feel my cheeks swelling up from the huge smile on my face when I felt Julio kiss me on the temple. "Just so you know, I wouldn't have missed that race for anything in the world, not when you're a participant." I turned to face him and was about to thank him when the lights went dim. I was instantly filled with excitement, expecting this to be romantic.

Then the DJ announced: "This is the couples skate only."

That is when I had chills, and Julio put out his hand to me, asking, "Will you skate with me to this song?"

"Of course, I replied, trying to control my eagerness." I took Julio's hand, and my heart was beating faster as he led me out onto the floor. We were skating to 'With or Without You' by U2. The lights were dim, and the floor was covered in big blue and purple circles from the spotlights above us. I turned myself around so I could skate backward and face Julio. He released my hand, and I placed both of my hands up on his shoulders. Just as I felt his hands on my waist, I was not disappointed at all. The couples skate totally lived up to my expectations, and it was romantic. I could feel every word in the lyrics of this song, and I shut the world out for this moment, with my eyes locked on Julio. We kept our eyes on one another even when the next song came on.

Julio just spun us around so that he was the one skating backward for this song instead of me. Now we were skating to 'If You Leave' by Orchestral Manoeuvres in the Dark. I looked up at Julio and felt myself blinking back the tears that would not stop coming. Julio leaned down, asking if I was okay? "I'm sorry Julio, the lyrics of this song at this moment are very overwhelming. I am so in love with you and... Julio lifted my chin and gently kissed me. The tears, along with the sadness, all disappeared the minute I felt his lips touch mine. We continued to skate around the rink locked in each other's arms until the end of this song.

Then Julio lifted my chin and said, "I will come back, Samantha. I'm scared of the unknown just like you, but I'm certain of my feelings for you. I won't forget about you." We pulled apart, and I was about to reach for his hand when Daphne came by, tugging me away by my arm.

"Daphne, where are we going?"

"To the arcade, it's Greg's treat."

When we arrived, Greg was at the entrance waiting for us, grinning, and Julio was right behind us.

"Come on, dude. I found it. Let's play."

"Found what?" I asked.

Julio replied to Greg. "You did? Where is it?"

"Over here, dude. We have to play." The minute we came around the corner, I saw the foosball table. The boys were thrilled with Greg's find and started playing immediately. Daphne and I watched them play until I reached into my pocket to grab my beeper and found two quarters. I pulled them out and showed them to Daphne.

"Do you want to play pinball?"

"Yes, I do, Sammy, let's go." We left the boys at the foosball table, and when we returned, Greg and Julio partnered up and were playing against Alex and Lewis.

"Where are Maria and Tonya?"

"They are in the bathroom, Sammy," Lewis answered. Then I saw the restrooms sign behind him. I headed for the bathroom with Daphne, but we slipped and fell outside the door. Greg and Julio came running over to us.

"Are you girls, okay?"

"Yes, Greg, we're fine, Sammy doesn't like to do much by herself, so she brought me with her," Daphne answered, giggling.

"What happened, Mi Corazón?"

"Julio, the floor's wet, and I slipped. When I was in the process of falling, I grabbed onto Daphne for support, and that wasn't the best idea because here we are on the floor together."

He tried not to laugh while saying, "Yeah, I see that, Mi Corazón. You didn't even make it inside the bathroom."

"Well, I didn't want you to miss my finest moment Julio. Not after you said, how much you like to watch me." Daphne and I went to giggling again, as Julio and Greg helped us up off the floor.

Tonya and Maria skated out of the bathroom a couple of minutes later and found us standing beside the foosball table. "Muñeca, where have you been?" I looked up at Julio, giving him pleading eyes.

Greg looked over at me, with a grin on his face before saying, "Tonya, she was on the floor with Daphne."

"But Julio told me she was playing pinball."

"Nope, I was on the floor just like Greg said."

"Muñeca, do you want to go back out on the floor to skate some more? Just us, girls?"

"Sure, let's do it," I replied while smiling back at the boys.

Then I took Daphne by the arm and told her, "Come on, it's time to get back on the floor." Julio and Greg looked as though they were about to burst with their held in laughter and eyebrows arched.

The four of us just stepped out onto the rink when the DJ announced: "This will be the final song." That's when the boys joined us, and everyone coupled up. The last song was 'Spring Love' by Stevie B. I noticed everyone in the rink was pouring onto the floor to skate to this song. This is freestyle music, and one of our favorite songs by one of our favorite artists. When the song was nearly over, Julio lifted my chin and kissed me for the last time on the floor. He left me feeling so happy that we came here, and we left the rink by the entrance into the arcade.

"Julio, what are we doing here?"

"You'll see, Mi Corazón." He took my hand and pulled me into the car, where we made out until the lights came on. The DJ made his final announcement while we were climbing out of the car.

When we arrived home, Julio and Greg wanted to go to the pool, but I had to walk Daisy first. Julio offered to come with me, and all four of us ended up walking back to my place. Carmen was in the living room with my mom when we walked in. "You girls are back already?"

"Yes, mom."

"How was it, Daphne?"

"Good."

"Can we go to the pool for an hour?"

"Daphne, you only have one hour, then we have to go."

"Sam, can you take Daisy outside first? She hasn't been out since this morning."

"No problem. I will take her out now." Daphne was in the linen closet, grabbing towels while I was placing the leash on Daisy. The four of us left out the backdoor together. Julio high-fived Greg and told him he'd catch him later. Daphne and Greg headed in the direction of the pool while Julio and I took Daisy out to the golf course. Once we were deep into the golf course, Julio took Daisy's leash off her collar. The two of them played chase until Julio ran up to me and picked me up to spin me around. Then he set me down and ran toward the lake with Daisy chasing him the whole way there. Even Daisy could not catch up to Julio when he was running that fast. I casually strolled over to the lake, taking my time when Julio ran up behind me and picked me up again, spinning me around and around. Julio set me down after the third turn kissing me slowly over and over again. My head was spinning, and I felt light on my feet. I just kept kissing him for as long as possible. When Daisy started barking, we pulled apart to see what's upsetting her. It turned out she was not upset at all. Daisy was letting us know Greg and Daphne were headed our way.

"Guys, I'm sorry to disturb you, but your mom-"

Greg interrupted Daphne to say, "Ms. Harris said something about you having to be home early tonight."

"Besides that, do you guys realize it's after eight o'clock?

"No way it can't be that late, Daphne."

"It is," Greg and Daphne said at the same time.

"Oh man, that means I might be grounded. Julio, I was supposed to be home by five-thirty."

"Then let's get you home, Mi Corazón" Julio hooked Daisy's leash to her collar and took my hand. The five of us headed back together. When Julio suddenly stopped and said, "Migs here," he pointed to a van parked in front of my building.

"Daphne, my ride has been here for over an hour. I won't be able to walk you upstairs." He kissed Daphne on the lips then jogged up to the van. We watched as the van pulled away before we continued walking back to my building. Julio kissed me then handed me Daisy's leash once we reached the top of the stairs. I walked inside with Daisy and Daphne.

"Finally, you're home, Sam."

"Yes, Mom. I am sorry. I lost track of time."

Carmen stood up and announced, "It's late; we're leaving." My mom and I hugged them both, and they left.

"Sam, please take your shower and get ready for bed. Oh, and pick out your clothes tonight. That way, it will be one less thing to worry about in the morning."

"Okay, Mom, I will, and I'll come by your room to say good night before I go to bed."

"Sounds good, Sam. I will expect to see you in a little bit." I walked into my room and went straight to my window. To my surprise, Julio was standing there below my window, looking up at me. He was smiling as he waved to me, which made me smile as I waved back.

The rest of the week went by so fast with SATs and going to bed early every night. Today was already the last day of school, and everyone was looking forward to getting this day over for their summer to begin. Except for me, I was sick to my stomach and filled with dread because it was the last day of school. Which meant this was my last day with Julio. He will be gone by tomorrow to start his new life in Anaheim. I felt depressed and upset. I tried to smile when I felt like I was about to cry.

I tried to keep my head up, even though I felt the weight of the world on my shoulders. I don't know how I managed to do it, but somehow, I made it through the day. When it was time to get on the school bus,

Julio was already there waiting for me. I sat down beside him, and he put his arm around me. Poor Julio listened to me cry on his shoulder the whole ride home. By the time we reached my doorstep, Julio was already asking if he could take Daisy outside for a walk. "Sure you can do that, Julio, do you mind if I go with you?"

"No, not at all. That's what I meant to say if we could take Daisy out for a walk now."

"Okay, so let me grab her leash, and we'll be on our way." Julio led us out to the golf course, and he was walking extremely fast, then all of a sudden, he just stopped.

"Is something wrong? Why did you stop walking?" He turned around to face me, then handed me a jewelry box.

"What is this?"

"It's a gift I bought you for your birthday."

When I opened the box, I found a gold necklace inside. "Julio, it's beautiful." He took the necklace out of the box and held it up to show me the heart hanging from it.

"I had the heart engraved on both sides. Do you mind if I read it to you, Samantha?"

"No, would you please."

"It says, Mi Corazón, wherever we go, you hold my heart." Then he turned it around and read, "Te Amo, Soccer Player."

"If I lift up my hair, can you put it on me, Julio?"

"Of course, I would love to."

After my necklace was on, I released my hair and hugged him. "Julio, the words you had engraved into the locket mean so much to me."

"I'm so glad you like it, Samantha."

"Julio, I love it. Why did you wait so long to give this to me?"
"Mi Corazón, I didn't get paid until three weeks after your birthday. Then I didn't have enough money to get the engraving until a month ago."

"Wow, that really makes this gift even more special. Thank you, Julio, I love you with all my heart." I bent my head down when I felt the teardrops starting. Julio placed his hand under my chin and lifted my head. He wiped away my tears and gently kissed my lips.

"You know I didn't give you that necklace to make you cry," and now he was grinning, trying to make me smile.

"I'm scared. You're going to forget about me, Julio."

"No, Mi Corazón. That's not possible."

He kissed me again and held me tight in his arms. We walked, talked, and kissed until midnight. That's when Alex showed up to the lake to tell us it was time to go.

Daisy was asleep with her head on my lap. Julio refused to wake her and insisted on carrying her back to my place even after she woke up. When I opened the backdoor, Julio kissed Daisy and told her, "I'm going to miss you, and you will always be my big girl." He sat Daisy down inside, and I shut the door behind her. I did not want Julio's last memory of us together to be of me crying, so I took in several deep breaths and let them out slowly. Finally, I felt calm enough to say good-bye. I barely made it inside when the tears showed up. I laid my head back against the door and slid down to the floor, crying. That is where my mom found me a few minutes later against the door. She bent down to hug me before helping me up off the floor.

Then we walked into my room, and she hugged me again. No matter how hard I tried, the tears would not stop. "Sam, do you want to talk about it now?" I was unable to speak, so I just shook my head no. My mom stood there a few minutes before saying, "You know where to find me if you need me. Do you want me to shut your door to give you some privacy." I nodded my head, yes, and she quietly shut my door on her way out. I slowly walked up to my window, looking out across the parking lot at Julio's building. Suddenly I felt like someone was staring at me, and I looked down and saw Julio. He was staring up at me with sadness in his eyes. I placed my hand against the window, and he placed his hand over his heart. We just stared at one another until Alex showed up. He waved to me before he put his arm over Julio's shoulder, and they left. No matter how hard I tried, I could not fall asleep. At five o'clock, I jumped out of bed and ran into my mom's room.

"Mom, I know it's incredibly early, but Julio's plane leaves at seven, and I want to know if I can go with Alex to drop the Sanchez boys off at the airport?"

"Yes, you can go, Sam but come straight home afterward. I want you to get some rest, and your brother should be home this afternoon."

"Okay, I will, mom, and thank you." I ran back to my room, got dressed, grabbed my purse, and ran over to Julio's place.

"Sammy, what are you doing here?"

"Alex, I want to go with you to take Julio to the airport."

"Did you ask your mom?"

"Yes, and she said yes."

"Then, you can go."

Julio was bringing his suitcase to the door. When he saw me standing there, he dropped his suitcase and pulled the door wide open. "Samantha, what are you doing here?"

Before I could answer him, he wrapped his arms around me and held me. "Julio, I want to go with you to the airport."

He eventually said, "Good, I want you to come too."

"Alex, Sammy is coming with us to the airport."

"I'm aware of that, Julio, and there is no way I would stop her from coming with us."

After the van was loaded up, we were on our way. Julio held me in his arms the whole way to the airport. Alex parked the van in the garage so we could walk inside with them. I had no idea we were walking them to the gate until we had to go through the metal detector. When we arrived, the boys checked in at the desk, then afterward, Julio and I sat down together on a bench.

"Please call me once you get there. Just let me know that you arrived safely."

"Samantha-"before Julio could finish what he was about to say, they called his row over the intercom. We stood up, and Julio pulled me into his arms. He held me for a moment then kissed me for the last time. My lips were left quivering, and I felt the tears in my eyes as he pulled away. While I stood there in front of him, trying not to cry. Julio lifted my chin to look into my eyes and asked, "Is it over, Samantha?" I stood there in agony, looking at him completely tongue-tied. Julio pulled his head away, and I saw the tears in his eyes. At that very moment, my heart broke into a thousand pieces as he kissed me on the cheek and whispered, "Te Amo, Mi Corazón, but I guess this is goodbye."

He turned his back to me and walked through the doorway to board his plane. Alex walked up behind me and said, "My little brother's mind is filled with you, Sammy."

"Alex, I can't imagine my life without him." The tears began pouring from my eyes, and Alex just held me, allowing me to cry.

"Sammy, I know you think your relationship is over, but it doesn't have to be. Just wait for Julio to call you, and go from there. I'm sure you two will figure something out. Now I need to get you home so you can get some sleep."

The End

Here is a look into the continuation of the MGX series *Book 2 Second Chances.*

Chapter 1 The Phone Call

My name is Samantha. My family calls me Sam, and my friends call me Sammy. Except for Tonya, she's like my sister and calls me Muñeca. Which means doll in Spanish. When I had a boyfriend, he called me his Corazón, which means heart in Spanish. I loved it. He's long gone now, and he broke my heart when he left. His name is Julio, and he has been gone about a month now to live in Anaheim, California. I don't believe in long distant relationships, so that's why we're no longer together. I thought if we broke up on the day that he left, it would spare us from the inevitable heartbreak. Guess what? I was wrong. My heart broke into a thousand pieces the day he left.

Today I woke up to my mom and my brother Tommy discussing yours truly. My mom asked my brother to take Daisy out for a walk. His response was, "Tell Sam to get up! It's her dog, so Daisy is her responsibility."

My mom replied: "You're right, Tommy, but she's devastated right now, so I'm giving her time to heal."

My brother sounded completely annoyed when he asked, "Heal from what? It's just puppy love. It's not real. Come on. Sammy is only 15 years old."

My mom sounded completely compassionate and filled with understanding when she simply said, "Tommy, heartbreak is devastating at any age."

"Mom! Seriously! You can't let Sam continue to spend her entire summer in her room. She needs to get over it already and go outside and get some fresh air. Tell her to go walk Daisy." I knew Tommy was right; I needed to start living again. I mean, what was I doing? I've been cooped up in my room feeling miserable over a guy who hasn't bothered to call me even once since he left.

That's when I climbed out of bed and went straight to the bathroom. I took a shower and put on shorts and a T-shirt. That in itself was already an accomplishment. I have been living in pajamas every day for about a month. I brushed my hair and had so many knots that my head was tender. I looked in the mirror and saw my eyes were a bit swollen and pink. I said aloud: "No more tears for someone who has forgotten I even exist." I put my hair up into a ponytail and grabbed Daisy's leash off the counter.

I took Daisy outside for a walk. When I arrived back home, I called up Tonya. She didn't answer, so I left her a message on her answering machine. I called Daphne, and Arturo answered the phone. "Hey, Sammy. How are you holding up?"

"I'm okay, I guess. I just want to get back to normal. You know what I mean?"

"Oh yeah. I definitely know where you're coming from. Michael has been gone over two weeks now."

"Gone where?"

"He is in LA at his dad's house."

"That's right. Sorry, I forgot."

"It's understandable; you must have been dealing with a lot. How is Julio? Does he like living in Anaheim?"

"I wouldn't know; he hasn't called me."

"Have you tried calling him?"

"Yes, but no one ever answers the phone."

"Oh, Sammy. I don't know what to say."

"Neither do I." I heard Arturo release a loud sigh, and I said, "You know what?"

"What?"

"I need to get out of this house and quit feeling all depressed, Arturo.

"Really? Me too. Let me go wake up, Daphne. I'll call you right back."

"Okay. Talk to you soon." After I hung up the phone, I walked straight into my brother's room.

"Hey, Tommy. Do you want breakfast?"

"No. I'm not making my bonging waffles this morning, Sam. You didn't even touch your plate the last time I made them for you."

"I'm sorry about that; I just didn't have an appetite. I do now, Tommy! I can make you pancakes."

"No, I want my bonging waffles."

"Okay. Then I will try making you waffles, Tommy."

"Nope! They won't be bonging."

"Okay, never mind. I'm sorry I bothered you."

I stood up to leave his room when Tommy said, "Wait." I stopped walking, and he said, "I'll make breakfast." He got up out of bed, and we walked out to the kitchen together. I grabbed the mixing bowl and a whisk. Tommy grabbed the waffle mix and the milk. As he prepared the batter, he told me to take a seat. I took a seat at the kitchen counter. "Talk to me, Sam, I'm your brother, and I've been where you're at. What's going on?"

"I called him, you know, Julio. He never answers the phone."

"Has he called you?" Tommy asked with a surprised tone to his voice.

"No." I crossed my arms over my chest. I was suddenly feeling frustrated.

"Then who were you talking to earlier, Sam?

"Arturo, he answered the phone when I called Daphne."

"How is he doing?"

"Not so good."

"Why? What happened?"

"Michael's spending the summer at his father's house in LA."

"Now is Michael, the guy with blond hair?"

I nodded my head, yes, and Tommy said, "Yeah, I remember him. That's Arturo's best friend."

I let out a sigh and asked, "What's the big deal about California? It's sunny here year-round too, and..."

"Forget about him and start having fun. It's summer, and I'm home. Let's cruise the Grove tonight, and we can eat at your favorite burger place." Tommy poured the batter into the waffle iron and set the bowl down on the counter.

He walked back over to me and said, "They have one in the Grove, Sam."

"What do they have?"

"Your favorite burger joint Sam."

"Really?"

"Yes. Really."

"What do you say, Sam?"

"Okay, let's go."

"You haven't ever cruised the Grove before at night, have you?"

"No. Why?"

"Oh, you'll see. It's where everyone goes to be seen."

"What are you talking about, Tommy?

"You'll see tonight; just be sure to dress up and act cool. Everyone dresses up. It's hard to explain, except that it's just different."

"How is it different?"

"Well, it's completely different from the daytime atmosphere. Everyone cruises around in their cool ride. They have a mega sound system so everyone can hear it as they drive by. Some people even have neon lights inside their car.

There's people everywhere walking around checking everybody out. When you think someone is cute, and they're checking you out, you say, 'Hey. What's up? Hopefully, you get a number or two. When you're in the car, you wink and jam out to your sound system. You have to show off a little bit and look cool doing it. You need to have tons of confidence. When you leave there, you feel like a celebrity or something. It's an awesome feeling."

"Okay, but there's only one problem, Tommy."

"What's that?"

"We don't have a cool car or a mega sound system. We only have Mom's car," I said, frowning.

"Okay, so we won't look cool cruising. We can park and walk around the Grove. It's the same thing, and we have to like strut, you know."

"I don't strut, Tommy."

"Then you just have to dress up and look cool. It'll be fun, Sam."

"Alright! Then I'll go, but I don't care about being cool. I just want to eat my favorite burger and fries with lots of cheese."

"That you can definitely do, but first eat your waffle." Tommy placed a waffle in front of me. It was so big; it took up the entire plate. I was definitely hungry because I ate the whole thing, and it was bonging. When I was finished eating, the phone rang. I grabbed it on the first ring.

It was Arturo. "Hey, Sammy. I was unable to get Daphne up yet. When she does get up, I will ask her about going out tonight."

I looked over at my brother and asked, "What about cruising the Grove tonight? My brother's home for the summer and he has been wanting to go there."

"Yeah, that sounds great, Sammy. I will ask Daphne when she wakes up." My brother suddenly had a surprised look on his face.

"Okay. Just give me a call back and let me know."

"I can totally do that, Sammy."

"Great. Talk to you soon. Bye, Arturo." I hung up the phone quickly before Tommy could refuse.

When I turned around to face Tommy, I noticed he was sulking with his arms crossed over his chest. He was still sitting down at the kitchen counter.

"What was that, Sam?"

"Tommy, to be honest with you, Arturo asked me to hang out first. The Grove sounds amazing, and I totally want to go. I even want to dress up and look cool with you.

"But...

"But what Sam?"

"But I also want to hang out with my friends. Plus, Arturo has the car and sound system for your cruising the Grove experience."

"Oh yeah! What kind of car does he drive?"

"He just bought a convertible Mustang. He even put a loud sound system in it. The trunk is filled with nothing but speakers."

"Now that will definitely get us seen," Tommy said, smiling.

"Wow. Tommy, you are so vain, dude."

"No, I'm just confident."

He stood up from the counter and dropped an ice cube down the back of my shirt. The ice cube fell out straight to the floor only after I danced around the kitchen. When I looked back at Tommy, he took off running to his bedroom. I banged on his bedroom door and said, "Don't worry, Tommy. I will get you back tonight, coward."

Daphne called me about an hour later. She was all excited about cruising the Grove tonight. She knew all about it. She also called it the place to be seen. I told her that I wanted to eat at my burger place while we were there.

Daphne was all excited about that, too, and said, "Greg can meet us there." Greg was at work until six o'clock. Arturo called me back, and he said he would be over to pick us up by seven. I told him we would be ready. Tommy and I watched TV with my mom until it was time to get dressed, and that's when Daphne called. She wanted to know what I was going to wear tonight. I really didn't know yet, so we both decided to wear a dress. I wanted to wear my hair in a French braid since it was so hot outside. That's when Daphne offered to come over and braid my hair and spike my bangs. Arturo and Daphne showed up by seven. Daphne got to work on my hair, and she offered to apply my makeup. I was surprised when I saw my reflection in the mirror. Daphne didn't go overboard with the makeup. My face still had a natural look with my eyes and lips enhanced with light colors of peach and tan. When I walked into my closet, I put on the first dress that caught my eye. The dress was turquoise with a thick black zipper that went down the middle. I put on a pair of black pantyhose, black slouch socks, and black leather boots that went just past my ankle. Daphne was wearing a blue spandex dress with a black short-sleeved jacket. She also had on black boots with a three-inch heel. We were totally ready for the Grove and to be seen. I walked into my brother's room. Tommy had his back to me, and I could hear him trying to suck in his gut to zip up his jeans.

"Tommy, those jeans are too tight." When he turned around, I thought I was going to throw up. "Dude, that's gross. You're totally bulging."

"That's what the girls like, Sammy."

"No, girls don't like that, Tommy. I'm not going anywhere with you dressed like that."

"Okay, fine. I'll take the sock out."

"You're wearing a sock?"

"I just wanted to see what it looks like. Lots of guys do that, Sam."

"You look stupid, Tommy! That's what it looks like!"

Daphne walked in, asking, "What's all the commotion about? Oh, Tommy," Daphne covered her mouth and walked out of the room.

"You see, Sam."

"What did I tell you? Girls like that."

"Tommy, she had to cover her mouth because she was about to throw up. Now take that sock out, and let's go." He turned his back to me and threw a pair of socks on his bed.

He walked inside his closet for a minute and shut the door. When he came out, he was wearing an aqua tank top, tan jeans, and a tan cotton jacket. He was also wearing tan leather espadrille shoes. "How do I look, Sam?"

"Better, now let's go, Tommy." When we walked out to the living room, Arturo was patiently waiting for us. He didn't look bad, but he wasn't dressed up. He was wearing blue jeans, high tops, and a faded polo shirt. My brother saw what Arturo was wearing and said, "Dude, we're going to the Grove. Don't you want to dress up for the ladies?"

"No, dude. I'm gay, and my boyfriend is in LA for the summer."

"That's Perfect. More ladies for me," Tommy said, sounding ecstatic. "In fact, you can be my wingman Arturo. What do you say?

Arturo had a confused look on his face when he said, "I guess that will be alright."

"Awesome, I like this night already," Tommy said as he rubbed his two hands together, smiling. He walked back to his room, and we heard him yell out, "Woo-hoo."

Arturo leaned over and asked, "Is he serious?"

I looked back at Arturo and answered, "I'm afraid so."

Daphne smiled when she added, "That's just Tommy being Tommy.

"Daphne's right Arturo. My brother is always thinking about how every situation can be used to his advantage to get chicks."

"Good to know," Arturo replied with the same confused look on his face.

Tommy walked back into the kitchen and yelled out, "Mom, we're leaving now!"

"Okay. Have fun, and bring your beepers."

"Got 'em, Mom!" Tommy responded as we walked out the door. Arturo waited until we were about two blocks away before he put the convertible top down. When he drove up the two blocks, it was like a huge traffic jam. My brother was all excited and shouted, "We're here!" I looked around to see where here was.

The traffic jam had the cars moving inch by inch. The passengers in the cars beside us would say, "Hey! What's up?" or "Aren't you cute?" I quickly realized this was the 'Check you out ride' Tommy was talking about.

Tommy had put in his mixed tape of his favorite freestyle jams. We were all waving to the different cars that drove by us. Girls often yelled out to Tommy and Arturo. My brother kept his hand on his chin, and occasionally he would look over at the girls. He just posed the whole time looking cool with a stiff lip. I laughed a few times when he said his lines to the girls. It usually went something like: "Baby, you got room for me in that car?" or "Hey, beautiful. You're smoking. You want to hang out later?" But my favorite Tommy line was definitely: "If you like what you see, let me get your number." Every time he said that I would burst out laughing in the backseat. It was so vain and totally Tommy. The whole time he had on his sunglasses, and it was nighttime.

The speakers were thumping in every car that drove by us. There were groups of girls dressed up like supermodels walking around everywhere. On every corner, there were groups of guys checking them out. Some girls would stop and talk to the guys, and some would just smile as they walked on by enjoying the attention.

Arturo finally pulled into a parking lot. The parking attendant handed Arturo a ticket. Then he pointed out the last available parking space in the lot. Once he was parked, Arturo put up the convertible top. We walked down the sidewalk, and I noticed several things. Everyone outside was in high school. There are plenty of nightclubs here, and the lines to get in were filled with college students.

Tommy suddenly stopped and said, "Sam, that's the center of the Grove." I looked over to where he was pointing and saw this huge staircase. It led to a big open bar on the second floor. It was filled with tons of people laughing and drinking frozen drinks.

Daphne's eyes lit up when she saw it. "That's the best spot in the Grove, Sammy. From there, you can see everything and everyone. When we turn twenty-one, we're hanging out there."

That's definitely the place to be seen." Daphne was all smiles as I turned around to look back at the Bar in the Center of the Grove. I felt excited as I began to picture us hanging out there one day.

We finally made it to my burger place. We placed our order then headed for the game room. Over the intercom, we heard, "Greg and Mig, your food is ready for pick up."

Daphne stopped walking and grabbed my arm. We walked back over to the counter; Greg wasn't there. I looked over at Daphne, and she was already scanning the restaurant for Greg. I saw her eyes comb every inch of the place. Then suddenly, her eyes lit up as she pointed toward the back of the room.

"Let's check there." Daphne headed for the back doors, and Greg spotted us as we walked outside. He was smiling and waving us over to his table. Daphne ran up to him and gave him a kiss. Greg just kept smiling up at her as she pulled her head away. You could tell he was so into Daphne. I stood at the table beside Daphne. Greg finally took his eyes off Daphne long enough to introduce me.

"Hi Sammy, do you remember my cousin Mig." I turned my head and looked over to my right and saw Mig smiling up at me.

"Yes, of course."

"Hello Sammy, you look beautiful tonight."

"Thank you. It's nice to see you again."

"Have a seat," Mig said as he pulled out the chair beside him. I sat down and felt completely nervous." Is this your first time here?" I looked back at Mig and noticed his smile. He had a dimple in his left cheek.

"Yeah, it is."

"So, what do you think, Sammy?"

I took a moment to think over his question and answered, "It's packed and kind of cool, I guess."

"Yeah, it is. What do you plan to do after you eat?"

I started to feel a bit nervous, and I bit down on my bottom lip before saying, "I don't know yet, Mig, first time here, remember?"

"They're going to head home after they eat," Greg retorted.

Mig gave Greg an annoyed look before asking, "Then what are your plans for tomorrow night, Sammy?"

I smiled and said, "I still don't know yet, Mig."

"We're going to be playing at the Bonfire tomorrow if you want to come. This time he was looking directly into my eyes when he was speaking to me. Mig has light brown eyes and brown, perfectly set eyebrows. His eyes and smile were captivating. "If you want to go and need a ride —" Before he could finish his sentence, they called our names over the intercom.

Daphne stood up and said, "Let's go, Sammy." Mig was smiling as I stood up from the table. Daphne latched onto my arm and looked back at Greg. Then I saw her fake a smile as we began to walk inside.

Which made me stop to look back at Greg. He was sitting up in his chair with an angry expression on his face. "Daphne, what's up with Greg?"

"It's nothing, let's go." When we arrived at the counter, I saw our trays waiting for us along with Arturo. They were loaded with big juicy burgers and fries. I went to the veggie station first. Followed by the cheese station second and smothered my fries in delicious hot melted cheese. My brother finally showed up and grabbed his tray from me. Once everybody had everything they needed, we all headed back outside to join Greg. Mig's eyes lit up when he saw me. I looked over at Greg, and he was frowning.

Then I heard my brother say, "Let me introduce you girls to my sister Sam." I looked over at my brother, who was standing between two girls.

They were totally Tommy's type. They were wearing tight short skirts and tank tops that revealed tons of cleavage and, of course, high heels. They joined us at the table and sat on either side of my brother. One of them was sitting in the chair beside Mig. I felt bummed about that. Daphne sat down beside Greg, and I sat beside her. Arturo sat down beside me and whispered, "There is no room for these girls in my car."

"Maybe we will get lucky, and Mig will take the girls with him."

"I don't think so, Sammy. I have noticed him looking at you." I smiled and didn't comment. Then I felt like someone was staring at me. I casually looked over at Mig from across the table. He was looking back at me. Then I turned my head and attention back to my food.

My brother was talking to the girls about school. He told them he just finished his first year in college. The girls were all excited when they heard that. They both just finished high school and were starting college when summer was over. My brother and the girls were in the middle of a conversation when I stood up.

"Where are you going, Sam?"

"Oh, I'm going to the arcade room, Tommy."

"Do you need any money?" I looked over at him and rolled my eyes. My brother thinks that girls like when a guy shows he can be generous.

"No, I'm fine," I answered, sounding completely annoyed and shaking my head.

Arturo and I walked over to the arcade room. When we sat down to play a tabletop game, Arturo started to laugh.

"Why are you laughing, Arturo?"

"Sammy, why were you so rude to your brother?"

"I don't know," I answered, smiling and trying not to laugh.

"Oh, I think you do know Sammy."

"Really, why do you think I was rude?"

"Obviously, you wanted to sit beside Mig, and the blond girl took your seat." I erupted into laughter because I wasn't expecting that to be his answer.

"I don't know what it is exactly, but I feel it, Sammy."

That grabbed my attention, and I stopped laughing to ask, "Feel what?"

"I don't know. It's like this strange feeling is in the atmosphere. Maybe it's the chemistry between you and Mig."

"No, right now, what you're feeling is my brother's aggravation. He's going to get even with me for being so rude to him."

"Yeah, I'm sure of that, Sammy."

"It's okay, I can handle it."

"Excuse me, Sammy. I'm going to the men's room."

We both stood up, and I walked over to the pinball machine. I inserted my quarter, and my first ball was released. That's when I pulled the knob all the way back and let it go. This sent the ball flying to the top of the table. Then a quarter was placed on the glass top in front of me. I looked over to my left, and Mig was smiling at me. "I have next game." I couldn't help it. I smiled back at him.

Then I turned my attention back to the pinball machine. After I saved the ball by pressing the flippers and sending the ball flying back up the table, I said, "It's yours when I'm finished." He just stayed there beside the machine staring at me.

When I looked over at him again, he didn't shy away or turn his head. I felt as though he wanted me to know he was staring at me. When I lost my last ball, Mig picked up his quarter off the glass top. It was a small room, and the pinball machine was long. There was just enough room for one person to stand in front of the machine to play.

As I turned to walk out from in front of the machine, Mig and I both had to turn sideways. He slid in behind me as I was moving past him. When he placed his hands on my waist as he slid by, I stopped and looked up at him. My mouth was dropped open, and my eyes were opened wide. I was about to ask him why he was touching me.

That's when he said, "I'm sorry." He put both of his hands up and continued to say, "I just didn't want to squish you against the machine." I just nodded my head to let him know I understood and moved the rest of the way past him.

That's when Arturo came back and asked, "Are you ready, Sammy?"

"Sure! Let's go, Arturo." I looked back at Mig and smiled, and he smiled back. I turned my head back around to face Arturo; he had a silly grin on his face. I knew what that silly grin was all about.

I rolled my eyes at Arturo, and he whispered, "Chemistry." We both laughed the whole way back to the table.

When we arrived, the girls were gone, and Tommy had a grin on his face. He said, "Okay, guys. I got what I came here for." Tommy waved a paper with a phone number written on it.

"So, does that mean we can go now, Tommy?"

"Yes, absolutely. Let's go, Sam."

Greg stood up and said, "Wait here a minute." He came back two minutes later with Mig. "We will walk you back to your car," Greg told Daphne as he leaned down and kissed her. Daphne just smiled and took Greg's hand.

Mig walked beside me as we headed back to Arturo's car. "It was nice seeing you again, Samantha."

"Yeah, it was nice seeing you too, Mig."

Arturo unlocked the doors, and Tommy pulled the seat forward. Daphne kissed Greg and climbed inside first. When I was about to climb into the car next, Mig kissed me on the cheek and said, "I hope to see you again tomorrow." The minute Mig kissed my cheek, I stopped and looked up at him. My mouth dropped open, but I was speechless. It was intense; he just stared back at me.

"Sam, let's go!" My brother said, and that cleared my head instantly. I climbed in the car and sat down beside Daphne in the backseat. My brother sat down on the passenger seat. Then he asked, "Are we going to put the top down?"

"No!" Daphne and I both shouted at the same time. We waved bye to Greg and Mig as we pulled away.

Daphne sat back in her seat and whispered, "I want to invite Greg over to hang out tonight. You know, back at the picnic tables, since Greg's staying at his cousin's house."

Now that got my attention. I turned my head from the window to look back at Daphne. "Oh, that's right, you aren't aware that his cousin. Mig lives just down the street from you."

"If you want to call him and invite him over for an hour, you can, Daphne. We should be back at my place in another 20 minutes at the most."

"Yeah, let's do that. But don't tell my brother Sammy, please. Arturo said he was dropping us off and going out to shoot some pool with Tommy and those girls."

"Those same girls from the burger place?"

Daphne nodded her head, yes, and I rolled my eyes.

"So, what do you say? Can I invite Greg over?"

"Sure, that's fine, Daphne. Just call him when we get home."

Arturo pulled into the parking lot and said, "Hey man, I don't think I'm going with you tonight. I just want to go home and call Michael. Tommy just sat there with a blank look on his face. That's when Arturo said, "You know because he's my boyfriend, and I miss him."

"Oh dude, that's cool. I just didn't realize that Michael was your boyfriend. We can totally hang out another time. Tommy climbed out of the car and pulled the seat forward. We climbed out of the back seat and waved bye to Arturo as he drove away. Daphne walked inside and grabbed the phone in the kitchen to call Greg. I headed to my room to listen to the stereo. Daphne yelled out, "Sammy! Come here!" I walked out to the kitchen and noticed she was covering the speaker on the phone with her hand.

"Who's on the phone, Daphne?"

"Greg, of course. He wants to come over, and he has to bring his cousin. Do you mind hanging out with Mig?"

"No, that's fine."

"Oh, that's great, Sammy. Thank you."

Daphne took her hand off the speaker and said, "Baby, get over here! I miss you already!" She hung up the phone and hugged me.

"Now, I need to touch up my makeup; they will be here in a couple of minutes." As Daphne and I walked into my room, the phone rang. I ran back to the kitchen to answer it.

When I heard "Hello, Samantha." I stayed quiet because I suddenly felt an explosion of emotions inside of me. I heard him exhale loudly into the phone before saying, "It's Julio, please speak to me, Samantha.

If you want to continue reading this story, purchase book 2

Miami Generation X

Second Chances

Available now at mgxbook.com

Glossary – Translation of Spanish Words into English

- **Abuela – Grandma**
- **Abuelo – Grandpa**
- **Hermano – Brother**
- **Muñeca – Doll**
- **Primo – Cousin**
- **Sobrino -Nephew**
- **Mi Hijo – My son**
- **Amigos- Friends**
- **Chancletas- Flip flops**
- **Por favor- Please**
- **Te Amo- I love you**
- **Mi Corazón – My heart**
- **Arroz con Pollo – Rice with chicken**
- **Hola- Hello**
- **Por favor -Please**

Translation of French Word into English

- **Pénible – Annoying**